HANDLE
WITH
Care

Saddler Cove
BOOK ONE

HANDLE
WITH

Saddler Cove
BOOK ONE

NINA CROFT

Entangled Publishing, LLC
2614 South Timberline Road
Suite 105, PMB 159
Fort Collins, CO 80525
rights@entangledpublishing.com

Amara is an imprint of Entangled Publishing, LLC.

Edited by Liz Pelletier
Cover design by Deranged Doctor Designs
Cover photography by Kaponia Aliaksei/Shutterstock

Manufactured in the United States of America

First Edition July 2018

For Rob, who makes everything possible.

Chapter One

Was she crazy?

Mimi Delaney paused, her hand half raised to open the door to O'Connor's Motorcycles. At the last moment, she was having a crisis of conscience.

Mimi was quite aware that through her long life—she'd be seventy in a couple of weeks' time—a lot of people had considered her crazy. But for the first time, she suspected they might be right.

She reminded herself that she was doing this for Emily, the sweetest granddaughter a woman could want. Taking a deep breath, she pushed open the door to the motorcycle shop.

And really, this was just a reconnoitering mission. If the boy was truly as bad as everyone said—though honestly, no one could be as bad as they said Tanner O'Connor was—then she'd walk away, no harm done, and find another way to bring a little adventure into her granddaughter's life.

The garage and shop were in the center of town—prime real estate. Rumor had it the O'Connor boys had bought it with a payout from their daddy dying in some sort of industrial accident while working in a factory in Virginia Beach. Others were sure it was bought from ill-gotten gains, drugs or prostitution, or worse. The money must have come from somewhere. The family had been dirt poor.

The door opened into a showroom, empty but for a single motorcycle on a podium in the center. She approached it cautiously, as she would an unknown stallion. It was huge, but the seat was quite low, so she could probably touch the ground—the women in her family had always been known for being tall—except poor Emily, who was knee-high to a flea. Probably from her father's side.

She walked around the monster machine, then reached out a hand and stroked a finger over the black and silver metal.

"Can I help you?"

The voice almost made her jump, but she was made of sterner stuff. She composed herself and turned around. And blew out her breath. This was her prey. But she was already having second thoughts. Dressed in faded jeans and a sleeveless white tank, he was big and muscular—and exuded an air of danger.

Now she was being fanciful.

He was also quite the most beautiful thing she had ever seen.

Something twisted inside her. Mimi hadn't had a man in thirty years, not since her husband had inconveniently died on her just before her fortieth birthday. She'd never thought much about sex in that time, but standing in front of this beautiful man, she felt every one of her seventy years. And a sense of melancholy and regret washed over her as she realized that she might never again feel a man's touch. That part of her life was over. Finished.

As she remained silent, his gaze wandered over her, one eyebrow raised, and she gathered her thoughts.

The idea had come to her last Sunday. She'd been walking back to the truck with Emily after lunch in town, when a low growling roar had approached from behind. They'd turned together as a huge dark red motorcycle had cruised past them.

And she'd caught a look in Emily's eyes. Longing.

Who would have thought her sweet granddaughter would have the hots for a tattooed ex-con who rode a Harley?

Of course Emily would never do anything about it. She was far too sensible and had never put a foot wrong. Mimi should be pleased about that. Because the boy was trouble. But seriously gorgeous trouble. If she was fifty years younger…

He cleared his throat.

Time to move on. "Mr. O'Connor?" Of course she knew who he was. Everyone knew Tanner O'Connor. But her brain had turned to mush.

"Yeah?" He'd obviously been working. Wiping his hands on a stained cloth, his body language screamed impatience. "As I said—can I help you?" His tone suggested he found it highly unlikely.

Like her, his dark blond hair was pulled back in a ponytail. The lower half of his face was covered by a short blond beard, his eyes were silver gray, and his cheekbones sharp. He was twenty-six but looked older—with a hardness to his features. Probably a couple of years in prison would do that.

She had another pang of doubt. She wanted Emily to have an adventure, but this might be the kind a woman never recovered from. Maybe she should just turn around and go.

"I'd ask if you were lost," he said, "but you're a local, so I'm guessing not."

"You know who I am?"

He raised a brow. "It's a small town, Mrs. Delaney. How could I not know one of our most prominent citizens? I'm guessing you've come to complain about something."

"You are?"

"That's usually what they come in here for."

"And do you do a lot of things worthy of complaint, Mr. O'Connor?"

He grinned then, and for a second the hard lines melted and he looked suddenly younger. Maybe what he would have been if life had treated him differently. "I do my best, ma'am. I don't like to disappoint the good folks of Saddler Cove."

She bit back a smile at that. How often did she have to stop herself from doing something just to aggravate the "good folks?" She reckoned they needed shaking up occasionally.

The grin was gone, his face settling back into its usual sullen lines. He tapped a foot, clearly trying to portray his impatience.

"I think your selling technique could use a little work, young man, if this is how you treat your customers."

Another lift of his brow. "You're a customer?" His tone reeked of disbelief.

"I am."

He scrubbed a hand over his beard as if to hide his expression. Was he finding her amusing?

"You need some work done. You have a motorcycle?"

"Not yet. Obviously, that's why I'm in here."

He cast her a look, then tossed the rag through the open door behind him and strolled toward her. He must have been half a foot taller than her, and for a brief moment she had to fight the urge to step back. Some of the stories she'd heard ran through her mind.

He'd stolen a car. Murdered his best friend in a drunken rampage. He'd killed a man in prison—though surely if that was the case, he'd still be locked up tight. No woman under the age of fifty was safe from him. Well, that left her out.

Small town gossip. She'd never given it any credence before, and she wasn't going to start now.

"So," he said, coming to a halt in front of her, "what sort of bike are you looking for?"

She waved a hand at the bike on the podium. "Something like this. Maybe in…pink?"

"You want a Harley? Ever ridden one?"

"No. Perhaps you could give me a few lessons."

Was that a glimmer of amusement in his eyes? "You think you could handle her?"

She studied the machine again. "I was a little worried I might not be able to reach the ground, but the seat seems low enough. And while I might be getting on in years, Mr. O'Connor, I'm still strong."

He looked her up and down, from her scuffed boots to her messy ponytail. "I can see that, ma'am." He tugged at his lower lip while he considered what to say next. "You know the town will probably lynch me if I sell you a hog."

"A hog?" She wanted a bike, not a pig. Well, she didn't *really* want a bike, but he didn't need to know that.

He nodded to the gleaming motorcycle. "That's what we call 'em."

"How odd." She bit back a smile at the thought of how the town would react. "I doubt they'll actually *lynch* you. Though I'm sure there'll be plenty of those good folks mighty dismayed."

"You've almost convinced me it's a good idea."

It was that one comment that persuaded her to go ahead with her plan. She had a strange notion that Tanner O'Connor did a lot of things just to deliberately dismay the townsfolk of Saddler Cove. As motives went, it wasn't a bad one.

"Do you usually expect your customers to convince you to sell them something?" she asked. "Is my money not good enough for you?"

He rubbed at a grease spot on his forehead, then at the little line between his eyes. "I guess so. You know what one of these babies goes for?"

"I have no idea."

"This particular bike is twenty-five thousand. More if you want her customized. You still want to buy her?"

Twenty-five thousand? For a secondhand bike?

She swallowed her shock. It was for a good cause, after all. And she wasn't expecting to actually buy the thing. "It's my birthday in a couple of weeks, and a woman is only seventy once, Mr. O'Connor."

He shook his head, then gave a shrug. "Let's go start the paperwork."

Chapter Two

Was she crazy?

Of course not—she was *sensible*.

Why hadn't she said yes? Maybe if she'd had a little warning. Ryan had told her he wanted to take her somewhere nice tonight, and she'd thought nothing of it. Her boyfriend was wealthy and often took her to nice places. Now, driving home afterward, Emily realized she should have read more into the comment.

As she headed up the long, curved drive that led to the ranch house, she caught sight of her grandmother entering the barn. Ryan had said he'd spotted her in town that afternoon. Leaving—of all places—the O'Connor's showroom. What would her grandmother be doing in a motorcycle shop?

Perhaps solving *that* mystery would take her mind off the catastrophe of her evening. She took the fork in the drive that led to the barn and pulled up in front of the wooden building. After switching off the engine, she sat for a moment. Mimi would no doubt want to know why she was back so early. It was only a little after eight. Maybe she should just go straight to the house—and hide.

But better to get it over with.

She climbed out of her sensible gray Honda and smoothed down her sensible tan linen dress.

Ryan had said she was "sensible." Just before he'd proposed. Apparently, it was what he liked best about her. She was sensible. Not beautiful. Not sassy and feisty and fun to be with. No, she was *sensible. Agh!*

Would she have said yes if he'd told her she was the most beautiful woman in the world? Of course that would have made him a liar—she wasn't beautiful, she was cute, and how she hated that word—but surely a little poetic license was allowed during a proposal.

The sweet smell of hay and horses filled her nostrils as she entered the barn, the familiar scents soothing her. Though it was only April, the weather had turned warm, and the horses were all out in the paddocks for the night, so the place was quiet and peaceful. She found Mimi in the tack room, sitting on an upturned feed bin and putting together a bridle. Dressed in jeans and a T-shirt, her long black hair pulled into a ponytail, she looked far younger than her sixty-nine years.

As Emily hovered in the doorway, her grandmother glanced up, one eyebrow raised—Emily had always wanted to be able to do that but had never managed it.

"I thought you were out with what's-his-name?"

Emily had been going out with Ryan for six months, and Mimi knew exactly what he was called. Though Mimi had never said it out loud, Emily knew her grandmother didn't like him. But Emily had no clue why—Ryan was rich, handsome, successful—Saddler Cove's most eligible bachelor. One day he would take over from his daddy as CEO of the family firm and no doubt from his uncle as head of the school board. If Saddler Cove had a first family, then Ryan's was it. He'd be his own boss.

He appeared the perfect boyfriend. Perfect husband material. A sensible woman would have said yes.

Grr.

She'd often wondered what Ryan saw in her. Now she knew.

"I left early," she said.

"Why? Are you not feeling well?" Mimi put the bridle down and stood up. She came over and put a hand to Emily's forehead. "You don't feel warm."

"I'm fine."

"Did you argue?"

Did she sound hopeful? "No, we didn't argue." Ryan had sort of been struck dumb, actually. An image flashed in her mind. Ryan sitting across from her, his mouth open, his hand still holding out the ring. It had clearly never occurred to him, not in a million years, that someone as sensible as Emily would turn such a catch down.

"So?"

She sighed. "Ryan asked me to marry him."

Mimi's eyes widened. She glanced past Emily as if to check that Ryan wasn't hovering somewhere behind her.

"I said no."

Mimi blew out her breath. "Praise the Lord."

Emily frowned. "Why don't you like him?"

"I don't dislike him, darling. He's just…boring. And you'd be bored out of your mind in no time."

"There are worse things than being bored."

"For some people, maybe. But not for you. You're a dreamer, sweetheart. You've just forgotten how to dream."

She hadn't forgotten, she'd just put aside her old dreams and made some new ones. She didn't want excitement and passion. She wanted…to be safe. And Mimi to be safe. And she wanted a family, babies. Lots of babies. And she'd keep them safe as well.

Mimi studied her, head cocked to one side. "So why did you say no to Saddler Cove's most eligible bachelor?"

She shuffled her feet, staring at the floor for a moment, then forced herself to look at her grandmother. "He told me I was sensible."

Mimi's lips twitched. "Well, you do give that impression, darling."

"I'm a teacher," she snapped. "I'm supposed to be sensible."

Mimi patted her arm. "Of course you are."

Emily scowled. One of them had to be sensible. You certainly couldn't rely on Mimi for that. The only sensible thing she'd done in her life was marry Emily's grandfather. And that hadn't lasted very long. She'd been alone since he'd died, though through her own choice, as she was fond of telling Emily—she'd had plenty of offers. Emily could believe it. Unlike Emily, she was beautiful, like Scarlett O'Hara with her black hair and green eyes.

"So, was he shocked?" she asked.

Emily grinned. "Speechless."

"Hah. I would have loved to have seen that. I'm glad. You did the right thing. You wouldn't have been happy. And you're too young to settle down. What you need is a fling or two."

Never going to happen.

Men didn't have flings with girls like her. An image flashed in her mind, though. Tanner O'Connor. Six-feet-four of bad boy biker. As different from Ryan as it was possible to get.

She'd had secret fantasies about Tanner since she was old enough to know what boys were for. She'd cried when he was sent to prison, convinced it was a travesty of justice and he was innocent. She'd been sixteen and in love—okay, maybe not in love—she'd never even had a proper conversation with him—but she'd had a huge crush. He was two years older than her and the coolest, baddest boy around. She'd watched from afar as he'd gone through just about every pretty girl in town, treating them mean, and they'd no doubt loved it. Rumor had it that he only dated girls who put out. If that were true, there'd been a lot of girls putting out back then. Emily had dreamed about being treated mean by Tanner O'Connor, but he hadn't even known she existed. But then she was hardly his type, too short, too curvy…too *sensible*.

More grr.

He'd been back six years, and he was badder than ever. She'd seen him last Sunday, and he was so hot she'd nearly melted in a puddle right there in front of Mimi. Definitely fling material, but sadly not for the town's first-grade teacher.

"Are you aware I have a morality clause in my contract?" she asked Mimi.

"You have? Is that even legal?"

"I suppose so. I never really thought about it. It never occurred to me that it would be an issue."

"Pity."

"Mimi!" But thinking about Tanner reminded her of something. "Ryan said he saw you in town this afternoon. Coming out of the O'Connor's shop."

"Yes. I might have dropped by."

When she didn't offer anything else, Emily frowned. "Why?"

"Why what, darling?"

"Why did you drop by the O'Connor's shop?"

Mimi wandered away, picked up the bridle she'd been working on, and hung it from one of the hooks around the room.

"What have you done?" Emily asked.

Mimi gave a small shrug of her shoulders. "I bought a hog."

A pig? "You're a vegetarian."

"Not that sort of hog. And really, I'd hardly buy a pig from the O'Connor's Motorcycle shop. A Harley Davidson."

"A Harley? A bike? You've bought a motorcycle?"

"It's a present to myself. I turn seventy next month and—"

"And that's just one reason why you shouldn't have bought a motorcycle. Seventy-year-old women do *not* ride Harleys."

"Says who?"

"Anyone. Everyone."

"Anyone *sensible*, you mean."

Low blow. "I don't believe this. You actually bought it."

"I handed over my check—which reminds me—I must talk to the bank tomorrow. Transfer some money. Hogs do not come cheap."

"How much?" Not that it mattered. The bike was going back.

"Twenty-five thousand."

"What?" The word came out as a shriek.

"I have the money, darling. It's just sitting in the bank. I might as well get some fun out of it."

Fun? She'd kill herself. Despite her height, Mimi weighed about a hundred and ten pounds. She'd never manage to handle a bike that size.

What sort of jackass would sell a seventy-year-old woman—who didn't even have a motorcycle license!—a Harley Davidson?

"Of course, I haven't got it yet. But that nice young man, Tanner O'Connor, told me he would order it tomorrow. Then another week or so for his brother to customize it for me. Pink with a black stallion on the fuel tank. I thought that would be nice."

Emily had stopped listening at the point when Mimi had mentioned Tanner O'Connor. The jackass had a name.

How dare he?

Most of the town reckoned he was bad to the bone, and maybe they were right. But even he wouldn't be that unethical. She turned on her heel and marched out of the barn. She was almost back at her car when Mimi called out.

"Where are you going?"

"To get that 'nice young man' to tear up your check."

Chapter Three

Tanner was in the workshop. The rest of the guys had gone home for the night, and he had the place to himself and was tuning up Aiden's bike. His little brother was racing on the weekends and making quite a name for himself. It was good for business.

He heard the ding of the door to the showroom opening. Maybe it was that crazy old woman coming back for her check. He'd given her until tomorrow to come to her senses, but maybe he'd overestimated her.

He grinned. She was something, that was for sure. More sass than most women half her age. He was almost tempted to sell her the hog, but lynching aside, he wouldn't have that on his conscience. Hell, he was pretty sure she'd never even been on a bike before. All the same, he had a reputation to uphold, so he'd prefer it to come from her. He couldn't be seen doing the honorable thing. That wasn't who he was, and the good folk of Saddler Cove would probably die of shock.

And good riddance to them.

He'd known exactly who she was. Saddler Cove was

a small town, and everyone knew everyone. Mrs. Miriam Delaney. She owned that ranch down Creek Road. Did some sort of therapy work for veterans with PTSD. Getting them to ride horses or some such crap.

She was also Emily Towson's grandmother. Sweet Emily Towson, whom he'd spent two years inside jerking off to. Better not tell her grandmother that piece of information. But she'd kept him sane. One good, clean thing to think about amid all the crap and the horror of his surroundings.

He'd come across her swimming in the creek in her bra and panties shortly before his life had gone to shit. And it was fair to say, she'd made an impression. He'd never noticed her before, she was too good for him, too quiet, and serious, and studious. But hell, he hadn't known what she was hiding beneath those sensible sweaters. A tiny waist and full breasts, slim legs. An ass to die for. She'd been all blond curls and dimples. She still was. After that, he'd often spotted her around town—okay, if he was honest, he might have gone looking once or twice—but he'd kept his distance. She was pretty and sweet, and he so did not do pretty and sweet. Some fantasies were best kept that way.

But when he went into the showroom, it wasn't Miriam Delaney, but the one man in all of Saddler Cove he'd prefer not to see: Sawyer Dean. He had his back to Tanner, staring at the motorcycle on the podium in the center of the room.

Oh hell no.

He thought about backing out, locking the door to the workshop behind him, and hoping his once-upon-a-time best friend would get the hint and fuck off. But Sawyer was already turning around. He wore a gray suit, a white shirt, and a dark red tie. His hair was immaculately cut. At first glance, he appeared the successful businessman he was supposed to be. Sawyer sold real estate and was good at it—he'd always been a smooth-talking bastard. Rumor had it that his father-in-law had set him up in business. Lanie, Sawyer's wife, had always been a spoiled brat.

But a closer look and the perfect image unraveled just a little. The tie was loosened, Sawyer's collar open, there was a slackness to his face, and he'd put on weight around his middle. He was twenty-six, the same age as Tanner, but looked older. And as Sawyer took a step closer, he swayed.

Shit. He was drunk.

Nothing new. When sober, Tanner presumed, the other man had way too much common sense to come near him.

He so did not need this. A few times over the years since Tanner had come back to Saddler Cove, Sawyer had come around, tried to talk as if they were still friends. Usually when he was drunk. Tanner reckoned Sawyer was looking for some sort of redemption, but he wasn't getting it here.

Never going to happen.

Sawyer came to a halt in front of him. "My old friend, Tanner."

"What do you want, Sawyer?"

"Maybe I want to buy a bike?" He waved a hand at the Harley on the podium behind him. "Maybe I want to do a little business with my old friend, Tanner. Hey, you remember that bike we did up together when we were fifteen."

"No." Of course he did. That had been a great summer. They'd gotten the bike for next to nothing, probably because it didn't work. They'd scrounged and stolen the parts. Taken it apart, put it back together. Got it working. It had been the start of a lifelong love affair for Tanner. Sawyer had always preferred cars, flashy sports cars. He hadn't been able to resist them. It had got him into trouble more than once when they were kids.

It had got Tanner into trouble as well, but he wasn't going there tonight.

"I thought we might go for a beer. For old time's sake."

He had to be kidding. Tanner took a step closer. He was a couple of inches taller than Sawyer, and he stared down, keeping his face expressionless. In the early years after he'd gotten out, he'd thought that maybe beating the shit out of Sawyer might make him feel a little better. At first, he hadn't because that would probably have been in violation of his parole, and he'd made a vow to himself that he was never going back to prison. Certainly not on account of a pathetic asshole like Sawyer. Later he hadn't done it because he had an inkling that was what Sawyer really wanted. The man was riddled with guilt, and maybe he knew he deserved to have the crap beaten out of him. Then he might get over his guilt, feel he'd paid for what he had done to Tanner. But they'd never be square. Tanner had paid with two years of his life. Two years that had changed him indelibly.

Before he went to prison, he'd believed he was tough. That first night, as the cell doors had clanged shut around him, he'd known he wasn't tough enough.

He'd been lucky. He had a cell mate who was one of the best people Tanner had ever met. Without Josh, he might not have survived those two years. All the same, he'd come out a different person. And not in a good way—you didn't survive prison by being good. He knew what the people of the town thought about him. And they were probably right.

So, no, he wasn't going to give Sawyer the satisfaction of getting over his guilt. Though Tanner's fists balled at his sides with the urge to punch him in the face. Break a few of those perfect teeth.

Sawyer blinked at him, didn't move, just stood there waiting.

Hell no.

Tanner was better than this. He breathed deeply and forced his muscles to relax. He hadn't been in a fight since he got out of prison, and he wasn't going to start now.

"Get the fuck out of my shop, Sawyer."

Sawyer's shoulders sagged. "I'm sorry."

"I know you are. You're just not fucking sorry enough. Now piss off and stay out of my way."

Sawyer opened his mouth and then closed it again. He gave a brief nod, turned, and walked away. Tanner stood for a minute after he'd gone, then crossed to the door and locked it, slid across the closed sign. He didn't want any more interruptions tonight. Sawyer had soured his mood.

He'd had anger management therapy in the joint. That first year he'd been bordering on crazy. Furious with Sawyer for betraying him. Furious with the town that was so quick to believe the worst of him. Furious with himself for allowing it all to happen. Though it wasn't as though he'd been in any position to change things. But underneath all his anger had been guilt. Dwain had been the best of them, and Dwain was dead, and Tanner was at least partly to blame for that. So maybe he deserved everything that came his way.

Fuck Sawyer for bringing the past back.

He headed to the workshop. He'd get a few more hours in on Aiden's bike. He always found working soothed him. That and some music. He grabbed his earbuds and flipped through his tracks. A nice soothing Brahms piano concerto. He grinned as the first lyrical notes flowed into his head.

He'd never hear the end of it if Aiden or Reese knew what he listened to. They were more heavy-rock types themselves. But this was something else he'd picked up in prison—maybe the only good thing to come out of his time. A love of classical music. They'd taught him to play the piano as part of the anger management thing, and apparently he was a natural. Whatever. He'd loved the music, found it did indeed offer an outlet for all the anger and pain and sorrow swirling around in his gut. He still played whenever he got the chance, but never when someone he knew might hear him. He had that reputation to uphold.

• • •

Emily pulled over to the side of the road and jabbed her foot on the brake. Her hands were tight on the wheel. In the ten-minute drive back into town, she'd managed to work herself up into a temper.

Which was just as well, because without the temper she was pretty sure she wouldn't have the nerve to face down Tanner O'Connor and tell him exactly what she thought of a man who would sell a seventy-year-old woman, with zero experience on a bike, what was the next best thing to a coffin on wheels.

Despite living in the same small town all their lives, she had never actually had a conversation with Tanner. Usually, she just gazed pathetically at him from afar. And the one time he'd actually said words to her, she'd clammed up and turned puce.

It didn't help that any face-to-face meeting with Tanner was always going to be colored by the fact that she had seen him naked. Of course, only in her dreams, but all the same, it was bound to make the meeting a little uncomfortable. She'd never admit to anyone that she fantasized about sex with Tanner O'Connor. Hot sex. Hot, dirty sex, and lots of it. And maybe if she was entirely honest with herself, her response to Ryan's proposal tonight was probably due in a large part to the fact that Ryan wasn't Tanner O'Connor. Not that she wanted to marry Tanner or anything. Certainly not. He wasn't marriage material. He was hot, greasy—no doubt kinky—sex material. And she'd known that if she married Ryan, then she really could not in good conscience go on fantasizing about sex with another man. It was almost adultery. And the sad thing was she wasn't ready to give up her dream lover.

And then Ryan had called her sensible. And she'd felt stupid, because she was being as far from sensible as it was possible to be. She was saying no to a man who was perfect marriage material, so she could go on fantasizing about sex with a man who didn't even know she was alive.

She'd never slept with Ryan. He hadn't pushed the issue, and the one time she'd gotten up her nerve to ask him if he wanted to, he'd said he respected her too much. *Ugh*. She banged her forehead against the steering wheel. She'd bet Tanner wouldn't respect her. At all.

She wasn't a virgin. She'd had a boyfriend in college, but no one since she'd moved back to Saddler Cove and started work. Maybe she was just frustrated. Maybe tomorrow she'd go see Ryan and suggest they have sex.

First, she needed to confront the man who had sold her grandmother a *hog*. Tell him what she thought about him— well, not everything she thought about him. Certainly not the naked thing. But she would make him tear up Mimi's check.

She'd parked outside the O'Connor's showroom with its big plate-glass window. Now she forced herself to get out and head to the door. It had a closed notice on it. Maybe she should take that as a sign that this was not meant to be and go home. Instead, she peered through the glass. The showroom was large, painted black and red, and only had one bike on show. A huge black monster on a podium in the center. She wouldn't have thought Saddler Cove was the sort of place to sell many motorcycles, but maybe they got customers from other places.

The business was owned by the three O'Connor brothers, Reese, Tanner, and Aiden. And they all appeared prosperous enough, so she presumed they must be making some money. Reese's daughter was in her class, a sweet girl, and she'd met Reese at the parents' evening. He was a single dad, and an ex-Navy SEAL, and as gorgeous as Tanner in his own way.

So was Aiden, the younger brother. But neither of them did funny things to her insides the way Tanner did. Something about all that brooding bad-boyness just did it for her.

The rat.

She couldn't see anyone around, and when she rattled on the door it was definitely locked. Was this a reprieve? But she didn't want a reprieve. She wanted this out and done with. She knew, deep down, that approaching Tanner O'Connor like this was not the most sensible of moves—she should come back when the shop was open and there would be other people around. But the frustration and anger had been building inside her since Ryan's comment. She didn't want to be sensible. Maybe she should let Mimi buy the bike and they could ride together, start up a motorcycle club, sell some drugs or some guns. She'd watched *Sons of Anarchy*. She'd swap her white sweater sets for black leather and…

She was prevaricating.

Don't be a wimp.

She banged on the door. When absolutely nothing happened, she stepped back and considered her next move. She looked up at the second floor, searching for any sign of life, but nothing moved. She was aware that Tanner lived above the shop, while his brothers still lived in the old family house across town. She couldn't see any sign of life up there. Could she shimmy up the drainpipe, peer in the window? Throw stones?

There had to be a way in. An alley ran alongside the building, and she headed down there, her feet slowing. Did she really want to show up on Tanner's doorstep? Maybe she should wait until morning and visit the shop. Keep everything official.

She'd just take a quick look.

At the end of the alley, there was a gate, which led into a yard. She counted five bikes. She knew they ran a garage, did repairs and customizing jobs as well as sales. This must be the workshop. She tried the gate, expecting—maybe hoping—it to be locked, but it swung open. She licked her lips.

There was probably no one here.

She stepped inside, and the gate swung shut behind her with a loud clang that would surely alert someone to her presence—if there was anyone here. Across the yard was an open garage door. A sound from inside made her jump. She stiffened her shoulders and marched forward. Then slowed as she got to the door.

There was still time to back out of this.

If half of the things they said about Tanner were true, then meeting him alone, at night, was not a sensible thing to do. The thought was enough to send her forward the last few steps.

It took a second for her eyes to adjust to the dimmer light, and she stood breathing in the pungent odor of oil and petrol. Not unpleasant. The place was big, maybe thirty feet by thirty feet. The walls were blocks and the floor concrete, as though no effort had been made to pretty the place up. She took another few steps in—picking her way across the oil-spotted floor. For a moment, she thought there was no one there. Then something clattered off to the left, and she went totally still. Someone was humming under their breath, something classical, the tune vaguely familiar, but her mind wasn't functioning sufficiently to identify it. Instead, she inched closer.

Holy moly.

There he was. Tanner O'Connor. At the sight of him, everything inside her clenched up tight. He had his back to her and seemed unaware of her presence. Probably something to do with the earbuds he wore, which gave her the chance to stare. She'd never been this close—or at least she couldn't remember being this close.

He was doing something with a wrench and a big black bike, leaning over the engine so his faded jeans were pulled tight across his ass. She wasn't the sort of girl to stare at men's asses, but she couldn't drag her gaze away. Maybe she'd start. Get some pin-ups for the teachers' staff room. Tanner's was perfect, tight, with lean hips and long legs.

Her skin heated up, and inside her tan dress, her nipples tightened, warmth settling in her belly.

Totally unprecedented.

She might have made a small noise, because he straightened and turned quickly. He still had the wrench in his hand, and his eyes widened as he took a step toward her. She instinctively took a step back, slipped on something, her feet going out from under her, her arms spiraling as she fought to stay upright. Wasn't happening. She hit the concrete floor with a crash, the air *whooshing* from her lungs.

She lay with her eyes closed. Way to go. How To Make An Entrance by Emily Towson.

She finally opened her eyes and then closed them again.

Holy *freaking* moly.

She peeked again. He was standing beside her, like really close—*if I reach out my hand I can touch him*—close. Her fingers curled in a fist at her side. From this angle, he appeared huge, like a giant towering over her. His jean-clad legs braced. She peered a little higher, her gaze snagging on the bulge at his groin, lovingly covered by the soft denim.

Look away, Emily, you're a pervert.

By force of will, she managed to drag her gaze away. The wrench was still held loosely in his hand, and she stared at that instead.

"Well, if it isn't little Emily Towson," he murmured.

She hated that. She wasn't so little. She would have stood up taller, if she'd been standing at all and not sprawled on the floor in an undignified heap at his feet. She pushed herself onto her elbows, then sat up, took stock. She wasn't hurt. Just her dignity was a little wounded. It occurred to her then that he actually recognized her. She'd thought he didn't know she existed.

At the realization—Tanner O'Connor actually knew her name—her heart, already thudding against her rib cage, double timed.

She risked another glance, found him staring down at her, eyes narrowed. He didn't look pleased to see her.

"What's the matter, Ms. Towson. You think I'm going to beat you to death with my wrench?"

She opened her mouth but couldn't make a sound come out.

"You've been listening to too much town gossip. I'm not likely to commit murder. At least not until I've had my evil way with you."

He was toying with her. She hoped. She cleared her throat. "Of course I don't think you're going to beat me to death." She scowled. "You could help me up."

"You think it's safe for a man like me to touch you?"

She rolled her eyes. "Oh, for goodness' sake." She made to push herself up on her own, but at the last moment, he reached out with his free hand. She hesitated briefly, but then slid her palm into his and allowed him to tug her to her feet. After she was up, she pulled at her hand, and he tightened his grip. She was actually holding hands with Tanner O'Connor.

"You okay?" he asked. "What the hell happened?"

She risked a glance at his face and really shouldn't have because he was the most beautiful man she had ever seen. And that could only be a distraction from her mission. Still she couldn't look away. His dark blond hair was pulled back into a ponytail, showing off his perfect bone structure: high cheekbones, and a big, straight nose. His eyes were blue-gray, and his lips were…moving again.

She shook herself. "Sorry? What?"

"I said are you okay? Did you have some sort of…fit?"

"Of course not. You surprised me, and I slipped on something." She peered behind her, and there was a puddle of grease on the floor, a skid mark through it where she'd lost her footing. She twisted around so she could see the back of her dress, and yup, a big black oil stain covered her bottom. She'd never really liked this dress anyway.

"I surprised you?" He sounded incredulous. "I'm busy working in my own garage when some woman creeps up on me from behind, with God knows what intentions, and yet *I'm* the one who surprised *you*?"

He had a valid point. So she decided to ignore it.

She tugged her hand, and this time he let her go. He was too close, so she took a careful step back and still had to crick her neck to look into his face. He'd taken off the headphones, and they hung around his neck. He had a nice neck and broad shoulders. The edge of a black and red tattoo could be seen peering out of the neckline of his vest top, and another ran down his left arm. She stared a little closer, trying to make out what the pattern was. Ryan didn't have tattoos. Neither had her boyfriend in college, and her hands itched to touch them, trace the intricate patterns.

"What are you doing here, anyway?" he asked. She started at the words, and he shook his head. "Christ, you're jumpy. You don't have to worry. I'm not really going to have my evil way with you."

She drew herself up tall, or as tall as she could, which was actually a pathetically inadequate five-foot-two. "I know that, Mr. O'Connor. I'm hardly your type."

His eyes narrowed at that. "And what do you think my type to be, Ms. Towson? Lap dancers and strippers?" His tone was definitely snarky. Had she hit a chord there somehow?

He didn't wait for an answer but crossed over to a bench,

tossed down his wrench, picked up a rag, and wiped the oil from his hands.

"There's a smudge on your cheek as well," she pointed out.

"Don't you like a bit of dirt, Ms. Towson?"

Actually, in her fantasies he was usually dirty as all hell. Greasy and sweaty and...

Don't go there.

He leaned back against the counter and folded his arms across his chest and considered her, his head cocked to one side. She had to fight the urge to squirm. He licked his lower lip with the tip of his tongue, and she almost groaned. He wasn't to know of all the other things he'd done with that tongue over the years. A little pulse started between her thighs, and she clamped them together and crossed her own arms over her chest just in case her traitorous nipples were showing.

His lips twitched; he was finding this amusing.

Was she so obvious?

"You know," he said. "I spent two years in a prison cell fantasizing about you. Every night, I'd lie in my bunk, close my eyes, shut out that fucking place, and I'd jerk myself off to the image of sexy little Emily Towson skinny-dipping in the creek. Sweetest pair of tits I have ever seen, then or since." His gaze dropped to her chest, and her breasts responded, swelling, aching. He licked his lips again and grinned. "So I guess that makes you my type after all."

She was speechless. Her mind a complete blank as she tried—and failed—to make any sense of his words.

"Not going to say anything?" he asked.

Finally, she came up with something. "I so was not skinny-dipping." She would never have had the nerve.

He gave a casual shrug. "Okay. That was a bit of poetic license. You were actually wearing this white cotton underwear. It was totally see-through and clung to your hard, little nipples. Probably sexier than being naked."

His tone was so matter-of-fact that for a second the words refused to make sense. She couldn't believe he was saying this. Was he lying? Did it matter?

"You never said anything."

"You were only sixteen. I put you on my to-do list for a later date." *His to-do list?* Was she supposed to be impressed? "Then you could say life got in the way."

He'd killed his best friend and gone to prison for it. Except, unlike the rest of the town, she'd never believed he'd been responsible for Dwain Forrester's death.

"Anyway, just wanted to clear up the whole 'not my type' thing. But despite that, you're safe with me."

Was that supposed to make her feel better? "What? You've thrown away your to-do list?" She tried for sarcasm, but it had never been her strong point.

"No, I've just written another one."

And she was clearly no longer on it. That was good. She didn't believe it, anyway. He was making fun of her. Tanner had always had a harem of beautiful girls after him. And she wasn't beautiful.

"So now that's cleared up," he said, "could we get back to what the hell you're doing here?" He straightened and came toward her again.

She took a few deep breaths, determined not to let him see her complete loss of composure. Time to get to the business of the night. His totally conscienceless sale of a totally inappropriate motorcycle to her grandmother.

"You sold my grandmother a motorcycle."

"Ah."

"Ah? Is that all you've got to say for yourself? She's seventy."

A smile tugged at his lips. "Not quite. She told me it was

her birthday in a couple of weeks."

He was still playing with her, and her temper roared back to life. Good, because she'd really been feeling a little weird.

"She's never even been on a bike in her life. You know there's absolutely no way she can drive one of those things. She'll kill herself. You really are as bad as they say you are."

And the smile vanished.

Chapter Four

Up until that point, Tanner had been planning to put her mind at rest, tell her that of course he wasn't selling her gran a hog. He wasn't that much of an idiot and had already cancelled the paperwork and torn up the check.

He'd guessed that's what she had come for the moment he'd turned around and seen her standing there.

Actually, maybe not from *that* moment. Maybe he'd given himself a few seconds to imagine that she'd been overcome by an irresistible urge to seduce him, and he'd finally find out what it felt like to be buried deep inside Emily Towson. Of course, he'd be a little reluctant, but she'd beg him, and in the end, he'd give in and he'd take her up against the wall, or on the hard concrete floor, or maybe straddling the back of the hog in the showroom where anyone passing by could see them if they peered through the glass. Him and little Emily, wouldn't that be something for the townsfolk to gossip about?

But of course, that's not why she had come.

All the same, he hadn't been able to resist teasing her just a little. She was shy, he'd always known that, and he found it a huge turn on. The one time he'd tried to talk to her—he'd seen her go into the hardware store, and somehow his feet had moved of their own accord and he'd found himself in the shop standing right next to her—she'd stood there all buttoned up, her mouth open, cheeks flushed, staring up at him as though he was a creature from another planet. And he might as well have been. He'd taken pity on her and backed away, but even so, he'd left the hardware store with a boner.

But this time, he'd seen the heat in her eyes when she'd looked at him. She might not be happy about it, but he reckoned sweet Emily Towson had the hots for the town bad boy. And was determined to hide it. So he'd told her about his fantasies, and he would swear she'd liked the idea.

But he'd made a decision a long time ago not to go there. He was bad news, and she was the epitome of a nice girl—and he wasn't going to fuck that up. Lately, he'd seen her around town with Ryan Forrester. Now that would be a match made in heaven.

Didn't change the fact that she fancied *him*, though.

But now she was pissing him off.

She wore a sort of brownish dress that left her arms bare but didn't cling anywhere and stopped at her knees. Matching shoes with a low heel. A slender gold chain around her throat was her only jewelry, and her hair was in some sort of bun thing, though a little straggly now after her tumble. She looked like what she was—a school teacher. She was only twenty-four but gave the impression of being older.

Where the hell did she get off making judgements about him?

Did she really believe he was stupid or mercenary enough to sell an old lady—who'd never ridden one before—a motorcycle? Though her grandmother was hardly a typical old lady—hell, he wouldn't be surprised if she *could* handle a hog. Unlike her granddaughter, who probably didn't even have the nerve to try.

"Well?" she said, dragging him from his thoughts.

She stood, hands on her hips, glaring at him, and he gave a shrug of his shoulders and shoved his hands in his pockets, so he wouldn't be tempted to pull her hair out of that bun. "It's just business, darling." Her eyes narrowed at that. She had beautiful eyes, big and blue as the summer sky. And a tiny, straight nose and small, full lips and actual dimples. She was so goddamn cute. More so when she was mad. Should he mention that? Probably not.

"Business?"

Another shrug. "Do you really think a man like me would turn down twenty-five-thousand bucks just because something might be a little...unethical?"

"A little unethical! It's death on wheels."

"Bullshit. She'll probably not even get it off the stand."

"If you think that, you don't know Mimi. You really can't do this. You *have* to tear up the check, right here, right now. In front of me, where I can see you do it."

Like he couldn't be trusted to say he'd done something? Hell, he'd almost forgotten she was part of this town. One of *them*. If she thought the worst of him, then let her have it.

"Never going to happen, sweetheart." She gritted her teeth at the sweetheart, but he continued before she could say anything. "It's easy money, and why would a man like me turn down easy money, huh?"

"She'll kill herself."

"But what a way to go." Okay, that was maybe a bit far—his goddamn mouth. Most of the time, he never thought before he opened it. He knew her grandmother was the only family she had. That she'd lost her parents in some sort of accident abroad when Emily was eleven. She was bound to feel protective of her grandma.

Her face had lost its color, and he suddenly felt like a

complete bastard. He'd liked her angry. He didn't like her like this.

"Anyway," he said slyly, "you've gotta think about why she wants the hog in the first place."

Her brows came together, a little line forming between them. "What do you mean? How could you possibly know what Mimi wants?"

"My guess is your gran needs a little excitement in her life. She doesn't look like the sort of woman happy to sit around and wait to get old. I reckon she's bored. Hell, she's got a granddaughter whose idea of excitement is probably wearing a white sweater set after Labor Day."

If anything, she went even paler. Her full lips compressed into a tight line. "What do you mean?"

"Well come on, darling, you've got to admit—excitement is not your middle name." He studied her a moment, curved his lips into a small smile. "No, if I had to take a gamble, I'd say your middle name would be something like…sensible."

Color flooded her face. It was as if he'd pressed some sort of button. She seemed to pull herself up, which still left her pretty small, and then she stalked toward him, coming to a halt only inches away, so he had to look down. The neckline of her dress was too high to see anything interesting, though.

"What did you call me?" she growled.

She was goddamn cute when she was angry. But what had gotten her so riled up? "Sensible?"

She stepped back, but probably only so she could look him in the eye without bending so far backward she'd topple over. Again. The top of her head came just to his chest. "I am *not* sensible. Why would you even say something like that?"

Hell, it wasn't that big a deal. There were worse things to be than sensible. "Nothing wrong with being sensible. Especially with you being a teacher and all."

That appeared to wind her up even more, tension in every

line of her body. "I'll have you know I do lots of un-sensible things. *Lots*."

"Name one."

"Oh!" She almost stamped her foot. And he could see her mind spinning, looking for something, coming up blank, and he chuckled. That didn't go down well.

Then her eyes widened. "I swam nearly naked in the creek."

"Hah, is that the best you can do? You swam *nearly* naked in the creek *eight* years ago."

"In front of the town's baddest boy."

"Yeah, but you didn't know I was there." And he wished she hadn't mentioned it, because an image flashed up of Emily coming out of the water, as good as naked, all lush curves and sweet innocence—up until then he hadn't even realized innocence could be a turn on.

She sniffed. "You think I would have cared?"

"Darling, I think you would have run a mile."

"I'm not scared of you."

And the nice thing was—it was true. She wasn't scared of him. Most of the town treated him like some sort of rabid dog who was likely to turn around and bite them if he got too close. Not Emily. She might be shy, but she was facing up to him, not budging.

"Maybe you should be." He licked his lower lip, and her eyes followed the movement. She was breathing hard now, whether from temper or something else he wasn't sure. Time to stoke the flames a little. "Maybe you should do the *sensible* thing and run right now. Sneak out the back door so you don't shock the neighbors. Little Miss *Sensible* spending time with a tattooed ex-con? Shocking. And never going to happen."

"You think I can't be shocking? You think I can't shock you?"

He spread his arms wide. "Do your best, baby."

She stared at him for a few seconds, her teeth gritted, hands balled into fists at her sides. What the hell was she going to do? He didn't think she knew herself, but from the look of determination on her face, he was going to find out soon.

She took a deep breath and closed the gap between them. He held himself very still as her hand reached out. For a second her palm splayed on his chest above his heart. Then her fingers curled into the material and she pulled him hard toward her. Her other hand came up and curved around the back of his head and dragged him down.

At first, his mind went blank; he had no clue what she was attempting. She growled in frustration, and he relaxed, allowed himself to be pulled, and she stood on tiptoes and pressed her lips to his. It was a brief kiss, and then she was gone.

"There," she said.

Oh no. Not that easy.

"*That* was supposed to shock me? A little peck like that."

She glared, pursed her lips, then seemed to sag a little. "Okay, maybe I can't shock you. I should go. I've said what I had to say." She sighed. "But really, I can't go out there like this. I have oil all over my dress." She turned slowly and yes, she did have a big black stain over her ass. But he wasn't sure what he was supposed to do about that.

"I suppose it's okay if I try and wash it out?"

He knew from experience that nothing was shifting that stain. But he gave a slow nod and waited for what was to come next. Something, he was sure. And his nerves tingled with anticipation. He hadn't had this much fun in...he couldn't remember. His brothers were constantly referring to him as a miserable bastard, and they weren't wrong. But he didn't feel miserable right now. He felt twitchy, on edge, excited...

She reached behind her and lowered the zipper.

Jesus.

Then she wriggled out of the dress until it pooled on the floor around her ankles. Leaving her in pale pink silk and lace that covered nothing. She was straight from his fantasies. Tiny waist, curvy hips, slender legs, and the most gorgeous pair of tits he'd seen in eight years. Full and round, and he could see her nipples poking through the lace.

Now what was he supposed to do?

. . .

Oh Lord. What have I done?

For a moment Emily's mind went completely blank. Refused to process the fact that she was nearly naked in front of Tanner O'Connor.

Yup, it was official—she was crazy.

But he'd said he fantasized about her. And then he'd made her mad. Called her sensible. And she'd needed to prove him wrong. To prove everyone wrong. To be someone else for a little while. Someone brave, who went after what she wanted.

But her anger was draining away. What if he didn't like what he saw? She was far from the tall, skinny model-types he was no doubt used to. Her skin heated up, and she swallowed, then risked a peek at his face.

He was standing perfectly still, his mouth hanging open, his eyes wide, and in the midst of her panic, she experienced a stab of elation. If nothing else, she had managed to shock him. And a wave of—probably misplaced—courage washed through her.

"Ha, got you!" she said. "Is that something a 'sensible' woman would do? Admit it, you're shocked."

He didn't deny it. He closed his mouth. Then opened it again, but no words came out. She'd stunned him speechless.

He shook his head. He was taking too long to answer—

maybe he was trying to work out how to turn her down gently—and her satisfaction and resolve were slipping away again. She looked at him, then down at her dress around her ankles, back to him. Nausea churned in her stomach.

"Nah." He broke the silence at last, his lips curving in a cocky grin. "I'm not shocked. Remember, I've seen it before. It will take more than that to shock me. Try again, sweetheart."

And just like that, the nausea cleared. More? She'd give him more. "Really? How about this, then?" She reached behind her and unclasped her bra. She could almost see him holding his breath as she peeled the material from her breasts. His gaze dropped. She held herself still, making no move to cover herself.

"Fuck, but you are beautiful." His voice was husky, and heat flared in his eyes. He liked what he saw, and the last of her fear drained away. He wanted her. Maybe not as much as she wanted him, or maybe more. Or perhaps he was just toying with her, and he'd start laughing any moment now. Or something worse.

She was playing a dangerous game. She knew his reputation, and she should be running a mile. Instead, she'd stripped in front of him. Now she had to take the consequences. She took a deep breath, pulled her shoulders back.

Something she couldn't quite identify flickered in his eyes. "You know where this is going?" he asked.

Did he think she was stupid? "No idea. Why don't you show me?" She shook her head. "For goodness sake, I might be sensible, but I'm not stupid. I'm nearly naked, I hope I know where it's going."

"And you want to go there?"

Emily glared at him. Why was he making this so hard? While she hadn't planned this, now she'd come this far, she didn't think she'd survive if he didn't make at least one of her fantasies come to life. "You know, in high school all the girls used to say you were easy. What do you want? A signed consent form? Yes, I want to go there."

He closed his eyes for a moment, and she held her breath. Then he grinned. "Thank Christ."

Reaching down, he grabbed the hem of his T-shirt, pulled it over his head, and tossed it away from him. She stared, quite unable to move, her gaze running over him, the broad chest, flat nipples, the rippling muscles of his belly, the little line of blond hair that disappeared inside his low-slung jeans. Lower. She could see the bulge in his jeans. He was already hard, and her mouth went dry, her pulse speeding up. Tanner O'Connor had a hard-on for her.

He stepped closer and reached down. Picking up her limp hand, he placed it on his chest. For a second, she literally couldn't move. Couldn't think. Then she stroked her palm over his skin, her nails scratching over his nipple, down his belly, resting on the waistband of his jeans. He laid his hand over hers to stop her downward movement, and her gaze shot to his face.

"Why?" he asked.

She licked her lips while she thought of her answer. Finally, she decided on the truth. "You're not the only one who has fantasies."

"You fantasized about me?" She nodded. "Sex with me?" It sounded like she'd shocked him again.

"Wow. Little Emily Towson had sexy thoughts about me. Who would have thought it?" He took another step closer, so close his body brushed against her bare breasts, and heat flashed through her. The warm scent of him filled her nostrils, fresh sweat and engine oil. Just as she had imagined.

"Did you touch yourself while you were thinking about me?" he asked.

"The first time I ever had an orgasm, I was thinking of you."

He groaned. "Jesus."

Had she *really* just said that? She released her hold on him, stepped back, and slapped her hands to her face. "I so did not just say that." She peeked through her fingers. "I did, didn't I?"

"Yeah, baby, and once said that sort of thing cannot be taken back. It's engraved in my memory." He was silent for a moment. "When you say used to—how long ago? When was the last time?"

Did she really want to admit this? But the word burst free. "Sunday."

"*This* Sunday?" She nodded, and he smiled. "I saw you in town. Did you see me, then go home and make yourself come?" She nodded again. She had a feeling she shouldn't be revealing this much of herself to him, but somehow couldn't help herself. "Jesus, that is so hot. But hell, enough talking about fantasies. Baby, I'm going to see you come for real. I'll be better than your fantasies. I'm going to fuck you so hard you won't be able to walk tomorrow. I'm going to—"

She wished he would just get on with it before she lost her nerve. "Honestly, you don't talk this much in my fantasies." Enough of the talking. "You definitely do more and say less."

With a grin, he cupped her breast in his big hand, and her nipple tightened. She held her breath. Second base with Tanner O'Connor. Who would have believed it? Not her.

His palm was hard and warm and rough, and she was melting from the inside. Her eyes drifted half closed as he lowered his head and kissed her nipple, sucking it into his mouth, teasing with his teeth, sending fire along her nerves, and she moaned and pushed into him.

He kissed her other breast, then the nipple. Then he raised his head and took her mouth in a deep kiss. His lips soft, then hard as his tongue pushed inside.

Tanner O'Connor's tongue was in her mouth.

And it was better than every fantasy rolled together.

Heat sank down through her body, and a pulse started between her thighs. This was so much more than she imagined.

She kissed him back, her hands coming up and gripping the back of his head, digging into his silky-soft hair, holding him while her tongue slid against his, the taste of him driving her wild.

He pulled back a little, and she gave a mewling cry of displeasure. "Condoms," he muttered.

"Condoms?" She didn't have any condoms. Would he expect her to have condoms?

"Don't worry," he said. "*I* have condoms. Somewhere. Don't move." He dug into his back pocket and pulled out his wallet. She held her breath as he opened it, took out a condom. *Hallelujah.*

Unable to resist, she reached out her hand and traced the tattoo around his right nipple. A sunburst. At her touch, a tremor ran through him. It made her feel a little better. He was far from immune to her. She trailed her finger down his chest; his skin was on fire. Finally, she reached his waistband and edged back enough to flick open the button on his jeans. She'd been peering up into his face, but now her gaze dropped to where she fumbled with his zipper.

"I want to see," she murmured.

Finally, he was free, and he groaned, then shoved his jeans and boxers down, kicked off his boots, dragged everything off, and he was naked. At last.

She blew out her breath.

Holy moly.

His dick was hard, vertical against his stomach, and as she stared, it twitched and pulsed.

"You're staring," he murmured.

"It's…bigger than I imagined."

He grinned. "Well, next time you play with yourself, you can get the details right."

She took a step closer. Her hand came out again, almost tentatively, and she touched him. His cock jerked, as if straining toward her, and she wrapped her fingers around him and squeezed. His skin was hot and silky smooth, and he groaned again.

Reluctantly, she released her hold and glanced to where he still held the condom in his hand. "Put it on."

He raised an eyebrow. "Bossy, aren't you?"

Not usually, but she had a feeling that if they slowed things down then one of them was going to decide this was a bad idea, and she couldn't bear it if he stopped now. "Please."

He tore the condom wrapper with his teeth and rolled it down over his cock. Then he glanced around. He was thinking too much. She didn't want him to change his mind. Not now. Then he wrapped his arms around her, slid them down her back, rubbed the curve of her ass—so good—then gripped her tight and lifted her off her feet.

A startled "Oh" fell from her mouth.

Her hands came up to grab his shoulders, her legs wrapping around his waist. She buried her nose in the skin at his throat. "You smell of oil and sweat and…man. Umm." She licked his skin; he tasted of salt, and heat pooled in her belly. His cock was pressed up against the softness of her, and she wanted more. He carried her over to the work bench at the edge of the room as though she weighed nothing, then balanced her *with one hand* while he swept the tools from the table and onto the floor with a loud clanging that barely registered in her foggy mind. He lowered her, resting her ass down on the cool metal surface.

"Lie back," he said, gently pushing her with his hand on

her shoulder.

She peered at him for a few seconds, then lowered herself so she lay staring up at the ceiling. He placed his hands on her breasts and squeezed, then tugged at her nipples, and pleasure flooded her. Lowering his head, he took one tight peak in his mouth, nipped with his teeth, then licked her, and she moaned for more.

One finger hooked in her pink lace panties, and he slowly stripped them down over her thighs, over her calves, over the shoes she still wore, tossed them away. She lifted onto her elbows to watch him. His cheeks were flushed, his eyes half closed.

Christ, he was beautiful.

A shiver ran through her as he trailed a finger through the curls at the base of her belly. Then he slid his hands between her thighs, parted them, so she was open to him. She couldn't move, couldn't look away, as he lowered his head. His breath whispered against her sex, and everything inside her clenched up tight. Then he touched her with his tongue, licking her, circling the most sensitive spot, and her spine arched, her hips lifting off the table. And nothing had ever felt this good, this frightening.

She gripped his head, her fingers threading in his silky hair as he French kissed her sex, stroking her with his tongue. She was writhing beneath him now, and he held her still with his hands on her hips as he sucked the little nub into his mouth, suckled her. She was so close now, she could feel the tension building. He bit down gently, and she exploded against his mouth, screaming as she came. He licked, then bit again, and she kept right on coming. Finally, the tremors racking her body faded. He kissed her one last time, then straightened.

"My turn."

The words hardly registered. She was totally boneless,

incapable of coherent thought. Sliding his hands under her ass, he picked her up easily, holding her against his chest. She clung to his shoulders as he backed her up to the wall, balancing her with one hand again while the other moved between their bodies, positioning himself at the entrance to her body, placing the tip of his cock inside her. A shiver ran through her at his touch, then he shoved hard and filled her.

And it was so indescribably good. Better than her fantasies. Better than anything she could have ever imagined, and she savored the sensation of him deep inside her, stretching her.

She'd gone all the way. With Tanner O'Connor.

For a moment, he didn't move.

"Don't stop." If he stopped now, she would die.

The corner of his mouth curled in a half smile. "No way am I stopping. Hold on tight, babe."

A shiver of fear prickled across her skin. So much naked power about to be unleashed. What had she done?

Too late now.

He pulled out—and her muscles tightened, fighting to hold him inside. Then he thrust back in, hard and fast. Then again. Harder and faster. Until she was mindless, aware of nothing but the hard body slamming into her. Over and over. The pleasure building at her center, radiating out. Her heart raced, her hands clawed at his shoulders, holding on tight as he sent her out of control.

Shifting her higher, he pressed her back against the wall, his hips grinding roughly against her core. So good. Then he lowered his head, bit down hard where her shoulder met her throat, and the sharp pain shot her over the edge. She came again. Harder than before. Pleasure exploding through her, the edges of her vision blurring.

She was only vaguely aware as he thrust one last time, spilling himself inside her. Her legs tightened around his waist, and he kept right on coming, hips pumping.

Finally, he went still, rested his head against her forehead, and she breathed again.

• • •

Best sex ever.

Who knew little Miss Sensible was going to be every fantasy he'd ever had rolled into one? Well, him, actually. After all, he'd been jerking off to thoughts of Emily Towson for the last eight years. Thank God that for once in his life the real world exceeded his imagination.

His legs were shaky, and he wrapped his arms around her, turned, and slid down the wall to sit on the floor with Emily in his lap. His body felt good, relaxed and at peace, but his mind filled with a sense of melancholy.

This was a one-off, as in never going to happen again; he was pretty sure she'd regret it once she came to her senses. Girls like Emily didn't date guys like him—they dated men like Ryan Forrester. But he'd bet his favorite hog—a Dyna Super Glide he'd customized himself—that Ryan had never made her come that hard, never made her scream his name. He had to bite back the urge to ask her—that would go down well.

Maybe it was time for her to leave before he said something monumentally stupid—it was only a matter of time.

She was awfully quiet. Was she working out how to get away from him? Did she think he was going to be a problem? Expect to see her again? That would be a bad idea.

But he wished briefly that he was a different person.

The sort of person who could be more than a one-off screw for a girl like Emily Towson.

Never going to happen.

Chapter Five

Emily kept her eyes tightly closed.

How was she ever going to look at him?

He'd had his mouth between her legs. The memory made her squirm a little, and the big muscular arms around her tightened.

But no one had ever done that for her before.

Holy moly. At the memory, a little pulse started between her thighs again.

Stop that, right now.

She'd screamed. It was a wonder no one had called the police. But maybe women screaming was a common occurrence in the O'Connor's workshop. In high school, he'd had a positive harem of girls. And while she wasn't aware of any current girlfriends, she presumed he must have one or more somewhere.

And she didn't like how that made her feel. It was none of her business who Tanner gave screaming orgasms to. This had been an aberration. Just a culmination of events, brought to a head by his using the dreaded "s" word.

If he hadn't said she was *sensible,* none of this would have happened.

Somehow, she had to get up, get dressed, and get out of there. Preferably without him seeing her. Yeah, like that was going to happen. She supposed she could ask him to close his eyes. He'd no doubt laugh in her face. But she'd never been entirely comfortable with nudity. Hers or anyone else's.

She hadn't told him to close his eyes when he'd been down *there.* He must have gotten a good eyeful. Ugh. She'd never understand how people could want to do that. Now she didn't think she'd ever get the memory of his mouth from her mind. It had felt so good. Better than good. She hadn't known her body was capable of so much sensation.

She'd had sex with Tanner O'Connor.

Would he tell everyone? Boast about it?

A shudder ran through her. He must have felt the movement, because he shifted her a little in his arms, jiggling her.

"You awake?"

Maybe she wasn't. Maybe it had all been a dream. "Yes."

"Good, because my legs are going numb. And this floor isn't meant for sitting on."

She forced her eyes open. She was sitting on Tanner's lap, her legs to the side, his stretched out in front. His were about twice as long as hers, tanned, muscular, with a light furring of golden hairs. His arms were around her, one curled around her waist, the other splayed across her hip. And she was still naked. So was he.

Naked, he'd been beyond anything she had ever imagined. All long, thick muscles and golden skin. She'd never thought of men as beautiful before, but Tanner was stunning.

All the same, she reckoned she'd lost her mind there for a while. Sex with Tanner O'Connor. How? Why?

"I can't believe we did that," she murmured.

"Are you sorry?" He sounded genuinely interested.

She nibbled on her lower lip. She'd always found it almost pathologically impossible to lie. "No. It was good. Are you? Sorry, I mean."

"Hell no. Best lay I've ever had."

Was that a compliment? Or something he told all his one-night stands? Send them away happy?

"But, maybe we'll keep this between ourselves, huh?"

She frowned while she thought about that. She twisted around on his lap, so she could look into his face. And then wished she hadn't, because he was so beautiful something twisted inside her. This close, his eyes had a black circle around the iris. She turned away quickly. "Are you ashamed of me?" she asked.

"Let's just say that I don't think it would do either of our reputations any good if the nice folk of Saddler Cove found out their Goody-Two-Shoes teacher lady got down and dirty with the town bad boy."

She wasn't a Goody-Two-Shoes. Hadn't she just proved that? She twisted again to tell him so when something nudged her in the ass. She'd stirred the sleeping monster. His penis was getting bigger.

Already?

Time to move.

She shot to her feet and made a straight line for where she could see her tan dress in a crumpled heap on the floor. She'd just about done a striptease. The poor man hadn't stood a chance.

Without bothering with underwear, she wriggled into the dress, twisting her arm behind her to tug up the zipper. Only when she was covered did she turn back. And again, wished she hadn't. He was still on the floor, long legs stretched out in front of him, his hand fisted around a truly impressive erection.

He grinned when he caught her gaze. "You look sexy as hell from the back."

She stood transfixed, couldn't drag her eyes from him, as he rose to his feet, hand still around himself. He was huge, and she had a sudden rush of heat and wetness between her thighs. That thing had been inside her. And it had felt so good.

"I'd suggest a round two," he said. "But no more condoms." He contemplated her for a second. "I don't suppose you'd consider a blow job?"

Her mouth dropped open.

"I take it that's a no."

He released himself and strolled toward her, totally unconcerned that he was naked with an erection sticking out in front of him. She envied him his insouciance. He stopped only inches away. He was so tall, she had to tilt her neck to look into his face. She couldn't seem to move as he lowered his head and kissed her. Just a brief touch of his lips.

"Goodbye, Emily Towson. Tonight has been surreal, and I'll never forget it. But maybe best if you don't come back."

When she still didn't move, he placed his hands on her shoulders, turned her around, and gently urged her to the door. Once she was through it, and into the yard, he released her, stepped back, and the door closed behind her.

He'd thrown her out.

How dare he?

And he still had her grandmother's check. But as she turned around, she heard the lock click.

He'd locked her out.

She glared at the door. Raised her fist to bang on it, then changed her mind. She would leave with what little dignity she had left. Mimi would just have to cancel the check.

But things could be worse. At least it sounded like he was no more eager for anyone to know about their little meeting than she was. That was good. Wasn't it? But she couldn't help thinking—what the hell was wrong with her?

Chapter Six

A week later and Tanner was still suffering the after-effects of his visit from Emily. He couldn't pick up a tool from that goddamn table without getting a hard-on. It was distracting as hell.

He hadn't seen her around town. They didn't exactly move in the same circles, so it wasn't surprising. And if he'd driven past the school a couple of times, then it was pure coincidence.

But God, she'd been hot. He wondered if she'd had any fantasies about him since that night.

He'd jerked himself off so many times his dick was sore. Was she the same? Lying in her bed at night, touching herself, her fingers all slippery and—

"Tanner, get your ass in here. Aiden's arrived."

He rubbed a hand through his hair and straightened from the bike he'd been working on. Reese stood in the doorway leading to the office. It was their monthly strategy meeting where they discussed anything to do with the business. And there was a lot going on right now—some difficult decisions to make.

They were doing well. It had been a gamble setting up the business in Saddler Cove. Both Aiden and Reese had wanted to open the shop in Richmond. It had been Tanner who had persuaded them to stay here. He hadn't wanted to leave. Despite everything, he loved Saddler Cove. During his time away, he'd longed for home, the fresh air, the sea. A small part of him knew that if he moved away, he would leave a whole load of baggage behind. Start afresh where people didn't look at him like he was a murderer. But he was too stubborn and ornery to let people drive him away. And maybe a little part of him believed he deserved whatever they could throw in his direction.

Anyway, he'd argued that their money would go a lot further here in Saddler Cove. They'd bought the place and still had cash left over for advertising, building a name for themselves. And for setting Aiden up on the racing circuit. He was bringing in a lot of business, and their reputation was growing. Tanner loved the work—it was his fantasy job— tinkering about with bikes all day long and people paying him to do it. Enough so he could indulge in his Harley obsession— as a kid he'd dreamed of owning a hog, and now he had three.

Most of their work came from outside Saddler Cove. People came a long way to buy from them, get the bikes customized. Then bringing them back for servicing. They employed three other mechanics now.

All the same, if it hadn't been for Keira, Reese's daughter, he didn't think his brother would have stayed. Hell, he would never have left the Navy and come back if it hadn't been for Keira. Reese managed the business side of things. He'd always been good with numbers, but there hadn't been the money for college. He'd joined the Navy when he was eighteen, a year before Tanner had gone to prison. He'd done well, seen a lot of action, been a Chief Petty Officer in the Navy SEALs when Keira's mother had died. Reese hadn't even known he had a daughter. But he'd come back as soon as he could and made a home for her.

Reese wanted the business to grow. Not so much for the money, but because he was bored and needed more of a challenge.

Aiden straightened from where he was leaning against the wall, and Tanner crossed to him, grabbed him in a bear hug. "Hey, bro. Great fucking race yesterday."

"Yeah. You got her running like a dream."

"I fucking did. It was all down to me." It was the goddamn truth—Aiden loved the racing but wasn't too keen on the work. Tanner kept the bikes running perfectly, giving Aiden an edge over his competitors.

He went to the big upright fridge in the corner of the office and got himself a cold beer, tossed one to Reese where he sat behind his desk. Didn't bother with one for Aiden—his little brother hadn't had a drink in six years. Not since Tanner had come home and talked some sense into him. He'd been drinking—among other things—himself into an early grave.

Tanner twisted the top off his beer and slumped on the sofa. Meetings were not his thing, but they were partners, so apparently his input was necessary.

Both Reese and Aiden took after their dad—black Irish. With dark hair and blue eyes. Aiden's hair was as long as Tanner's and pulled back in a ponytail. He looked totally badass. He'd gone a little crazy when Tanner had been sent away. Then their father had died in an accident at work, and Aiden, still only seventeen and in high school, had ended up in the foster system. He'd gotten mixed up with some bad people. Drink, drugs—you name it and Aiden had tried it. Tanner had made him see the error of his ways, and he was clean now and doing well on the race circuit.

Tanner had gotten his coloring from his mother. He

could vaguely remember her. He'd been six when she had died. In childbirth. They'd lost the baby as well. That's when his father had gone to pieces, taken to drink, and never really recovered. He'd still managed to make sure they were fed and clothed, but only just enough to keep them out of the hands of social services.

But they'd grown up as kids of the town drunk.

"So what's happening?" he asked.

"I've found us a site in Richmond."

Reese wanted to expand. Tanner had known this was coming. And he was happy to go along with it, as long as they didn't expect him to move to Richmond. He hated cities and all the people crammed in together.

He listened while Reese went through the details. "You plan to move there?"

Reese shrugged. "Not yet. Keira likes it here. I don't want her unsettled. I'll commute for now, see how it goes. Probably put a manager in there, and I'll oversee both places from here."

Tanner could understand that. Keira hadn't had the easiest of childhoods, and she was only just beginning to come out of her shell. She was a sweet kid, but more than a little screwed up—which meant she fit right into this family. She was six and had started school this year. Which meant she was in first grade. Which meant Emily was her teacher.

He wouldn't mind teaching Emily a thing or two. He had a flashback to her expression when he'd suggested the blow job. From her look of shock, he doubted she'd ever had that pretty mouth around a dick. She hadn't been a virgin, but she'd seemed surprised at her own response. She'd probably only fucked in bed. With the lights off. The way she'd stared at his dick… He shifted in his seat as his jeans got a little snug.

"Tanner!"

He jumped. "What?"

"You said you had something you wanted to discuss?"

He rubbed at his scalp, getting his mind away from where it wasn't supposed to go. But the fact was he was back to fantasizing about Emily with a vengeance. It was doing his head in. Now he'd had the real thing, he couldn't get the feel of her, the taste of her, out of his mind.

Maybe he needed to go out, let off some steam, find himself a different type of woman. One who knew the score. The idea didn't appeal.

"Tanner? Are you with us or off in some fucking dream world?"

More like off in some dream world fucking. "Piss off," he said, swallowing the last of his beer. But there was something he needed to talk about. "Remember I told you about Josh? He needed a job and a place to stay if he had any chance of getting parole?"

"Yeah," Reese said. "You also said it was a formality, would never come to anything as it was unlikely he'd get parole."

Tanner had met Josh his first night in prison. He hadn't realized back then how lucky he was. He might not have survived without Josh telling him how things worked. Of course, that had taken a little time. Josh was essentially a loner and hadn't been happy sharing with anyone, let alone a crappy eighteen-year-old kid who didn't know his ass from his elbow. But somehow, they'd become unlikely friends. He owed his sanity, if not even his life, to Josh. And now he had the chance to repay some of what he owed the man.

"Well, he has. And he'll be here next week."

"Are you sure that's a good idea?" Reese asked. "How old is this guy, anyway? I got the impression he was pretty old."

He didn't actually know. It wasn't something they'd

discussed. They tended to steer clear of personal stuff, though they'd talked about most everything else. He had to be close to seventy. He'd done forty years of a life sentence, and he'd been twenty-eight when he went inside. "Sixty-eight, I think."

"Can he work?"

"We'll find out, because he's getting a job. It's not negotiable."

But Josh didn't act like an old guy. He worked out a lot. Not much else to do inside, and Josh had said it kept the dark thoughts at bay. That and reading. He'd taught Tanner to love books. He didn't think he'd ever voluntarily read a book before he'd gone inside. But in two years, he reckoned he'd read just about every book in the prison library—some more than once.

"I suppose he can help out in the workshop," Reese said. "We're a man down with Danny leaving. Where's he going to stay?"

"I'm giving him the apartment."

"What?"

"He's been inside for forty years. He'll need some space and somewhere he can be alone." It was what Tanner had craved when he'd first come out. Still did, occasionally, though he was getting better. And he'd only been inside for two years. How the hell did someone stay sane for forty?

"And where are you going?"

"I thought I'd move back home for a little while."

"You're not fucking sharing with me," Aiden said. "You snore."

"It's his house as much as ours," Reese pointed out—always the sensible one. "But Keira's got your old room, and I'm not moving her out of it."

"I wouldn't ask you to. There's the attic room. I thought I'd clear that out and put a bed in there. It's all I need."

Anyway, it wouldn't be for too long. He was thinking of buying his own place. He could afford it now. Somewhere out of town. With a big yard and a view. And he'd maybe buy himself a piano and be able to play it where no one could hear him.

"Okay, but you're responsible for this guy." Reese frowned. "What was he in for, anyway?"

"Murder."

"Great," Reese said. "I don't suppose he was innocent."

"Nope." While the vast majority of prison inmates would swear they were innocent, Josh had never denied his guilt. Though he'd never spoken about the crime that had locked him away. And Tanner hadn't asked.

"If word gets out, there's going to be a few unhappy townsfolk. Why do I get the idea you're not too bothered about that?"

"The townsfolk can go fuck themselves." Except Emily. She could fuck him. Except he'd told her never again, and that was still good advice.

Emily was the white picket fence, happily-ever-after type. And that was as far from what he was as you could possibly get.

He still hadn't told her grandmother that he'd torn up her check and cancelled the order. Did he secretly hope Emily would come and chew him out about it again? Was that why he'd worked late every night for the last week?

Never going to happen.

He reckoned she'd stay as far away as she could.

And he'd do the same.

Which meant no loitering by the school gates or following her into the hardware store.

All he needed was a little willpower.

If only he believed it was going to be that easy. Willpower was one thing he was seriously lacking when it came to Emily.

Chapter Seven

Josh couldn't shift the sense of unreality that had enveloped him since he'd stepped through the gates that morning. The clothes they'd given him felt all wrong, and he rubbed at the collar of his shirt—he'd taken the tie off as he'd walked away, hearing the gate clang shut behind him. What the hell did someone like him need with a goddamn tie?

It was late spring, but the bus was air-conditioned and cool, though out the window the sky was a deep blue and the sun bright. The bus was pretty full, but the seat next to him was empty. You'd think no one wanted to sit by him. Maybe he was giving fuck-off vibes. He'd perfected the art a long time ago.

There were still a couple of hours to go, and he forced himself to relax, watch the passing scenery, and accept that the lump in his stomach was fear.

Fear of being free.

He was a goddamn prison cliché.

Institutionalized.

That's what they called it.

So many years, he'd slept when he was told to sleep, eaten when he was told to eat, pissed when he was told to piss. His whole life had been ordered for him. Now there was no one to tell him anything. And he felt like he had vertigo, that he was falling, tumbling through the sky with the Earth nowhere in sight.

He was on his way to Saddler Cove. Tanner's hometown. The place that had screwed that boy up good and proper. Because they thought he wasn't good enough.

What the hell were the inhabitants of Saddler Cove going to make of a sixty-eight-year-old black ex-con who'd spent forty years inside for a murder he'd definitely committed? While the actual memory of the act had always been blurred, he'd never had any doubt of his guilt.

He'd read a lot in prison, and he'd come to realize that murder had been inevitable—he'd been a ticking bomb waiting to explode. He was just glad that when the explosion had finally happened, the man in front of him had deserved to die. Even if the judge and jury hadn't exactly seen it that way.

He'd worked in the workshop at the prison for the last twenty years. He knew his way around and might even be able to do something useful. But that wasn't why Tanner had offered him the job.

Tanner was one of the good guys, whatever he thought. He'd visited Josh once a month without fail over the past six years, bringing him new books, talking about what was going on on the outside, staying away from anything personal. His only visitor—Josh's family were long gone, dead, or vanished.

Forty fucking years.

The world had moved on without him, and he didn't think he could run fast enough to catch up. Even if he wanted to try. Those forty years had broken him in some indefinable way. Left him a shell.

He pulled a battered copy of *The Count of Monte Cristo* out of the duffel bag between his legs and tried to concentrate on the words. Otherwise, he was in danger of doing Tanner a favor, getting out at the next stop, and just walking till he dropped. But he'd promised he'd see Tanner first, give this thing a chance. If it didn't work out, then walking was still an option.

When the bus pulled up in Saddler Cove, his heart was beating fast and his hands were clammy. He wiped them on his pants leg, then picked up his duffel and shuffled down the aisle. The bus was almost empty now, nearly at the end of the line. It seemed fitting.

It was late afternoon, but all the same the warmth hit him as he stepped onto the concrete parking lot. The town was small, Tanner had warned him of that. Josh had lived in the city before, except for the years in Nam, and that had hardly endeared him to the countryside. They'd driven through the town to the bus depot. It had taken five minutes. Low-rise buildings on either side of a wide road. It looked clean and pretty, with lots of green areas. Far off, the way they had come, he could see a backdrop of mountains. He breathed in the air, clean and fresh with a hint of salt. They were close to the ocean. He'd never actually seen the ocean.

He glanced around, and his gaze locked on the tall figure strolling toward him. Dressed in jeans, scuffed boots, a white tee that showed off his tats, Tanner looked nothing like a prosperous business owner and everything like a badass ex-con. Maybe he'd lied about the job. But whatever, the parole board had believed him, and that's what mattered.

Tanner stopped in front of him, and a wide grin spread across his face. It was weird seeing Tanner smile. He wasn't the smiley type. More the miserable bastard type. They stared at each other for long moments. Josh had never believed this day would come. That was how he'd survived the years inside.

By leaving hope behind. A long way behind. And now he didn't know what to feel.

"It's good to see you here," Tanner said.

"Shit. Don't go all mushy on me, man."

"Fuck you. Not a chance." He grabbed the duffel from Josh—did he think he was too old to carry his own bag—but was moving away before Josh could complain, and he followed in a brisk walk. There were a few other people around who invariably followed their movements in a surreptitious way. As though they didn't like what they were seeing, but were too polite to be openly antagonistic. Josh could live with that—he didn't give a toss what they thought as long as they kept it to themselves.

Tanner led the way along the sidewalk, past a diner that promised all-day breakfast—as much as you could eat for five dollars. Josh had precisely one hundred and six dollars to show for a lifetime of hard labor. Five dollars for breakfast seemed excessive.

Finally, Tanner headed down an alley. He stopped at a dark blue door, pulled the keys out of his pocket, and let them into a hallway with a narrow staircase.

"This apartment came with the showroom and garage," he said. "I've been using it, but it's yours for as long as you need it."

"I've kicked you out of your own home?"

"Yeah, you bastard." Tanner headed up the stairs as he continued. "I'm moving in with my brothers."

At the top of the stairs, he unlocked another door and led the way into a big living area. Josh dropped his jacket on a chair and crossed the room to stare out of the wide bay window. It looked out onto the street. And he stared for long minutes. Too much. He didn't know what to do with all this space, and his heart rate sped up again.

He'd wait until he was left alone and then he was off.

Tanner could have his place back. This wasn't for him.

He turned as Tanner shoved a beer into his hand, and he wrapped his fingers around the icy bottle.

"Welcome to Saddler Cove," Tanner said, raising his own bottle. "Don't even think about walking out without talking to me first."

For a moment he couldn't move, then he slowly lifted the bottle to his mouth. The beer was cold and delicious, and he drank half in one gulp. And some of the tension drained out of him. He tossed Tanner a wry look. "*'Get busy living or get busy dying.'* Is that what you're suggesting?" It was a game they'd played in their cell at night. Identifying quotes from their favorite books.

Tanner grinned. "*Rita Hayworth and the Shawshank Redemption*—very fitting. And that's exactly what I mean." He emptied his beer and put the bottle down on the table. "Come on, you can get settled in later. Right now, I want to show you something."

"What?"

"Wait and see."

He followed Tanner out and back down to the alley that ran alongside the building. At the far end, a shiny black truck was parked, O'Connor Bros printed on the side in silver. Tanner climbed into the driver's seat, leaned over, and pushed open the passenger door.

"You've done well for yourself," Josh said as he got in. The truck looked new.

"Remember, my daddy died?"

"Yeah."

"It was an accident at work. We got compensation in exchange for keeping our mouths shut. We used that to buy the business."

"An asshole would have frittered it away on booze and women."

He grinned. "I did a bit of that when I got out. But it grows old quickly."

With the grin, Tanner looked younger now than he had when he'd gotten released. Tanner hadn't taken the time inside well. Some people didn't. Too independent and stubborn. Hell, it had taken Josh fifteen years before he'd accepted that it was his life. And he'd spent a hell of a lot of that fifteen years in solitary. It had been a learning experience. There was no such thing as easy time, but there was definitely harder time.

They drove through the town. At one point, Tanner slowed the truck as they passed a woman walking along the sidewalk. Small and pretty, in a navy-blue dress, she glanced at the truck and then looked quickly away.

"Friend of yours?" he asked Tanner.

"Hardly. Emily Towson, the town's first-grade teacher. A good woman. Far too good for the likes of me."

There was no bitterness behind the words, just a wry acceptance of the way things were. And maybe he was right. Why try and fight the system? It always won.

They were out of town now, driving along a dirt road that wound along the edge of a creek, flat blue water, hardly moving.

Where the hell were they going?

Finally, Tanner pulled the truck to a halt and parked, turned off the engine. "The first day I got out, I came here. It helped."

Josh sat staring ahead. They were parked in the shadow of a huge sand dune. "Where exactly is here?"

Tanner waved a hand. "Follow that path. You'll see." He pulled a book out of the side panel—a paperback copy of *Don Quixote*. "Take as long as you want. I'll be waiting here."

For a moment, he considered arguing, but he was programmed to take the course of least resistance, and he opened the door and jumped down from the cab.

He stood, breathing slowly, unable to shake the sense of futility. In the early years, he'd often imagined this day. Dreamed of how it would feel to be free. But as the years passed, the dreams had come less frequently, until one day he'd stopped dreaming altogether.

Dreams were for people with hope. People with a future. He had neither.

Tanner banged on the truck window. "Go," he mouthed.

Josh shrugged but headed off. It wasn't as though he had anything else to do.

He'd have been better off if they'd never let him go. If he'd died in prison. At least there he wouldn't be tormented by all the things he would never have. A home, a wife, children. Before he'd joined the army, he'd had the same dreams and hopes as other men.

All long gone. Nothing but a distant memory.

It was cooler now, a slight breeze brushing against his skin. And the salt tang was stronger. He rolled up his sleeves as he headed down the track Tanner had pointed to. It skirted the edge of a sand dune. And as he came around the other side, his feet faltered. The ocean was in front of him, as far as he could see. Huge and empty and endless, lined by a pale-yellow beach that went on for miles with no one in sight. Waves rolled in from the sea, curling and cresting and crashing on to the sand with a constant roar that filled his ears.

So vast.

The sight filled him with an awareness of his own insignificance. Like he was nothing, a speck of sand that would soon be washed away. His chest felt hollow, empty, and his eyes ached.

He moved slowly forward, his feet hesitant at first. But something was drawing him on, and soon he was walking faster, then running, racing along the sand at the edge of the ocean. He couldn't remember the last time he had run. Finally, when his legs ached, he slowed and stopped, turning to face the immensity of the ocean. He was alone and free. His eyes stung, and he rubbed them with the back of his hand. Too much salt spray in the air? That was it. He never cried, at least he couldn't remember the last time. Certainly not since he'd killed a man.

At the thought, something inside him snapped, and he crashed to his knees, a cry ripped from his throat. And he knelt there, as though in prayer, his body wracked by sobs. He didn't know what he was crying for: the life he'd taken or the one he had lost. Or maybe the one that might be his. If he could dredge up the courage to accept what had been offered.

Was he brave enough to overcome his fears? To dream again?

Finally, the tears dried, and he shifted so he sat on the soft sand, watching the ebb and flow of the waves.

He had never understood why Tanner had insisted on coming back to the town that had treated him so badly. Now he could see.

He stayed for a long time, not thinking, just being, until the sun disappeared in a blaze of crimson, and a huge heavy moon was rising over the horizon.

Then he pushed himself to his feet and headed back the way he had come. He was going to come back and swim in the ocean. Submerge himself in the water.

For the first time he could remember, he thought there might be some things worth living for.

He'd give it a go.

Chapter Eight

Emily took a gulp of punch from her plastic tumbler and wished she'd not agreed to come. She'd gotten the invite from Susanne Defray, who'd been her best friend in high school, even if they had drifted apart a little now. Susanne had married a man from Richmond when she was twenty. Now she was back home and divorced, though thankfully— she said—without children. She was going to make up for lost time. She'd said there was a whole group of them going to the Founders' Parade and the dance afterward together. That it would be fun. Unfortunately, the obvious organizers of the group were Susanne's cousin, Lanie Dean, and her husband, Sawyer. Emily had never really liked Sawyer.

Maybe because he'd supposedly been Tanner's best friend back when he got into trouble, and Sawyer hadn't stuck around long enough to even say goodbye. At the time, Emily had been deep in her Tanner crush—completely gone now, of course—and she'd seen Sawyer's act as a cruel betrayal. He'd abandoned his friend when he needed him the most. Apparently, Sawyer had left town the afternoon before the accident and hadn't turned back up until Tanner was convicted and carted off to prison. Staying with his uncle in Richmond.

And it just didn't ring true to Emily. Him, Tanner, and Dwain had always been thick as thieves, always together. And why would Sawyer have left town then, in the middle of graduation week? It didn't make sense. And Sawyer had already been in trouble for drunk driving, which made his disappearance out of town just a little convenient. But no one else had ever questioned it, and Sawyer had never even been called at the trial. A travesty of justice, she'd considered, but she'd been sixteen at the time, and no one was listening to her.

These days, Sawyer was still drinking too much. He was the sort of guy you never saw totally drunk, but often not quite sober. And she could see Lanie throwing him dark glances every so often. But Sawyer wasn't the problem. How had she forgotten that Lanie was Ryan's cousin? Which of course meant he was part of the group. And everyone was treating them as if they were still a couple. Even Ryan. *Especially* Ryan.

Even if he hadn't asked her to marry him, she would have finished with him anyway. How could she go out with one man and sleep with another?

Okay, maybe not sleep. Definitely not sleep.

But Ryan was totally ignoring the fact that they were finished. Just pretending it hadn't happened. And it was driving her crazy. He was at her side now, so close he kept bumping arms as he drank. She edged away, and he followed her right along.

"You look beautiful tonight."

She gritted her teeth. Unfortunately, she'd been brought up far too well to ignore him. "Thank you, Ryan. You look nice as well."

Where was Mimi? Maybe she could get a lift home. Ryan had picked her up and driven her here—that was when she'd realized the evening was on a fast downhill slope to Horribleville.

Mimi had ridden her stallion, Frankie, in the parade and then afterward gone to dinner with a couple of friends and claimed that she didn't want Emily cramping her style. That was a low blow. But Mimi reckoned she'd been a complete wet blanket for weeks. Three weeks exactly, to be precise. It was exactly three weeks since she'd crept back into the house, so Mimi wouldn't catch her coming home covered in grease and completely without underwear.

Mimi said she should go out and have fun.

Grr. She didn't want to have fun. She didn't want to think about having fun. And she certainly didn't want to think about the last time she'd had fun—if that was the right word to describe her one-night stand with Tanner.

Lanie approached at that moment. "We're all heading over to the dance now," she said with a tight, brittle smile. There were whispers around town that her and Sawyer's marriage was in trouble.

"I'm feeling a little tired. I might go see if I can find my grandmother and get a lift home."

"No, you must come. Just for a short while."

Had Ryan put her up to this? Probably.

Lanie hooked her arm in Emily's, and she was towed along. She really did want to go home. She didn't feel right. Listless, she hadn't been sleeping well since…that night. But she didn't want to offend Lanie, and in the end, it was easier to just give in.

The dance was in the town square. Lights had been strung all around and a podium set up at the far side, where the band would play. They were getting ready now, setting up their instruments, three guys and a woman. They'd played at the Founders' Celebrations dance for the last three years.

She edged away from Ryan and crossed to where Susanne stood tapping her feet to the music coming over the speakers while the band set up.

"Can I ask you something?" Emily said.

"What is it?"

"Who asked you to ask me tonight?"

"Lanie."

"But I hardly know Lanie." They didn't move in the same circles. Lanie was a couple of years older and a stay-at-home mom.

Susanne moved closer. "Between you and me, honey, I think Ryan put her up to it. I think he wants to get back together with you. And you were such a nice couple. Why not give him another chance? Whatever he did wrong, I'm sure he's sorry." She quirked a brow. "What did he do, anyway?"

What was she supposed to say—he asked me to marry him? Susanne would probably think she was mad. Turning down Saddler Cove's most eligible bachelor. Or maybe not. Susanne was a little anti-marriage at the moment. All men were apparently cheating, lying bastards. Only good for one thing. "We just weren't suited."

"Well, clearly Ryan doesn't agree."

She shrugged. "He'll find someone else." Or he would if he would stop staring at her. It was creepy. She turned away and went still.

The square was filling up. But a group of four men stood off to one side. Separate as though the rest of the population were giving them a wide berth. With a little shock of surprise, she recognized the O'Connor brothers, together with a tall, black man, taller even than the brothers, with a long lanky frame. Handsome, almost distinguished, she couldn't tell his age; it could have been anything from fifty to seventy.

Susanne edged closer and whispered in her ear. "Is that

the man they've employed at O'Connor's? I heard he was some sort of serial killer who's been in prison all his life and is likely to murder all us innocent folk in our beds."

"And no doubt torture us and eat our babies. You shouldn't listen to gossip. Anyway, I'm sure the O'Connors wouldn't employ anyone dangerous."

"Are you serious? The O'Connors *are* dangerous." Susanne sounded as though the idea didn't put her off in the least. But then, she'd been married for four years to an insurance salesman whose idea of a fun Saturday night was watching a ballgame on TV. Probably Susanne was more than ready for a little danger. Or a lot of danger.

The tall man said something to Tanner and then he turned and walked away, heading back toward the garage. She'd heard that he was staying in Tanner's place while Tanner had moved back home.

"They're something else, aren't they?" Susanne's voice was laced with longing.

The three men were talking together, huddled in a little group, and for a moment she allowed herself to stare. They seemed almost alien, something apart from the people of Saddler Cove. But with an air of confidence and ease as though they knew they didn't belong and didn't care. Was that true, or was that something they'd fostered? Aiden, the youngest, had been in her year in high school. She remembered him being teased because his dad was a drunk and his clothes were never quite right. Though no one had ever touched him, because then they might have incurred the wrath of his big brothers, and no one had wanted that. They'd had reputations even then.

A bottle of beer dangled from Tanner's hand. He lifted it to his lips, and she watched the movement of his throat as he swallowed. He was dressed the same as the night in the garage, in faded jeans that hung low on his hips and a white tank, but at least it was clean tonight. His hair was loose, not quite reaching his shoulders. She remembered the feel of it under her fingers as she'd gripped onto him while he…

Don't go there.

She took no notice of the inner voice, and her mind filled with a flashback of his blond head between her thighs. It had been the most erotic thing she had ever seen.

She hadn't laid eyes on Tanner since, except for a brief glimpse one evening as he'd driven past her. He hadn't stopped. Of course he hadn't stopped. She'd never been his type, and that wasn't about to change. And guess what—she didn't want to be.

Susanne nudged her in the side. "You're staring," she said. "I do believe you've got the hots for the O'Connors."

"I have not," she said with as much dignity as she could muster, considering her panties were soaking from the memory of Tanner's mouth just there.

"Hmm, but which one?" Susanne mused. "Maybe all of them. What would that be like?" She fanned herself. "Shit, I think I just came at the thought."

"Susanne!"

"Come on. Can't you imagine it? Just for a night. One hot night of super-hot sex."

"You know you're treating them as sex objects. If it was the other way around, you'd be screaming about sexism."

She sighed. "You're right. I suppose we could talk first. Perhaps we could ask them about the serial killer in our midst."

Emily remembered why she had liked Susanne so much. She'd never taken anything seriously. And it looked like her marriage hadn't changed that. It would be nice to have her friend back. Most of her circle had gone to college and moved away. She hadn't really clicked with anyone in the three years since she'd been back from college. She was friendly with a couple of the other teachers, but not close. Not close enough to talk about…say…screwing the town bad boy.

Susanne sighed. "Okay, maybe all three is more than I could handle. I'd probably spontaneously combust. If I had to pick it would be…" She studied them, head cocked to one side. Emily couldn't believe they were oblivious to the weight of her hungry stare. "…Aiden."

"Why Aiden?" Not that he wasn't hot, but no more than the others, and obviously she was biased.

"Tanner's sexy as hell, but I prefer my men tall, dark, and handsome."

"What about Reese?"

"Reese is nice, but he's also a single daddy, and I ain't looking to be no surrogate mother."

Reese's daughter was in Emily's class this year. Keira was a sweet child, though overly quiet. Not surprising when she had lost her mother so recently.

Susanne was beautiful, with long chestnut curls and a killer body, tall and slender, exactly what Emily had always wanted to be. She reckoned Susanne could get any man if she set her mind to it. Emily was beyond relieved she wasn't going after Tanner. She presumed he was with some nameless, faceless woman—she could live with that. But not Susanne.

"Oh my God," Susanne gasped. "They're heading this way."

They were. Led by Reese. And now she looked down and saw Keira was clinging to his hand. The little girl had been hidden behind a sea of jean-clad legs. Emily's gaze flashed to Tanner behind them. She wasn't ready for this. In fact, she could already feel heat washing over her skin, her throat locking up.

"Hey, teacher lady," Reese said, coming to a halt in front of her. "Keira wanted to say hi."

Emily shook herself, did her best to ignore the looming,

brooding figure of Tanner behind him. She stepped closer and held out her hand. Keira shook it, her expression solemn.

"Hi, Ms. Towson."

She cleared her throat. "Hi, Keira. Did you enjoy the parade?"

She nodded. "I sat on Uncle Tanner's shoulders and saw everything."

Her gaze flicked to Tanner. He had nice shoulders. He returned the look, his face expressionless as he took another gulp from his beer bottle. Obviously, he'd been telling the truth when he said they should forget that night. Clearly he'd had no trouble forgetting it. A little niggle of irritation poked her in the belly. She did her best to ignore it, but at least it cut through the worst of her nerves.

"That was very nice of Uncle Tanner."

"He didn't want to come, but I made him."

"Don't you like parades, Uncle Tanner?" she asked, holding his gaze and willing him to make some sort of response. Though she had no clue why.

"No."

God, he was surly.

"Tanner's a miserable bastard," Aiden said. "Ignore him. Me and Reese here are much better company."

Susanne nudged her in the side.

"Do you remember Susanne? She was in our year in high school. She's just moved back from Richmond."

"I do." Aiden said, his gaze wandering over her. "Didn't we have a thing in school?"

Obviously, he had about as much charm as Tanner. Emily was pretty sure they hadn't. Susanne would have told her back then if she'd bagged an O'Connor. Before Susanne could answer, Lanie approached, Sawyer at her side. "We're all going for some supper," she said. "Ryan insisted we wait for you, Emily."

She opened her mouth to snap something—probably that Ryan could wait forever, but Sawyer spoke before she could get the words out.

"Perhaps you would all like to join us," he said.

A complete silence followed the invitation. As though the words had been spoken in a foreign language. Then Tanner snorted. "You've got to be fucking kidding me." He was glaring at Sawyer, and something dark passed between the two men.

Aiden stepped forward, closer to Sawyer than was polite, and any hint of amusement was gone from his face. "I think we'll take a rain check on dinner. Another time, perhaps. Or maybe never."

Sawyer opened his mouth to answer, but Lanie glared at him, with something close to desperation in her eyes. She grabbed hold of her husband's arm and tugged. "Come on, Sawyer. We need to get back to the others."

For a moment, Emily thought he was going to resist. Then the tension went out of him and he allowed himself to be dragged away. It occurred to Emily, for the first time, that if she was right about Tanner's innocence, and she was sure she was, then likely Lanie had her suspicions as well. How could she not? Had she known what had really happened? Emily didn't think so, Lanie wasn't a bad person, but the other woman must have had doubts over the years. They would have eaten away at her, goading her every time she set eyes on Tanner, every time Sawyer drank.

She glanced at Tanner. His jaw was clenched, his fists balled at his side. He caught her watching him and snarled. "Why don't you go with your nice friends, Ms. Towson. Ryan is waiting for you."

The atmosphere had changed, and a chill ran through her despite the warm night. "I think I will. Goodnight," she said to the group, not looking at Tanner—she had a feeling it wouldn't take much for him to act like a complete ass.

"See you around, teacher lady," Reese said.

"Bye, Ms. Towson."

"Bye, Keira."

She nodded to the group in general, turned on her heel, and walked away, tugging Susanne with her.

"Aw, damn," Susanne muttered. "We should have stayed. I was making progress."

Emily snorted in disbelief. "He couldn't even remember if you had a thing in high school. That is not progress."

• • •

Tanner tried not to watch her go, but for some reason he couldn't take his eyes off the sway of her ass. She was wearing a blue-and-white striped dress that covered her from neck to knees. About as far from sexy as you could get. But he'd seen beneath the clothes. He knew what she looked like sprawled out across his work bench, thighs open, breasts... Shit, he'd told himself so many times...forget Emily Towson. But he was pretty sure she hadn't forgotten; she'd gone all pink and wide-eyed when she'd seen him.

"I like Ms. Towson," Keira piped up. She was a nice kid and clearly had good taste. "Maybe you should ask Ms. Towson on a date, Daddy."

That finally dragged Tanner's attention from Emily's disappearing ass.

"Maybe I should," Reese answered.

Not in this fucking lifetime.

As far as Tanner was aware, Reese wasn't looking for a mother for Keira. But what did he know? It would certainly make life easier. Reese was spending a small fortune on nannies and babysitters. He insisted on the best for Keira, and Tanner couldn't blame him. And it must be hard on

Keira in a household with three guys. So yeah, it would make sense. But no way was he marrying Emily.

"Don't even think about it," he growled in a low voice.

Reese shrugged. "Why not? She's young, pretty. She obviously loves kids, and I think she was giving me the eye back there."

"No, she wasn't." Had she been? She'd better not have been. It was Tanner she'd been fantasizing about for years. Not Reese. He rubbed a hand through his hair. She wouldn't fantasize about two men. That wasn't like her...was it?

He shut off the thoughts. She was making him crazy. He glanced up to find his brothers and Keira all regarding him with expressions from amusement to curiosity. Yeah, he was so goddamn funny.

"You staking a claim?" Reese asked. They'd always had an agreement they wouldn't go after the same girl. But he wasn't going after Emily. And neither was Reese.

"No. You heard. She's going out with Ryan Forrester."

Reese shrugged. "I could get her away from Forrester."

Tanner narrowed his eyes, took a step closer, and poked Reese in the chest. "Don't go near Emily Towson." Then he spun around and stalked away. He suspected he heard a chuckle follow him—yeah, he was so funny.

He went back to the truck and pulled another Bud from the cooler, popped the top, and stood for a moment. He didn't know what to do. He should go back to the garage and do some work. That would take his mind off stuff. And by stuff, he meant Emily. Instead, he wandered around the outside of the square, perfectly aware of the people shifting out of his way, avoiding contact, and he felt his face falling into its normal truculent lines.

The weird thing was, he loved this town, its proximity to the sea, the wide open grassy plains, the creeks, the mountains in the distance. But also, the town itself. It had a sense of age and permanence. It fitted into the land as though it belonged. It hadn't been designed but had grown organically, weathered and aged, until it was almost part of the landscape itself.

It was just a pity the town didn't love him. Christ, he was maudlin.

He was deep in his miserable thoughts when he almost crashed into someone who didn't get out of his way.

Shit, I do not need this right now.

Jed Forrester. The most influential man in the town, head of the school board, council member. And Dwain's father. Until Dwain had been killed. Thrown out of an open-top car, straight into an oak tree head first. He hadn't stood a chance. They'd been celebrating graduation and freedom. That had turned out to be an ironic joke.

Tanner never blamed Dwain's father for what had happened to Tanner. He blamed himself, mostly, and Sawyer partly. Forrester had been so stricken by grief that he'd had to lash out at something. Tanner had been the obvious choice. That didn't mean Tanner forgave him. He wasn't the forgiving sort. Or liked him. The man was an uptight asshole. He was also Sawyer's father-in-law. Maybe there was some justice in the world.

They stared at each other for long moments. Tanner suspected that Forrester made every bit as much effort to avoid these encounters as he did. They did not raise happy memories for either one. He could guess what Forrester wanted to talk about, and he needed to keep his temper.

"Can you guarantee this man will not be a danger to the people here?"

Straight to business. He obviously didn't want to waste time chatting. He became aware they had an audience. "Which man?" Okay, he was being an ass, but it sort of came naturally after so much practice.

Forrester was tall, lean, ascetic looking. His lips thin,

his eyes cold. It must have been hard losing your only son, so Tanner tried to cut him some slack. He'd known bringing Josh here would cause ripples, and he'd done it anyway. As Josh was on parole, it had to be registered with the town hall. Luckily, Gracie, the mayor's secretary, had put the paperwork through for him. She'd been a girlfriend way back in high school and still held a soft spot for him.

He blew out his breath. "He's a good man who made a mistake over forty years ago. He's nearly seventy—he's not a danger to anyone."

It was...probably true. If Josh was a danger to anyone, it was likely himself. He was struggling to adjust to the outside. But hell, Tanner had struggled and he'd only been inside for two years. He couldn't even begin to imagine what forty would be like. So far, Josh had been working, keeping to himself, and taking long walks on the beach.

Forrester nodded once, then turned and walked away. Tanner glanced around, glared at a few obviously nosy bastards, and then shoved his hands in his pockets and moved on.

Tables had been set up at one side of the square, and the local diner was doing good business. He caught sight of Sawyer and searched his table. Emily had her back to him. She was seated beside Ryan Forrester, and something dark uncoiled in his gut. Early on in prison, they'd sent him for anger management therapy. Hell, he'd needed it. He'd been spitting mad at everything and everyone, including himself. They'd taught him to breathe through his rage. They'd also taught him the piano. There would be a few startled expressions if he got up on the podium and started banging out a Mozart concerto. He was totally tempted.

Now he breathed slowly and forced the anger back down. She wasn't his. He had no right to any say in who she had dinner with. Except when he looked closely, he could tell instantly that she was not happy. Her shoulders were rigid, and she was leaning away from her companion as she spoke. Ryan placed a hand on her arm, and she immediately swiped it off. Tanner took a step forward. How dare the bastard touch her when she clearly didn't want to be touched? But before he could take another step, she got to her feet and dropped her napkin on the table. She said something to the group in general, he couldn't hear the words, then pushed her chair back, grabbed her bag, and weaved her way out through the crowd of tables.

Tanner waited for a moment, then followed her, like a goddamn stalker, but his legs seemed to be moving of their own accord. Once away from the square, she paused on the sidewalk, pulled her phone out of her bag, and made a call. She continued on her way, and he continued right after her. He was just making sure she didn't come to any harm, get into any trouble—not that there was a lot of trouble to get into on the main street of Saddler Cove. Finally, she came to a halt outside the Ocean View—the nicest restaurant in town. Not that Tanner had ever been in there. It was a suit-and-tie sort of place. If she went in, he'd have to give up his stalker activities for the night.

He took a swig of beer. Drinking on the sidewalk was prohibited in Saddler Cove, but they made an exception for holidays, so he was probably safe. Though they might make an exception to the exception for him.

But she didn't go in, just moved to the edge of the sidewalk and leaned against the wall as if she was waiting for someone.

No one was going to touch her here. He should go. Instead, he tossed his empty bottle in the trash can and swaggered over. Across town, he heard the band start up— maybe he should ask her for a dance.

She'd been reading something on her phone, and she glanced up as he stopped in front of her. Her eyes widened, and she glanced behind him, presumably to check if he was alone. The streets were quiet—almost everyone was in the town square having what passed for fun in their tiny town.

"Tanner."

Just the way she said his name, sort of breathless, made him hard. He nodded. "Emily."

"What are you doing here?" Her eyes narrowed. "Did you follow me?"

"You looked a little upset. I was just making sure no one else followed you."

"You mean Ryan? He's being a total pain in the…"

"Ass?"

"Yes." She pressed her finger to the spot between her brows. "I don't know what's wrong with me. I'm usually so…" She took a couple of deep breaths. "He was making me so angry."

"I thought he was your boyfriend?"

"Not anymore. It's over between me and Ryan. It was over before that night you and I…"

He decided to help her out. "Had hot, dirty sex on top of the work bench in my garage. Then up against the wall in my garage."

She gritted her teeth but gave a quick nod.

"Why was it over with Mr. Perfect? Did he finish with you?" Maybe she'd needed some sort of affirmation of herself as a sexy woman. He wanted to beat Ryan for that, though he had ultimately benefited from it.

"None of your business."

"Come on, Em. I'm curious."

Her face took on a mutinous expression, lips pursed. "He said I was *sensible* and then he asked me to marry him."

Tanner managed to choke back the laugh, but she must have seen it on his face.

"It's not funny."

He'd proposed? That made Tanner want to growl. But she had a point. It sounded as though Ryan had fucked up on the proposal. Tanner certainly wasn't sorry. Ryan's loss, his gain. "Let me get this straight. If he hadn't called you sensible, you would have said yes?"

"Probably not. He told me he'd decided it was time to settle down, and I was a nice, sensible woman, and would make him a suitable wife. Or something like that. I sort of stopped listening at 'sensible.' What sort of man starts a proposal by saying you're sensible?"

"An asshole?"

"Yes. Exactly. I said I didn't think we were suited and walked out. Then when I got home, Mimi told me she'd bought a bike from you, and then she more than hinted that I was sensible, too. So when you said it as well, I just…sort of blew."

"Actually, you kissed me, then you stripped, then you threw yourself at me. I didn't stand a chance." He had an image of her standing naked in front of him, challenging him to do something, and almost groaned.

"I did not throw myself at you."

He just stood there, one eyebrow raised.

She folded her arms across her chest. "Anyway. I thought you were pretending that never happened?"

"Believe me, I'm trying. But I keep getting these little flashbacks at the most inappropriate times. Like when I'm picking up a tool from my work bench and there you are, all soft and naked and panting for me."

Why did he do this to himself? His dick was almost painfully hard.

She was staring at him wide-eyed, her pink lips slightly parted. She didn't move. He cast a quick look around the street—it was empty—then he closed the space between them, lowered his head, and kissed her before she could even have an idea of his intentions. He half expected her to pull back and run away, but her lips softened, then parted under his, and he slipped his tongue inside, sliding it along the length of hers. He kissed her until they both ran out of air. He hadn't thought kissing was such a big deal, but he could kiss Emily all night.

"Hmm," he whispered against her skin, "you taste of strawberries and cream."

She blinked up at him. "You taste of beer."

He looked around again, spotted a deep doorway to the hardware store behind her. Just one more kiss, then they'd go back to the forgetting thing. And maybe a quick squeeze. The music drifted across town. "You want to dance?"

She blinked at him as though she didn't know what the word meant, and he slid his arms around her waist and turned her in a spin. Her hands gripped his shoulder, and she was pressed against him, soft against his hardness, and he groaned into her hair. But she made no move to pull away, and he slowed the spin, maneuvering her back and into the doorway. For a minute he held her, swaying to the music. Christ, he didn't know how to dance, but he could pretend. Not for too long. He had a feeling that if he wanted another kiss, he'd better be quick, because any moment she'd remember who he was and where they were. And then she'd be gone.

Stepping back, he cupped her cheek and kissed her again, his tongue playing with hers as he gently urged her back. She didn't fight him, instead sinking into him, soft and pliant. Finally, he backed her against the doorway and deepened the kiss. He pressed his body against hers, feeling the softness of her breasts, and she moaned into his mouth, her hands coming up to grip his shoulders. He nuzzled her neck, licked then sucked the soft skin. He lifted one leg, pushed it between hers under her stripy skirt so she rode the hard muscle of his thigh. He was pressed right up against her sex, and she liked it, he could tell, rubbing herself against him, almost purring. He was going to make her come and then he'd...

He could hardly take her back to his place, not with his brothers and Keira there. And he could equally not screw the town's first-grade teacher in a doorway on a main street. But Christ, he wanted to.

She went still in his arms and then punched him on the shoulder. "Let me go. Now."

He lowered his leg, released his hold, and turned around. The restaurant door had opened, and three women walked out. He recognized the middle one as Emily's grandmother.

Emily was smoothing her dress down. Her hair had come loose and hung in a mass of honey curls to her shoulders. She had glorious hair but usually wore it tied back tight. She looked a little...undone. It suited her.

"I have to go," she said. "I don't suppose you could..."

"Hide until you've gone?" Well, that put him in his place. But what else did he expect? "Yeah. Get out of here. We wouldn't want the nice people seeing little Ms. Sensible with me, now would we?"

Her lips formed an O of outrage. He reckoned he'd learned how to push her buttons. But he wouldn't be doing it again. From now on, no more stalking.

• • •

Emily tried to shake of the niggle of guilt. She'd offended him, and she hadn't meant to. After all, he was the one who'd said they should keep their little encounter to themselves.

A taxi drove up, and Mimi's friends climbed into the back, leaving Mimi alone on the sidewalk. She glanced across as Emily appeared out of the shadows. "Hello, darling. Are you hiding?"

She shrugged. "I thought Ryan might have followed me.

He was being a pain." She took a deep breath. She wasn't ashamed of Tanner. Even if he was ashamed of her. "And Mr. O'Connor was just keeping me company while I waited."

"Mr. O'Connor? Really? In the doorway of Dee's Hardware store? What a novel idea. And is he going to come out, or stay skulking in the shadows?"

She had no clue. Emily glanced back over her shoulders. Maybe he'd just ignore them and stay there. But he strolled out of the doorway, hands in his pockets as though he hadn't a care in the world.

"Evening, ma'am." He nodded to Mimi.

"You must call me Mimi," her gran said. "Everyone does."

Tanner's lips curled as though he found the idea amusing, but he never said anything.

"Well, thank you for keeping Emily company, Mr. O'Connor. Happy Founders' Day, now we must be going." She took Emily's arm. "But don't think I have forgotten about my motorcycle. The bank informs me that my check has not been cleared. Is my money not good enough?" She didn't give him a chance to answer, just continued, "I will be visiting your place of business very shortly to find out exactly what's going on."

Emily had forgotten all about the bike. But he clearly hadn't taken the money. She peered over her shoulder as Mimi hustled her away. He was standing watching them, a frown between his eyes. Mimi could have that effect.

They were silent until halfway home. "Anything you want to tell me about, Emily?"

She chewed on her nail, something she hadn't done since fourth grade. "No?" She had an idea that wouldn't work. But Mimi couldn't know anything. There had been nothing incriminating to see tonight. Mimi couldn't know that she was hot and wet and frustrated. It had just been a kiss. Okay, a kiss and a grope and a big strong leg between her thighs. She could have ridden that leg to paradise. She snorted.

"What are you finding so amusing?"

"Nothing, Gran."

"Hmm, there's something between you and that Tanner boy. What were you up to when you were both waiting for me in the doorway? Out of sight. And you come out looking like you've just been kissed."

"Nothing, Gran."

"You didn't sell yourself for twenty-five thousand dollars, did you?" Mimi sounded more intrigued than anything else.

"Gran! What a terrible thing to say."

"Well, just be careful. A sensible girl would keep her distance from trouble like Tanner O'Connor, however good his kisses."

Hah. She had a feeling that from now on, the *S* word was going to be everyone's go-to word for riling her up.

"That's not a problem." She sniffed. "Mr. O'Connor has no intention of being seen with me. He believes it would be bad for his reputation."

Mimi laughed out loud. "Hah. I'm beginning to like that boy."

Chapter Nine

A week later, Emily opened her eyes to find her bedroom lit with bright sunshine. She normally woke as the sun rose, but glancing at her clock on the bedside table, she saw it was ten o'clock. She sat up and stared. She hadn't been to bed late, hadn't drunk anything more than a glass of wine with dinner last night. But her head felt muzzy. She'd been feeling more than a little weird for a while now. Since before she saw Tanner at the Founders' Celebrations. But hadn't thought much of it.

It was Sunday. There was nothing she had to get up for, though she usually helped with the chores around the ranch on the weekends. A cold cup of coffee stood on the bedside table. Mimi must have brought it up and decided not to wake her.

She sat up, and everything around her swum. Her stomach lurched. She swallowed, then swung her legs out of the bed. Then she was up and running. Shoving open the bathroom door and leaning over the toilet bowl, only just making it as the contents of her stomach forcibly removed themselves. She stayed where she was for a moment, then slowly straightened.

And threw up again.

What the heck?

Five minutes later, she was pretty sure she wasn't going to heave again. Mainly because there was nothing left in her stomach.

Food poisoning?

They'd had fish last night. Fish could be dodgy at this time of year. Couldn't it?

Five minutes after that and she felt as right as rain. Nothing but a glitch.

Head hanging over the toilet bowl the following morning, she knew she wasn't going to be able to convince herself of the glitch thing again.

But she couldn't even get her brain to focus on the alternative.

They'd used a condom.

But she was throwing up—classic sign. And while her periods had never been regular, she was pretty sure she should have had one by now. Probably all the upset about breaking up with Ryan. Except she wasn't upset. Not really. It had actually been a relief.

Maybe this was some sort of phantom pregnancy. *Agh!* There, her brain had said the *P* word, now it could never be taken back. It was out there loose in her head, free to cause havoc.

This couldn't be happening.

They'd used a goddamn condom.

Sensible people like her did *not* get pregnant.

She had a morality clause in her contract, for goodness sake. And she'd never in a million years thought it might come to apply to her. But she had a funny idea that being a single mother, pregnant by Tanner O'Connor, might well be in violation of that clause.

She straightened, then slid down the wall to crouch on the bathroom floor, arms wrapped around her knees.

She loved children, and she'd always believed that one day she would have babies of her own. That was probably the main reason she had started going out with Ryan. Because he was such fabulous father material. Stable, good job, nice family—if you ignored Lanie and Sawyer—at a point in his life where he wanted to settle down himself. He'd told her that on their first date. In the end, it hadn't been enough.

She wanted love and passion and marriage and babies and happily ever after.

An image popped up in her mind. Tanner. Long hair, beard, tattoos, presumably no intention of ever settling down. Gorgeous, sexy as hell, but as far from fabulous father material as it was possible to get. No white picket fences in Tanner's future.

And that was beside the point. She didn't love Tanner. She didn't even know him. She'd just had this huge crush on him because he was hot and unattainable. And then briefly, he'd been hot and attainable.

Anyway, he didn't want anything to do with her.

And that was good, because she didn't want anything to do with him. Really, she didn't. It could never work between them, even if either of them wanted it to.

They were just too different.

But she was getting ahead of herself. She had to find out if this was really happening first. Maybe it was just a phantom echo brought on by…subconscious guilt?

No way was she going into the drug store in Saddler Cove and buying a pregnancy test—it would be all over town in minutes. She considered asking Susanne for help, but she didn't want to involve anyone else at this point. Which meant she was going to have to go out of town. Which meant she would have to wait until the following Saturday.

It was the longest week of her life.

Luckily, the sickness passed quickly, and she was able to function okay. But the wait was driving her crazy.

By the time Saturday morning came, she was a nervous wreck. Once she was through her morning ritual of throwing up, she stripped off her pajamas and had a quick shower. After dressing in a pale pink linen dress and white strappy sandals, she headed downstairs. Mimi was nowhere to be found, and she made her way to the barn.

Up until her grandfather's death, this had been a working ranch, breeding and raising beef cattle. But after her husband had died, Mimi hadn't been interested in carrying on the family tradition—she was a vegetarian. But she loved horses and was brilliant with them. She now ran the place as an equine therapy center, treating people with PTSD, usually veterans. Mimi had lost her only brother in Vietnam, and it was a cause close to her heart. There was no one here right now, but the horses still needed to be worked. She also employed a manager who looked after the land and the barns and stables, but Mimi did most of the work with the horses herself. She claimed it was what kept her young.

Emily leaned on the fence and watched as Mimi rode the youngster around the indoor school, horse and rider as one. This was a chestnut mare Mimi had taken on as a rescue case. A year ago, she had been underweight, vicious, having no trust in humans, until Mimi worked her magic. Now there seemed an unspoken communication between the two.

Emily loved horses and was happy to work with them on the ground, but she hadn't ridden since a fall when she was eleven. The accident had been shortly after she'd found out about the death of her parents, and the two things had become inextricably mixed in her mind. She still had the pony, though. She loved her, just hadn't wanted to ride again.

Mimi brought the mare to a halt close to where Emily waited and swung out of the saddle.

"She's looking so well," Emily said.

"Yes, she's ready to go out into the world. I'll put the word out and we'll see if we can't find her a good home." Mimi rarely kept the horses she saved, claiming they needed to make room for the next horse in need. Emily suspected that Mimi just didn't like to care too deeply for anything. She'd lost so many people. Emily couldn't even begin to imagine what it would be like to lose a child. And Mimi had lost her only daughter when that plane had gone down in Africa, killing both of Emily's parents outright. "Are you okay?" Mimi asked. "You've seemed a little off this week."

"I'm fine. Just the heat." She reached across and stroked her hand down the mare's nose, and she whickered. "I need a few things. I'm going to head into Virginia Beach. Is there anything I can get you?"

"You want me to come along?"

"No." Gosh, had she said that too quickly. The last thing she needed was Mimi suspecting something was wrong. "I'm sure you have lots to do."

"Actually, I do. And I'm going to pop into town and see your young man."

"My young man?" Did she mean Ryan?

"Tanner O'Connor. Find out what he's doing about my hog."

"Nothing, hopefully." It had better be nothing. And why had Mimi called him her young man? She couldn't know. Actually, there was very little *to* know. Except for the thing that Emily didn't even know yet. She groaned, she was in such a mess.

"Are you sure you're all right?" Mimi asked.

"Of course. I'm going to get going. I might see if Susanne

wants to meet for lunch afterward."

"Sounds nice."

"I'll see you at dinner."

The drive to Virginia Beach took just under an hour—she was a careful driver. She parked up in the center, close to the beach. Instead of going straight for the shops, she headed for the long stretch of golden sand. It was busy, the sand covered with bright-colored umbrellas and family groups. She preferred the quiet, stark beauty of the beaches close to Saddler Cove. Thankfully, they'd never really been a tourist destination and they retained their wildness.

When she could put it off no longer, she headed for the biggest drugstore she could find. She wanted anonymity.

They'd used a condom.

Of course it was going to be negative. This was just a precaution, so when she threw up tomorrow morning she could start worrying that she was seriously ill.

She couldn't shake the feeling she was being watched as she hovered over the pregnancy testing kits. Why did there have to be so many? What was the difference? Finally, she picked the most expensive because she had no other criteria to go on. Then she went back and picked the next expensive one. Better to be sure.

Once her purchases were safely camouflaged in a white paper bag, she set off again.

Should she go home? But she didn't think she could wait that long. Instead, she headed for the town library and then to the ladies' room. She had the place to herself. She got out the box and read the instructions, which wouldn't seem to gel in her head.

All you have to do is pee on a stick. So go pee.

She did. First one. Then the second test. She laid them carefully on the tank behind her, faced firmly forward, and stared at her watch. The seconds ticked by.

She had to look.

But it would be negative. She couldn't be pregnant. Her egg would never have accepted Tanner's seed. Some things were not meant to be, just unnatural.

Turning slowly, she whimpered.

She picked up the first test and shook it, but the blue line refused to waver. Then the second.

Not happening.

Once, just once, she'd done something spontaneous, and look what happened. It wasn't fair. She'd always been so good, so careful, and where was her payback for that? Nowhere. But one little walk on the wild side, and she'd be paying for the rest of her life.

And she hated that she thought that way. She didn't want any child of hers to ever, ever, get an inkling that they weren't wanted 100 percent. At least by one of their parents.

Because one thing she was sure of, Tanner O'Connor was not ready for fatherhood.

She got to her feet, picked up the sticks, shook them a couple of times—just in case—then tossed them in the trash. Could she pretend this had never happened? Just go on with her life and hope no one noticed her getting bigger and bigger.

At least this would put Ryan off. He'd phoned twice this week. Talk about *treat them mean to keep them keen.* He'd certainly never been this devoted when she was going out with him.

She left the library and walked along the seafront. Trying to decide what her next move should be.

She had a horrible feeling she was going to lose her job. And it wasn't as though she didn't need the money. She'd had a small trust fund from her parents, mainly a compensation payout from the charity they'd been working for, but that had gone to her college education. Mimi wasn't poor, but all her money went back into the ranch—the twenty-five thousand for the hog was actually earmarked for a new indoor riding school.

But it wasn't just the money. She loved her job, it was what she'd trained to do, and she couldn't imagine doing anything else. She could move away and get a similar job in a different town—presumably without the morality clause— but she couldn't leave Mimi, and Mimi would never leave her beloved ranch, and Emily wouldn't ask her to.

Mimi had been diagnosed with recurring and remitting MS thirteen years ago—the doctors believed the first bout had been brought on by stress after Emily's parents were killed. She was in remission now, but Emily would never put her through the stress of even thinking about moving.

Never going to happen.

Her head hurt.

She glanced at her watch. It was already after one. Her stomach rumbled, empty from the bout of vomiting. Morning sickness—she could give it its real name now.

The thing that was really screwing her up, though, was what to tell Tanner. She had a strong belief that a child deserved to have two parents whenever possible. But two loving parents.

So while she knew she had to tell him he was going to be a father, she was 100 percent sure he would be totally dismayed. And probably in denial. Might even claim she was trying to trap him. But it had been his crappy condom, after all. If anyone had done the trapping, it wasn't her.

Except I did throw myself at him.

She groaned.

She could go around and around in circles. She was going to tear herself apart thinking about this. The only way to put a stop to that was to get it over with now.

Without thinking it was a really bad idea, she pulled out her phone and called directory inquires. She was going to track down her baby's father and tell him the good news.

Chapter Ten

Mimi hesitated a moment at the door, chewing on her lower lip.

Truth was, she was feeling just a little bit guilty, and that wasn't something she was used to. Once, a long time ago, she'd done something she was ashamed of, something she would probably never recover from, and she'd take the burden of that regret to her grave. Afterward, she'd sworn to herself that she would never put herself in a situation where she might be ashamed of the outcome again. That had been over fifty years ago, but she'd pretty much kept to her promise.

Now, she'd broken her own rule and meddled in something that was none of her business, and she had to decide just how much of a mess she'd made of things.

She pushed open the door and stepped into the showroom. The place looked the same, except the bike on the podium had changed. To her untutored eye it appeared the same model, but this one was painted red with orange flames along the gas tank.

Two men stood behind the counter. Clearly, they'd been

talking but stopped when they heard the door. Both turned her way.

One was Tanner O'Connor, looking much the same as the last time she'd seen him, in jeans stained with oil and a white T-shirt, also stained. He didn't look particularly happy to see her, his face set in sullen lines.

She turned her attention to the man beside him and guessed who he must be straight away. She'd heard the rumors—the whole town was talking about him. How Tanner O'Connor had gone too far this time, bringing a serial killer into their town. They'd all be murdered in their beds... She hadn't paid the gossip much mind, but now she studied the man as she walked toward the counter.

He was tall and lean, with a starkly handsome face and dark eyes that sent a shiver through her. She wasn't a fanciful woman, but those eyes held a hint of restlessness, as though he'd seen everything and was still coming to terms with it. His skin was dark, and his hair cut close to his head and white at the temples.

And suddenly she was pleased that for once she'd made the effort to change out of her work clothes before heading into town. And she had no clue where that thought had come from.

She came to a halt in front of the counter, addressed Tanner. "Where's my hog, Mr. O'Connor?"

Did his lips twitch at that? "Not going to happen, lady."

"We entered a contractual agreement. You took my check. You—"

"I tore up the check."

She'd suspected something like that when it hadn't cleared from her bank account. "And why would you do that?"

He opened his mouth to answer when the phone on the wall behind him rang. "Just a moment." He turned and picked it up, listened for a moment, glanced at her, a frown forming between his eyes. Then he turned so his back was to her and spoke quietly, so she had to strain to hear.

"What's the matter... Can't you tell me what this is about... There's a roadhouse this side of Virginia Beach, The Ball and Chain. I'll meet you there in an hour."

Her ears perked up at the Virginia Beach. Who else had gone to Virginia Beach that morning? Was she reading things in that weren't there? This could be pure coincidence. Just her guilty conscience putting one and one together and getting a hundred.

He put the phone down and turned back to them. Did he give her a weird look? Was she being paranoid? Probably.

"I have to go out," he said to the other man. "Deal with this." He waved a hand in her direction and then, without giving either of them a chance to say another word, he disappeared out the door at the back of the showroom.

She pursed her lips, then eyed up the other man. "So, Mr...?"

"Simpson. Joshua Simpson, ma'am."

"I'll call you Josh, if I may, and you must call me Mimi, everyone does."

His eyes widened a little, and she thought it was doubtful he'd be calling her Mimi anytime soon.

"So how can I help you, ma'am?"

"Mimi." She hated being called ma'am—it made her feel every one of her seventy years.

He just nodded.

"A little over a month ago, I came here and bought a motorcycle from Mr. O'Connor. I signed a contract and I paid by check. Granted, Mr. O'Connor said it might take a couple of weeks, but it's been four now, and I'd like to know where my motorcycle is."

"Let me go look in the office."

She followed him across the showroom and leaned in

the doorway while he went to the desk and leafed through a pile of paperwork. He obviously came to her contract at the bottom and glanced up at her. He held it out, and she stepped forward and took it. A great big "cancelled" was stamped right across it, and stapled to the top was her check—torn in half.

"I think your order was cancelled, ma'am."

This time she didn't put him right. "And can you tell me why it was cancelled?"

"No clue, ma'am. You'll have to take it up with Mr. O'Connor."

"But Mr. O'Connor is not here."

"No, ma'am."

"Is my money not good enough?"

"I'm sure it is, ma'am."

"And yet my contract has been cancelled, my check torn up, and I have no motorcycle. Tell me, have you met my granddaughter, Josh?"

"No, ma'am. Should I have?"

"I wondered whether she'd been in here and requested that the order be cancelled."

"Why would she do that?"

"She was a little unhappy about my purchasing a motorcycle—she seemed to think that a woman my age couldn't handle something so…powerful." He didn't respond. "What do you think, Josh? Could a woman my age handle a hog?"

His lips twitched at her use of the word. And she had the sudden urge to see him smile properly. She was guessing he wasn't a man who smiled easily. "I don't know, ma'am."

She tried to remember what she'd heard about him. But probably it was a mixture of exaggerated half truths and downright lies, depending on who was doing the gossiping. But they all agreed—he was a dangerous man. And she could see that; there was a sense of everything coiled in tight, held under control. Shut down.

She'd seen the same thing in many of the veterans she worked with, though with them it tended to be closer to the surface. This man had had years to perfect his control. She studied his face. His body was that of a much younger man, but hard lines bracketed his mouth. She guessed he was close to her own age.

"Did you fight in Vietnam, Joshua?"

His eyes narrowed. "Why would you ask that?"

"You have the look of a soldier. That's all."

"I haven't been a soldier for over forty years, ma'am." He nodded to the paperwork she still held. "You want to take that with you?"

It was a dismissal. Had she upset him with her questions? She took the paperwork and placed it in her bag. "You can tell Mr. O'Connor that this is not the last he'll hear on the subject."

"I'll tell him that," he said drily.

She turned to go, but hesitated, for some reason reluctant to leave. "Do you ride, Joshua?"

"Motorcycles?"

"Horses."

"No, ma'am. They never offered me no riding lessons in prison."

"I have a ranch just outside town. I run an equine therapy center. If you get some time off, perhaps you would like to pay us a visit."

"What the hell's an equine therapy center?"

"We work with veterans who are suffering with PTSD— that's post-traumatic stress disorder."

"I know what it is."

"They spend time with the horses. I thought you might find it interesting. Considering your past."

For the first time, she saw some real emotion in his eyes. A flash of anger. "You think I need to be rehabilitated? Lady, I've had forty years of rehabilitation, and this is as good as it gets."

Forty years. Had he been in prison all that time? She couldn't even begin to understand what that would do to a person. He was doing pretty well. Considering. Maybe it was time to go.

"Welcome to Saddler Cove, Joshua. I do hope you change your mind and come out to visit me. Anyone will tell you the way." And she turned and headed for the exit.

"Never going to happen, crazy lady."

The muttered words followed her through the door.

She called back over her shoulder. "Never is a long time, Josh, and I can be very tenacious."

She was still thinking about him as she headed back to her car and didn't see the man walking toward her. She almost crashed into him but stopped at the last second. Looking up, she went still.

He'd stopped as well. For a moment, she thought he would move on without speaking. It was what they usually did when they could get away with it. When no one was watching, and they didn't have to keep up the pretense. Even after all this time, she couldn't look at him without something twisting up her insides. A mix of sadness, and regret, and guilt. And anger.

"Miriam."

"Jed." She nodded briskly and made to move on, but he stopped her with a hand on her arm, and a shiver of shock ran through her. They avoided touching even at social events they both attended. It was hard to avoid each other completely in such a small town. Jed Forrester. He was head of the school board now and on a number of committees. It was why she shunned such things.

"I've been wanting to talk to you," he said. "Meaning to talk to you."

"What about?"

He cleared his throat. "I thought we might...go out sometime. Have dinner. Talk."

Was he insane? "I can't."

Something crossed his face, some echo of her own mixed-up emotions. She'd always wondered how what they'd done had affected him. They'd never spoken. Not afterward. She didn't blame him—or maybe she did, and that was just something she told herself. But they'd both been sixteen, and back then it just didn't happen. Not to people like them. However much they thought they were in love. And they had been—totally, madly, crazily in love. Looking at the aging, tired man in front to her, it seemed like another lifetime. Two different people. They'd both lost children since. Maybe it had been punishment for past sins.

They'd had no other choice.

But she knew in her heart that wasn't true.

You always had a choice.

"Why, Miriam? It's been so long. We're both alone. I thought we could be...friends."

"Just leave me alone, Jed. I can never be your friend." And she pushed past and walked away.

• • •

What the hell did she want?

Tanner had a bad feeling about this. He was aware that Emily wouldn't contact him unless it was something important. And how weird that she'd phoned when her grandmother was in the shop. The old woman had been pissed about the Harley. Had Josh managed to calm her down? He didn't think customer service was Josh's strong suit, but what did he know.

Emily had sounded...hell, he didn't know what she sounded like. He didn't know her well enough to read the nuances in her voice. But she had sounded as though she'd been crying.

What the hell would make her cry?

Tanner drove just within the speed limit and pulled up into the parking lot of The Ball and Chain with five minutes to spare. The place was owned by his maternal uncle, Benjamin Fohler. Ben had been med-boarded out of the Marines four years ago with one leg and a pension. He'd come back and bought this place. He'd lived abroad most of Tanner's childhood, and the O'Connor brothers hadn't known him, but he'd introduced himself into their lives when he'd moved back. He claimed Tanner and his brothers were the only family he had, and he wanted the chance to get to know them.

Tanner liked the man. He was tough as shit and took no crap from anyone, including Tanner. He also had a piano and was one of the few people in the immediate vicinity who was aware that Tanner played. Ben was a big jazz fan and often had live music in the club. He'd given Tanner a key and let him come and go as he liked. He'd come here sometimes when the place was closed, play until whatever bad mood was riding him disappeared. Yeah, anger management.

He'd thought it was a place he could meet with Emily and talk in private. He doubted she would want to be seen with him.

The club was closed during the day, and the parking lot was empty except for a small gray car parked in the far corner. He drove the truck across and parked a few spaces down from the car, turned off the engine. Something churned in his stomach.

Fear?

He felt like he was tilting on the edge of a precipice. Because really, there was only one thing he could think of that Emily would want to talk to him about and that would make her cry.

Shit.

He swallowed and then jumped down from the cab just as she climbed out of her car. Her face was pale, but there was no sign she'd been crying. She cast him a quick glance. "Thanks for coming."

"No problem." Actually, he had a feeling it was going to be a fucking great big problem. "Let's go inside. You look like you need a drink."

He took her around the back and tried the door at the rear. It opened, which meant someone was around. But his uncle wouldn't mind, and the staff all knew him and were used to him coming.

He led her down the corridor and into the large bar area where he spotted Ben behind the bar stock-taking. He turned as they approached and smiled, looked past Tanner to Emily, and quirked a brow.

"Not here to play today?"

"Not today." He turned to Emily. "This is Ben. He's my mother's brother, and he owns this place."

Ben nodded. "Emily."

"Emily is a…friend. We just needed somewhere to talk. Is that okay?"

"Of course. You want a drink, Emily?"

She looked like she needed a drink, but she shook her head. "I don't suppose I could have a cup of tea? Black tea?"

He raised a brow but nodded. "I'll get it for you."

Tanner ducked behind the bar and helped himself to a bottle of Bud from the fridge. He needed it, even if she didn't. He came back and gestured to one of the booths that lined the big room.

"What did he mean about you playing?" she asked.

"Nothing." He waited until she was seated, then slid into the seat across from her. "What is it, Emily?"

She opened her mouth and then closed it again as Ben approached with a steaming cup of tea, which he placed in front of her before leaving them alone.

She stared at it for a moment, then looked straight into his face. "I'm pregnant."

At the words, his heart rate picked up, even though he'd been expecting it. What else would upset her this much? What would make her approach him?

"Are you sure?"

"I just bought a test. Two tests, actually. They both came out positive. I'm definitely pregnant."

That must be why she'd gone to Virginia Beach. So she could buy a pregnancy test without anyone from town knowing. Hell, if she had bought one in the drugstore back home, the whole of Saddler Cove would have been reeling with the news that their first-grade teacher was pregnant.

"Is it mine?" he asked.

She bit her lip and nodded. He was betting she wished it was anyone else's but his.

"Aren't you seeing Ryan Forrester?" He didn't know why he was pushing this. If it wasn't his, she was hardly likely to pretend it was. He was the last person she would choose to be her baby's father. Strangely though, he didn't want Emily pregnant with Ryan's baby. The man was an asshole.

"Not any longer. And besides, we never…" She shrugged. "It's yours."

Even in the midst of a catastrophe of epic proportions, he was still glad that she hadn't fucked dickhead Ryan. He took a gulp of beer, trying to get his brain to work again. He seemed incapable of coherent thought.

"I don't understand," she said, her voice so woebegone.

"We used protection. How did this happen?"

He had a few ideas. Well, just one, actually. He gave an almost-guilty shrug. "The condom might have been a little... old."

She frowned. "How old?"

"Three years, at a guess."

"Three years!" She groaned, then her frown deepened until she had a distinct line between her brows. "What were you doing with a three-year-old condom?"

"Nothing. That's the problem. Well, nothing until you came along."

"You mean you hadn't been with a woman for three years?"

He shrugged again. "It's no big deal." Actually, it was a huge deal. Gargantuan. Maybe if he'd been getting some regularly, he might have been capable of keeping his dick in his pants when Little Miss Sensible started her striptease in his garage. And they wouldn't now be sitting here talking about babies.

Shit.

"Are you going to have it?"

She'd been staring at the table, tracing patterns on the steel with her fingertip. Now her gaze flew to his face. "Of course I'm going to have...him or her." She picked up the cup and took a small sip, put it down again. "I won't let you persuade me to get rid of this baby, so don't try."

Where the hell did she get off presuming he was the sort of man who would try and get rid of his own kid?

"I understand that you'll want nothing to do with the baby," she continued. "I just needed to tell you, and I wanted to get it over with."

"You understand nothing, lady."

She blinked at him, those big blue eyes suddenly wary, and he realized how angry he'd sounded. He had to rein that back, get a grip on his emotions. No point in getting angry. But she had to know he would take his share of responsibility. He took a deep breath. This didn't have to be a total disaster. There was no reason why it had to be a big deal.

"Look, I know you'll probably want to keep quiet about... us. I won't make trouble, I'll stay in the background. But if it's my kid, then I'll pay my way—no one needs to know where the money comes from."

She'd gone still. "*If* it's your kid?" She glared at him. "You don't believe me? What do you want—some sort of paternity test before you hand over your crappy money?"

"Of course I don't want a paternity test. I believe you." He tried to make his tone soothing.

"Big of you."

They were both silent for a few minutes. He drank the rest of his beer and waited. As the silence lengthened, he shifted in his seat. Finally, he broke. "This doesn't have to be a big deal," he said. "You'll have the baby, you can tell people what you like about the father, you—"

"Perhaps you'd like me to tell people that I don't know who the baby's father is? Would that suit you?" Her voice had risen, and he was glad he'd brought her somewhere they could talk privately, because he had a strange idea that she was about to blow. Hormones? He'd heard pregnant woman could be a little moody, but surely not already. He felt like he was sitting across from an unexploded bomb that might go off at any moment.

"Of course, it wouldn't suit me." He was trying the soothing again, but he suspected they were way beyond that. Anyway, why was she getting all heated up? She was hardly likely to want all her nice friends and colleagues to know she'd been slumming it with Tanner O'Connor.

"So what would suit you?" She didn't give him a chance to answer. "How about you go away and forget we ever had this conversation?"

Christ, what was the right answer? "If that's what you want," he said cautiously.

She took no notice. "And you can just continue on with your life and pretend I don't exist. We don't exist. That's probably for the best, don't you think?" This time he'd learned his lesson and kept quiet. "I mean, the last thing I would want in my life is a scruffy, greasy, surly...loser."

Loser? He supposed she could have said worse. And he decided to cut her some slack—she was clearly a little upset. And that was the understatement of the century. "Exactly. But I will pay my way. That way you can go back to work if that's what you want. Or you can stay at home and look after the baby. Whatever you want."

"There's a big problem with that," she almost snarled. Her face had gone blotchy, and he wanted to tell her to calm down, that this wasn't good for her or the baby, but he had an idea that might light the fuse for the explosion.

"There is?"

"I have a morality clause in my contract. Do you even know what one of those is?"

Actually, he had no goddamn clue. He shook his head.

"It means they'll fire me. It means as an unwed mother, I would be considered unfit to teach the children. I will lose my job." Yup, that sounded like something the good folk of Saddler Cove might insist upon. Pompous pricks. "And guess what?" she continued, "I love my job. You get to go on with your greasy life as if nothing's happened. As if you didn't have a crummy three-year-old condom in your wallet. And I lose my job. How is any of this remotely fair?"

"Then we get married."

He had no clue where those words came from.

For a moment, she just stared at him. "What did you just say?"

He wasn't sure he could get the words out a second time. "We get married. Then they can't sack you." Though maybe marrying Tanner O'Connor would be seen as far more immoral than having a baby without a husband.

Her eyes narrowed to daggers. "Why would I want to marry a man who goes out of his way to piss everybody off? A man who clearly doesn't know how to use a condom or a razor?" She waved a hand at his face, and he automatically touched his scruff of a beard. But she wasn't finished. "A man who would sell a seventy-year-old woman a dangerous motorcycle? Of course we can't get married. How would that help anything?"

Maybe she had a point. But what the hell did she want from him?

He was just trying to work out how to ask when she shoved herself to her feet. "I have to go. I just had to tell you. But now maybe you can just forget I ever mentioned it."

Then she turned and stomped away.

Chapter Eleven

She'd lost it spectacularly back there.

She'd called him a loser. She shouldn't have said that, because Tanner wasn't a loser. Not at all. Against all the odds, he'd made a success of his life.

Maybe she should have waited a while before telling him. Just until it had really sunk into her own brain. And then she could have explained the situation in a rational manner. Like a reasonable human being instead of a mad harpy.

He'd looked almost frightened. As though she might explode all over him.

But really, she'd expected him to just walk away. Maybe suggest she have an abortion and get rid of the problem. Either way, she'd been sure he would want nothing to do with her or the baby. And then, with telling him behind her, she could have started to work out what her best options were.

Instead, Tanner O'Connor had asked her to marry him. Okay. It hadn't exactly been a proposal, but he had suggested they get married. Unfortunately, by that time, she'd been too wound up to even take it in. Anyway, he clearly hadn't meant it—he'd looked almost as shocked as her when the words fell out.

And really, anyone less like husband material she had never come across.

However much she was attracted to Tanner, the sad truth was, she was pregnant by Saddler Cove's least eligible bachelor.

She was quite aware of the big black truck trailing her all the way back to Saddler Cove. She was driving slowly—she wasn't the best of drivers under normal circumstances—and these were hardly that. He could have easily overtaken. But he didn't, he stayed a safe distance behind, until she turned off on the drive to the ranch. Then he parked. When she pulled up outside the house, she glanced back just as he was pulling away.

Was he making sure she got home safely? She had probably come across as a little irrational. Okay, a lot irrational. But then, he hadn't acted according to how she'd expected things to go, and that had knocked her off balance, and she'd gotten scared and...

She climbed out of the car and headed for the steps up to the house. Then changed her mind and took the path that led to the barn. It was the middle of the afternoon, and the horses were all inside out of the heat and flies of the hottest part of the day. She headed for Beauty's box. This was where she came when she was scared or troubled or anything really. She'd gotten Beauty as a one-year-old at the annual pony auction on the nearby island of Chincoteague. Emily had been six at the time, but it was love at first sight, and she'd begged her grandmother for the filly. That was the first year her parents went away—they were both doctors and had volunteered for disaster relief. It was something they'd always wanted to do but had put on hold when she was born. She supposed she should be grateful they'd stuck around for so long. Anyway, Mimi had seen that she needed something to distract her and had bought her Beauty on the understanding that she would care for the mare herself. And she had.

She'd looked after her, trained her, ridden her every day until she was eleven. That was the year her parents had been killed. Flying between hospitals in a tropical storm, in a small plane, in Africa.

Not long after she got that news, she'd stopped riding. At the time, she hadn't really understood why. Now she'd come to see that she hadn't wanted to take the risk and leave Mimi with no one. But Beauty was still the one she ran to when she needed a little unconditional love.

The mare was nearly twenty, but still the most beautiful horse in the whole world. Emily let herself into the loose box and stroked her silky black nose. "I messed up, Beauty."

The horse whickered against her skin.

She had no one to blame for this but herself. Okay, maybe Tanner was a little to blame with his three-year-old condom. Had he really not been with a woman in three years? That was hard to believe. He had such a reputation as a man whore.

But anyway, she was the one who had thrown herself at him. Now she had to sort out the consequences and do what was right for the only truly blameless one in all this. Her baby. Their baby.

She patted her stomach. It was sinking in. She was going to have a baby.

And really, she was much better off than most people in her circumstances, even if she might be about to lose her job. She was pretty certain that a baby outside of marriage would be in breach of the morality clause in her contract. When she'd signed it, it had never occurred to her in a million years that it might become an issue. That wasn't who she was. So, she was going to lose her job, and that hurt big time, because she loved her job and she was good at it. And she didn't consider herself immoral. But she was luckier than most—money would be short, but she would have a home, and while Mimi would be disappointed, she would still stand behind her 100 percent.

Tanner had said he would give her money. And stay out of her life. She didn't want him in her life—he was her fantasy lover, who she was pretty sure would get bored with her in no time. All the same, the offer to just send money and go on about his life had made her so angry. That her life was going to be turned upside down while his would go on with hardly a ripple.

Then he'd mentioned marriage and she'd gotten even angrier. She'd been a little…irrational. Could she blame it on pregnancy hormones? It was a little early, though maybe not. She was throwing up every morning, after all.

"I was horrible to him, Beauty." He'd said they should get married, and she'd just lost it, because it was so…impossible. Obviously, being tied to her legally was the last thing he wanted. But she hadn't needed to be so nasty about it.

She didn't want to marry because she was pregnant.

But she did want her baby to have a father. A tattooed ex-con with an attitude problem might not be what everyone dreamed of as their baby's daddy, but that didn't change the fact of the matter. That was what she had, and she'd make the best of it.

So she was going to apologize and suggest they try again.

For their baby's sake.

Giving Beauty a last pat, she headed out. She considered phoning, but she didn't have a private number. And the shop would be closed by now. She'd heard that he'd moved out of the apartment and was back to sharing with his brothers. Which meant she'd likely have to see them. And she just wasn't ready for that yet. Maybe never would be, but it couldn't be helped.

But as she walked out of the barn, Tanner's big black truck pulled up. He stopped the engine and climbed down from the cab. A quiver ran through her. The familiar reaction of almost overwhelming shyness and instant attraction he always managed to induce. Even in these horrible circumstances, he still turned her on hot and hard. She was hard-wired to react to him, that was all. Too many years of fantasizing. You couldn't switch that stuff off.

As he sauntered toward her, hands shoved in his pockets, dark glasses over his eyes, she couldn't read any expression on his face. He stopped in front of her. "I came to apologize."

She twisted her hands in front of her, needing something to hold on to. "I was just on my way to come and see you and do the same."

"You've got nothing to apologize for."

She sniffed. "You mean, apart from turning into an irrational sniping woman? Who accused you of never shaving?"

"Actually, that part was a little scary." He gave a shrug. "I presumed it was hormones or something. Anyway," he added, stroking his fingers down the scruff on his jawline, and she had a very inconvenient flashback to how soft that hair had felt against her inner thighs while he'd—she cut off the thought. It wasn't helping. "I don't shave."

For a moment, there was silence. This man was a virtual stranger, and yet they'd connected on a level so fundamental it was doing her head in. There was a life growing inside her. Part her and part Tanner.

For the first time, the amazingness of that struck her. She forgot, for a moment, that they didn't know each other, they weren't married, they were polar opposites, and she had a morality clause in her contract so very soon she'd be out of work, and just concentrated on the fact that they'd made a new life together. That was beyond awesome.

"We're going to have a baby," she said.

"So it seems."

"And whatever we do from now on, the baby has to come first." She searched his face, wished he'd take off the glasses. He looked like such a badass standing there. All muscle and tattoos and bad attitude. What did she know about him, really? Except he'd spent two years in prison for a crime she was pretty sure he hadn't committed. That he'd come back to Saddler Cove bitter and hating everyone, and that he hardly ever smiled.

That was sad.

"We should talk," she said. "Nothing deep and meaningful or anything. Just what we're going to do now."

He nodded. Obviously, the strong, silent type.

"You want to walk?" She didn't wait for an answer. "Let's walk."

She led the way around the back of the barn, not waiting to see if he followed but sensing his presence close behind her. She took the path beside the creek that ran behind the house, and he fell into step beside her. It was late afternoon, the heat was going out of the day, and she didn't speak for a while, just let the atmosphere soothe her. She loved this place. The ranch, the wild coastline, even Saddler Cove with its small-town mentality and stupid outdated morality clauses.

They walked for about five minutes, then came to a bench her grandfather had made that looked out over the creek and to the distant mountains to the north. She sat, and he came down beside her. It was one of her favorite places when she wanted to think. And just another hundred feet along the creek was the spot she used to swim when she was younger. Where Tanner had no doubt seen her in her underwear just before he went to prison.

There was something she wanted to know. "Why did you come back here?"

"What, today?"

"No, when you…" God, was it impolite to bring this up? She really wasn't sure of the etiquette with ex-cons. Should you pretend it had never happened?

He twisted slightly so he could look into her face and took off the dark glasses at last, hooking them in the neckline of his T-shirt. He had beautiful eyes, though she still couldn't tell what he was thinking. She guessed he'd perfected the art of keeping his thoughts to himself. Only letting people see what he wanted them to see. He came across as wild and undisciplined when you didn't know him, but even after their short acquaintance, she reckoned that wasn't who he was. It was a facade to hide the real Tanner O'Connor.

As to who that was—maybe she'd never know.

"When I got out of prison?" he finished for her with a sardonic smile.

"I just wondered. You could have gone anywhere and started your business. The people here…" She didn't know how to put it.

"Are a load of assholes who will always think of me as a deadbeat loser who'll never make anything of himself. A loser who should have died instead of Dwain Forrester?"

A tinge of bitterness was making its way through his not-quite-impervious demeanor. She'd thought he didn't care what the people thought about him, but now she could see that wasn't the case.

"I shouldn't have called you a loser. It's not true. And no one thinks that," she said. Though she wasn't entirely sure that was the truth. She wondered if she should tell him she believed he was innocent, that she'd always had her doubts. But she didn't think now was the time. "It was a horrible accident that could have happened to any number of young people." Though it had totally shocked the town at the time. Dwain was Jed Forrester's only son. The richest family in

Saddler Cove. Dwain had been a nice guy, good-looking, easy-going, everyone had loved him. His only fault—if you listened to most of the town—was his friendship with Tanner. Emily had been sixteen at the time, and she remembered thinking how unfair it all was. "You were just unlucky."

"Dwain was unluckier."

They'd taken Dwain's father's sports car for a joyride. Without permission. There were rumors that they'd both been drinking, but she didn't think that had ever been proven. All the same, Tanner had ended up charged with aggravated manslaughter.

"So why did you come back?" she asked.

"The simple answer—it's my home and I love it here."

"What's the unsimple answer?"

He grinned. "That I won't let the fuckers chase me off, and I'll show the bastards that I can make it no matter what they think of me. Despite them."

Whew. It made her wonder how much of his badass attitude was a show. And how much was for real. She was guessing she'd find out over the next few months. Maybe it was her duty to find out before the baby was born. She thought all children had the right to know both their parents, if possible. But maybe Tanner's bitterness went too deep and he would do more harm than good.

She hoped not. But there was so much bitterness there. She took a deep breath. "I think we should keep quiet about the baby for now."

"You do? Now that's a surprise." He could do sarcasm extremely well. "We wouldn't want the townspeople to discover their nice little first-grade teacher was pregnant."

"Well, it's not something I'm going to be able to hide forever. Perhaps they won't fire me. I'll worry about that later. Right now…" She shrugged. "I just need time to come to terms with it myself—without anyone else interfering." She cast him a look. "Except you, of course." She took a deep breath. Maybe he'd just say no. That he didn't want to be involved at all, except for the financial help that he had already offered and which she hoped she wouldn't need. "I think we need to spend some time getting to know one another."

"You do? You want to get to know me? Are you sure? Maybe things might go easier for you if people don't know who your baby's father is."

"I've thought about this. And perhaps you're right. But…I want to do the right thing."

"Little Miss Perfect."

She had a rush of anger again. "Stop that. Right now. The last thing I need to deal with at the moment is your persecution complex."

His jaw tensed, and his eyes narrowed. "I don't have a—"

"Yes, you do. And perhaps it's justified. But I don't blame you for this. It was as much my doing as yours."

"Yeah—you did that cute little striptease thing."

"Shut up. All I'm saying is we did it together, and now we have to deal. I lost my parents when I was eleven, and I missed them, and if at all possible I would like my baby to have his mom *and* his dad. Not together, together," she added hurriedly. "I know the last thing you really want is to marry someone like me. But both of us there for him or her."

"I lost my mom when I was six," he said.

She'd forgotten that. She reached out and rested her hand on his thigh, gave it a quick pat, and withdrew. "Then you know what I mean."

"Yeah, I know." She glanced at his face. For once the sullen attitude was absent. "So how do we do this?" he asked.

She nibbled on her lips for a moment. "I suppose we just spend time together. See if we can get along enough for it to be more of a good thing than a bad. And to give you time to decide if you want to be in our lives. I know this has come as a shock."

He grinned then, and something twisted low down in her belly. "Yeah, just a little."

"We could take it in turns to choose what to do. Things we each enjoy and can maybe share. Something out of town so…"

"…people don't see us together," he finished for her.

"Yes. But that's as much—maybe more—for you as for me. Probably more. If a few weeks down the line, you decide you don't want anything to do with us, then you can walk away from this and no one will be the wiser."

"Is that what you hope?"

"Gosh. You are so touchy. No. I told you what I want—for my baby to have a mom and a dad who get along together. Are you willing to at least try?"

He didn't answer immediately, and in some ways, she liked that. Liked that he was clearly thinking about his answer. Finally, he nodded. "Yeah. I'm willing to try. But I've got to warn you—even my brothers reckon I'm a moody bastard, so don't expect this to be easy."

"Believe me. I don't."

But for the first time since this whole thing had started, she felt a little hint of optimism.

Just don't try and think of everything that could go wrong.

Chapter Twelve

Riding his bike usually made him feel better, made him forget the bad stuff. But not today. His mind was churning as he turned his Harley Davidson Super Glide into the drive of the ranch.

His first date with Emily Towson, the soon-to-be mother of his baby.

It seemed more than a little surreal.

In the week since she'd told him, Tanner had occasionally believed that he'd come to terms with the notion. Then it would come crashing in on him again.

He was going to be a father.

Yeah, totally fucking surreal.

And she wanted him to be part of its life. Whatever it was, he or she. And at the same time—she'd given him the chance to back out if that was what he wanted. It occurred to him, frequently, that Emily was way too good for him. She was a genuinely nice person. And he'd fucked up her life with his three-year-old condom. Probably before that. It had all started when he'd taken her grandmother's check for a Harley he had no intention of selling her. He was still actually waiting for the fallout—Josh had said that Mimi had promised to return. He wasn't looking forward to that. Wasn't even sure if he could look the woman in the face after he'd knocked up her granddaughter.

One thing at a time.

Get through the first date, first.

She must have been keeping watch for him as she emerged from the front door as he pulled up in front of the house. She was dressed in a black and white dress, sleeveless, finishing just above the knee. She looked…nice.

Maybe he should have made more of an effort on his appearance, but it had never occurred to him. And perhaps that said it all. Did she look a little dubious as she watched him from the top of the sweeping stairway?

Hell, this was as good as he got. Clean jeans and T-shirt, his best boots, and a leather jacket. She'd asked him to meet her here and she would drive them wherever they were going. Maybe it was some fancy restaurant and they wouldn't even let him through the door.

He switched off the engine and swung his leg over the bike. As he pulled off his helmet, he caught the brief flicker of a frown on her face.

"Am I not smart enough for you, princess?" he said, then wished he could take the words back. Of course he wasn't smart enough for her.

Her face cleared, and she shook her head. "No. It was just the bike. It made me think of Mimi and the bike you sold her. She hasn't said anything, and it hasn't turned up…"

"I tore up the check."

"What? Because of me?"

He shrugged. Let her think that. "So where are we going?"

She smiled. "It's a surprise. But come on. We don't want

to be late, and I don't drive very fast."

"We can go on the bike if you like. I can go as fast as you want."

A look of alarm flashed across her face. She glanced down at her dress, then back at him. "I don't think so. No, we'll go in my car."

She led the way to the small gray sedan she'd been driving the other day. She appeared a little nervous, kept shooting him sneaky sideways glances. She was probably regretting even telling him she was pregnant. Probably regretting suggesting this getting-to-know-you stuff.

He actually felt more than a little nervous himself. He didn't do dates. Had no clue how he was supposed to behave. He cleared his throat. "You look smart enough for both of us," he said.

She peered at him across the top of the car. "This isn't a date like that. You don't have to say nice things to me."

No, he supposed it wasn't really a proper date. She didn't date guys like him. Christ, he was pathetic. He forced the feeling down. He couldn't start getting maudlin this early on or they'd never make it through the evening. And he wanted this to work. The thought took him by surprise.

"Maybe I want to," he said as he climbed into the passenger seat beside her. The car was small, and he nearly didn't fit. "You do look nice. Very school-teacherish."

She turned and glared at him. "Don't you dare say sensible."

He held up his hands in mock alarm. "I promise. Never mention it again. Except to say that Ryan's loss was my gain." With a start of shock, he realized that despite the outcome, and the baby, he wasn't sorry he'd fucked Emily. It had been a once-in-a-lifetime fantasy come true for him, and he'd never regret it. So thank you, Ryan.

She was silent for a minute while she switched on the

engine and reversed out of her parking spot, the tip of her tongue peeking out between her lips as she concentrated. When they were out on the road, she relaxed a little, her grip not so tight on the wheel. Did he make her nervous?

She sighed. "It's so weird to think if he hadn't said that, maybe *we* wouldn't be here now."

"No, you'd likely still be picking out sensible wedding rings with asshole Ryan."

She giggled, and he liked the sound. He didn't think he'd ever heard her giggle before. Made her sound younger. Hell, she was only twenty-four.

"So how are you feeling?" he asked. "You know...?" He shrugged. "I did a bit of reading, and pregnancy does not sound fun."

"You did? I'm impressed. And I'm still throwing up every morning. That's how I suspected I was pregnant in the first place. Just sick in the mornings, though. After that, I'm okay."

He knew there was all sorts of other stuff, tender breasts, bloating... Maybe he would wait until they were a little more comfortable around each other before he asked about her breasts getting bigger.

"And I don't have much appetite," she said. "At least I might get rid of that last ten pounds I've never managed to lose. Except I'm going to be huge, so I might as well not bother." She sighed again.

"You never needed to lose weight. You're perfect."

"Hah."

They were quiet then. He relaxed back in his seat and tried to think of things other than Emily's breasts.

He was worried about Josh. The job was working out fine—he was more than capable of doing the work and was conscientious, did what was needed. But he spent too much time alone. Maybe that was inevitable. His brothers had repeated some of the gossip around town—the serial killer stuff was especially interesting. Assholes.

Maybe Josh would have done better in some bigger place, where he wouldn't have stood out so much. Perhaps once Reese had the Richmond shop set up and functioning, Josh could move there. Or maybe he just needed more time. Tanner knew he spent a lot of time on the beach, walking or just sitting and watching the waves. Perhaps that was what he needed. Not company. Hell, he'd spent forty years with way too much company. Now he wanted to be alone. But Tanner still worried.

"You've gone all serious," Emily said from beside him.

"I was thinking about Josh."

"The man you have working for you?"

"Yeah. He's a good guy. I might not have made it inside without him."

"Now you want to pay that back. That's why you helped him?"

"Hell no. I helped him because there was no one else. And he's my friend." He grinned. "I don't have many."

"Mimi likes him," she said.

"Yeah?"

"She said she went in to check up on her Harley on Saturday and met him then. It must have been when you came to meet me."

"She came in just as you phoned with the good news."

She was driving into the city now, and he let her concentrate. She didn't seem the most confident of drivers. Maybe she didn't do much of it, just from the ranch to town. He hadn't heard rumors of her going away much. Not since she came back from college. Even then, she'd come home for weekends. He realized that without consciously doing it, he'd kept tabs on Emily over the years.

Finally, they pulled up into the parking lot of the festival hall. A poster as they entered showed a man sitting at a grand piano. Mozart's piano concerto no. 21. Tanner almost smiled—it was one of his favorites. He'd never been to a live recital before, and anticipation turned in his stomach. Did she know of his secret vice?

She parked, switched off the engine, and wiped her hands down her thighs. "I hope this is okay. I know it's probably not your favorite." Obviously not. "I was given tickets and I love Mozart. And you know music is supposed to be good for the baby."

"Don't worry. I can probably sit still and not embarrass you for a couple of hours."

In fact, he didn't feel conspicuous as they moved through the busy foyer. He was guessing there were a lot of students in the audience—all casually dressed. It was only when they took their seats in the area in front of the stage that he felt a little out of place. Obviously, these were the pricier seats, and that was reflected in the clientele, mostly middle-aged to old and well-dressed. He didn't let it bother him. He'd been worried about tonight, and this was turning into a totally unexpected treat. There was an orchestra beneath the stage, and he could hear them tuning up.

"I'm sure you'll recognize it when it starts," Emily whispered in his ear, though she didn't sound convinced. "It a very popular piece." In fact, she sounded worried. Probably thought a Neanderthal like him would be bored out of his mind.

"I'm fine. I can always take a nap."

He had no intention of sleeping. This was a piece he played, though not very well. It was a little beyond his ability, but he loved it. And it would be great to hear it played live by someone who could do it justice.

The lights lowered, and the orchestra went silent as a man walked on to the stage from the side. The guy was dressed in a tuxedo, long tails, and he gave a small bow to the crowd and then took the seat at the piano.

Staring at that piano, Tanner's fingers itched with the need to play. If his life had been different, he would have loved this. But while he was good—a natural, his teacher had told him—he'd never be this good—he'd started too late in life. All the same, playing and listening to music was one of the few things which gave him pleasure.

Then the music started, and he lost himself, letting the music flow over him and through him. And the time passed without him realizing.

The lights came up, and Emily touched him on the arm. "Are you okay."

He couldn't even pretend he hadn't found it moving. "I'm great. That was...wonderful."

A smile broke out on her face. Relief, probably. "I'm glad. I have to go to the bathroom. You can wait here, or we can go get a drink."

"Do you want a drink?"

She shook her head.

"I'll wait here, then."

He peered around as he waited. The man on his right was wearing a dark suit and tie. In fact, all the men in his row were wearing suits. He must stand out like a grease monkey at a...Mozart concert.

Would it have hurt him to dress up a little for her? He'd bet she was regretting bringing him here.

He didn't care for himself—they could think what they liked, but he didn't want Emily to feel self-conscious just because she was pregnant by a guy who didn't even own a suit.

Then again, maybe she needed to get used to it.

They had been mostly silent on the drive back.

He'd been reliving the music in his head. So powerful. It had been one of the best evenings of his life, and he would always be grateful to her for giving it to him. And he knew this was something they could share in the future, that could maybe forge a bond between them.

She pulled up in front of the house, switched off the engine, and killed the lights. She turned to him and was just about to speak when the door to the house opened and Mimi appeared on the porch. She stared at the car for a moment and then disappeared inside.

Emily sighed. "I'd invite you in, but there's something I need to do, and I've put it off long enough."

His stomach churned. "You're going to tell your grandmother?"

She nodded. "I think she's probably already guessed. My morning ritual vomiting is hard to miss."

"Will she be angry? Do you want me to come with you?"

In the dim light, he could see her smile. It was probably the last thing she wanted. "Thank you, but no."

He swallowed. "Are you going to tell her who the father is?"

"Yes. She probably saw your bike anyway."

Probably. He rubbed at his chest—it had suddenly become too tight—then looked away, not wanting to see the embarrassment pinkening her cheeks.

She climbed out, and he followed, came around the back of the car. He stopped in front of her. He hadn't touched her all evening. Now he gave into the urge and cupped her cheeks. He lowered his head and kissed her on the forehead. "I had a good time tonight." Then he backed up and grinned. "I bet that surprised you."

"Maybe a little. But I hoped." She shrugged. "I suspect you're not the philistine you pretend to be."

The strange thing was, if it hadn't been for his time inside, then he probably would have been just that. It had been a dark time, but also a time for contemplation and change and growing up. And he'd learned about music and reading. It had changed him, and on balance he'd come out a better person. Not that he'd let anyone else see that. But all the same, he couldn't belittle the evening. "Maybe not. Good luck with your grandmother."

"Thank you. And I'll see you next week?"

"Yes."

And he turned and walked away. She was still standing there, watching him as he revved the engine and headed home.

Was she worried about telling her grandmother? Maybe he should have insisted he go with her. A shudder ran through him at the thought. Miriam Delaney was a forceful woman and was unlikely to be happy with Emily's news.

He wouldn't be at all surprised if she came after him with a shotgun.

• • •

Emily stood by her car and watched until Tanner had disappeared around the bend in the road. Then she heaved a huge sigh and headed into the house.

The evening had gone far better than she'd ever hoped. It had been a risk, but Tanner had seemed to truly enjoy himself. She didn't think he was pretending.

She'd had second and third thoughts about taking him to the concert. Really, she'd worried that he'd hate it, feel out of place, be bored out of his mind. But in the end, she'd gone with her first thought—that maybe he would enjoy the music, and it could be something they could share going forward.

So many people went to concerts just to be seen but had

no real feeling for the music. Tanner had been engrossed. And he certainly hadn't given the impression of feeling out of place. The opposite. He had such a composure about him, as though the rest of the world could think what they liked, and it didn't affect him.

She suspected much of his surliness was an act. She'd seen the brief glimpses of bitterness. All the same, his composure was impressive, and she wished she had just a little of his insouciance. She had an idea she was going to need it in the coming months.

Maybe it would be contagious, and if she spent enough time with Tanner then some of it would rub off on her. And when they told her she was fired, she could just smile in their faces.

Thankfully, the night had gone much better than expected. She was feeling optimistic, so she might as well get the next hurdle over with. She found Mimi in the living room, sitting on the sofa, feet curled up under her, a glass of brandy in her hand. She was wearing a long black dress and looked ageless and elegant.

Emily had a sudden yearning for a good stiff drink herself, but that wouldn't be happening for a long time soon.

"You're up late," she said, taking the seat across from Mimi.

"Time enough to sleep when you're dead," Mimi replied.

"Hah." She had no clue how her grandmother was going to take this. She was a law unto herself. She'd always told Emily to go her own way and not worry about what other people thought. But she might think this situation smacked of stupidity. Okay, better to get it over with quickly. "I'm pregnant."

Mimi looked at her over the rim of her glass. "I gathered."

"What gave it away?"

"Your mother was exactly the same—every morning like

clockwork. Luckily, it only lasted the first couple of months. Fingers crossed you'll be the same."

"You're not angry? Or disappointed? Or…?"

"There are worse things, and I know you. You'll do the right thing."

"I'm trying." Trouble was—what was the right thing? She felt deeply that a baby should have the chance to know both its parents, but really, Tanner was far from ideal father material. She sensed that there was so much good inside him, so much more than he revealed to the world. But that hardly mattered while he continued to stick his middle finger up at the whole town every opportunity he got. What would it be like growing up with a father like that?

"Stop chewing your lip," Mimi said.

She stopped. It was a bad habit she'd had from childhood whenever she'd gotten nervous or upset.

"You haven't asked who the father is," she said.

"I didn't need to. I saw the hog out there when I got home." She sniffed. "For a moment, I thought he might have delivered my motorcycle."

"Never going to happen," she said.

"Hah. Anyway, I'm glad the baby's not Ryan's. I was worried at first."

"Why? Ryan would seem the more obvious choice for father of your only grandchild's illegitimate baby." And she'd at least been in a relationship with Ryan—people might have been more understanding than a one-night stand with Tanner O'Connor.

"Because he might have persuaded you to marry him."

"You think I would have done the *sensible* thing?"

"Maybe. For the baby. But it would never have worked."

"And you don't think Tanner will persuade me?" Mimi gave her a wry look, and she sniffed. "For your information, Tanner said he would marry me."

"There's a good man in there somewhere."

"Yes. Deep down. I suspect too deep down for me to get to him."

"Yet you're seeing him?"

"We decided we would try and be friends for the baby's sake." She yawned. It had gone better than she'd thought. Mimi didn't seem disappointed or angry. "Time for bed." She pushed herself to her feet.

"First, there's something I need to confess," Mimi said.

She frowned. "There is?" Emily couldn't think what.

"It's my fault."

"What's your fault?"

"The baby."

"How could it possibly be your fault?"

Mimi looked a little discomforted. She gave a shrug of her shoulders. "I never wanted the motorcycle—not really. I prefer a horse any day. And that young man took a lot of persuading to sell me one. He only did it in the end to annoy the town."

"But why?"

"Because I knew you would get all riled up and go make a scene."

"Why would you want that?"

"Because I was worried about you. I was terrified you were going to marry Ryan, because he was safe, and I knew you would regret it. Since your parents died you've always picked the safe path. I just wanted to give you another option." She gave another shrug. "I saw the way you looked at him. That day when he passed us in the street and you thought no one was looking."

Her eyes narrowed. She couldn't believe this. Mimi matchmaking. And with Tanner O'Connor, of all people. That was more irresponsible than buying a hog. "How did I look at him?" She wasn't sure she wanted to know the answer to that one.

"Like you looked at Beauty that day at the pony auction. When you were six years old. Like he was all you wanted, and you would die happy if you could just have him for your own."

Crap. That was so embarrassing. And she didn't have a thing to say. Because it was true. But without Mimi noticing and interfering it would have been a secret she took with her to the grave. When she remained silent, Mimi drained her brandy, got to her feet, came toward her, and stopped, hands on her hips.

"But honestly, Emily, it was supposed to be a goddamn fling. A fling. Not a goddamn baby." She shook her head, turned, and headed for the door. Emily heard the muttered words just as it slammed behind her. "History goddamn repeating itself."

And what did that mean?

Chapter Thirteen

Week two of the getting-to-know-you situation. It was the following Saturday. Emily had spent the week throwing up and teaching school.

Mimi had been quiet about the baby, except to ask if she had thought about a gynecologist and that she would come along with her and hold her hand if she wanted. Emily had been putting it off, but she supposed she couldn't do that forever.

She was glad Mimi had offered. She didn't want to go alone, but she really didn't think Tanner was quite ready for hand-holding. If he would ever be.

She hadn't expected to hear from him every day or anything, but as the days passed and nothing, she wondered if that meant he had made up his mind and was bowing out of the fatherhood role. Or maybe he'd finally realized she was too boring for him.

And she'd been trying not to think about how that made her feel. Sort of weepy and pathetic and crazy and...

Finally, he called on Thursday and asked if she fancied

a trip down the coast on Saturday. He had somewhere he needed to go, apparently. Something to do with work. He'd said dress casual—no dresses allowed, so she was wearing jeans and sneakers and a white T-shirt with a pink heart on it.

She was ready and waiting for him, sitting on the porch swing at the allotted time.

Mimi was loitering in the background, and Emily had an idea that she planned to confront Tanner and...truth was, she had no clue what. Maybe ask what his intentions were. Perhaps confess the whole I-never-wanted-a-hog thing. Emily hoped not, because that might turn out very embarrassing for her. Though she had already confessed to Tanner that she'd fantasized about him. She'd even told him she gave herself orgasms while thinking about him. How could she have done that? So totally, totally embarrassing.

He drove up at two o'clock exactly. On his hog. She'd somehow thought he'd come in the truck. Maybe he was expecting her to drive. He must be expecting her to drive. The bike was black and silver and made this noise like a hungry lion as he gunned up the driveway and pulled up at the bottom of the steps.

He switched off the engine and pulled off his helmet. His hair was in a neat ponytail. He wore faded jeans and a black leather jacket, and he swung himself off from the beast with a lithe grace. His legs were long, his hips narrow, and his shoulders, under the black leather, broad. She sighed.

After grabbing a bundle of something from the back of the bike, he headed toward her. Watching him stroll up the steps with that casual, easy grace made things twist low down inside her. Her breasts ached, and her skin flushed. No doubt that was hormones.

She rose to her feet so she wouldn't feel at a disadvantage. And still felt at a disadvantage—he was more than a foot taller than her.

"Hi," he said, taking off his dark glasses and halting in front of her. "Ready to go?"

She nodded.

He shook out the bundle. It turned out to be a spare helmet and a leather jacket. "They're Aiden's from when he was a kid. They should fit."

She took them without saying a word and remained where she was, the gear in her hand, not moving while she stared down at the bike. It was huge. And while the seat was quite close to the ground, she really wasn't sure she wanted to get on it. And she'd have to sit right up close to Tanner and wrap her arms around him and press her breasts up against his back. She'd been doing such a good job of not remembering what Tanner had felt like all up close and personal, and she was betting this would bring it all flooding back.

She swallowed. "I'm not sure…"

Suddenly he looked from her to the bike. "Christ, I didn't think. Hell, is it even safe? It won't…fall out or anything?"

For a moment, she had no clue what he meant, and then she giggled. "What, you mean if I open my legs too wide? You wish."

His face went serious at that. "Actually, I don't wish. I never even thought about kids. Hell, or getting married. But now that it's happening, I wouldn't want anything to go wrong. Hell, I'm sorry. We can take your car. Or I can go back and get the truck."

Warmth washed through her at his words. This was the first sign that he cared about the baby and didn't just see it as a huge inconvenience. The thought gave her hope. "No. Really. I was just shocked. I've never been on a motorcycle before."

"Never?" He sounded as though that was an inconceivable idea. "I suppose all your boyfriends have nice safe cars."

She could feel her eyes narrowing. "Why would that be?"

He held up his hands in mock defense. "Oh no, we're not getting into *that* conversation again. But hell, you've led a sheltered life. You need to live a little." He looked her up and down and winked. "Before you get too big. If you're sure it's safe."

She glanced down at herself, expecting to have suddenly grown huge, but there was no sign of the little one in there. Hopefully wouldn't be for a while.

The door opened behind her, and she turned slightly as Mimi came out. She was wearing her usual work gear of Levi's, T-shirt, and cowboy boots, and she didn't look like anyone's idea of a nice cuddly grandmother. Tall and model thin, and not for the first time Emily wondered if she had done something super-wrong in a former life to end up so vertically challenged. Why couldn't she have taken after her grandmother?

She'd hoped to avoid this meeting for a while longer, but she supposed it had to be done. Mimi came across to stand by her side and look at Tanner, who did a good job of not squirming. Though his face settled into that sullen look, which she now recognized as his I'm-a-badass-and-don't-forget-it expression. It didn't faze her grandmother. She was made of sterner stuff.

Emily cleared her throat. "I believe the two of you have met," she said.

"We have," Mimi replied. "In fact, we entered into a contractual agreement, which I believe Mr. O'Connor broke."

His lips actually curled up at that. "Call me Tanner, ma'am."

"Only if you call me Mimi."

"I'll try."

"Hmm. I believe you and my granddaughter are going to have a baby together, that makes us family of sorts. I will be inviting you to lunch in the near future, where I expect to get to know you better. Be prepared."

"I will, ma'am…Mimi."

Hopefully that was it and they could go, but Mimi hesitated a moment longer. "And how is Josh settling in?" she asked.

For a moment surprise flashed across his face. "I don't know," he replied. "He keeps to himself. He'll talk when he's ready." He shrugged. "I'm not sure I did the right thing bringing him to Saddler Cove. The people…"

"Can be charming when they want to. But I fear Josh is a little outside their comfort zone. They'll get used to him."

"They never got used to me." He glanced up at the sky and crossed his arms before settling his gaze back on Mimi.

"That may well be your own fault. You don't exactly go out of your way to convince them you're not who they think you are. A little humility would go a long way."

He half grinned at that. His teeth white in his tanned face, his eyes crinkling at the corners, and there was that weird little tummy twist again. "Humility has never been a strong point of mine, ma'am."

"No. I suspect not. But maybe in light of your change in circumstances"—she waved a hand in the general direction of Emily's stomach—"you might want to cultivate a little. You would be the last person to want your child growing up with the stigma of an irresponsible parent."

"Mimi!" It was hardly Tanner's fault that his father had been the town drunk.

Mimi shrugged. "I'm sure Tanner doesn't mind a little straight-talking. Do you, Tanner?"

"No, ma'am."

"I think I've said enough but say hello to Joshua for me. He has a good friend in you." She smiled. "And warn him he will be invited for lunch as well."

"You know," Tanner murmured as they watched Mimi

walk away. "I reckon your gran could handle a hog. I reckon she could handle just about anything."

Emily wondered whether she should mention that Mimi had set them up, that really this whole situation was Mimi's fault. But maybe she'd wait a little longer. "She's the best person I know."

"You were lucky."

She studied him for a moment. It was a strange thing to say. Because she hadn't been lucky. She'd lost both her parents. But things could have been so much worse. She still had Mimi.

She followed him down the steps, then placed her new helmet on the seat while she shrugged into the leather jacket. It was a little snug across her breasts but otherwise fit well. Tanner picked up the helmet and placed it on her head, and she held herself still while he tightened the strap under her chin.

"Okay?"

She nodded. Though she was in no way sure that was true. She was a little bit scared, her pulse racing, her heart thumping. "Is there anything I should or shouldn't do?" she asked.

"Just hold onto me tight. If I lean into a corner, then go with me." He stepped back and studied her. "You look cute."

"Great. Because I always aspire to be cute."

"Cute works for me." Did it? Or had she been some sort of novelty after all the tall, skinny women he usually dated? Though if he'd been telling the truth—and why would he lie—he hadn't dated anyone in three years.

He put his own helmet on and then slung his leg over the seat, making it look effortless. She examined the bike for a minute, nibbling on her lower lip. He twisted around so he could see her and patted the leather behind him. "Come on, Teach, show me how wild you can be."

"Hah." But she shuffled a little closer. She so wanted to be cool here, but she had an idea she was going to look like an idiot. Try to get on and fall over the other side or…

She took a deep breath and swung her leg over the seat behind him, and then settled herself onto the leather. She wriggled a bit, sliding closer to Tanner. He switched on the engine, and she nearly jumped out of her skin as the vibrations shivered up through her body.

A bit closer, and she was almost touching him, her thighs parted so she was pressed up against his butt. She couldn't do this. She was going to go into meltdown. Then he did something, and the engine throbbed beneath her, and automatically her hands went to his waist. He took hold of her hands and slid them around him, so she was wrapped tight, the hard muscles of his belly clenched beneath her fingers.

And they were moving, slowly at first, smooth, and she had the feeling she was sitting on some powerful beast. Right now, the power was reined in, but all she had to do was loosen her grip on the reins and they would be off and flying. Did she want that?

Hell yes.

She squeezed with her fingers, and he must had gotten the message, because he increased the speed a little as they passed through the gates and onto the road.

He turned his head and mouthed the word: *ready?*

She nodded, held him a little tighter, and then they were flying. She bit back a scream of shock rather than fear. She trusted Tanner. Which was a weird thought because really, she hardly knew him. But she did, at some deep, basic level that went beyond mere knowledge.

The ride was exhilarating, snatching her breath from her lungs, and she pushed aside all her thoughts and worries for the future and just lived in the moment.

She rested her cheek against the smooth leather of his

jacket. He was so hard, and big, and he'd always been so beyond her that this seemed a little weird. She was pregnant with Tanner's baby, and she was riding along on the back of his Harley, hugging him as tight as a woman could hug a man—even if it wasn't for real.

He didn't want her like that. She had a flashback to the nice platonic peck on the forehead he'd given her last Saturday before he'd left. That was obviously all she could expect from him now. And that was good, because sex would only complicate matters. But oh God, she felt so horny right now. If she could only get a little closer. She wriggled on the seat, pressing closer, trying to ease the throb between her thighs...

Something was changing. They were pulling over onto the side of the road. Tanner switched off the engine and twisted so he could see her.

"Are you all right?" he asked. "You were wriggling."

Hah. She'd just been about to give herself an orgasm on the back of a bike. So no, things were not all right. In fact—if that ever came to light, she might go up in flames and die of embarrassment. She nodded.

"Do you need to go to the bathroom or something?" When she didn't say anything, he continued, "I read that pregnant women need to...you know...pee more often. I don't want you to be uncomfortable because you're too embarrassed to mention it."

She cleared her throat. "I'm not and I won't. I was just getting comfortable. I'm good."

"Okay."

Then they were off again. This time she held on tight, because hey, she wasn't going to risk falling off, but not that tight. And she watched the scenery. They were driving along the coast road, just passing the bridge to Chincoteague Island. It was the annual pony swim soon, when they swam the wild ponies over from the nearby Assateague Island, and she always went with Mimi, who was on the organizing committee. It was a tradition that had gone on for many years. The wild pony herds of Assateague were thought to be the descendants of a group of horses who were shipwrecked in a Spanish galleon just off the coast hundreds of years ago. They ran wild and proliferated, and each year they were rounded up and swum across the narrow channel between Assateague and Chincoteague. Most of the youngsters were auctioned off—that was where she had bought her mare, Beauty—and the adults returned to Chincoteague. It kept the herd in sustainable numbers and also raised money for the Chincoteague fire department. As well as being a huge tourist draw for the area.

She somehow managed to switch off after that and relax, letting her mind go blank and just enjoying the brand-new experience of riding on the back of a Harley with a gorgeous guy.

It was probably thirty minutes later when the bike entered the small coastal town of Freedom Bay. Tanner drove straight through the town and pulled up outside a big double metal gate on the outskirts. "Freddie's Scrapyard" was written on a faded sign above the gate.

Tanner parked the bike and switched off the engine. She didn't think she could move, her legs locked in place, her hands still gripped around his waist like claws. Tanner pulled off his helmet and twisted to look at her. "You can let go now, Emily." She didn't move. "I mean, you don't have to. I kind of like you holding on to me that way."

She could hear the amusement in his voice. And she slowly uncurled her fingers from around his waist.

"Are you okay? I'm sorry about the bike. It was a mistake. I didn't think…"

"No, I'm fine. I absolutely loved the ride. In fact, I might pop into the shop and buy one myself any day now." She unfastened her helmet with fingers that were shaking slightly and tugged it off, ran a hand through her hair.

"I'll get you a discount," he said with a grin. He shifted and somehow managed to swing his leg over and get off the bike without her moving. Which was good. She wasn't quite ready to move yet.

He took the helmet from her, then came back, placing a finger under her chin, and at his touch a shiver ran through her. He raised her face, so she looked him in the eye. "You sure you're okay?"

"I'm not ill and I'm not delicate. I grew up on a ranch. I'm not going to fall apart."

He nodded. "Okay then. Off you get."

When she still didn't move, he smirked, then placed his hands on her waist, lifted her up high, and placed her down on the ground. He kept hold for a minute while her legs steadied, the heat of his palms burning through the denim of her jeans. Probably branding her forever.

"I'm okay now. I think."

"Shit, I'm so irre-fucking-sponsible. I'll arrange a ride back for you."

"No, you won't. I told you. I loved it. A first. I'm looking forward to the ride back."

He studied her for what seemed like a long time and then gave a grudging nod.

"Tell me about this date," she said. "A scrapyard? That's another first for me."

He looked slightly shamefaced. "Sorry, I had been planning to take you to dinner at Ben's place, but Freddie phoned me on Wednesday and told me he had a few items that might be of interest to me coming in this morning. A couple of old bikes I can use for parts on a Harley I'm working on."

"Is that what you do? Fix up old bikes?"

"Mainly I do up vintage Harleys—they can go for more than the new ones if you get it right and authentic."

"Wow." She knew from Mimi that the one she'd been buying had cost a whopping twenty-five thousand. That was a lot of money.

"So, are you up for grubbing about in the muck and the grease with me?"

"Is this some sort of test? See what the mother of your baby is made of? You think I can't get dirty."

A slow smile spread across his face. "Hell, babe, I've seen you get good and dirty." Then he shrugged. "But maybe a little. Last week you showed me what your life was like—all la-di-da classical shit. Now it's my turn."

Ha, she'd show him. She'd helped Pete, the handyman at the ranch, fix the machinery from an early age. Passing him wrenches and fetching him tools. She wasn't scared of a little muck and work. "Lead the way," she said.

He took her to the side and through a smaller metal gate that led into a huge yard area absolutely cram-packed with… scrap. Mostly old cars piled on top of each other. A crane and a crusher machine stood to one side but were silent, and the air was heavy with the smells of gas and diesel and rust. A man around Tanner's age, dressed in gray coveralls, emerged from a small building. A big smile split his face when he saw Tanner, and he hurried across.

Emily watched as the two men hugged.˙ They parted and stepped back from each other, though a smile stayed on Tanner's face. He looked relaxed, more relaxed than he ever seemed back in Saddler Cove.

"Hey, my man, how you doing?"

"Good," Tanner replied. "And you?"

"Business is doing great." He turned to Emily. "Is this your girl? She looks too good for you."

Tanner didn't say yes or no to that, but at least he didn't

deny it outright. And why did she care? She wasn't his girl. Didn't want to be his girl. She stepped forward and held out her hand. "I'm Emily," she said.

He took her hand in his much bigger one and shook it vigorously. "Freddie."

"Nice to meet you."

He turned back to Tanner. "Definitely too good for you."

"So where are these bikes?"

"Follow me." He led the way across the yard and into a lean-to shed that provided a little shade from the hot sun. Three motorcycles stood there. Even to Emily's untrained eyes they looked a sorry state, the leather rotted away in places, the paint dull and chipped. Tires torn, one wheel twisted. "A couple of dudes found them moldering away in an old barn after their daddy died. Must have been in there for years. I got the lot for five hundred."

Tanner was walking around the bikes, running his fingers over the metalwork almost lovingly.

"You're looking a little wistful there, girl," Freddie said. "You worried Tanner loves his bikes more than you? You can always leave him and go out with me instead."

She wasn't worried because she knew it. "I'll think about it," she said.

"No, you won't," Tanner replied, coming back to them and slinging a possessive arm around her shoulder. "I'll give you a thousand for whatever I can get off them."

He held out his free hand, and Freddie shook it. "It's a deal." He nodded across the shed. "There are a couple of crates back there, and help yourself to tools. I'll leave you to it."

She liked the feel of Tanner's arm around her, the casual possessiveness. She didn't like that she liked it. But she would worry about that later.

"He seems nice," she said.

"I met him inside. Doing two years for grand theft auto."

"Oh." She looked around. "The bikes aren't stolen, are they?" She didn't want Tanner getting into trouble. She might cope with the father of her baby being an ex-con, but not an actual convict.

He cast her a look of disbelief. "Who the hell would steal this pile of crap? Come on, we've got work to do."

And he wasn't lying. For the next few hours, they worked. She handed him tools when he asked, put things in the crate. Even added a bit of muscle on a particularly stiff bolt.

Freddie had brought them mugs of coffee at one point and lingered while they drank it. "I hear Josh got his parole at last. He's working for you?"

"Yeah. A few weeks now."

"He settling in all right?"

"Not sure. You should come over, have a drink one night. Might cheer him up to see a familiar face."

"Yeah, like some sort of old school reunion. Sweet. But maybe I will one night." He turned to Emily. "Hey, did you know about Tanner's time away? Am I telling stories I shouldn't?"

"Emily knows. She's from Saddler Cove."

He grinned. "You fraternizing with the enemy now?"

"Yeah."

"Well, I'd say it's worth it for this one. Now, I'll leave you two to work. Let me know when you're ready to leave."

Finally the two crates were full, and all that was left was a pile of metal and moldy leather. Tanner straightened from his hunkered position and stretched, raising his arms above his head and revealing a strip of golden skin and ridged abs at his waist as his T-shirt rose up. She tried not to stare. Really, she did. But holy moly he was hot. Hottest thing she had ever seen.

She wiped her sweaty palms down her thighs. The sun

was nearly down, but her temperature was up.

"You've got oil on your clothes," he pointed out.

"So do you. And on your face."

"Yeah, but the last time you had oil on your clothes you stripped off right in front of me."

She snorted. "Yes, and look what happened. The end of my life as I know it."

His face closed up, and the smile blanked from his eyes. "I'm sorry for that. For fucking up your life, I mean. I have a habit of doing that."

"Don't be so melodramatic. According to Mimi, my life needed to change."

"I bet she didn't envisage this scenario, though."

"Well, she should have. You do know she set us up, right?"

"What?"

"She didn't like Ryan, and she thought I needed a fling—a little excitement in my life. So she went and bought a motorcycle, knowing I would go straight over to your place and call you out on it."

"Really?" He sounded skeptical.

"Yes, really. She confessed last week after I told her I was pregnant. Apparently, she was worried about me—with my boring little life."

"She probably wasn't expecting a baby, though."

"No, she probably thought a man like you would never get caught out like that."

He frowned. "A man like me?"

"Well, you do have a bit of a reputation. My God, you had the harem in high school."

"The what?" He looked bewildered.

"That's what they called them, your little—well, actually not so little—group of girlfriends."

"I was eighteen." He scrubbed a hand through his hair. "I can't believe this. Your gran set us up. The devious…"

"Get used to it."

He blew out his breath, obviously deciding to change the subject. "You like crabs?" he asked.

She nodded. "I love crabs! I've had to cut back, because too much seafood is bad for the baby."

"Sure? Maybe we shouldn't—"

"Some is fine, though" she interrupted. She'd told the truth—crabs were her favorite. "Honest. Some is good."

"Well, I know where we can get the sweetest crabs in the whole of Virginia. And they won't care if you've got a bit of dirt on you. Plus, it's on the way home."

"Sounds like a plan."

Chapter Fourteen

Josh shoved his hands into his pockets as he walked away from the diner, trying to decide if he was pissed off or relieved.

Tanner had told him the rumors going around—that he was some sort of serial killer and likely to murder everyone in their beds. But it was Saturday night, and Tanner had said he needed to get out more. Mix with people. Though he hadn't seen Tanner doing much mixing with the population of Saddler Cove.

Most of the customers at the shop came from out of town—they had developed an excellent reputation, and the business was doing well. Which was good. At least it meant he didn't have to worry that Tanner had made up the job. Was paying him money he couldn't afford. He was kept busy. Which he liked—stopped him thinking too much.

So he'd decided to go out for dinner. Which was a first. He'd chosen the diner, as the other restaurants in town were way too fancy. But when he'd stepped through the door, the place had gone quiet. And he'd almost turned around and walked out again. Except he was hungry.

Then a waitress with dark hair and dark eyes, in a pink dress with a name tag across her chest—María José—had sidled up to him as though he might produce an axe from under his shirt at any moment and start hacking the whole joint to pieces. She'd told him they were full-up, when it was clear the place was half empty.

He'd thought about making some sort of comment. But he couldn't really blame them. He was outside their comfort zone. And he could tell Tanner he'd tried.

Or maybe he wouldn't tell Tanner, because he might come over here and make a fuss, and that was the last thing Josh wanted or needed.

In the end, he'd turned around and walked out without a word and had almost heard the sighs of relief as he opened the door.

He was relieved, too, he decided. On balance. He'd go back to the apartment, make a sandwich, and drive the truck to the beach. Tanner had given him a lesson, left him a set of keys, told him he could use the truck whenever he wanted.

"Josh."

Someone called out his name from behind him. And he stopped, more out of shock than anything else. A woman's voice. He didn't know any women. Didn't know anyone except Tanner and his two brothers and a couple of mechanics who also worked in the garage. And it definitely wasn't any of those.

He turned slowly. It was the woman who'd visited the shop a couple of weeks back. The one who'd told him to call her Mimi.

She was beautiful, tall and slender, with black hair and green eyes. And she'd seemed…nice. Quirky but nice. And a little crazy. She'd been pissed off that Tanner had cancelled her order for a Harley. And she'd invited him to visit. He'd guessed she wanted to do some therapy on him. Thought he needed saving. He'd met plenty like that in prison. Do-gooders who were actually incapable of doing any fucking good at all.

Tonight, she was wearing faded jeans that clung to her slender figure and were tucked into fancy cowboy boots. And a black T-shirt with a silver horse's head.

What did she want?

She came to a halt in front of him and smiled. "Joshua. I was just coming to the shop."

"Tanner's not here right now. He's out."

"I know. Out with my granddaughter, actually."

That was interesting. "She a pretty little thing—blond—dresses like a school teacher?"

"She *is* a school teacher."

"Figures."

That was the woman Tanner had slowed down for that first night. It looked like Tanner had a girlfriend. He'd kept quiet about that. Then what she'd said sank in a little further. "So why were you coming to the shop?"

"To see you, of course."

"To see me about what?"

She shrugged. "I was alone, and I presumed you were similarly alone, and I thought we might go to the diner, have some food."

He just stopped short of scratching his head. "Why?"

"Because that's what people do."

"Not that I've noticed. Not in this town." What the hell did she want from him?

"That's because they are afraid of you. This is a small town, and most people are a little intimidated by anyone who's…"

"A serial killer?" he suggested. "Maybe they're right to be afraid."

"Don't be silly—I know you're not a serial killer. I was

going to say different from them. So, what do you say?"

"About what?"

"Joining me in the diner for a meal where we can talk like civilized people."

"The diner's full," he said.

Her black brows drew together. "The diner is never full."

"It is tonight. Waitress told me so herself."

Her eyes widened as she thought about that and no doubt came to the correct conclusion. "Really. Well, we'll see about that. Come along."

"No."

She'd half turned, now she paused, turned back. "No?"

"I ain't going back there. And I don't plan to be your good deed for the week. I'll see you around, ma'am."

"It's Mimi. And I can see that you really haven't talked to many people in this town. I am not a do-gooder." She pursed her lips. "I was lonely."

The admission made him hesitate. Not many people would own up to being lonely. Did he believe her? But why the hell would she lie about something like that? And for what purpose? He didn't believe for a second that she wanted to spend time with him.

"I'm sure you have lots of friends in town."

"Some. None I want to see right now. Come on, you still need to eat."

"I was going to make a sandwich and take it down to the beach." And why had he told her that?

"That sounds better than the stuffy diner. But we can buy a couple of sandwiches from the convenience store and drive in my truck."

We? The night was turning surreal. And somehow, he found himself walking beside her along the sidewalk. A few people said hello as they passed, and Mimi nodded but didn't slow. He could feel their eyes on him, almost sense their disbelief. At the convenience store, she headed straight for the cooler section. "Anything you prefer?" she asked.

"No." He'd learned to eat anything and everything inside. He was not fussy.

"I'm a vegetarian," she said. "Have been since my husband died—he ran a beef ranch—it didn't seem viable before that. But the choices can be limited in a town like this. I might be the only vegetarian in Saddler Cove. Cheese do?"

"Yeah."

He'd stopped thinking by this point.

"Good, then grab a couple of bottles of water."

He did as he was told—he reckoned most people did when this woman was involved—and trailed her to the counter. At the last minute, his brain started working and he pulled some notes out of his pocket and slammed them on the counter. He wasn't anybody's charity case. She raised a brow but didn't argue.

Her truck was parked close by. Not a fancy thing like Tanner drove, but old, the red paint faded. Maybe you didn't need fancy status symbols when you'd been born rich and never known anything else. She opened the driver's door, climbed in, then leaned across and pushed open the passenger side.

He hesitated, standing on the street with his bag of food. It wasn't as though he had anything else to do, and he had to admit he was curious. And he hadn't been curious in a long time. That more than anything made him shrug and climb in, shut the door behind him.

They were both quiet as she started the engine and pulled into traffic.

He hadn't been this close to a woman in…he didn't like to think. Tanner had offered to go with him to a bar in Virginia Beach and help find him some pussy. Not happening. Maybe twenty years ago. Not now. Tanner had said the first thing he'd done when he got out was go get laid, though he reckoned Tanner hadn't needed to go looking very far. He'd seen the women that came into the store, all dressed up and trying to tempt him. As far as he was aware, Tanner didn't have anything to do with any of them.

She didn't smell of any fancy perfume, but soap and something else he couldn't identify. He breathed in deeply.

"Horses," she said from beside him. "Best scent in the world."

"I'll take your word for it, ma'am…Mimi."

"I still haven't given up on you coming to the ranch."

He frowned. "Why are you bothering with me?"

"Truth?"

"Why the hell not?"

"I don't know. But I find you…interesting."

"I'm not some fucking object of curiosity."

She gave him a sideways glance. "Of course you're not," she said soothingly. But he didn't want to be soothed. He wanted out. He realized he was angry, and that it might be the first real emotion he'd felt in as long as he could remember.

"But when you've lived in a small town for any length of time," she continued, "you'll realize that interesting people are to be cultivated."

"Not sure I want to be cultivated." He wasn't even sure what it would involve. But some of his anger subsided.

She pulled up in the same place Tanner had that first night, and they both got out without speaking again. He grabbed the bag and headed down the now-familiar track to the beach. The evening was warm, but a cool breeze blew in from the sea, heavy with the salt tang of the water. He could feel his mood levelling out, the last of the anger dissipating. He loved this place.

They had the beach to themselves, except for a couple of seagulls wheeling high overhead and, far out to sea, a boat of some kind. He'd like a boat. He'd go out there, just far enough so he couldn't see the land, water all around him.

"You come here often?" she asked.

"Yeah. I never even knew places like this existed. I grew up in the city."

"A city boy? Sit down. I'm hungry. I've been working all day."

He sank down onto the sand, legs stretched out in front of him, then rummaged in the bag and handed her a sandwich. He decided not to question the evening anymore. Just go along with the flow. She sat beside him, her legs curled under her, and they ate in silence. Josh washed the last mouthful down with water and tucked the rubbish back in the bag, then leaned back on his arms and stared out to sea. The boat had disappeared now.

"How old are you, Josh?"

"Sixty-eight. How about you?"

"Seventy."

"No way." He'd thought her around fifty. He twisted so he could study her. She did have lines at the corner of her eyes, but otherwise her face was smooth, and her hair showed no gray, though that could be dye. All the same, it was hard to believe she was the same age as him. "Got a picture in your attic somewhere?"

She chuckled. "I do believe that was a compliment?" Then she considered him, her head cocked to one side. "You're quite well-read, aren't you?"

"You mean for a black ex-con?"

"No, I mean for anyone. I'm guessing you've read more than the vast majority of the people in this town."

"Wasn't a lot else to do inside."

"You were in for forty years?" He nodded. "Goodness. Yes, plenty of time for reading."

"Yeah, I read every single book in the goddamned library. Most more than once."

"I suppose it must be hard getting used to the outside

again."

"You could say I've become a little institutionalized."

"Nothing that time and some good sea air can't resolve."

He laughed at that. But as they sat side by side on the sand and watched the sun turn the sky to orange and pink, he believed maybe she might be right.

. . .

Tanner couldn't drag his gaze away as Emily licked the crab juice from her fingers with a small, pointed tongue. Desire hit him hard and fast, twisting knots in his stomach and making his dick jerk in his pants. He shifted uncomfortably, glad that particular part of his anatomy was safely hidden beneath the table.

While she'd said she wanted to get to know him, he was quite aware it was only because of the baby. Otherwise, no way would they be sitting here together. He might be good for a hookup, but he was hardly boyfriend material.

Having said that, he was pretty sure she'd enjoyed herself that night. Hell, she'd screamed like she enjoyed herself.

At the memory, his dick stiffened to attention.

Not good. Think of something else.

"Do you ride horses?" he asked. "You know, what with you growing up on the ranch and all."

She wiped her fingers on the napkin and turned her gaze on him. "I used to. Not anymore."

"Why did you stop?"

She gave a shrug, looked away for a moment. "I don't really know. Well, I do sort of. But it's not a very good reason. I stopped after my parents were killed."

He'd known her mom and dad were dead. It had been big news in the town at the time. They'd been away somewhere. He didn't know the details. "How did they die?"

"They were both doctors. They worked for this organization that did humanitarian work, disaster relief mainly, but also monitoring outbreaks of infectious diseases. Their plane went down in a tropical storm. Both killed outright, or so we were told. Anyway, shortly after that...I fell off Beauty—she's my pony. It wasn't even a bad fall, but I used it as an excuse and just stopped. My mom's death nearly killed Mimi. She was her only child. I can't even imagine what it must be like." In what he was sure was an unconscious gesture, her hand moved to rest on her stomach. "And I kept thinking. What if I died, too, and she would have nobody?"

"So you stopped riding to reduce the chances of anything bad happening to you—so Mimi would be okay. Figures." She was way too nice. He hadn't known nice like her existed in the world.

"It was around then she was diagnosed with remitting and recurring MS as well. The first attack was brought on by the stress, and I just wanted to do anything I could to make things a little bit easier."

"I didn't know she had MS."

"She doesn't keep it a secret, but she doesn't let it control her life, either. She's been in remission for a few years now. She's strong. My not riding used to drive her insane." She paused, took a sip of her iced water. "Mimi still rides just about every day, and she thought there was something seriously wrong with me. And in some ways, she was right. You shouldn't let fear rule your life. But it just became habit. Have you ever been on a horse?"

"Never."

"You'll have to come and let Mimi give you a lesson."

"Yeah." *Not.*

"You'd probably be a natural. It's all about balance. And you must be good at that."

"But my bike stops when I tell it to."

"So do Mimi's horses. They're very well trained." She smiled. "Don't tell me I've found something you're scared of?"

"I'm scared of lots of things."

"Like what?"

He smiled. "Your grandmother terrifies me."

"Hah. What else?"

"I'm scared of something going wrong with the baby. I did this reading and—shit, there's a whole load of stuff that can happen—and maybe I shouldn't have mentioned that."

"I've probably been reading the same stuff. But nothing will go wrong." She sounded so sure. "What else?"

He looked away for a moment, suddenly uncomfortable. He'd never talked about this stuff with anyone, but she wanted to get to know him, so... "I'm shit-scared of failing and having the whole town of Saddler Cove say I told you so."

"Oh. You don't like them very much, do you?"

She was right there. "My mom died when I was six. My dad fell to pieces and never really got over it. He was a drunk."

"He must have loved your mom very much."

"I guess. I don't really remember her much. Just feelings. Up until she died, the house was a happy place, seemed to be filled with light. We were poor, but it didn't matter. After she died, it was like the lights went out. I remember going to school and the other kids laughing because my clothes were dirty, or my socks didn't match."

Her face softened. But he didn't want her pity. "That must have been hard."

He shrugged as though it hadn't mattered. But it had. "I learned to fight back. I was always fighting." He tugged at his lower lip—he didn't want to talk anymore, but he had to finish now that he'd started. "My dad lost his job, so money was even tighter. You know, you hear all this stuff about small towns and them looking after each other. Yeah, well. No one looked after my dad."

"So you decided to show them you didn't care?"

"I decided to show them they were right. If they thought I was so goddamned bad, then I was going to give them bad."

"Yet you were never in trouble before…"

He cast her a look. "Before I got locked up for killing my best friend?"

For the first time in his life, he wished he could open up to someone about that night. But he wasn't going there. It was in the past, and best it stayed that way. The truth wouldn't change anything for the better, anyway. Not now.

"I'm sorry."

"Don't be. The funny thing was, after I went inside, my dad cleaned up his act. Maybe he realized what a shit father he'd been. There was only Aiden left at home—Reese was in the Navy back then. Dad got a job, was sorting himself out. Then he was killed." He ran a hand through his hair. What was he telling her all this fucking shit for? She didn't want to know. But her expression was so earnest, and she reached out a hand and rested it on his arm. Squeezed.

"I remember when they told me, and just thinking what the hell was the point in anything?" He shook his head. "When I got out, and we had the compensation money, Reese and Aiden both wanted to move to Richmond. I persuaded them to stay. You know the town board tried to stop us opening the shop?"

"No. Why would they do that? They're always trying to bring new businesses to the town."

"Because it was us. Maybe they didn't want a business run by the O'Connors in their nice, tidy little town."

"Maybe you make them feel uncomfortable."

"I certainly hope so."

"You're still trying to show them that you don't give a damn?"

"I don't give a damn."

"Yes, you do."

"Change the subject."

She searched his face, and he kept his expression bland. "I have an appointment with a doctor next week. About the baby. Do you want to come?"

Why was she asking? "You feeling sorry for me, Teach?"

"No. And I understand if you don't want to come along. But I just thought I would give you the chance. It's in Richmond."

"Was that so no one will know you?"

She nodded. "The doctor was recommended to me, but yes, a little bit. I'm not ready for people to know just yet."

Did she really want him there? And why was he being so goddamned pathetic? Did he *want* to go? He wasn't sure, but he didn't want her to go alone.

"Mimi will come with me if you don't. It's not a problem." She sounded unworried, but something flickered in her eyes.

Hell, he was no good at this. Didn't know what to do for the best. But the fact was, he wanted to go. He wanted to hold her hand. "I'd like to come. I can drive if you like. Not the bike." It didn't seem right, going for a baby appointment on a bike.

"Okay." She smothered a yawn with her hand.

"Come on. I'll get you home."

"I haven't been sleeping too well. Apparently, that's normal. Some weird hormonal thing. Mimi says it will get better."

Driving back to Saddler Cove, with her arms wrapped around his middle and her curves flush against his back, he felt at peace, and it occurred to him that if only they could do this alone, then they might make it work.

But how likely was that to happen?

And once it became communal knowledge, he had an idea that things might go to shit really quickly.

Chapter Fifteen

What the hell was he doing here?

But time was running out for a quick getaway. A big yellow and black bus was pulling into the school yard.

Keira tugged on his hand. "Smile, Uncle Tanner."

He glanced down at her. She had a worried little frown line between her eyes. "What, honey?"

"Daddy said I should keep reminding you to smile. So you don't scare the other mommies."

Daddy had said that, had he? Tanner bared his teeth, and Keira giggled.

Goddamn fucking Reese for setting him up for this. He was probably sitting somewhere laughing his head off. He'd kill the bastard. Duped by his own brother.

Reese should be here. He was the one who'd signed up for this. Tanner hadn't. Never would have in a million years. Chaperoning a bunch of first- and second-grade kids on a field trip. Hardly his scene. Though actually, it wasn't the kids he minded so much—he liked kids—it was the mothers. A few of them were eying him up as if he were some sort of rabid dog in their midst. The rest were just eyeing him up. He wasn't sure which was worse.

He hadn't felt this terrified since his first night in prison. *Breathe.*

Tanner glanced around uneasily, his gaze skittering away from a blond woman around his age. She was holding the hands of two small boys and staring at him as though they had some sort of connection. Did they? He was sure he recognized her from high school, and he was equally sure they'd had a thing at one point, but damned if he could remember the details. She smiled, and he looked away. Avoid eye contact. That was the way to get through this.

He hunched his shoulders, trying to appear inconspicuous, an impossible task when he was at least a foot taller than everyone else.

Just suck it up.

Reese was trying hard to be a good father, and apparently all the parents—well, usually the mothers, but Keira didn't have a mother—took turns at this sort of thing. But Reese was stuck in Richmond. On purpose, Tanner suspected.

Josh was quite capable of taking care of the shop, Reese had said to Tanner's initial refusal. There was no reason for Tanner to say no. And the trip would be cancelled if he didn't go—they needed a certain number of chaperones—and it would be Keira's fault, and all the other kids would hate her, and besides, she'd been looking forward to it. Reese knew how to press his buttons.

"Thank you, Uncle Tanner."

He sighed. He could do this. "So where are we going, exactly?"

"Ms. Towson's house."

He went still. The one little ray of sunshine in an otherwise really crappy situation was that Emily was Keira's teacher and therefore he might get to see her. Even if she would be surrounded by kids and their mothers. "Really?"

"Yes. She lives on a ranch, and she's going to show us the horses and the chickens. And she has a pony." She blinked up at him. "I'd like a pony, Uncle Tanner."

Dangerous topic. If he wasn't careful, he'd be promising all sorts of things. Keira had that effect on him.

But he was saved from answering by the school door opening.

And there she was. Walking together with some nerdy-looking guy—who appeared around Tanner's age—reading from a clipboard. Then she glanced up, looking straight into his eyes, and almost tripped over and fell. The man beside her grabbed her arm, stopping her fall, and Tanner had to stifle his instinctive growl.

Luckily, Emily brushed away the man's hand. She gripped the clipboard to her chest and moved to the front of the bus, casting him a wary little glance as she passed.

Was she worried he was going to embarrass her? Ask her how the baby was?

"Come on." Keira tugged on his hand, dragging him toward the bus and Emily.

He stopped beside her. She looked so cute with her clipboard. "Hey, Teach."

"I didn't expect you here," she said. Her cheeks had that pretty little flush, and she couldn't meet his gaze.

"I'm standing in for Reese. He got stuck in a meeting in Richmond."

"Oh. Well, good." She smiled brightly. "I hope you enjoy the trip, Mr. O'Connor."

People were crowding behind him, and he had to move, up the steps and into the bus. He stopped at the top, unsure where to go.

"You have to sit in the back with the other mommies," Keira said.

He did? For a second, he clung to Keira's hand. She squeezed it, tugged free, and then patted his arm. "Don't worry. I'll keep a look out. Make sure you're all right." She rummaged in her bag and pulled out a book—*Alice in Wonderland*. "Here. You can read this in case no one talks to you. And remember to smile."

Crap.

He nodded and made his way toward the back of the bus. The women fell silent as he passed, then started talking quickly and quietly. He tried not to listen, because he really didn't want to hear what they were saying. He had zero doubt that he was the topic of conversation. He found two empty seats and sat down. Staying on the outside so no one would be tempted to sit beside him. Not that he thought there was much risk of that. Then he opened the book at random and stared at words. He'd read it before—it had been in the prison library, though there had been fewer pictures in that copy.

Keira was up at the front, chatting with the other kids. She seemed popular, which was a relief. She caught his gaze—she was keeping an eye on him, as promised—and waggled her fingers. He sat back and turned his attention to Emily. She was standing by the driver, staring fixedly at her clipboard, but then one of the boys said something to her, and she smiled and nodded.

"Everyone sitting down?" she asked.

"Yes, Ms. Towson," they replied in unison.

"Then we're ready to go."

She shifted from foot to foot for a second as if undecided where to sit. Then her shoulders stiffened, her lips tightened, and she headed down the aisle. She stopped beside his seat, and he struggled to keep the shock from his face. "Is this seat taken?"

"Hell no." She raised an eyebrow. "No, ma'am."

A smile flashed in her eyes as he shifted along the seat,

and she came down beside him as the engine rumbled to life and the bus pulled away from the school.

After a minute, she cleared her throat. "Good book?" she asked, nodding to the paperback clutched in his hand.

"Keira lent it to me." He smiled. "And it seems apt. *'"But I don't want to go among mad people," Alice remarked.'*"

"You think we're mad? And that's very impressive. Especially as the book's upside down."

He glanced down. "So it is. But I've read it before. It was in the prison library."

"And you learned it by heart. I'm even more impressed."

"Not all of it. But it was a…thing I used to do with Josh—guess the quote. We read the same books—didn't have much choice."

They were silent for a few minutes. She craned her neck to look behind her and then back at him. "You know, I think I recognize at least a couple of members of your high school harem here."

He cast her a narrow-eyed look, but didn't comment. He hadn't had a goddamn harem. Not that he could remember.

"You were certainly busy back then," she added cheerfully.

He shrugged. *"Gather ye rosebuds while ye may."*

She giggled, then looked around almost guiltily, no doubt in case anyone had heard. "I can't believe you're quoting poetry about your harem."

"I never had a harem," he growled. "I was a perfectly normal eighteen-year-old."

She patted his thigh. "Of course you were, Tanner."

"Okay. Well, maybe I was just practicing. So I'd get it right when it mattered." And there was that flush again, turning her cheeks pink. He loved that she'd seen him naked and yet he could still make her blush with just a few words. He leaned a little closer, and her eyes widened. "Did I get it right, Teach?"

She swallowed, licked her lips, and heat shot through him. Then she sniffed. "I'd give you a B+ at best—there was definitely room for improvement."

"Hah." That was why she'd screamed so loud. "You want to help me practice, Ms. Towson? Give me a little extra... tutoring?"

She pursed her lips, but was saved from answering as the bus slowed and then turned into the ranch driveway. "Ah. We're here." She rose to her feet, smoothing her skirt. "Well, it was nice talking to you, Mr. O'Connor."

He was smiling as she walked away. Keira would be proud.

Once they were out of the bus, he stayed at the edge of the group while Emily explained that there was going to be a tour, followed by a picnic, and afterward, her grandmother would give a riding display on her stallion, Frankie. Then the bus would take them all back to school.

"Why don't you just bring up the rear, Mr. O'Connor?" she said at the end of her speech. "You can make sure there are no stragglers. That no one gets left behind."

"And eaten by the horses."

She blinked at him. "Exactly."

He let the rest of them move away and took up position at the back. Actually, it wasn't a bad way to spend an afternoon. Emily had a cute ass, and he could follow it around for hours.

They stopped at one of the stalls, where a small black horse stood with its head over the door. "This is my pony, Beauty," Emily said. "I got her when I was the same age as you are now."

There were sighs all around at that. Tanner guessed there were going to be a few hassled parents tonight.

Keira put up her hand. "Can I stroke her, Ms. Towson?"

"Of course you can. Just move slowly so you don't startle

her."

Keira's eyes were wide, her lower lip clenched in her teeth as she reached up, touched her fingertip to the pony's black nose.

They moved on, though Keira lingered, glancing back at the black pony longingly. Yup, Reese was in trouble. His brother was going to have to think of some really good reasons why Keira couldn't have a pony. He could almost feel sorry for his brother. Almost, but not quite.

Emily was so great with the kids, always having two of them clinging to her hands, but changing at regular intervals so everyone got a turn. They clearly loved her, staring up with rapt attention while she introduced the rest of the animals and explained their backgrounds.

Seeing her surrounded by the children, Tanner could understand why she was so desperate to keep her job. She was obviously a brilliant teacher and loved interacting with the kids. And she might lose all that because of him.

Never going to happen.

He turned his attention back to better things. Her ass. That ass had been naked on his workbench. His dick twitched at the memory, and he shoved his hands in his pockets and shifted. It seemed wrong thinking about Emily naked when she was surrounded by six- and seven-year-olds. All the same, he couldn't help but wonder if he'd ever get to see her naked again. It seemed unlikely. She wanted to be his friend. She'd given no indication she wanted anything more.

"I didn't expect to see you here, Mr. O'Connor." He jumped. Emily's grandmother had crept up on him while he'd been thinking about Emily's naked ass. Not good.

"I think it came as a surprise to most people, ma'am."

"Call me Mimi." She nodded across to where Emily crouched beside a little girl, whispering something as the child giggled. "She's a natural teacher. I don't know where she got it from—I always preferred horses—but working with children was all she ever wanted to do. She'll be a good mother."

Just as well. "Hopefully that might make up for the poor thing's crappy father."

She gave a short laugh, then studied him for a moment. "Did Emily tell you about the morality clause in her teaching contract? That she could lose her job?"

"Yes, ma'am." A wave of anger rippled through him that they might try and take the job she loved from her. It was a travesty. Just the thought that anyone might consider Emily immoral was crazy. And he felt so fucking powerless—he couldn't get involved, it would only make things worse. And anyway, she didn't want his help. She wasn't even ready for anyone to know she was pregnant, and certainly not by him.

"We won't let that happen, will we, Mr. O'Connor?"

What could he say? "No, ma'am."

And he wished it was that easy, but nothing ever went smoothly for him.

• • •

Emily glanced behind her. Mimi was strolling beside Tanner, their heads close together. His hair was loose, almost reaching his shoulders. It made him look sexy as hell and slightly dangerous. She loved his hair; her fingers had itched to touch it while she'd sat next to him on the bus.

Nerves fluttered in her belly. What were they talking about?

In fact, the whole day was making her twitchy, as though at any moment her nice, safe world would come crashing around her ears. Not that her world was particularly safe anymore—it was like she was two different people, but so far, she was keeping them apart. Now with Tanner here, the two separate parts of her life were on a collision course.

She could sense his gaze focused on her. As she walked, as she talked, as she introduced her pony to the children. His attention never wavered.

He'd flirted with her on the bus. Like a real couple. And he'd quoted poetry—Robert Herrick. There was so much more to him than he let on to the world. Why was he so determined to ensure everyone saw the worst in him?

He'd looked so out of place when she'd first seen him— almost scared.

She would have found it funny, except she didn't.

She'd seen the way the other women watched him. One in particular. Marlene Jackson had been a cheerleader, two years ahead of Emily in school, so she hadn't known her well. She'd been in the same year as Tanner, and if Emily remembered rightly, she'd been with him for a time. Tall, slim, perfectly groomed, the other woman awoke every insecurity Emily believed she had put behind her when she left high school. She was also the mother of six-year-old twins and should know better. But she was positively drooling. Luckily, Tanner was acting as if he didn't even know she existed.

Here with the children around her, he was a reminder that she might lose her job. This was the third year she'd organized the field trip to the ranch. The kids loved it. Her chest ached when she realized it might be the last.

She rubbed at the spot between her eyes where a headache was forming. This was the final week of the school year, and the children had all been in a frenzy of excitement. Which at least took her mind off things. Only two more days, and then she could relax. Hide. Decide what her next move should be. Though that would depend on Tanner to a big extent, and how much of a part he wanted to play in their lives. The thought scared her.

While he might have flirted with her on the bus, that

didn't mean he was ready for anything more. And for some reason she wasn't prepared to articulate, she desperately wanted him to *want* to be a father to her baby.

The picnic had been set up on the lawn in front of the house, under the shade of the huge oak trees. Everyone was getting tucked in, and there were enough helpers to make sure everything went smoothly. She slipped off, heading to the house. Her throat was dry from too much talking, and she needed the bathroom and a moment alone.

As she came out of the house ten minutes later, she spotted Tanner's tall figure disappearing into the barn—he was hard to miss. Without thinking, she followed him. She stood for a moment just inside the door as her eyes adjusted to the dim light. He was leaning against the wall, arms folded across his broad chest, watching her out of hooded eyes. All her fantasies in one stunning package.

"You following me, Teach?"

His voice was a low, husky drawl, and she nodded, somehow unwilling to lie. She'd never been a good liar, anyway, and she just wanted to put all the subterfuge aside for a few minutes. Actually, what she really wanted was for him to wrap his arms around her and tell her everything was going to work out.

She walked past him, casting him a sideways glance, and into an empty stall, where they'd be hidden if anyone came into the barn. She turned to find he was standing just behind her.

A small smile quirked his lips and crinkled his eyes, and she melted inside. He didn't smile enough. "You going to give me that extra tutoring now?" he asked.

She took a step closer, so she could breathe in the warm scent of him—soap, and fresh sweat, and a hint of diesel. "I think you know you don't need any extra tutoring. You were pretty good." He raised an eyebrow. "Okay, you were *very* good."

"*We* were very good. The best."

He didn't mean that. She could never compete with the beautiful women he'd had before. He was just being kind. Except kind wasn't a word she'd ever have associated with Tanner.

He curled his hand around the back of her neck, his touch sending shivers across her skin, and drew her closer. "You're thinking too much." He lowered his head and nipped the skin of her throat, and tingles prickled down her spine. "Way too much." He placed a soft kiss on her neck. "How long do you think we have before some kid comes looking for teacher?"

"Probably about thirty seconds."

He nibbled his way up her neck and jaw. "Let's not waste them, then."

He touched her lips with his. The kiss was gentle for all of a second, and then his mouth hardened on hers, his tongue sliding inside, and her hands came up to cling to his shoulders. Pressing herself against him, she found him already hard, and her insides melted, a pulse starting between her thighs. He kissed her cheek, her ear, his lips trailing fire down the skin her throat.

"Christ, you make me lose control," he murmured.

She did? She liked that, but then he was kissing her again, stripping the thoughts from her mind.

"Ms. Towson!"

She went still. Had they been caught in the act? But the voice had come from outside, though she doubted it would stay that way. Tanner pulled back a little, and for a moment, he rested his forehead against hers, his breathing ragged.

"I guess the lesson is over." He kissed her on the forehead, then stepped away, and she had to bite back her growl of frustration. "It's probably just as well," he said. "Right now, I'd like nothing more than to get you naked and fuck every bad thought, every worry, from your head. But I don't think this is the time or the place." He urged her gently in the direction of the door. "Off you go. I'll be out in a minute. When I've…" He shrugged and waved a hand down his body, where she could see his erection pressing at his fly.

She blushed. Then turned and walked away. Because what else could she do?

He was right. So right. Her brain was starting to function again.

No doubt it was going to come out about her and Tanner eventually. It was impossible to keep secrets in a town like Saddler Cove, and the last thing she needed was someone spotting her messing about with the father of her illegitimate baby during a school field trip. Not if she wanted any chance of keeping her job.

Besides, until they decided how they were going to move forward—whether Tanner wanted to be part of her baby's life—a physical relationship was not a good idea. It just complicated things.

Maybe there would never be a right time and place for them.

Chapter Sixteen

"You fancy coming out for a couple of beers tonight?" Tanner asked, fully expecting a negative answer. Though Josh had seemed more relaxed the last couple of weeks. Some of the tenseness had eased out of him.

"Can't. I've got a book to read."

"You need to read fewer books and drink more beer." He thought for a moment, trying to select the perfect quote. *"'Finally, from so little sleeping and so much reading, his brain dried up and he went completely out of his mind.'"*

Josh snorted. *"Don Quixote."*

"Yeah, and your brain is drying up. What do you say? We can drive out to Ben's place."

Josh shrugged. "Why not?"

What the hell? It was a first, and Tanner worked to keep the grin from his face.

They'd been setting a display. A pink Harley—trying to up their female custom. It was pretty, though. Maybe he'd get one for Emily after the baby—though maybe not—he'd liked her on the back of his bike.

He was meeting her tomorrow. It was her turn to choose their date, though "date" still didn't seem the right word. They were hardly dating. They'd had two more since the day of the field trip, and she hadn't yet seemed inclined to follow up on that interrupted kiss.

She'd taken him to a movie but obviously kept him in mind when she'd picked the film. He'd mentioned to her that he loved the old classics, especially Hitchcock, and they had been doing a run on them at the cinema in Virginia Beach. He'd enjoyed it.

The following Saturday he'd taken her to an open-air rock concert. He'd been tempted to take her dancing, because the fact was, he was fighting a growing urge to have her in his arms again. And he'd been resisting, because that wasn't what this was about. It was about getting to know each other, so they could be good parents to their baby.

He reckoned they were doing okay, except for his inconvenient need to get in her pants again. So he was keeping his hands to himself, and he'd avoided the bike, as that was a little too much up close and personal.

The doctor's appointment had gone well. And she'd invited him for the next one in a couple of weeks' time, so she obviously hadn't decided to cut him from her life.

Things were going better than expected. Though he knew she was still worried about it all coming out, and maybe losing her job. She loved her job, that had been drummed into him the day of the field trip, and he hated that it might be his fault she lost it.

"Shit." Tanner groaned as the door was pushed open and a tall figure stepped inside. Sawyer.

"A friend of yours?" Josh asked from beside him.

"A long time ago. But not anymore."

It was Friday afternoon, nearly closing time, and from the looks of it Sawyer had already had a good deal to drink. He stood just inside the door, swaying slightly, waving a hand as he caught sight of Tanner behind the counter. Then frowning as he took in Josh standing beside him.

"You want me to deal with him?" Josh murmured.

Tanner was tempted. So tempted. He ran a hand through his hair and sighed. "No. But stay there." Maybe Sawyer wouldn't be quite such an asshole if he had an audience. The last thing Sawyer would want was anyone else knowing his guilty little secret.

"Okay, boss."

Sawyer swayed as he walked. When he halted in front of Tanner, he put a hand on the counter for balance. He'd obviously had more than a few.

"You planning on taking my old man's position as town drunk?" Tanner asked.

Sawyer winced. "Maybe. You want to come for a drink with me, Tanner, my old buddy?" He didn't wait for an answer. "No, of course you don't."

Tanner shook his head. "Go home, Sawyer."

"What, to my lovely loving wife? And my beautiful son?"

"Yeah."

"And don't forget my wonderful father-in-law. Saddler Cove's most upstanding citizen." He leaned a little closer, so Tanner could smell the stink of alcohol on his breath, and he stepped back. "He doesn't like you, you know."

"Really."

That was hardly news. Sawyer's father-in-law had been the main voice against the O'Connors getting permission to open the shop. In the end, it had gone through, though it had been a close thing. But then, Jed Forrester was also the father of the boy Tanner had gone to prison for killing. And he'd never forgive him.

Tanner didn't blame him for that.

Dwain had been his only son. And a golden boy. His only

fault had been being friends with the likes of Tanner. And it had killed him. Or that was the story most people believed.

"Is this your new friend?" Sawyer asked, waving a hand toward Josh. Then inched along so he was opposite the other man. "You know, me and Tanner used to be friends. Not anymore. Tanner likes to hold a grudge. Don't you, Tanner?"

A fucking grudge? Was he serious? He would so like to punch Sawyer right now. But he really would not give him the satisfaction.

"Why don't you both come out for a drink with me? We can talk about old times."

"Fuck off, Sawyer. Or I'll call Lanie and tell her to come pick your sorry fucking ass off my floor."

For a moment, he suspected he was going to have to carry through with his threat. And the last person he wanted to talk to was Lanie. She was another one who would never forgive him. Though he suspected with Lanie, it was more out of fear that maybe her life was built on a shitload of lies, and if she poked at it, then it all might just come tumbling around her. He reckoned she'd forced herself to believe Sawyer's version of that night, but he also suspected that she had her doubts. The night at the Founders' Parade, he'd seen the expression in her eyes. The usual hatred had been replaced with dread.

"You really want Lanie wondering why her husband wants to be friends with the man who killed her brother?" Tanner asked.

Sawyer pursed his lips. "Maybe she should be asking." He gave a shrug. "It doesn't matter, anyway. She's left me."

"What?"

"Walked out last night." He gave a short laugh. "She said I drink too much, and why was that? I think she might have seen through me at last."

Suddenly the tension went out of Tanner. He didn't want to deal with this. "Go home, Sawyer. It's over."

Finally, he shrugged. "I'll go. But you're wrong. It's never over."

Tanner blew out his breath as Sawyer turned and walked away. The door closing behind him.

"You want to tell me what that was all about?" Josh asked.

"Fuck all. The man's a dickhead."

"Yeah. A dickhead who used to be your friend."

Never again. But Tanner had a sinking feeling he hadn't seen the last of his old buddy.

• • •

"Are you sure this is a good idea?" Emily asked as they made their way along the sidewalk toward the O'Connor's showroom. "He's scared of you, you know. And we're just getting comfortable with each other and—"

"It's an excellent idea. It's about time we got to know each other better."

As they came up to the shop, the door opened, and they hesitated. A man stepped out. Sawyer Dean. She hadn't seen him since the night of the Founders' Parade. He'd been a little the worse for drink that night. And it looked like he'd been drinking again. He squinted at them, his gaze resting on Emily.

"Little Emily Towson. Are you going to see my old friend, Tanner? Now why would that be? What's a nice girl like you doing with Tanner, eh?"

"Mr. Dean," Mimi snapped. "Go home before you fall down."

"That's what Tanner told me. Though I suspect he might have been thinking of pushing me down." He swiped his sleeve across his face. "We used to be friends, you know."

"Home."

He held Mimi's gaze before glancing down. "Yes, ma'am."

They watched him weave his way down the sidewalk. Mimi had a frown on her face. "Now, what do you suppose that was about?"

"I don't know." Though she had a few ideas. But whatever had happened that night long ago was Tanner's secret to keep or tell. "They *did* used to be friends."

"Hmm. That's a troubled young man."

Guilt was a hard thing to live with. "He's married to Lanie Forrester," she said. "That can't be easy."

"Really, Emily. I do believe that was a bitchy comment."

She grinned. "Blame it on the hormones."

When they entered the shop, her eyes caught on Tanner. He'd clearly been working, his white T-shirt stained with grease, his hair pulled back into a ponytail. A smile broke his face as he caught sight of her, quickly transforming into a frown as he studied her. He came out from behind the counter and walked over. She never got tired of just looking at him. "Are you all right?" he asked. "Nothing wrong…"

"I'm fine. We just popped in because Mimi has something to ask you. Both of you, actually." She waved a hand to encompass Josh, who was sidling away.

Mimi called out to him. "Don't you run off. This involves you as well."

He stopped, glanced around, and then came back slowly. There was a wary expression in his dark eyes, but also maybe a hint of amusement.

"Why don't you come out here and meet my granddaughter," Mimi said.

Emily had seen Josh at a distance, but they'd never been introduced. She was aware that Mimi had some interest in the man, but she'd presumed that she wanted to help him. Mimi had a strong belief in the healing powers of horses. And in fact, her equine therapy program was well known throughout the country, and they got referrals from all over the States.

Now she had an inkling that maybe there was more to this than helping someone in trouble. That Mimi was interested in him as a man, and that was quite mind-boggling. She'd never known Mimi to show an interest in any man. Josh was certainly good-looking. A little taller than Tanner, he had the lean physique of a much younger man. His eyes were wary as he stepped out from behind the counter.

She held out her hand, and he shook it briefly. "I should get back to work," he muttered.

"No, you shouldn't. Not quite yet." Mimi looked between the two of them. "Emily and I would like you both to come to lunch at the ranch on Sunday."

Tanner looked slightly alarmed. But he swallowed and nodded. "That would be…great."

Mimi grinned. "Of course it will. As long as we don't let Emily cook. She's really not very good." She turned to Josh, raised an eyebrow.

"I don't think—"

"Nonsense. Of course you'll come." She tapped Tanner on the arm. "See that he does. I'm taking your success or failure in this as a direct reflection on your character. Don't let me down."

Tanner nodded. "He'll come."

"Good. Now let's go, Emily."

"I'll still see you tomorrow night?" she said as Mimi dragged her away.

"Seven o'clock your place. Right?"

"Yes. 'Night."

Once outside the shop, she cast a sideways glance at Mimi. "You like him?" she asked.

"Tanner?"

She swatted her arm. "You know exactly who I mean. Josh."

"He's an interesting man."

Emily could read nothing from her expression. "How interesting?"

Mimi gave a small smile. "Interesting enough."

"I've never known you to chase a man before."

"I'm hardly chasing, darling."

"Hah," Emily scoffed. "You almost roped him back there when he tried to make his escape."

"Okay, chasing a little." She shrugged. "But maybe I've never met one worth chasing. And Joshua intrigues me."

"Well, it's good to have an interest. But be careful."

They came to a halt by the car, and Mimi turned to her, expression annoyed. "Humph. You're not falling in with all that bunkum about Josh being a serial killer and likely to kill us all in our beds?"

"No. He did kill someone, though. Tanner told me. That's what he was in prison for. But it's not that. Tanner says he's damaged. He says you see it a lot on the inside. Long-term prisoners. They get to a point where prison is their whole life and they can't function on the outside. Or worse, they don't even want to. And Josh was inside for forty years. I can't even imagine that."

"Institutionalized."

"Yes—that's the word Tanner used."

"He's a bright man."

"He said he read a lot in prison, and now he can't get over the bad habit. But I know he's worried about Josh."

"With good reason." She banged the side of the truck with her fist, and Emily winced. "Sorry," Mimi said, "but it makes my blood boil when I think about what this country did to our men. Sent them off to fight, brought them back damaged, and pretty much ignored any responsibility. There are so many cases like Josh who should have been helped, not punished."

"Things are better now, though, aren't they?"

"A little. At least they are acknowledging that the problem exists." She opened the driver's door and climbed in. Emily walked around and got in beside her, fastened her seat belt. "Don't worry," Mimi continued. "Josh will be all right. He's a survivor—he's had to be. He just needs time to understand he can have a good life on the outside. And friends to help him realize that." She grinned. "And horse riding. Lots of horse riding."

That was her gran's answer to everything, and maybe not a bad one. Perhaps Emily should try it. Get over her fear... maybe that would help her face up to everything else that was going on in her life.

"So how is it going with Tanner?" Mimi asked.

"Good. Mostly. If we could keep this just between ourselves, then I'm sure it would work."

"You're worried the town will look down on you when it all comes out."

She frowned. "No. Not for me, anyway. Maybe for the baby a little. If Tanner would just…"

"Change? Wear a suit? Cut his hair?" Mimi's tone was sharp.

"I don't want to change the way he looks." She loved the way he looked. And he'd better not cut his hair. "I don't want to change anything. I just wish he'd let other people see what he's really like. When he's with me he's…nice. I enjoy his company and I convince myself that he could be a good daddy to my baby. But he's also really bitter. He hates the people in Saddler Cove, and sometimes I wonder if that includes me."

"They did treat his whole family abominably. If his father had been given more help, or even if social services had gotten involved, things might have gone better for those boys."

"But there's more. He feels guilty about what happened to Dwain. But not only guilt, sadness—he was his best friend, after all. And then there's Sawyer. Tanner hates him, and they were always such close friends, the three of them. I can't help but think that something else happened. Something we don't know about."

"I remember thinking the same at the time. But I did nothing, and that makes me as bad, if not worse, than everyone else."

"What could you have done? He pretty much owned up to it."

"I don't know." Mimi gazed off into the distance for several beats. "Anyway, it's in the past now."

"Not for Tanner. I truly believe he's a good man—look at what he's done for Josh—but I think if it came to a choice between something that would piss off the town and something that would help them, he'd piss them off every time. Is that who I want as an example for my child?"

Mimi patted her arm. "It's who you've got, sweetheart."

"For now. But he'll back off if I ask him to."

"Will you?"

"Honestly? I don't know yet."

Chapter Seventeen

Emily was sitting on the porch swing as Tanner parked in front of the house and switched off the engine. She was wearing a white dress, and her hair for once was loose about her shoulders. For a minute he sat, watching her, something twisting inside him. She was so beautiful he ached. A beauty he recognized was as much internal as external; she radiated a goodness. And he'd defiled that goodness.

She had tempted him, but he doubted the people around here would see it that way. This was down to him. Though that wouldn't exonerate her. No, she'd likely be dragged down to his level, which was about as far down as you could go. And he hated that he'd done that to her.

And the sad fact was that if the opportunity came again, he'd be all over her in a second, and be damned that she was way too good for him and always would be.

"This place is something else," Josh said from beside him, pulling him out of his less-than-happy thoughts. "I didn't know places like this existed."

In fact, the house wasn't huge and ostentatious, but it

sprawled across the landscape as though it was a part of the land. A wide veranda ran all the way around it, providing shade, and a green lawn stretched out in front, surrounded by flower borders, full of color at this time of year. He knew fuck-all about flowers. But they looked pretty.

And there was his girl, sitting in the middle of it all as if she belonged. Which she did. And she wasn't his girl.

He thought things were going okay. Last night she'd taken him to another concert. She'd sort of apologized but said she'd thought he enjoyed the first one, and it was the season, and she could get tickets… He'd fucking loved it.

He'd always thought of his love of classical music as some sort of dirty little secret, and he had no doubt that he'd be subjected to all sorts of ribbing if his brothers ever found out. But the truth was, it soothed his soul. If he even had one anymore.

When he'd dropped her off back here afterward, he'd almost kissed her. But hadn't quite dared. He didn't want to break the fragile truce between them. That night in the garage, she'd told him she fantasized about him. Had that changed once she'd had him for real? It didn't seem she had, from the way she'd kissed him in her barn.

Maybe he'd been a disappointment, but he didn't think so.

Maybe it was hormones, and she just didn't feel like that anymore. He'd likely put her off sex for life.

Or maybe she was getting to know him, and realizing she wanted nothing to do with him, and she didn't want her baby to have anything to do with him, because he was bad and no good to anyone and…

"Are we going to sit here all day?" Josh asked.

"No, we're going in." He glanced at his friend. "You scared?"

"Should I be?"

"*I* am." Tanner gave a visible shudder.

Josh's eyes narrowed. "What are you not telling me?"

Tanner gave a shrug. He wasn't one for sharing, but the subject was likely to come up over lunch, so Josh might as well be prepared. "Emily's pregnant."

"She is? Is that a good thing?"

"It's an unexpected thing. Right now, I'm not sure about anything else." He rubbed a hand over his scalp, then his beard. "We're sort of spending some time getting to know each other—but I'm pretty sure that she's deciding whether she wants me in her baby's life."

"You want to be?"

He didn't have to think about his answer. "Yes."

"And you want her as well."

It wasn't a question, but he answered anyway. "She's too good for me. I'd fuck up her life. I fuck up everything."

"You haven't fucked up the business—that's doing well. And Aiden says you pretty much saved his life when you came back."

"He just needed someone to talk some sense into him."

"And you haven't fucked up me. I'd probably still be in my cell, if you hadn't helped out. I don't think I ever thanked you for that. So…thanks."

Tanner shot him an amused glance. "We're going to get all crappy and emotional and shit, aren't we? Maybe we should just get out of here and go drown our sorrows." He had an idea the afternoon terrified Josh almost as much as him. All the same, he'd agreed to come, when he could quite easily have dug in and refused.

"That sounds like a great idea."

At that moment, someone rapped on the window. Emily. He hadn't even noticed her coming across. He rolled down the window.

"Are you going to sit in there all day?" she asked.

"Sorry, Teach," Tanner replied. "Just trying to work out which one of us is the most scared."

Josh snorted but remained quiet.

"Two big strong men like you, scared of two little women like us. I don't think so. Man up. Lunch is nearly ready. Mimi has made mimosas."

She turned and headed back. Tanner turned to Josh. "We'd better go."

"Yeah."

Tanner pushed open his truck door and climbed out. "Mimosas, though. What the fuck's a mimosa?"

"Beats me," Josh said as they headed toward the house. "Really, though—last night I spent the evening looking up articles on etiquette so at least I'd know which knife to use."

Tanner let out a short laugh. "That's goddamn pathetic." At the same time, he decided to keep a close eye on Josh—maybe get some clues. Shit, he'd never had to worry about which knife to use—there had only ever been one.

"Tell me about it," Josh muttered.

Josh had dressed in a pair of dark gray pants and a white shirt. The neck was open, his sleeves rolled up. He looked as smart as Tanner had ever seen him. Tanner, on the other hand, was wearing his usual jeans and a tee. If people didn't like him the way he was, they could...the truth was they could wave him goodbye and say we don't want your sorry ass in our lives. And he'd promised her that if she asked he would back off gracefully. He would never make this harder for her than it had to be.

At the same time, his stomach tied up in knots at the idea of walking away.

Emily had disappeared inside, but as they got to the door, it opened as if by magic. A man stood in the doorway. About Tanner's height and broad at the shoulder, with short military-cut hair, a scowl on his face, and more than a hint of disapproval in his eyes. He gestured them inside, then waved at a door opposite. "Through there."

Another guest? But he didn't follow them.

Tanner pushed open the door. It led into a spacious drawing room, which he presumed ran along the back of the house. French windows opened onto a shady stretch of veranda where the two women were sitting. Mimi waved a hand, and they headed over. A table had been set for four, with a white tablecloth and a flower display in the center and crystal glasses. And lots of knives. Off to the left were two floral sofas with a low table in between, where Mimi and Emily sat, presiding over a jug and glasses.

He sat down beside Emily, letting Josh have the seat beside Mimi. He felt scruffy and inadequate in the elegant setting. "Who was the guy who let us in?" he asked. He hadn't seemed to like them. Best find out who your enemies were sooner rather than later.

"That's Jeremy," Emily replied. "He's Mimi's foreman on the ranch. But he loves to cook. So he helps out now and then when we have guests."

"He looks like a soldier."

"That's because he was in the military," Mimi said. "A Navy SEAL, actually. Jeremy came to the ranch for one of my courses and decided he didn't want to leave. Pestered me mercilessly until I offered him a job. He works with the horses, mostly, but cooking is his passion, and he offered to make lunch."

Mimi leaned across and picked up the jug, poured them all tall glasses of something orange and fizzy. A mimosa, at a guess. He took a small sip. It tasted okay. At least it was cold.

"Would you prefer a beer?" Emily asked him quietly.

"Nah. This is good. Never had one before."

"We usually have them on Sundays. It's become a bit of a tradition. It's champagne and orange juice."

"Well, who woulda ever thought Tanner O'Connor would be sitting on a veranda sipping champagne with Emily Towson," he teased with a wink that made her blush adorably.

"I'm just drinking orange juice," she said, raising her glass. Of course. She hadn't touched any alcohol since she'd found out about the baby.

The soldier appeared in the doorway. "Lunch is ready."

"Thank you, Jeremy. I cannot wait to see what you've been cooking up in there for an hour. Smells delicious," Mimi said with a big smile and turned to the rest of her guests. "Shall we?" She rose and headed for the table, Josh following her. Tanner got up and held out his hand to Emily. She glanced at it and then slipped her palm in his, and he tugged her to her feet. "How are you feeling?" he asked quietly.

"Sick," she replied. She had lost weight. He thought pregnant people usually got bigger. Was she okay?

"Maybe we should go see your doctor again."

She flashed him a surprised glance as she sat down. "No need. It's normal."

What the hell did he know what was normal or not? But for that matter, what did she know? She hadn't had a baby before either. He wasn't the only one in the dark.

Lunch was some sort of vegetarian concoction. But it was good. A sort of lasagna with roasted vegetables and lots of cheese. And a big salad. The knives and forks were pretty straightforward, and he copied the two women's actions as they shook out their napkins and laid them on their laps. He caught Josh's eye at that point—he was doing the same—and nearly sniggered.

They didn't talk much as they ate. Well, he and Emily didn't, but Josh and Mimi made up for it. They were discussing some book Mimi had lent him last week. Tanner hadn't realized the two had spent so much time together. He glanced at Emily and raised a brow, but she just smiled serenely. She was good at that.

They drank red wine with the meal, though Emily had water. And Tanner stuck to one glass, as he had to drive back later, and the last thing he wanted was a DUI.

There was peach cobbler for dessert with whipped cream. He decided that one of his brothers was going to have to take a cooking class. If nothing else, it wasn't fair on little Keira having to eat the crap they produced. Or more usually, the crap they brought in.

"That was great," he said after the last mouthful went down.

"Not too scary, then?" Mimi raised an eyebrow in his direction. Emily must have told her what he'd said.

He shrugged. "Not yet."

"Well, make sure you tell Jeremy you enjoyed his food. He likes to be appreciated."

Jeremy appeared at that moment. "There's a call for you, Em," he said, sounding way too informal for Tanner's liking. "Ryan."

"Oh."

Ryan Forrester, he presumed. She didn't look pleased or displeased. She should tell the bastard to piss off. But she stood up, placed her napkin on the table. "I'll be right back."

She shouldn't be going. He watched her until she disappeared, then turned back to Mimi and Josh, who were both watching him, Mimi with amusement twinkling in her green eyes.

"Ryan is her old boyfriend," he said to Josh. Then he frowned. "He is 'old,' isn't he?" he asked Mimi. For all he knew, she could still be seeing the bastard. After all, *they* weren't going out with each other in any normal sense of the word.

"I believe so. And if it's any consolation, I would prefer her to be pregnant by you than married to Ryan Forrester."

Really? That was interesting. Though Emily had told him that her gran had set them up. He still had no clue why. "But not married to me?" He didn't know where that question had come from.

She studied him, head cocked to one side. "Do you want to marry Emily?"

Did he? Christ, he didn't know what he wanted anymore. Except not to let Emily down. "I want to do what's right."

The fact was, he was beginning to want more than that. Because what if what was right was getting out of her life? And the baby's. And staying out. He did *not* want to do that.

He was scared because he wasn't sure he could manage it now. He'd known from the beginning that he should stay away from Emily. That he would fuck up her life. And he'd tried. He'd told her to forget that night. And he'd meant it. Except, if he were honest, even before she'd told him she was pregnant, he'd been itching to hunt her down. Stake a claim. That night at the Founders' Parade. When he had kissed her. He'd pretty much known then that he was a goner, and he was going to have to have her again or go quietly insane.

Once had definitely not been enough.

"Not a bad answer," Mimi said. "The real difficult part is actually knowing what's right. And at the moment, I'm not sure that you are right for Emily." She studied him over the rim of her wineglass. "And do you know why that is?"

He could make a guess. "Because I'm Tanner O'Connor."

She smiled at the answer. "And what does that mean?"

"That I'm a miserable bastard with an attitude problem, and just about everybody in town either hates me or distrusts me. It means I'm not good enough."

"No, it doesn't. It means that you believe you're not good enough. Which is not quite the same thing, but might as well be if you can't get over it." She put down her glass and rose to her feet. "Now, I'm going to show Josh around the ranch.

See if I can't persuade him on the idea of horse riding." She turned her attention to the other man. Thankfully.

"No way," Josh muttered but pushed his chair back and got to his feet.

Tanner chuckled. It was nice to see someone else the focus of Mimi's attention. "Ride 'em, cowboy."

"Go to hell."

Mimi ignored the comments. "You," she said, pointing a finger at Tanner, "wait for Emily. Jeremy has no doubt set up coffee in the drawing room, and she'll join you as soon as she's finished with Ryan. If she hasn't fallen asleep in the telephone conversation. I'll give you one credit, Tanner O'Connor. At least you aren't boring." She hooked her hand in the crook of Josh's arm and somehow maneuvered him across the terrace and down a set of steps. Tanner watched as they crossed the smooth lawn. As they disappeared around the side of the house, he stretched out his legs and considered what she'd said.

Mostly he reckoned she was right. Maybe he'd had it drummed into him for so long, and so many times, that he wasn't good enough that deep down he'd started to believe it. And if the thought had needed any help taking root, then Dwain's death had made that happen.

He ran a hand around the back of his neck, trying to ease the tension.

At least he wasn't boring.

He smiled at the thought. Well, it was something to work with.

Where was Emily? He didn't believe for a moment she would have fallen asleep; she was far too good-mannered. He stood up and wandered back to the French doors, peered inside. Coffee had been set up on a table at the edge of the room, and he headed over. Before he got there, his gaze snagged on something in the far corner. He stopped. A grand piano. He'd never played one before, and somehow his feet moved in that direction. He ran his fingers along the silky-smooth wood, then flicked open the lid, revealing the keyboard. He played an A minor chord, and almost jumped as the notes sounded loud in the silence of the house.

He glanced around, but no one was nearby to hear.

Without conscious thought, he sank down onto the bench, stared at the black and white keys. Then lowered his hands and started to play. As the swell of the music filled the room, he lost himself completely.

Chapter Eighteen

She was tall for a woman but still only came to just over his shoulder. Her arm was tucked inside his, and she was steering him in the direction she wanted him to go.

And Josh let her. He liked that she seemed so confident, to know what she wanted and how to get it.

The sun was warm on his back, there was the faint hum of insects in the air, and a whiff of salt filled his nostrils, mixed with the sweetness of flowers that lined the lawn. He reckoned they weren't far from the sea. If he could have envisaged paradise when he was locked in the grayness of his little cell, then this would have been it. The colors were so vivid, the blue of the sky, the green lawns.

The last couple of weeks, something had changed inside him. Up until then, he hadn't really recognized his constant companion.

Fear.

Fear of being free, of fucking up, of closed-in spaces, and wide-open spaces. Of never enjoying anything because he was too fucking scared it would be taken away again. That he'd been locked away too long and now would never fit. Fear that the world had moved on without him.

Spending time with Mimi had been a revelation. Seeing how she lived—fearlessly going after what she wanted, standing up for the things she believed in and loved—had made him recognize that his own fears were petrifying him, locking him into a dark place.

And once he'd recognized his fears for what they were, they had lost some of their power. At some time over the past couple of weeks, those fears had loosened their hold on him. Not totally. They were still lingering, and maybe he would never be entirely free of them. But perhaps he could be free of their control. Maybe he could find a life worth living. Somewhere like this, with nature all around him and the smell of the sea on the air.

He cast a glance down at the woman at his side. What did she want with him? She was so far beyond him that under normal circumstances he would never have even noticed her existence. But she'd made him notice, and now he couldn't stop thinking about her.

They were around the same age, but that was the only similarity. Their lives couldn't have been more different. She had grown up among all this, never wanting for anything. He'd never had anything. He'd spent the first eighteen years of his life somehow surviving on the streets of New York, then five years in the Army. And that was a blur. He'd made sergeant, but only because everyone around him had died. Hell, he'd even gotten a medal—not that that had ever helped with anything. He'd been injured out just before the end of the war, spent nearly a year in the hospital.

After that, it had just been a struggle to survive.

No one wanted to employ a black guy with a limp, even if he did have a medal. He couldn't blame them. He'd been a screwed-up mess. But then, so had most of the men who had come back from that war. And so he'd been drunk whenever he could afford it.

Drunk when he'd killed a man.

Maybe the man had deserved to die. But it hadn't been Josh's life to take, and he'd paid the price. Never questioned that the price was fair and just. A life for a life.

She led him out of the sunshine and into the relative darkness of a huge barn. He breathed in a warm, musky scent. Horses, he presumed. Stalls lined either side of the barn, probably twelve in all, each with an occupant. He knew nothing about horses. Had never been near one in his life before. Wasn't sure he wanted to go near one now. They were fucking huge.

She patted his arm as if sensing his unease. "We'll start small," she said, heading off to the nearest stall. The half doors were open, and as if sensing their approach, the occupant appeared, letting out a low nicker.

"This is Beauty," Mimi said. "She's Emily's horse. Though she doesn't ride now."

The horse was small, at least smaller than the others he could see, and black, with a white star across her forehead and dark eyes. She stared back at him. Almost expectantly.

"Wait a moment." Mimi disappeared through an open doorway next to the stall. She came back a second later and handed him a carrot.

"Really?" He looked at the horse, and she curled her lip. "You want me to get that close?"

"Oh, I want you to get a hell of a lot closer than that. But there's no hurry. This will do to begin with."

He shuffled closer.

"Show no fear," she murmured. "They'll sense it. Something I think your friend Tanner learned at an early age. He was such a cute little boy. I remember him from when I used to drop Emily off at school. But always fighting."

"Better than letting them beat you down."

"Probably. Unfortunately, it's entrenched, and his natural reaction to the majority of people is aggression. Show them he doesn't give a shit what they think of him before they even have the chance to form an opinion."

"He doesn't fight anymore." Tanner had told him he hadn't been in a fight since he got out of prison.

"Perhaps not actual physical fights, but the attitude is still there. And I'm sure he has good reasons. But I don't want that for Emily. So maybe it's time for him to learn a new way."

Poor Tanner. He had no chance against those two.

He gingerly held out the carrot at arm's length.

"On the flat of your palm," she said. "Or you may lose your fingers."

He almost snatched his hand away but forced himself to uncurl his fingers and hold his breath. The horse's mouth was soft and gentle as she took the gift.

"There. You mastered your fear. There's hope for you yet."

She led him to the next and the next, giving their names and a few details.

"Do they live in here all the time?" he asked. It didn't seem much better than a prison cell.

"No. We just bring them in at this time of year in the heat of the day. Away from the flies. They go out in the morning and at night. And the rest of the year they are out all the time. We actually close for July and August. It's too hot to work, and it gives them a break, so they come back fresh. But we're full-up over the autumn and winter. Sadly."

"Why sadly?"

"Well, in an ideal world there would be no one in need of our help. Unfortunately, there seem to be more than ever. But at least the world is now admitting that there is a problem." She cast him a look. "Did you know one study showed that four out of five Vietnam vets had symptoms of PTSD twenty-five years after the end of the war? And that up to one in ten prison inmates have prior military service?"

"I've read the statistics," he said.

"You can't send a man—or a woman—to war and expect them to come back unchanged."

He glanced away.

Was she talking specifically about him? He wasn't sure he was ready to go there. Maybe never would be. But all she did was move to the last stall, this one a little away from the others.

"And finally, best until last, this is the love of my life, Frankie. He's a stallion quarter horse."

"Isn't that dangerous?"

"He likes to think so. But no, it's a matter of knowing how to handle him. Like most men, I suspect."

He wondered if she'd "handled" many men. He was presuming she must be divorced or widowed. He didn't think there was a man in her life right now. As far as he could tell, her only family was Emily.

"Come on," she said. "Let's walk." She took his arm again—he liked the feeling—and led him out the back end of the barn. A path ran along a creek, and as they walked side by side, a sense of peace washed over him.

Finally they came to a place where a flat rock edged the bank. She released her hold on his arm and sat down. She wore some sort of strappy sandals and she kicked them off and dangled her feet in the water.

"Lovely," she murmured, then peered up at him still standing. "Join me?"

It almost seemed like a turning point. For a few seconds, he stood and looked around. Like he was taking a step into the unknown. Dangerous territory, and for a moment, he couldn't force his feet to move. There was that fear again.

Then he took a step forward. And another.

He sank down beside her and tugged off his boots, then his socks, rolled up his pants, and put his feet in the cool, slow-flowing water.

"There, that wasn't so hard. Was it?"

"You'll never know."

He found himself staring at her feet. They were long and slender, like the rest of her. The nails unpainted.

"I like having you here," she murmured.

"Why?"

"I'm not sure. But I've learned not to question things too closely. Just accept them as a gift."

He snorted. He'd never thought of himself as a gift before. She sounded a little melancholy. But how could you be sad when you were surrounded by all this?

"I take it Tanner told you that he and Emily are having a baby?"

"Yeah. Just as we arrived. It was a...surprise. But he's a good man. The best. Look what he's done for me."

"I do, and it gives me hope."

"Are you disappointed?"

She turned to him, her eyes widening. "Disappointed? Why should I be?"

"Well, these sorts of things don't usually happen to... people like you."

She leaned over, trailing her fingers in the water. "You'd be surprised."

And he held his tongue, waiting for her to continue. He sensed she had something she wanted to say, but she wasn't sure how, or maybe even that she should.

"I've never talked about this with anyone," she said eventually. "Not Emily, not Liam—that was my husband. He's been dead thirty years. But this thing with Emily has brought it all back."

Again, he wanted to ask why? Why him?

"Maybe because I know you won't judge," she said, almost as if he'd asked the question out loud. "Because you've also done things you don't talk about."

Yeah, that was the truth.

She withdrew her hand and wiped it down her dress, then rested it in her lap. "Anyway, now I've decided to talk, I don't know what to say."

He remained silent, just staring at the water swooshing back and forth around her feet.

"When I was sixteen, I got pregnant."

He'd been expecting something similar. Hell, it happened all the time, though he could see that back then, for a girl from a good family it might have been a big deal. "I was impetuous, and I thought I was in love—or maybe I just wanted to be in love—I don't remember now, except that I wanted to experience everything." She twirled a strand of hair around her finger. Black. "It was so long ago. Another life." She shook herself. "My brother had died the year before. In Vietnam. And that had affected me deeply. We were close. He was only twenty. And I remember being filled with a sense that everything could change so easily. Snatched from you in a second. So I grabbed at every bit of life I could. And got rather more than I bargained for."

"Who was he?"

She shrugged. "It doesn't matter. But he's still around. I look at him sometimes and wonder how and why? I find it inconceivable." She gave him a sideways glance. "At least with age, I've developed a little taste. He was sixteen as well. Marriage was never an option. We were just both too young. It would have ruined our lives. I still remember the arguments my parents gave me. All the same, I went to him. I told him I wanted to keep the baby, get married, we would work it out somehow. He told me his family would disown him. That we were too young. That it would ruin our lives. He was like a goddamn fucking parrot."

The language took him by surprise. He'd never heard her swear before. And it gave him an inkling of how the situation had affected her. How it still did. Maybe it had festered over the years.

"The next day his family shipped him off somewhere. I don't even remember where. I didn't see him for years. When I did, there was nothing. No feelings between us. Maybe there never had been. Or maybe I'd just blanked them from my mind. Now I can only be glad that he behaved the way he did. Marriage between us would never have worked."

"And what happened to the baby?"

He was expecting her to say she'd had an abortion.

"It was a boy." The words seemed ripped from her throat. Raw and still painful. "They sent me to my aunt's in Maryland before I started to show. Then, for the last month, to a home for unwed mothers. Run by the Catholic Church. It put me off nuns for life. I wanted to keep the baby. But they took him from me. I should have tried harder. Run away. But I didn't, and I've regretted it ever since." She took a deep breath. "So there it is. My deep, dark secret. That I don't want to be a secret anymore."

"It's not so bad. Lots of girls get pregnant." At least, where he'd come from. Though most of them had ended up having backstreet abortions.

"I'm not ashamed of that part. Maybe I should be, but I never was. But I gave away my baby. Or rather I allowed them to take him from me. I didn't fight for him. Though I cried for twenty-four hours solid afterward. Such a long time ago, and I can still remember the feel of him, the smell of him. I'd begged them, and they let me hold him just for a few minutes. Maybe that was a mistake." They were silent for a moment. "As I said, a long time ago, but I decided then and there no one would ever tell me what to do again." She blew out her breath, as though relieved she'd gotten her story out. "Anyway, this thing with Emily has brought it all back, and I've made a decision."

"You have?"

"I've decided to look him up. They changed the law, and these days, you can do that. Send a message, and it's up to him whether he answers. He'll be fifty-four now. It's hard to believe. He'll probably want nothing to do with me. But I have to try. Some things you don't get over." She looked at him. "What do you think?"

Hell if he knew. "I think..." Actually, he had no clue.

"I know. I've thought of the downsides. What if he never even knew he was adopted? What if he knows and he hates me because I abandoned him? What if he had a horrible childhood and it's all my fault? What if I get my hopes up and he's...already dead?"

"Jesus, woman. Stop. Do it or don't do it. But don't drive yourself crazy thinking about it."

She smiled. "You're right." She jumped to her feet. "I'm glad I told you. You know, the Catholics have it right in one thing. Confession is good for the soul. I feel much better."

She held her hand out to him, and he looked up at her. Then placed his palm in hers and allowed her to pull him to his feet. "Come on, get your shoes on," she said. "We'll walk some more, we need to give the young ones some time alone to talk. And now I've told you my secret, and you can tell me yours. All about how you once killed a man."

Jesus. Never going to happen.

Chapter Nineteen

Ugh.

There was one good thing about being pregnant. Once it came out, as it must do soon, Ryan would stop pestering her. She really hadn't thought he cared that much. Just that he'd decided the time was right to marry, so he'd looked around for the most suitable candidate. And lucky her.

She thought that because it was pretty much what he'd told her when he proposed.

Now, all of a sudden, he'd fallen madly in love with her.

He couldn't live without her.

It was crazy. He was crazy. And annoying. He wanted her to give him another chance.

Was it just that she was the one who got away? Ryan had a competitive streak. Maybe he just couldn't stand the thought of not winning.

Anyway, another chance wasn't an option. And he'd hardly want her pregnant with another man's baby. The time was coming when she would have to tell someone—the school board, at least, and she was not looking forward to that. And once she'd told them, then the whole town would know, because that's how Saddler Cove worked. But before then, she needed to figure out just what sort of role Tanner was going to play in her and her baby's lives. What role he *wanted* to play.

Part of her was worried that he'd decide it was better for them all if he backed away. That deep down he believed that having no father was better than having Tanner O'Connor. And a small part of her suspected he was right. And that there was a whole load of heartache waiting up ahead if she kept up this thing with Tanner.

But bad attitude and all, she liked him.

More than liked him. It was becoming harder to deny the desire she felt for him. Harder to shut down the memories of the one night they'd had together. She dreamed of him. The feel of his hands on her skin and his kisses and...

But Tanner was his own worst enemy. He believed he was bad, almost reveled in it, and if she couldn't break through that, then there was no hope of a future for them as parents.

She was scared. Scared to talk to him in case he said it was over.

But maybe that was for the best, and she could move on with her life. Plan a different future for her and the baby. She swallowed. One without a father.

Either way, she was going to be brave and talk to him. She hated to be sensible, but she was going to have to be. Try and push through that barrier and find out what Tanner was thinking underneath, where it mattered.

And thinking of unlikely couples, she'd seen Mimi and Josh head into the barn, arm in arm. What was going on there?

Tanner had told her that Josh had pretty much saved his life. That without the other man, he might not have survived his time. He'd been so angry. And young and stupid. Josh had taught him the unspoken rules. How to navigate the prison's unofficial politics. He'd also encouraged him to read and learn new things. To expand his mind.

She just hoped Mimi wouldn't be hurt.

Or Josh, for that matter.

As she headed down the stairs, the sound of piano music drifted out of the drawing room. At first she thought it was a record—she recognized it as the piano concerto she'd heard with Tanner on their first date. Then a wrong note. A pause, and the music started again. She walked slowly down the rest of the stairs and across the hall, hesitating in the doorway. Tanner sat at the piano, his long fingers moving over the keys. He hit another wrong note and swore, then started playing again, and this time it was faultless, and she closed her eyes and let the music soothe her fears.

He couldn't be all bad if he could produce something so beautiful.

And where on earth had he learned? He was good. She'd heard enough to recognize that. He wasn't technically perfect, but he made up for that in feeling.

Finally, the music fell silent, and she opened her eyes and found him watching her. "Sorry," he said. "I couldn't resist. I've never played a grand piano before."

"Don't be. It hasn't been played since my father died, although Mimi keeps it tuned and…" She was babbling. "I didn't know you played."

"I bet it's the last thing you'd have thought I could do."

"Maybe not the last." But pretty close. "How? When?"

"In prison." He grinned. "It was part of my anger management therapy."

"Really?"

"Yeah. Believe it or not, but apparently, I had anger issues when I went inside. Anyway, there was this local pianist. He used to come in once a week. Said he wanted to give something back. And he gave lessons. He took a liking to me, said I was a natural."

"Did it help?"

He looked thoughtful for a moment. "Yeah. It did. Still does. If you'd ever asked me if I'd like classical music, I would have said—hell no. But I find it…soothing."

"Where do you play? You must practice. You're good." He was better than good. There was a magic to his playing.

"I go to Ben's place. He has a piano and lets me play when the club is closed. Occasionally when it's open. Not classical then, though. Jazz. I like that as well."

She remembered now. At the bar when she'd told him she was pregnant. His uncle had asked if he wanted to play. She hadn't known what he meant, and her mind had been on other things.

She closed the distance between them, came to a halt only inches away, trying to get her head around this new facet of his personality. Tanner the piano player. "You're not angry anymore?"

"Only sometimes. Like when Ryan fucking Forrester calls up my girl like he's got the goddamn right to talk to her."

Butterflies swirled in her belly. His girl? "He still wants to marry me."

He turned on the stool so he was facing her, his eyes narrowed. "And what did you say?"

"That he needs to look for someone a little more sensible. And since when am I *your girl*?"

He looked up at her. It wasn't often she saw him from this angle—normally he was looking down at her. He was so beautiful she ached. And suddenly she just wanted to forget sensible for a while. Forget everything, the baby, the school board…

"Since you stripped off and offered yourself to me," he said. "I haven't been able to get the image out of my head."

Her heart tripped. "Really?" Not that she'd been able to tell. Except for a couple of measly kisses, he'd been treating her like a sister since.

"Yeah. I've been trying so fucking hard, but baby, being with you, and not touching you…is hell."

She swallowed. Her mouth dry, her skin hot, her breasts all achy. She could do this. Be bold. "Touch me, then."

His eyes narrowed, and he searched her face. What he saw there made him groan, and he reached out almost tentatively and rested his hands on her hips, pulling her slowly between his legs. His palms seemed to burn through the material of her dress as she inched forward, and a longing welled up inside her so strong she swayed toward him. He leaned in to her and rested his head against her breasts for long minutes. Not moving, and she put her hand to the back of his head and dug her fingers in the silky strands of his hair, holding him closer.

Finally he pushed her away slightly, stared into her eyes. "You sure? 'Cos, baby, I want this so bad, and if you say no now"—he paused, gave her a wink—"you might put my therapy right back to the beginning."

"I won't say no."

"Then come here." He gave her a tug and a little twist, and she ended up on his knee. His hand curved behind her head, drawing her closer so her senses filled with the scent of him, warm, clean, male. Then he kissed her, and rational thought abandoned her, leaving pure feeling. The softness of his lips, the warm, wet velvet of his tongue, filling her, stroking against hers, heating her blood until it all but boiled in her veins. The hardness of his fingers digging into her flesh.

Finally, he ran out of air. He lifted his head and glanced around as if remembering where he was. "Jesus, I'd forgotten. Josh and your gran."

"Gone for a walk."

All the same, maybe they should take this someplace else. She wriggled off his lap and held out her hand. He slipped his palm into hers, and she pulled him along, out of the room and up the stairs, along the corridor, and stopped in front of the door to her room. She'd never had a boy here. Only a fantasy one, anyway. She pushed open the door and tugged him inside. Then dropped her hold on his hand and turned to face him. He was looking around, well, mainly at the queen-sized bed with the purple and grey cover.

"Is this your room?"

She nodded.

"It's nice." He crossed to the window and peered outside. "You're sure your gran's not coming back to catch us?"

No, she wasn't, and part of her was terrified. But she wanted this. Needed this. "Tanner, shut up and take off your shirt."

His eyes widened, and a slow smile spread across his face. "My, aren't we the forward one."

"Please." Actually, she couldn't believe she was being so forward, but she needed to see him naked.

"Okay. But lock the door. I know she can probably kick it down, but I'd feel safer."

She laughed and backed up and clicked the door lock without taking her eyes off him.

"What was it you wanted?" he asked with a wicked glint in his eye.

"Tanner!"

He raised his hands in mock surrender. "Okay." Then holding her gaze, he grabbed the hem of his T-shirt and pulled it over his head, dropped it onto the floor.

Her breath caught as she stared. That first night had been too frantic for her to really take him in. Now she looked her fill. He was all long, lean lines, golden skin over hard muscle. His jeans were loose and hung low on his hips, and his flat stomach was ridged with more muscle, with a line of golden fur that disappeared inside his waistband, and her fingers itched with the need to stroke down that line, follow where it led. She could feel her breathing speed up, her heart racing.

She cleared her throat. "The rest."

He made a small noise, and her gaze flew to his face. His eyes were dark, heavy-lidded, his lips slightly parted, nostrils flaring. "You're gonna undo me looking at me like that."

"I want to undo you." Actually, she wasn't quite sure what that involved, but it sounded good.

"Are you ready?"

She nodded, having lost the ability to speak as his hand went to the button on his jeans. She held her breath as he flicked it open. Didn't let it go as he lowered his zipper. Finally she had to breathe, and the air left her in a *whoosh*.

He kicked off his boots and socks, then slowly pushed his jeans and boxers down over his thighs. He was teasing her. Taking it slow.

He was already hard. Almost vertical against his belly, the head flushed with blood. And everything inside her tightened, heated up. A little pulse started between her thighs, and she pressed them together. She'd never thought of penises as beautiful before, but he was totally and utterly beautiful. He shoved the jeans the rest of the way off and he was naked. And quite the most stunning thing she had ever seen.

"You're going to make me blush if you keep looking at me like that," he murmured.

Her gaze shot to his face, and she gave herself a little shake. "It's probably hormones or something."

"Probably." He gave her a long, hot look, so the fires in her belly burned hotter. "Come here." He crooked his finger at her, and she took a shaky step. Maybe this was a mistake, because her feelings were threatening to overwhelm her. Perhaps the last thing she should be doing was making important decisions right now, because in all honesty, her hormones were all over the place. No doubt screaming at her to get a daddy for her baby. Make sure they had a provider.

Or maybe she was just kidding herself, and she'd had the hots for Tanner O'Connor from the moment she'd realized what boys were for. And maybe she was overthinking this and should just make the most of the opportunity. Because afterward, they would talk, and who knew what would happen after that.

So she took another shaky step, and another. Finally came to a halt in front of him, with only inches between them. She reached out a hand and stroked her fingers across the tattoo on his chest, then down his left arm. Later, she'd examine them, discover what the intricate designs actually were, but right now, she had better things to do.

She trailed her finger down over the ridges on his belly, following the line of blond hair. The back of her hand grazed his erection, and she heard his indrawn breath. But she didn't look up, all her concentration on the long, thick length of him. She fluttered her fingers over the swollen head, and it jerked and twitched beneath her touch. Then she wrapped her hands around him and squeezed.

He muttered something under his breath as he gripped her shoulders. She released him as he turned her around. He found the zipper at the back of her dress and lowered it, tugging the dress from her shoulders until it fell to the floor. Then his sure fingers were on the fastener of her bra, and she groaned as he released it and peeled the material from her too-sensitive breasts. He turned her back and stood looking down at her. Heat bloomed across her skin. She was shy, as she hadn't been last time. Then she'd been too fueled by righteous indignation to feel any embarrassment. Also, she knew her body was changing, though so far it was more internal feelings than actual physical change. She felt different inside.

He cupped her breasts, stroking the pads of his thumbs over her nipples, and she felt it in her sex, heat pooling between her thighs.

"They're bigger." He dropped a kiss on one breast, then the other. "So beautiful," he murmured against her skin, and she ached for him.

He raised his head and kissed her on the mouth, his lips parting hers, his tongue sliding inside. Then he trailed butterfly kisses along her jawline, to her ear, the tip of his tongue dipping inside, sending shivers running through her.

"I want to take this slow," he whispered. "But I'm really scared your gran is going to come back and stop us." She let out a startled giggle, and he grinned back. "I know. It's like being a teenager again. I sort of like it."

"Me too." Though really, she'd never actually done this as a teenager. She was determined to make up for lost time.

His hands slid down over her ass, and he picked her up. Her fingers clung to his shoulders, her legs wrapping around his waist, as he walked the few steps to the bed and lowered her gently to the mattress. Then stood looking down at her. "Jesus, I never thought I would be this lucky. Emily fucking Towson. You are the…" He shook his head. "Christ, I'm scared I'm going to mess this up. I want it to be good for you and I'm so turned on right now, I might explode."

He took a deep breath, and she could almost see him taking control of himself. Part of her wanted him wild, but a small part was afraid. He was so big and strong and masculine. Alien in this room that had been her private sanctuary for so long. So she stayed still, waited for him, every nerve-ending alert, her skin sensitive, her nipples tight with need. She'd never felt like this before. Not even the first time.

His hands wrapped around her ankles, and he parted her

legs, came down on his knees between them.

"I've never done it without a rubber before. That's all right, isn't it? I'm clean. I had a medical a few months back, and I haven't been with anyone since. Well, except you. I have condoms if you'd prefer."

"No. There's no need." She liked the idea of him being inside her with nothing between them. "Anyway, I've sort of lost my faith in condoms."

"Hey, I did buy new ones. But I'm glad. It's sort of like a first."

As he came down on one elbow, his hair slid forward over his cheek, and she reached up, running her fingers through the silky stands, hooking it behind his ear. She found him watching her, and her body clenched in anticipation. Then he paused, poised over her, a frown flashing across his face. "Can I hurt you? Is it all right to...?" He waved a hand down over his body, to where his dick twitched.

God, he was sweet, and she'd never expected that, but really, if he didn't get inside her soon, then she'd scream.

"Tanner," she said. "Do it. Now."

A look of surprise flashed across his face and then he smiled, looking suddenly boyish. "Yes, ma'am."

She expected him to come down on top of her, but instead he lay on his side facing her, then pulled one of her legs over his hips. He reached between her thighs, his fingers unerringly finding her sex, pushing through the folds, groaning as he found her so wet. She should be embarrassed, but she wasn't. She liked that he knew she wanted him. Then she felt him nudging at the entrance to her body, scalding hot. He parted her with his fingers and then pushed inside her, so slowly.

He was so big, she was stretched, filled. When he was in as far as he could go, his fingers moved over her, slippery with her desire. He found her clit and rubbed over it, and she almost jumped at the sensation. In this position, he could touch her freely, and she felt exposed as she never had before.

"Relax," he murmured. "I'm going to make you come. Then I'm going to come. But you need to first, so just let it all go."

She made a conscious effort to relax her tense muscles. He pulled out, the drag of his flesh against hers exquisite. Then pushed back in. He went easier this time, as though her body was making room for him. His fingers fluttered over her gently as if learning her responses. She sighed as pleasure washed over her, and he dropped a kiss on her lips. He got into a rhythm then, his fingers playing over her, circling her as he pushed in and out. She concentrated on the sensation of him moving in and out, everything else pushed from her mind, just the slow burn of pleasure building inside her, coalescing on that one spot where his fingers teased and rubbed. Everything was tingling, and her hips were rising and falling with his rhythm, and she knew she would break soon, everything so intense.

Her eyes fluttered closed as he pressed harder, massaging little circles, and her spine arched, and she shattered. He came up over her then, balancing on his elbows and shoving inside her, hard and fast. And she opened her eyes because she didn't want to miss a moment of this. He must have been teetering on the edge, because he came quickly, his head back, his muscles locked, his skin gleaming with sweat. And she watched as he fell apart.

Finally he stopped moving and collapsed onto his side, face-to-face with her, dragging her close to him so she could hear the rapid beat of his heart. His legs still tangled around hers, his shaft still deep inside her. His eyes were sated and sleepy. Then he tucked her head against his shoulder and a sigh ran through him. She felt safe, pulled against his hard body. Just her and Tanner. No one else intruding.

For a moment, she wished they could just go away together, far away from Saddler Cove and the people who had done such an excellent job of making him believe he wasn't good enough. Away from here, he might forget that he was supposed to be a bad boy. Become the man he should have been. If his mother hadn't died. If his father hadn't drunk himself stupid.

And if he hadn't gone to prison for killing his best friend.

But she couldn't leave Mimi. She had no one else. And besides, she didn't think Tanner would leave. He'd come back for a reason. This was his home.

"You're doing that thinking thing again," he said, his voice rumbling in his chest beneath her head.

As she pulled away a little, so she could see into his face, he slipped out of her, leaving her empty and once again alone. "I was just wishing we could shut out the whole world. Things are so simple when it's just the two of us."

His body stilled. "Are you worried about telling the good folks of Saddler Cove that you've got a little O'Connor growing inside you?"

"Maybe a little. It's complicated."

"Not really."

Maybe it wasn't. After a minute, he relaxed against her again.

Something had been building in the back of her mind since he'd turned up today. She'd put it off a little while longer. In case he totally rejected her idea. She was enjoying lying here with him, his hand stroking circles over her hip, her body still glowing in the aftermath of the best sex ever. "Anyway, I'm not the only one worrying. Back in the car, earlier, when you arrived. You said that you were scared? What of?"

"That you were going to tell me that you thought I should back out. That you didn't want me in the baby's life. In your life."

She blinked at him. She'd been worried he wouldn't want to be part of *their* lives. "She's your baby, too."

He latched onto the word. "She?"

Emily gave a shrug. "I decided it was rude calling it 'it,' so I'm alternating until I know."

"Will you ask?"

"I'm not sure it matters. But it might make thinking of names a little easier." She pursed her lips. "So you've decided? For sure? You want to be a father to our baby. We won't cramp your style or anything?"

"Hell, I don't think I've got a style to cramp. The way I see it is, we're in this together. It's not something I ever wanted... that's not even right. It's just so totally beyond anything I ever imagined. But I wouldn't change it now. And if you think it's best I back out, if you think I'll harm her life, I will. But it will kill me. So yes, I want to be a father to our baby."

Some of the tension knotting her insides loosened. She'd hoped, but she hadn't really known what he was thinking. Hadn't even known until that afternoon that he still wanted her.

"I don't want you to back out. In fact, I think..." But at the last moment, she couldn't make herself say the words. It was a stupid idea. And of course, he'd say no—in fact, he'd probably laugh and then it would make things difficult between them and...

"Come on, Emily, spit it out. What do you think?"

"I think we should get married."

Chapter Twenty

Aiden punched him on the arm. "What the hell's the matter with you? You're even more of a miserable bastard than usual. Cheer the fuck up."

Tanner ignored him. He didn't want to cheer up. He'd never considered himself a coward, but he was fighting the urge to turn around and go home. Hide away.

The Fourth of July. Usually he avoided occasions like this. When the whole town got together to celebrate. He'd never felt particularly like celebrating with the town.

But tonight was *the* night. He and Emily were going to announce that they were getting married.

It was a week since she'd proposed to him. And he'd said yes.

Everything seemed unreal. Him getting married at all. It had never been in his plans. And not just getting married, but getting married to Emily Towson. The town good girl. Who up to now had never put a foot wrong.

But somehow, despite his brain telling him it was a really bad idea, he'd found himself saying yes. The word just came out of nowhere.

It was for the baby. And for Emily. If she was getting married, then presumably the school board wouldn't be able to fire her for breaking the morality clause in her contract. Except he had this weird notion that maybe the good townsfolk of Saddler Cove would think it more immoral that she was marrying him than they ever would about her being pregnant out of wedlock. What sort of fucked up town had a morality clause in their teachers' contracts, anyway? They might as well be back in the dark ages.

But lying in that bed, naked, his mind and body sated with post-coital bliss, it had seemed like anything was possible.

She'd suggested getting it over with in one fell swoop. Everyone would be here. They could share their happy news with a few people, and within minutes it would be around the whole town. The thought made nausea churn in his stomach.

He'd once promised himself that he'd never give a shit what they thought about him again. Hell, he'd gone out of his way to ensure they thought bad things. The badder the better. Now, for the first time since he'd come back after prison, he just wished... Hell, he didn't know what he wished. That things were somehow different. That he was the sort of man a woman like Emily would be proud of.

But he wasn't.

He patted his jean pocket, checking for the hundredth time that the ring was still there. They hadn't talked about a ring. But it had suddenly occurred to him that afternoon that she should have a ring. It would make it all a little more... believable.

When he'd said yes, she'd seemed relieved. Not ecstatically happy or anything, but what had he expected?

He cast a quick glance down at himself. Maybe he should have dressed differently, smarter. But he still didn't have anything smart. They were just going to have to take him as he was. He was in his usual jeans and a white T-shirt. Boots. But he was clean. This was as good as he got.

Hell no matter how he dressed, no one in this town was going to be happy about this.

"You're scowling, bro."

He scowled harder. He'd hoped to sneak out of the house without his brother. Aiden kept away from these things as much as he did. Reese had taken Keira to watch the parade, and hopefully they would be heading home by now. He'd arranged to meet Emily in the town square at nine o'clock. He was five minutes late already. But Aiden had caught him as he was leaving and insisted on tagging along. Nosy bastard.

Maybe he should warn him what was about to go down.

"Look, there's something I need to tell you." He ran a hand through his hair, at the last minute, though, he chickened out. Couldn't get the words out of his mouth and he just shrugged, shoved his hands in his pockets—his finger grazing the ring. Would she like it? Or would she think it a stupid idea? He picked up his pace.

"Tanner?"

"Later," he muttered.

The town was decorated in red, white, and blue, and he could hear music up ahead. This had been a stupid idea. They didn't need to tell anyone. It was nobody's business but theirs, anyway. They should have just gotten married quietly, the town would have found out soon enough. And that way they wouldn't have been able to talk her out of it. Which he was sure they would try.

He stopped abruptly, and Aiden ran into the back of him.

Was that what he was afraid of?

They'd been getting on okay. Better than okay. He had a flashback to Sunday. The feel of her beneath him, the sensation of being buried deep inside her. He hadn't seen her since, though they'd talked on the phone and texted.

Arranging tonight.

As they approached the square, the streets got busier. People gave him and his brother a wide berth, as though they were somehow dangerous, and he could feel his expression becoming more set.

There was a dance in the town square every year after the parade. Lights had been strung all around, and a podium set up at the far side where the band would play. They were getting ready now, setting up their instruments, three guys and a woman.

The square was busy, and he searched the crowd for Emily.

"Are we going to dance, bro?" Aiden asked.

Tanner ignored him, because he'd caught sight of Emily. She was standing at the edge of the square. Alone, gnawing on her lower lip as she looked around her. She probably thought he wasn't going to show.

Then she saw him, and relief swept over her features.

She was wearing a blue dress that hid her sexy curves and ended below the knee. Her hair was tied back somehow, and she looked very...teacherish. At least she didn't look pregnant. Though according to the stuff he'd been reading, she would start to show anytime now.

It still screwed with his head.

He took a deep breath and headed over, making his way around the outside of the square and stopping in front of her.

"I thought you might have changed your mind," she said. "And decided not to come."

"Nearly."

She bit her lip some more. Very distracting. "You want to back out?"

He realized she meant of the marriage. "Hell no." Just this.

"Good. I think." She didn't sound sure.

"You having second thoughts?"

"And third and fourth."

At least she was being honest.

"Hi, Emily."

He'd forgotten about Aiden.

She forced a smile. "Hi, Aiden."

God, he wished he could just take her away somewhere they could be alone. He always messed up when other people were involved. He turned to Aiden. "Go get me a beer," he said. "And a soda for Emily."

Aiden opened his mouth, shut it again as Tanner shot him a warning look. He looked between the two of them, his eyes widening, then he nodded once, turned, and walked away.

Tanner searched her face. She looked pale but composed. And she'd managed to nibble off all her lipstick. He felt like he was the center of attention and everyone was watching, but when he looked around no one had noticed them yet. That wouldn't last.

He reached out, took her hand, and tugged her down the side street away from their audience. Once they were alone, he leaned down and kissed her. Because he wanted to make the worry disappear from her eyes, and this was the way they communicated best.

For a moment, she was stiff against him, then she melted. He cupped her face, backed her up until she hit the wall behind her, and then he kissed her some more. He fucking loved the taste of her and the feel of her. Even her smell, like vanilla, so sweet.

She was breathless by the time he raised his head. But the worry was gone from her eyes. "Say the word, babe, and we can forget this, head back to my place and—"

She smiled. "You don't have a place."

Shit, no, he didn't. And no doubt Reese and Keira would be home by now. "Head back to your place?" he suggested.

"Mimi is there. She doesn't like to leave the horses in case they get spooked by the fireworks. And Josh is visiting. I think there's something going on between those two."

No going there, then.

He took a deep breath. He could do this. For her.

"I got you something," he said. He pulled the ring out of his pocket and held it out to her.

Emily stared at it as though she had no clue what it was.

"I know it's not a real engagement or anything. But I thought it might make it more believable."

She reached out slowly and took it from him. She blinked a couple of times, and he had no clue what she was thinking. Had it been a stupid idea? Because it wasn't a proper engagement. She was only with him because she was pregnant, and this might be the best way to keep her job. Otherwise she probably would have nothing to do with him.

She slipped the ring onto her finger and lifted her hand. "It's beautiful, Tanner. You didn't have to."

He shrugged. "You should have a ring."

It was a sapphire—at least it matched her dress. Just a simple single stone on a white gold band. He'd thought the simplicity would suit her. It had cost more than a Harley, though he wasn't going to tell Emily that.

In the square, the music started up. He blew out his breath. "Are you ready for this, then?"

"No."

"Me neither. Come on, let's go shock the whole of Saddler Cove."

She hesitated as they reached the edge of the square, and he stopped and looked down at her. A little line was forming between her brows, and he had the distinct impression that she was screwing up her nerves to say something. She licked her lips and heat flashed through him.

"What is it?"

She swallowed. "Do you think you could..." She gave a little shrug. "When we tell people, can you sort of look as though you care about me. I know they're going to find out about the baby soon enough. But it would be nice if they didn't think..."

"You'd totally trapped me into marrying you?"

Alarm flared in her face. "You don't think that. Do you?"

It occurred to him then that she had her own insecurities. "Hell no. If anyone's trapped, it's you. Maybe that's what we should tell everyone. That I used a dodgy condom to trap you into marrying me."

She giggled, and some of the tension went out of her figure. "Somehow I doubt they'll believe that. Unless you were looking for a sensible wife, of course. Then I'm your girl."

"Yeah, a sensible wife who accosts a man in his own garage, strips off bare-assed naked, then kisses him senseless."

"I did, didn't I?"

Now was not the right time to think about her little striptease. He had to keep his wits about him tonight. "So you want people to think we're in love?"

Her eyes widened as though she hadn't expected him to use the *L* word, and some expression flashed in her face, a hint of wistfulness, perhaps. "How good an actor are you?" she asked.

"Let's go see." He wrapped his arm around her shoulder and pulled her close to his side as they walked out of the shadows and into the light of the square. The band was playing something slow. Christ, he didn't think he'd ever danced with a woman before. "I don't know how to dance," he muttered as they halted and turned to each other.

"Everyone knows how to dance."

"Not me."

"Just hold on tight," she said. Then she slipped her arms

around his waist, closed the space between them, and rested her head on his chest. For a moment, he just stood, paralyzed, then he wrapped his arms around her and held her close.

He emptied his mind of everything but the feel of the woman in his arms. They weren't dancing, just swaying to the music. She was all soft curves and warmth, and her hair smelled of strawberries. Her breasts pressed against his chest, and he felt himself harden. She raised her head, her cheeks were pink, and he gave a small shrug. "Sorry," he murmured.

"Don't be. I like it."

She laid her head back and they swayed to the music. He was almost sorry when it stopped. A new song started. Faster. Time to go spread the good news. As he loosened his hold and stepped back, he became aware that they were the center of attention.

He searched the faces. Most wore slightly stunned expressions of disbelief. He found Aiden in the crowd. His brother was grinning like an idiot. He held up a bottle of beer, and Tanner grabbed Emily's hand and made his way over.

"That was a first," Aiden said, handing him the beer and a coke to Emily. "The sight of my big brother actually dancing. With a lady."

Emily peered at him as if asking permission, and he sighed and gave a small nod.

She held out her left hand with the sapphire. "You can be the first to congratulate us," she said. "We're getting married."

Aiden glanced between the two of them. "You're fucking kidding me."

Tanner shook his head and took a gulp of his beer.

"You're not fucking kidding me?" Now he sounded bewildered.

"Nope."

"Holy crap." He looked Emily up and down, and she

squirmed. "You're pregnant?"

Jesus. Even his own brother believed a woman wouldn't marry him unless she had to.

"How the hell did that happen?" Aiden continued.

"What?" he growled. "You don't know?"

"Not you and teacher lady? It's beyond my comprehension. I think I might have to go lie down." Then he started laughing.

. . .

Emily blew out her breath and pulled herself together. If she was perfectly honest, she found Aiden O'Connor more than a little intimidating. Frightening, even. In a way she'd never found Tanner.

Aiden had been in the same year as her at school, though they'd moved in different circles, and he'd always been a little wild. Then after Tanner was sent down, he'd become a lot wild. It was common knowledge that his father had taken less than no notice of what any of his sons were up to. And she suspected that Tanner had been more of a father to his little brother than his real father ever had. After their father had died, Aiden had gone into the foster system and pretty much disappeared from sight. All sorts of rumors had surrounded him: he'd become a drug dealer, an arms dealer, joined a motorcycle club…

And looking at him, she could well believe it.

He was six-feet-four of badass attitude, with a ring through his lip and tattoos down his arms. In black jeans and a black T-shirt. Even laughing his head off, he looked lean, mean, and capable of anything.

"Fuck off," Tanner growled. He grabbed Emily's hand and dragged her off. "Fucking asshole," he muttered. She could still hear Aiden laughing as they walked away.

"Well, that went well," she said. "Who next?"

It was clear that word was going around. She could sense all the attention focused on her, and not in a nice way. Her skin prickled. She searched for a friendly face, finally found Susanne. She would have to do and was probably as friendly as she was going to find tonight. How would Tanner perform? She didn't believe for a moment that anyone would believe that a man like Tanner could fall in love with a woman like her. She wasn't in his league. But at least they could try. She knew she'd get a whole load of pity and disapproval once the news of the baby got out, but first, could they just pretend they had a normal relationship?

She squeezed Tanner's arm and urged him in Susanne's direction, only realizing she wasn't alone as they halted in front of her, and she almost turned around and ran in the opposite direction. Lanie stood by her side, a look of disbelief on her face as she took in their hands entwined together.

Emily gripped him harder. "Hi," she said brightly.

There were a few seconds of silence, and then Susanne cleared her throat. "So, are you two together now?" she asked.

Emily held out her hand and showed off her ring. It really was a beautiful ring. Both sets of eyes widened and then dropped to her stomach, and she sucked in her breath. Though she wasn't showing yet.

"We're getting married." She squeezed Tanner's arm and willed him to say something. She cast him a quick sideways glance and almost groaned. He'd adopted his sullen, fuck-you attitude.

Lanie glared at her, though Emily couldn't quite decipher the expression in her eyes. Hatred, certainly, but also fear. Finally, she shook her head and turned and walked away without saying a word.

"Sorry," Susanne muttered. "But you know..."

Of course she knew. Tanner had supposedly killed Lanie's

brother. Or so everyone said. Emily couldn't even begin to imagine how that must feel. They'd accused him of stealing the car, but that had never stuck. The car had belonged to Jed Forrester, Dwain's father, and it was much more likely that Dwain had just "borrowed" the keys as he had done many times in the past. Usually so Sawyer could drive it.

Now she could well believe Sawyer had stolen it and driven while under the influence. He already had at least one DUI under his belt at eighteen, and he'd been stopped for speeding countless times. Only the fact that his uncle was the sheriff had stopped him getting in greater trouble. But Sawyer hadn't been there that night. He'd been out of town.

Tanner, on the other hand, had always been more interested in two wheels than four. Back then he'd had a great big monster of a bike.

Dwain had a broken arm at the time, in plaster up to the elbow from an accident on the football field, so no way was he driving. Which meant it had to be Tanner. And he'd not denied it. At least not in court.

He hadn't been drinking, but all the same they'd got him on aggravated manslaughter. And everyone had nodded their heads and said it had only been a matter of time. Emily had cried her eyes out when he'd been sentenced. Mimi had found her and asked her what was wrong, but she'd just sniffed and said a boy at school had upset her.

"Yes, we're together," she said, keeping the smile on her face. When Tanner remained silent, she nudged him in the side with her elbow.

"Oomph." He cast her a surprised look, and she had to fight the urge to kick him in the shins. She guessed his sullen look was totally ingrained in his character now and he was hardly aware he was doing it. An automatic response when he met…well, anyone. He was indiscriminate with his scowling. Young, old, they were all on the receiving end of Tanner's sweet nature.

"You're a crap actor," she muttered under her breath.

His eyes widened at the words, as if he'd totally forgotten that he'd promised to at least look as though he cared. He wrapped his arm around her shoulder and pulled her close. "Emily has made me the happiest man in the whole world. I never for a moment believed that someone like Em could love a man like me."

"Me neither, bro." Aiden had come up beside them, drawn, no doubt, by the small crowd who had gathered at a distance. He was still grinning, eyes twinkling with amusement. Susanne was looking decidedly skeptical, and there was a lot of negative energy wafting across from the onlookers. Maybe it was up to her to do the acting.

"Of course I love you, baby," she cooed. "There's so much of you to love."

"Are you saying I'm fat?" He smiled down at her, his eyes crinkling in humor. He knew exactly what she thought of his body, and her cheeks heated at the memory.

She dug her fingers into the lean muscle at his waist. She doubted there was an ounce of fat anywhere on his body. "No."

"Or were you talking about some other part of my anatomy? If you're not careful, you'll be shocking these good people with your forward nature." He dropped a kiss on her forehead. "They probably think you're a good girl, but they don't know you like I do."

He was teasing her. It was sort of cute and very un-Tanner-like. She had a quick peek around. There were a lot of open mouths. She was betting that Saddler Cove had never seen this side of Tanner before.

She turned her attention back to him—his eyes gleamed down at her as if in challenge. He thought she was going to back down. "I am a good girl. Isn't that how you like them,

Tanner?"

She shifted a little, so she faced him, then rested her hand on the soft cotton of his T-shirt, right over his heart. He winked at her, then lowered his head and kissed her. She knew it was supposed to be an act, but the second his lips touched hers, she melted. Her surroundings faded as his other hand came up to frame her face, and his big body curved over hers as he deepened the kiss. His tongue pushed inside for the briefest moment, filling her mouth, sending heat flooding every corner of her body, and her knees went weak, so she clung to his shoulders.

Slowly, she became aware of her surroundings, the music in the background, the utter silence of the people around her. The fact that Tanner's erection was pressing into her belly.

Holy moly.

She'd nearly lost it in front of the whole town. She'd been ready to lie down right there in the middle of the square and...

She cleared her throat, edged away, hoping that a little space between them might get her brain working again. Tanner shifted a little, so he stood slightly behind her. "Don't want to embarrass you, baby," he whispered in her ear.

In front of her, Susanne was fanning herself. Aiden was still grinning, but there was a look of speculation in his eyes.

"Can I see the ring?" Susanne asked, and Emily held out her hand again. "Oh. My. God. It's huge. And real pretty. So how long have you two been dating?"

"A few months. Since I split up from Ryan."

"Oh my God, Ryan is going to be totally gutted."

"Good," Tanner muttered.

"That's why you warned Reese off her," Aiden said. "You had your own eyes on her. And more than eyes, I'm guessing."

What did that mean? Why would he have had to warn

Reese? She must have looked a little confused.

Aiden grinned. "Keira likes you. That's enough for our big brother to get a hard-on these days."

"Shut up, Aiden."

"Anyway," Aiden continued, taking no notice. "He said he was going to ask you out, and Tanner here nearly bit his head off. Now we know why. He had the hots for you himself. He should have just said."

"If you don't shut the fuck up, Aiden, I'm going to shut you up."

"You could try."

She slapped him on the arm. "Tanner. Play nice."

"For you, baby, anything." He shook his head and grinned down at her, and she almost lost it again. When he smiled like that, the hard lines smoothed away. He looked years younger. An image of what he would have been if his life hadn't gone to shit. She wished she could somehow keep him that way.

"Congratulations," Susanne said. "Maybe we can meet for coffee tomorrow, and you can tell me all about it."

"Yes, of course. I'll give you a call. Now I think we're going to circulate and maybe dance again." And then maybe run away and hide until it all the speculation was over with. Except it was never going to be over. She might as well get used to it. But she'd never felt comfortable being the center of attention. And you didn't get more centerstage than this.

They made their way around the outside of the dance floor. No one actually spoke to them, but everyone watched.

Tanner got another beer and a coke for her, she held it tightly clutched in her hands as though it might give her some protection. They found an empty chair and Emily sat down—she was already noticing that she tired easier than she used to—Tanner taking up position behind her, one hand resting possessively on her shoulder. Finally one or two people got up the nerve to come and say hi, and she smiled, showed off her ring, tried to ignore the looks of curiosity. John, the second-grade teacher who'd been with them on the field trip to the ranch and who she suspected had been trying to get up the nerve to ask her out, was the first. He was a nice man, good-looking in a nerdy sort of way. Nerdy men had never done it for her.

The contrast couldn't have been more clear. John, clean-shaven, glasses, short hair, suit and tie. Tanner with his faded jeans, T-shirt, hair in a ponytail, and short beard. But Tanner was the one who made her melt, filled her with longing, made her fingers itch to loosen his hair, stroke her fingers through the silky strands, press herself against him. She was losing it again. Hormones, that's what it was. Baby hormones. But why would they make her weak with longing? Surely with a baby inside her she should have lost the urge to procreate.

"I think he likes you," Tanner said as John walked away.

She shrugged. "He's not my type."

He looked down at her, his gray eyes gleaming in the darkness. "What is your type?"

"You are."

He hunkered down beside her, took her hand, played with her fingers. Clearly he had something on his mind. "Shit, you make me want…" He trailed off, released her hand, and scrubbed his fingers through his hair. "I never wanted anyone like I want you. Girls were always easy to get."

"I was pretty easy." She had an image of stripping off in front of him. Throwing herself at him.

"Hell, you're not easy. Not in any way that matters. You're the hardest thing I've ever done, and I'm terrified of getting it wrong. And I know I should back off a little on the sex stuff, because you're probably feeling all sorts of weird things right now. But Christ, I want you."

She didn't know what to say. Wasn't sure she even believed him. "I—" She broke off as she spotted a figure weaving his way through the crowd, and her heart sank. She'd had enough drama for one night. Her nerves were raw. "Sawyer's coming this way," she said.

"Great." Tanner exhaled, then straightened, turning to watch Sawyer's approach. "I suppose it's too much to expect him to be sober."

Actually, he looked pretty steady on his feet. And his suit was clean and uncrumpled, his tie still knotted, his sandy hair neatly combed. She got to her feet as he stopped in front of them. Maybe they might need a quick getaway.

He didn't look at Tanner, concentrated on her, his gaze fixed on her face. "Lanie just told me that the two of you are getting married. I wanted to say congratulations, and I hope you'll both be very happy." He leaned down and kissed Emily on the cheek. "Look after him," he said quietly. Then he straightened and without another word, he turned and walked away.

"That was a little odd," she said, glancing at Tanner, who had his sullen expression back on.

"Yeah." He was watching Sawyer's retreating back with a scowl on his face.

"What happened between you two?"

A wary expression crossed his face. "Nothing happened."

"You were best friends. Before…"

"Before I stole a car and killed my other best friend?" He shook his head. "Let's not talk about it. Not tonight. Come on, I think we've been on show long enough. Mission accomplished. I'll take you home."

As he put his arm around her shoulder, someone grabbed him from the other side and pulled him away from her, so she stumbled and let out a squeak of surprise. As she righted herself, she caught sight of Ryan, just as he pulled back his fist.

"You bastard, you got her pregnant."

Chapter Twenty-One

"Well, things could have been worse," Mimi said matter-of-factly.

Emily glanced across from the passenger seat and glared. "How? How could they have been worse?" She certainly couldn't come up with anything. It had been a nightmare. She still broke out in a sweat thinking about it. She hated violence; it made her all shaky and nauseous. And right now, she had enough of that without any outside help.

"Tanner could have fought back. In which case, things could have got very messy. We might have even needed to buy new chairs for next year's celebrations."

She could tell that Mimi found the whole thing very amusing. "Tanner could hardly fight back. He was out cold." Not from Ryan's punch, but he'd stepped backward, tripped over a chair, crashed into a table, and brought the whole thing down, finally smashing his head on the sidewalk as he landed. She'd thought he was dead. She might even have screamed a little bit.

"Exactly," Mimi said. "Praise the Lord for small mercies.

I can't imagine he would have not reacted. He doesn't seem the turn-the-other-cheek type."

No. He'd been furious when he had finally come to, but more that Ryan had risked knocking her over than from the actual punch. But luckily by that point Ryan was long gone. Dragged away by his friends, most of whom had cast her blistering looks of disbelief and resentment as they went.

Well, she'd known it wasn't going to be easy.

That was five days ago. She hadn't seen Tanner since, but then, she hadn't been into town. Not that she would have seen him even then, because according to Josh—who Mimi spoke to most days—he'd been in Richmond. They were opening a new shop, and there were lots of last minute things to do. Josh had been left in charge.

Emily reckoned Tanner was staying out of the way until his temper had cooled. And maybe he was a bit embarrassed, because he was supposed to be tough and Ryan had knocked him out. Sort of.

Apparently, he was back now and not a moment too soon.

She'd been sick all week. And not just in the mornings. According to Mimi, she was right on target. It had to get worse before it got better sort of thing. But she felt sick and tired and listless. She'd had lots of phone calls. Everyone wanted to call and…congratulate—it didn't seem quite the right word—her on her engagement. Ask her if they had set a date, and she knew what was behind that question.

No one had actually come out and asked if she was pregnant, and she hadn't volunteered the information. But Mimi had come back from lunch with a few of her friends and said that the town was positively agog with the news that nice little Emily Towson, who had always seemed such a sensible girl—*grrr*—had broken Ryan Forrester's heart and gotten herself in trouble with Tanner O'Connor on the rebound.

What about Tanner getting in trouble with her?

Then today she'd got a call from Freda Riley, the school secretary, who'd said the school board wanted a meeting with her. Just informal to talk over a few…issues with her contract.

She'd hoped that by marrying Tanner, the morality clause wouldn't even come up. That had obviously been wishful thinking.

"You don't think they'll fire me today, do you?" she asked Mimi.

"Probably not today. They need a proper meeting and votes and things for that. They probably just want to talk to you. Check if you plan to come back next term. They'll have heard the rumors and probably want to confirm whether they need to start looking for a new first-grade teacher."

Her chest ached at the thought. The baby was due next spring, and she'd hoped to be able to work up until the Easter break. Then maybe have the rest of the semester off and back to work after the summer break. Mimi had promised to help with childcare.

If she had a job.

It was time to see just how supportive Tanner planned to be. As her fiancé, he had every right to attend this informal meeting and give her some moral support.

Mimi pulled the truck up outside the showroom, and Emily sat for a moment, her hand on her stomach, which was churning, her meager lunch threatening an escape job. She unscrewed the top from the bottle of water in her hand and took a gulp.

"Are you okay?" Mimi asked. "You want me to go in and get him?"

"No. I have to ask him first."

"Maybe asking isn't the right thing to do. Just tell him."

She shook her head. "It's his choice." But he would come. He'd said he wanted to help any way he could. She took a deep breath and opened the door, climbed down.

"You want me to wait?" Mimi asked.

"No. I'll see you at home." Tanner would no doubt take her home after the meeting.

Josh was behind the counter in the showroom. "Is he here?" she asked.

"In the workshop. You want me to tell him you're here?"

"No, I'll go through." She headed through the door at the back. And stopped. The sound of a piano concerto filled the air. There were three other mechanics working in the room, though her gaze went straight to Tanner. He was hunkered down with his back to her, working on a bike.

Everyone else had stopped work and was staring at her. She recognized them all. They were all local boys—one had been in her year at school. Another had a daughter in her class last year.

She forced a smile and cleared her throat. Tanner straightened and turned slowly, a smile spreading across his face as he saw her. He glanced around. "You lot got nothing to do?"

"Sorry, boss."

"You want to come through?" he said to her, then turned without waiting for an answer and headed for a door in the opposite wall. It led into some sort of staff room, with a couple of sofas and a coffee machine on a table. Here the music was louder.

"Chopin," she said. "Very classy."

He grinned. "Yeah. Aiden came in an hour ago and nearly walked straight out again. Thought he'd come to the wrong place." He gave a shrug. "I thought they might as well get used to it." He waved a hand toward the coffee machine. "You want one?" he asked.

Just the thought made her contemplate puking. "No."

He poured himself one and came back to her, sat down on the sofa, and patted the seat beside him. "You look pale.

Are you all right?"

"Just a little sicker than usual. Mimi says it will pass." She perched herself on the edge of the sofa. It didn't look particularly clean, as though lots of greasy overalls had sat on it.

"I'm sorry," he muttered.

"Don't be, it's not your fault."

"Actually, it is."

"Maybe." She twisted slightly so she could look at him, reached up, and stroked a finger over the mark on his forehead. "How about you? Are you okay?"

"Yeah. I still can't believe that fucker knocked me out."

She smiled. "I think you did that yourself." She let her hand drop to her side, then cleared her throat. "I have a favor to ask."

"Then ask away."

"I'm on my way to a meeting. With the school board. Just an informal one. And I thought…I hoped…" She gave a shrug. "I thought you might come with me."

A look of horror flashed across his face. "No way."

Her heart sank. It hadn't really occurred to her that he might say no. It was only a meeting. So they could stand solid together. "Please, Tanner. It's important."

He ran a hand through his hair. "Really. If it's important, then you don't want me there."

She bit her lip. "I don't want to go alone."

"You think they know about the baby?"

"Not *know*. But I'm sure everyone has guessed."

"Yeah, like your old boyfriend Ryan. Because why else would you agree to marry me?" He put his cup down—he hadn't touched his coffee. "You know who the head of the board is?"

"Of course I do."

"Jed fucking Forrester. He hates my guts and the rest of me. The best thing I can do for you is stay as far away from that meeting as possible."

"Don't you think it's time to put the past behind you?"

"You think Jed is going to think that way? Hell no. As far as he's concerned, because of me his son is dead, and you can't put that sort of past behind you and move on. It's with you forever." He got to his feet and paced the small room. Ran his hands through his hair, came back to stand in front of her.

"Look, what the hell right do they have to pull this morality shit on you? You're better than all of them. You think they're all so goddamned perfect? You don't have to go crawling to those assholes, and I certainly have no intention of doing it."

"I signed the contract."

"Tell them to fuck their contract and fuck their job. You don't need it. I make enough to keep us."

"But I love my job, Tanner. It's what I trained for, and I'm good at it."

"Then get a different one. We can move to Richmond. I can work at the new place."

"I thought you didn't want to move. I thought you wanted to stay in Saddler Cove?"

He shrugged. "That was before the other night. I saw the way they looked at you. I've lived with that all my life—I don't want it for you. And today. You shouldn't have to let them put you down."

"I can't move to Richmond." And truthfully, she didn't want to, this was her home. "I can't leave Mimi. I was hoping after we get...married then you'd move into the ranch."

"Hell, I haven't even thought that far."

"And I can't commute to Richmond. Not with a new baby. Please, Tanner. Just come with me this once. I won't ask again."

He glanced away, but when he looked back, his expression had settled into its usual sullen lines, and she knew she was beaten. "I can't. You're better off without me."

Maybe she was. But she knew he could be nice if he wanted to. He clearly didn't want to. She pushed herself up and wiped her hands down her skirt. She didn't look at him as she headed for the door, and he didn't come after her. She pasted a smile on her face as she walked through the workshop, feeling everyone's gaze on her. She'd better get used to it.

Her eyes were pricking as she crossed the showroom. Goddamn baby hormones. She nodded quickly to Josh and let herself out and onto the street.

As she came out of the door, a man stepped out of the shadows. Ryan. She so wasn't ready for this. She just wanted to get this meeting over with, then go home and lick her wounds and hide for a while. Maybe throw up.

She sighed. "What is it, Ryan?"

"I saw your grandmother drop you off. I thought we might talk."

"There's nothing to say. And I can't. I have a meeting to go to."

"I know. My uncle told me. I'll walk with you. I won't make a nuisance of myself. I promise. There's just something I wanted to say."

She shrugged, too emotionally exhausted to argue. They were silent for a minute as they walked, and she waited for him to say his piece. No doubt some sort of condemnation. How could you...

"A woman like you," he started. "You probably think you don't have options. I just wanted to say that you do."

"I do?"

"I still want to marry you, Emily."

Shock stopped her in her tracks, and she turned to face him. "I'm pregnant, Ryan."

"So I gathered."

"With Tanner O'Connor's baby." She started to walk

again, and he kept pace beside her.

"You made a mistake. That doesn't mean you have to throw your life away."

"I'm keeping the baby."

"I would never expect you to do anything differently. But if you marry me, then I'll bring him or her up as my own." When she didn't say anything—because she really couldn't think of anything to say—he continued, "Look, I'm quite aware that I totally botched it when I asked you to marry me. I knew you didn't love me like I love you, and I thought it was the best approach. If I'd done better, then you might not have…"

Gone straight over to Tanner's garage, stripped, and thrown herself at him. But she kept that to herself. It was clear that Ryan was genuine. And while there was no way she would even consider his proposal, she didn't want to hurt him any more than necessary.

"I'm sorry, Ryan, but I'm marrying Tanner."

"But why? I could understand it if you had no other options, but you do."

He sounded so mystified that she decided to offer the one answer she was certain would make him back off. "Because I love him."

• • •

Tanner stood in the doorway of the showroom and watched her walk away, her head bent slightly toward the man beside her as she listened to whatever he had to say. He wanted to run after them, rip Ryan away from her, punch him in the nose. Not in retribution for the punch the other night, just to get him away from Emily. But violence never solved anything.

He'd fucked up. He knew that, but surely she could see that he'd be no help. He couldn't even believe she wanted him there. She must know he was more likely to put their backs up than help her case.

All the same, he'd come after her, not knowing what he was going to say or whether he was going to give in. Just knowing he couldn't bear the thought of that expression on her face. Defeat. He was supposed to be helping her.

But how the fuck could he? On her own she might have a chance of sweet-talking them. He'd just be a reminder.

Then he'd seen her with Ryan and he'd stopped in his tracks. For a moment, he presumed she'd arranged the meeting, but that was just stupid. She'd wanted *him* to go with her, so she would have hardly invited another man to meet her here. So Ryan had just turned up, and Emily was way too nice to tell him to piss off.

Ryan in his sharp blue suit, his short hair, not a grease stain anywhere.

Maybe she didn't want to tell him to piss off.

Ryan still wanted her. Enough to put up with another man's baby?

It didn't matter. It was never going to happen. The baby was his. And Emily was his. And Ryan fucking Forrester could go fuck himself.

But the moment had passed. He wouldn't go after her tonight. Because he was right. And if she wanted any chance of keeping her job, then she was better off alone.

He stepped back into the showroom and turned to find Josh regarding him thoughtfully. "You fuck up?" he asked.

"No more than usual."

"You care for her, don't you? I mean more than just the baby."

He shrugged. "She's too good for me."

"Probably."

He snorted. "Thanks."

"It doesn't matter. If you keep on thinking she's too good for you, then you'll keep on fucking up."

"What are you? A goddamn relationship counselor?"

"The only one you've got."

Actually, he had three now with Josh. His brothers had oscillated between disbelief and amusement since the other night. And were a constant stream of unsolicited advice. What the hell did either of them know? Though the funny thing was, he'd found himself listening to the advice. Hoping he'd glean a little something to help him make it work with Emily. Pathetic or what?

"Anyway," he said. "What about you and Mimi?"

Josh shifted and looked away. "What about us?"

"You in a relationship?"

"Hell no. She's just a do-gooder who sees me as a charity case."

"Yet every time I turn around, there the two of you are. It's sweet, really."

"Fuck you."

"As I'm sort of family now, I think I should ask what your intentions are."

"Maybe you should ask Mimi."

A shudder ran through him. He was scared of Emily's grandmother. She intimidated him as no one else could. Maybe because he knew, deep down, that she had the power to stop his relationship with Emily point-blank. For now, she appeared to be supporting him. That might change after his fuck-up today.

"Actually," Josh said, "I'm going out there tomorrow. I'm going to ride a horse."

"You're fucking kidding me."

"Nope. You can ride along if you like. Apologize to your girl. Take her some flowers."

He picked up a wrench and hunkered down in front of a bike needing new brakes. "And see you on a horse? Count me in."

Chapter Twenty-Two

He felt an idiot with his big bunch of flowers.

The woman in the shop had given him a sly grin. Did she know he was off to do some serious groveling?

He hadn't made any extra effort with his clothes. He wasn't Ryan Forrester, and if she wanted someone who wore suits then maybe it was better they find out now.

For once, Aiden wasn't off racing somewhere. Tanner had left him in charge; his little bro could do some work for a change and earn his keep. He was happy enough spending the money. Racing was an expensive business.

"Come on, cowboy," he said to Josh. "Let's do this."

"I feel sick. Maybe we should head home instead."

"Hell no. I'm apologizing, and you're riding a horse. And I think I have the easier task."

"I wouldn't be so sure."

No, actually, he wasn't at all sure either.

He kept seeing her disappearing off down the road last night, side by side with the town's most eligible bachelor. As opposed to the town's most ineligible bachelor. But it was *his* ring on her finger. He could sort this out.

He'd explain that she just had to understand who he was. They'd get married and that would put an end to the stupid morality clause. But he was never going to be the type to wear a suit and a tie and bow and scrape to all the high and mighty townsfolk. It wouldn't do any good, anyway. They'd decided a long time ago that he wasn't worth a shit, and a change of clothes wouldn't alter that.

As they climbed the steps to the front porch, the door opened. His breath caught, but it was Mimi who stood there, not Emily.

She looked the two of them up and down, an eyebrow raising at the bunch of flowers in his hands. "Morning, ma'am."

"I wasn't expecting you," she said, and the look she sent him suggested he wasn't particularly welcome.

"I came to see Emily." Christ, maybe she wouldn't even let him through the door. He tried to look past her but couldn't see inside.

"I never thought you a coward, Mr. O'Connor. Was I wrong?"

He shuffled his feet, gripped his poor flowers tighter. "I hope not, ma'am."

"Hmm. She's on the back terrace. Don't upset her any more, or you'll deal with me." She opened the door wider to let him through, and he moved quickly, before she changed her mind.

He made his way through the house, casting a slightly envious look at the grand piano as he passed—if he lived here he could play every day—and out onto the terrace. She was sitting at the table, her fingers wrapped around a cup, gazing into the distance. But she looked at him as he stepped through the French doors.

Her eyes were red, and in that moment, he felt like the

biggest shit in the world. In the next moment, he had a violent urge to punch someone. Lots of someones. Just about the whole population of crappy Saddler Cove for doing this to her. Couldn't they see she was the best of all of them?

He hurried across, tossing the flowers on the table as she rose to her feet. He didn't wait for her to speak, just wrapped his arms around her and pulled her close. For a second, she pressed herself against him. Her arms slipped around his waist, and she laid her head on his chest.

They stayed like that for maybe a minute. Then he put his hands on her arms and put her away from him slightly, so he could look down into her face.

"I'm sorry," he said.

Her eyes narrowed. "What for?"

He couldn't lie. "For not going to the meeting last night— though that was for the best—they hate me. And I suppose for getting you into this mess."

She sniffed. "I did my share."

Yeah. She was no helpless victim. "Well, then, for being the sort of man I am, I guess. Anyone else and they wouldn't be putting you through this. What happened?"

She pulled free and stepped back. Sitting down, she reached for the coffeepot and poured him a cup. Probably giving herself time to think. He sank down across from her and took the drink.

"Thank you for the flowers," she said. "They're beautiful."

"I was going to get you roses, but I thought these suited you better." They were a bunch of mixed wildflowers.

"I'm hardly wild."

"Come on, Emily, what did they say?"

She took a deep breath. "That they don't think an ex-con is a suitable husband for their first-grade teacher. That you'll be a bad influence on me and that will rub off on the children. That I'm not a fit teacher, and I could still be in breach of their morality clause even if we get married."

His stomach sank. "Bastards. So much for paying for your crimes. I did warn you."

"But it's so unfair."

"Jed Forrester lost his son. He probably doesn't see it like that."

Suddenly, she looked fierce. "It was an accident. Maybe stupid, but no worse than a lot of the stuff kids get up to. It was just a tragic accident. Dwain died, but that doesn't mean you have to pay all your life."

He had to force the next words out. But he owed it to her. "Do you want to call it off?" She'd been staring at her hands, twisting the ring on her finger—at least she was still wearing it—but now she looked across at him and he forced himself to continue. "I know the only reason you're marrying me is to get past the morality clause in your contract and keep your job. If that's not going to work, then you can still stop this now. Forget the marriage thing."

He held his breath as he waited for her answer.

"Is that what you want?" she asked.

Maybe he should make it easy on her and say yes. Then she could walk away without a backward glance. But he couldn't do it. Could not physically get the words out of his mouth. So he shook his head. "No. It's not what I want. But you have to know what you're getting yourself into. To the people in this town, I'll never be anything other than the son of the town drunk and a murdering ex-con."

"You'll be my husband and the father of my baby."

She sounded so fierce that something relaxed inside him at her words. The tight coil of tension that had been squeezing his insides since she'd walked out last night loosened. He'd been so sure he'd lost her, and he really wasn't ready to examine why that idea hurt so much.

She licked her lips and studied him. "I'm not ashamed of

you, Tanner. But maybe you could just try…" She shrugged as though she couldn't come up with the words she needed, and he decided to help her out.

"Not to embarrass you?"

She frowned. "I don't embarrass that easily. But perhaps you could just try and not piss people off so much. I know you do it on purpose. You get this look on your face."

"A look?"

"Sort of mean and sullen and…" She shrugged again. "Maybe you could try…smiling more."

He blew out his breath. She'd said exactly what his brothers and Keira had been telling him. "That's all? You don't want me to change my clothes, wear a suit, maybe cut my hair. Just smile more?"

She nodded. "Nothing else. Just smile."

"I'll try." And he would, because he couldn't bear being responsible for her crying again. He knew from his reading that she was probably a little hormonal right now, and he had to take more care. Make allowances. Smile. He tried it, a big one with lots of teeth, and she giggled.

Definitely worth the effort.

His smile faltered. "I saw you with Ryan last night."

Her eyes widened. "You came after me?"

He shrugged. "I knew I'd acted like a jerk—I'm not saying I was wrong—I wasn't—it would have been a mistake to go with you. But I could have handled it better. So I came to say I was sorry. You were with Ryan." He hadn't meant to make it sound like an accusation. But he was pretty sure it did.

"He wanted to talk to me."

"What about? I don't suppose to apologize for punching your fiancé. I owe him one, by the way."

"Actually, he wanted to ask me to marry him."

"What did you say?" He tried not to hold his breath, like his whole universe depended on her answer, but he couldn't exhale to save his life. He was drowning in her gaze, waiting for her to breathe life into him again.

"That I was already spoken for."

He let out his breath, a little light-headed now. "Well, I suppose it would have been the sensible choice."

"Probably."

"But we know you're not a sensible girl."

She smiled at that. "No."

He sighed. "It's not going to be easy. I'm not an easy man." He scrubbed a hand through his hair. "But we'll get through this. We'll get you an appointment with a lawyer. See where we stand."

"I hadn't thought of that."

He leaned across and kissed her on the lips, lingered longer than he meant to. He wished he could take her to bed, make her forget, but maybe now was not the time. A hotel. That's what they needed. A night out in Virginia Beach and a hotel room with no interruptions.

He smiled. "Now. How about we go watch Josh get on a horse?"

• • •

"Are you sure about this?" Mimi asked.

"No."

She grinned, and the expression smoothed the creases from her face, making her look younger.

He still had no clue why she had taken an interest in him. He no longer believed that she was just some do-gooder getting a notch on her bedpost, as it were. She seemed to genuinely like him. And he found her easier to talk to than he could have ever imagined. He hadn't realized how closed-up he'd become. They talked about everything, from current events, to books, to movies—he hadn't seen most of the ones she mentioned. She told him about the history of the town, the ponies on the nearby island of Assateague who'd been shipwrecked on a Spanish galleon hundreds of years ago. She knew everyone and divulged the details of the people of the town, who was who, who was doing who.

She'd occasionally asked him about his past, though she never pushed the issue when he changed the subject. She'd talked about her work with veterans, and he knew she believed strongly in the power of words. Of getting things out in the open.

But the fact was, he didn't need to. He'd read enough to know that he'd been a classic case of PTSD when he'd come back from Nam. The knowledge had come too late to make a difference. And anyway, it would hardly have been a defense. Back then, the country hadn't supported its veterans, hadn't recognized PTSD. He was pretty sure there'd been no equine therapy around forty years ago.

Fact: he'd been a black man who killed an unarmed white man. Had things been the other way around, then he doubted he'd have spent forty years inside. But he tried not to be bitter. Things were changing—he'd seen that since he came out—maybe not fast enough, but they were different than when he was locked away.

And he was over it now, had come to peace with who he was and what he had done. He'd told Mimi that much.

He'd started fantasizing about kissing her. Which he was sure was the last thing she wanted. She hadn't given him any encouragement in that direction. But once he'd had the thought, it wouldn't go away.

She was beautiful, despite her age, or maybe because of it. Tall and slender, toned from all the hard work she did every day, and the long hours spent in the saddle for pleasure. She had high cheekbones and green eyes that still sparkled when she spoke of the things she loved, and she'd admitted her long black hair was her one vanity and came out of a bottle.

He rubbed a hand over his own graying scalp.

Christ, he hadn't had a woman in forty years. Had seriously considered he was past all that. The first few years inside had been hard. He'd missed sex. But as the years passed, the memory faded. The need subdued. Now it was like his body had come alive. That morning he'd woken with a boner. The first in more years than he could remember.

He'd taken a cold shower.

It probably didn't even work anymore. He was scared to try.

And why the hell was he even thinking about it?

Of course she wasn't interested in him like that. A wealthy, beautiful white woman and a black ex-con who hadn't been handsome even when he was young.

Anyway, she was seventy. Seventy-year-old women didn't still do it. Did they?

What the hell did he know?

He was probably just trying to take his mind off what awaited him in the barn. Had he been crazy to agree to this?

He'd never had anything to do with horses. Now he was going to get on one.

He followed her out of the bright sunshine and into the relative shade of the barn.

They passed Jeremy in one of the stalls, bandaging a big brown horse that bared its teeth as its eyes met Josh's. Could he ask for a horse without teeth? Probably not.

They came to a halt in front of a stall.

"This is Jasmine," Mimi said. "She's a fourteen-year-old mare I bred myself. She's a total sweetie and will look after you."

She looked huge. A strange sort of pale brown color with a black mane and tail.

"I had Jeremy tack her up for you. Next time you can do

it yourself, but I thought it would give you less time to back out if she was ready to go."

He peered down at her. "You think I'm going to back out?"

"You're like a skittish colt that's going to bolt at the first opportunity." She opened the stable door and stepped inside. He hesitated for a moment, then followed her in. "Horses can sense that sort of thing," she continued, "but Jasmine's used to beginners, she makes allowances."

"That's good."

"Go say hello. Approach her from the side, move slowly and stroke your hand along her neck."

He did as he was told, his hand reaching out gingerly. The coat was soft and silky-smooth and beneath it he could feel the hardness of muscle. He breathed in. This close his nostrils filled with the warm musky scent of animal, overlaid with oil and leather. A sense of peace washed over him. Maybe she was right, and this was good for the soul.

"Right, let's go."

She handed him the reins and then headed out, leaving him with the animal. For a moment he hesitated, then he gave a shrug. "You wanna go for a ride, Jasmine?"

She looked at him out of the corner of her eye and then followed Mimi without any action from him. She definitely knew who was in charge. He had hold of the reins and had no choice but to go along.

Mimi was waiting for him at a gate and as he passed, she slapped a cowboy hat into his hand. He'd never worn a cowboy hat in his life. He'd never even met a real cowboy— they were something you saw in the movies. He settled it on his head.

The back of the barn led directly into a riding area. Big. He'd been hoping for somewhere smaller, just in case Jasmine decided to take off with him. But the area must have been nearly a hundred feet long, plenty of room to get up steam.

He came to a halt just inside, or rather Jasmine came to a halt and he stopped beside her. Mimi strolled up to them, one hand tucked in the pocket of her tight blue jeans. She'd put a cowboy hat on her own head, and he was betting it looked way better than his did.

"This is the cinch," she said, pulling on the strap of leather that went around the horse's middle. "Just check it's tight before you get on or you'll end up on the floor rather than your horse's back." She turned to look at him. "You're always responsible for your own safety. Never forget that." She took his hand and placed it on the cinch. "Feel how tight it is."

He felt. He certainly didn't want to end up on the floor. Well, that wasn't quite true. Actually, he didn't want to *leave* the floor. But he'd agreed to this—though she'd sort of goaded him into it—and he wasn't going to back out now.

At one point in his life, he'd believed he was never getting out of prison. He'd resigned himself to the fact that the rest of his existence would be bound within those gray prison walls. He'd hardly lived before. Drafted at eighteen, then a few years in Nam, a haze of boredom intercepted by moments of overwhelming horror. Then afterward, his life had been dulled by drink and drugs, anything that helped him get through the days. And then prison. Hard at first. Mostly fighting. He'd been so angry.

He'd read enough to know why. But finally, he'd settled to some sort of peace. He didn't know what happiness was, but the anger had faded, and he'd found his own coping mechanisms. Books. Music. He'd even made friends. Done a little good where he could. He'd saved Tanner. The boy had been on a path to self-destruction, with no clue how to survive on the inside. And that one thing had maybe made it worthwhile.

Tanner had repaid him.

He was out.

So he reckoned this was Tanner's fault.

"What are you thinking?" Mimi asked.

"That I'm going to whup Tanner's ass."

"Why?"

"His fault. I'd still be in my nice cozy prison cell if Tanner hadn't offered me this job." Actually, though, the job offer had come through Tanner's brother, Reese, who was a decorated war hero and so a little more impressive than an ex-con. Whatever—it was down to Tanner.

"I didn't know that."

"I'd been turned down for parole so many times. Probably they had no idea what to do with me on the outside. But once I had a guaranteed place to live and a job, they were happy to get rid of me."

"That was kind of him."

"He's a good boy. Don't forget that."

"You mean when he behaves like a total idiot and makes my granddaughter cry?"

"Yeah. Those sorts of times. I'm sure there'll be many. He's not an easy man."

"The interesting ones never are." Did she give him a look then? Did she consider him interesting? Maybe he was just a novelty.

"Okay, enough chatter. Up you get."

The moment of truth. A tingle of excitement ran through him.

"Hands on the pommel," she said, taking his left hand and putting it on the sticky-up bit at the front of the saddle. "Put your foot in the stirrup. No, your other foot, or you'll end up facing her tail."

He had this horrible image of going straight over the top and onto the ground on the other side. At least the ground looked soft. "You do realize I'm sixty-eight," he said, looking down at her. "My bones are likely to snap like twigs."

"Nonsense. I'm seventy and I haven't broken a bone in… at least three years. Now up." And with that, she placed her hand right on his ass, and he almost shot into the air. Just as he was about to catapult over the other side, she grabbed the back of his pants and steadied him. He somehow managed to get his other leg over and he came down with a ball-crunching slam.

But he was up.

He closed his eyes for a moment. Somewhere along the way he'd dropped the reins. He had no way to steer or stop this thing. If he didn't move, not a twitch, maybe she wouldn't either.

"Ride 'em, cowboy."

He opened his eyes at the sound of Tanner's voice, sounding enormously amused. He was standing by the railings, Emily at his side. An inane grin on his face.

"Ignore him," Mimi said. "You're doing extremely well."

"I haven't actually moved yet," he pointed out.

She took hold of his foot and moved it back slightly. "That's better." Then she handed him the reins. "Keep your hold loose. If you want to turn, just rest the reins along her neck."

"What if I want to stop?" Right now, that seemed more important than turning. Why had he agreed to this? He couldn't remember.

"She's actually trained to voice commands. Just say whoa and she'll stop."

"Really?" Sounded too good to be true.

"Relax, Josh. Close your eyes for a moment and breathe deeply and slowly." He did as he was told. He felt much better with his eyes closed. "Now open them." He knew it had been too good to last. "And squeeze gently."

Nothing happened.

"Maybe a little less gently than that."

He squeezed again, and this time they moved smoothly forward. Shit, he was riding. But he wanted to check the brakes before he went any farther.

"Whoa." And she actually stopped.

"You need to go a little farther than that," Tanner called out.

"Do you want to have a go?" Mimi snapped.

"Hell no."

"Should we get away from them?" Mimi asked.

He looked back at Tanner's grinning face. "Hell yeah."

"Then follow me."

She led the way out through the gate to the back of the house and the walk they'd done along the creek the other day. Josh didn't do anything at all—the horse seemed happy to just follow. He was riding. Solo. The sun was warm on his back, the movement of the horse rhythmic, and a sense of peace washed over him. In that moment, he was happy. He almost didn't recognize the emotion. Maybe the answer was to just live in the moment.

"So, Josh," Mimi murmured. "Perhaps now's a good time to tell me about the man you killed."

Well, she had warned him she was tenacious.

Chapter Twenty-Three

"It's a girl," the doctor said.

"Really? You can tell from that?" Tanner leaned in closer to the screen and stared, an expression of such concentration on his face that Emily felt a smile tugging at her lips.

"And is everything okay?" he asked.

"She's perfect," the doctor replied.

"Shit." He ran a hand through his hair. "Wow. A girl."

She hadn't known whether he'd had any preferences. If he had, he'd kept them to himself. But from the grin on his face, she decided he was happy with the outcome. He looked like a different man when he smiled. If only she could find a way to keep that smile on his face.

This was the twelve-week dating scan. They'd decided they would ask the sex of the baby, if only to narrow down their name choosing.

The baby looked about the size of a plum. Hard to believe something so small could cause so much havoc.

It was two weeks since he'd come to the ranch. She'd been sort of avoiding him. She'd been busy helping Mimi, who was on the organizing committee for the pony swim on the nearby island of Chincoteague. It was a huge tourist draw for the area, and there was a lot to organize. The swim was tomorrow, and so far everything was going really well. Mimi was riding with the saltwater cowboys, herding the horses over from Assateague to Chincoteague, where the foals would be auctioned off at the end of the week. And she'd asked if Emily would go with Josh, show him around.

Tanner phoned every day to ask how she was, which was sort of cute. She'd actually been feeling like crap, still throwing up every morning and sometimes every afternoon and evening as well. She was losing weight rather than putting it on. Then yesterday, she'd woken up and felt wonderful. And she'd been feeling pretty good ever since. Well, good enough to face Tanner, anyway. Not that she had a choice. He'd insisted on driving her to the scan. And on the drive, he'd told her all about the baby, how big it was right now, that it had all its features, that it looked like a little human being.

He was taking his fatherhood role very seriously. Which was sweet.

"Would you like a print of the scan?" the doctor asked, handing her a wipe to clean the gel from her skin.

"Can we have two?" Tanner said.

"Of course."

The doctor stepped out of the room, and as the door closed behind her, Tanner turned from the screen, a big grin on his face. "We're going to have a girl." He reached across and touched her belly lightly. "She's in here, all warm and safe." He took the wipe from her hand and gently stroked it over her skin. Then he lowered his head and kissed her right there where his hand had been. Just a brief caress, but at his touch warmth washed through her. "I think there's a little bump showing?"

She swallowed. Almost overcome with need. She'd

missed his touch. They hadn't really touched since that day they'd made love when she had asked him to marry her. She placed her hand over his, pressing his palm against her skin.

But then the doctor returned, and the moment was gone. Emily pushed herself up and went behind the screen to change back into her own clothes. Her hand rested on her stomach. A girl. A daughter. She hoped she took after her daddy, because then she'd be a real beauty.

"You're really feeling better?" he asked as he helped her into the truck five minutes later.

She nodded. "I haven't been sick in nearly forty-eight hours."

"I'm glad." He was silent for a minute as he settled in the driver's seat and switched on the engine. Then he turned to her. "You want to go out for dinner on Saturday?" he asked. "We could drive into Richmond, maybe stay the night somewhere."

"You mean a hotel?"

"Yeah. A hotel. Just you and me."

A whole night with Tanner. Alone. Nobody to butt in and remind them what a bad idea this was. She could touch him. He could touch her. They could make love. Her nipples hardened at the thought, and tingles ran down through her belly, a little pulse jumping between her thighs.

"That would be nice. We can talk." They needed to discuss the wedding. She didn't want to leave it too long. She'd prefer she didn't look pregnant in the wedding photographs, though she supposed they could always photoshop them.

"Maybe we could find a few minutes to talk. But I'm expecting to be busy with other things."

"Other things?"

He took his eyes from the road for a second and cast her an over-the-top leer. She giggled.

"I like it when you laugh."

"Well, I haven't felt much like laughing recently."

"I know. And I'm sorry." He was silent for a moment. "Have you heard anything from the school board yet?"

"Not yet." It would be soon, though. There were only a few weeks before school started, and if they were going to sack her they'd need to start looking for another teacher. Unless they'd already started looking.

"That's probably good, then. Maybe they're not going to push it."

"Maybe."

But she remembered Jed Forrester's face at that last meeting, and she suspected he was going to push it as far as he could. But she'd try not to worry about that until it happened.

In fact, she didn't have much time to worry. That evening, she was roped into running one of the stalls at the Chincoteague Fireman's Carnival, which was run every evening throughout the week of the pony swim.

Mrs. Watson, the fire chief's wife, was usually in charge of selling raffle tickets. Unfortunately, she was being operated on tonight for acute appendicitis. So now it was Emily's job. She was happy to stand in. She usually ended up doing something at the carnival anyway.

And it had been a good evening so far. In fact, she was feeling all warm and fuzzy. Two people had actually congratulated her on her engagement to Tanner. And they'd both sounded genuine.

Tom Bailey, the music teacher at the school, let slip that Tanner was behind the scholarship that had been set up to pay for extra music lessons for the kids. Apparently, Tom had promised Tanner that the donation would remain anonymous—but he'd presumed as Tanner's fiancée, she would know all about it. Nope.

And then Mrs. Summers, the superintendent from the Saddler Cove Seniors Club, had come up to her, patted her on the arm, and told her she'd got herself a good man. A little probing and Emily had discovered that Tanner had been servicing the Club's bus for the last five years. Free of charge. Not only that, but only last month, he'd rushed straight out and fixed it for them when they'd broken down in Virginia Beach. He'd never mentioned *that* to Emily.

Clearly Tanner didn't hate everyone in Saddler Cove, but, equally clear, he liked to keep his good deeds close to his chest. God forbid anyone should catch him doing something nice.

She was humming to herself and tidying up the booth when someone stopped beside her, and she looked up, a smile spreading across her face before she could stop it. Tanner stood there in his usual jeans and T-shirt, hair pulled back in a ponytail, Keira holding onto his hand. He looked so goddamned cute with the little girl.

"Hi, Keira," she said.

"Hi, Ms. Towson."

Keira actually looked more like Tanner than she did her father. She had Tanner's dark blond hair and gray eyes. Presumably from his mother. His father had been black-haired and blue-eyed like the other two O'Connor boys.

She turned her attention to Tanner. He'd only dropped her off at the ranch a few hours ago. She shouldn't feel this thrilled to see him again so soon. But just looking at him caused a little fizz of excitement in her blood.

"I didn't realize you'd be here," Tanner said. "You never mentioned it."

Was there a slight accusation in his voice? In his eyes. Maybe he'd thought she wouldn't want him along. Wouldn't want to be seen with him. Just about the whole of Saddler

Cove was here tonight. Ryan had already been around and bought some raffle tickets from her.

She looked over Tanner's shoulder to make sure that he wasn't still around, but there was no one she knew in sight, and she breathed a little easier. The last thing she needed was Tanner getting all riled up. Because Jed Forrester was here as well. No doubt he'd jump at any sign that Tanner was not a suitable husband for his town's first-grade teacher.

While she loved the way Tanner looked, just for once, she wished he didn't look quite so...bad boy. That he could pretend, just for a few hours, that he *did* care what people thought about him. More to the point, what her boss thought about him. So maybe she'd just have a teeny chance of keeping her job.

Was it so wrong to want Tanner *and* her job?

"Mrs. Watson had a medical emergency this afternoon," she said. "I was asked to stand in for her." She smiled. "Can I tempt you into a raffle ticket? You can win a pony."

Keira's eyes widened. "A pony? A real pony?"

"They do it every year. The first foal to complete the swim gets named King or Queen Neptune, and he or she is given away in the raffle. It's to raise money for the fire department."

"Why the hell would I want to win a pony?" Tanner sounded baffled.

"Uncle Tanner. *I* want to win a pony."

"No, you don't. We have nowhere to put a pony."

"Please, Uncle Tanner."

He was looking almost scared now. Clearly, he couldn't say no to the little girl. She decided to help him out. "They've sold over ten thousand tickets so far," she said. "You're probably safe."

"I'd better be." He pulled a wad of cash out of his pocket and placed it on the table. She counted it and then filled ten tickets out and handed them to Tanner.

• • •

Tanner looked at the tickets in his hand. The way his luck was going, he'd probably win the fucking thing. They'd have to keep it in the back yard.

"I didn't know you were coming tonight, either," Emily said.

Was she sorry he was here? She'd smiled when she first saw him, but then she'd gotten that worried expression on her face. Nibbling her lip like she expected something bad to happen. Probably ashamed of him because he didn't look all smart and dressed up like Ryan fucking Forrester. He'd seen him earlier, all smug in his smart suit. He'd caught sight of Tanner, but then taken one look at Keira, and turned and walked the other way.

Tanner had seen Jed Forrester as well. The man had looked straight through him as if he didn't exist. He should be used to it by now, but for some reason, tonight it rubbed him the wrong way. He'd gotten good at ignoring the looks he received from the townspeople, but tonight they niggled at him, grating on his nerves. The fucking unfairness of it.

Since when had he expected life to be fair?

He'd done his best to ignore it, because he didn't want to spoil Keira's evening. This was her first pony swim, and she was bubbling with excitement.

Christ, he'd been on such a high that afternoon. He was going to have a daughter. And he'd never thought that would happen, but now it was, and he wouldn't change it for anything. Or her mother. When he'd gotten back after dropping Emily at home, he'd tried to do some work. He couldn't stop taking the ultrasound photo out of his pocket. And he was happy. Then he started worrying. What if people ostracized his daughter because of him? He knew what it was like to have the other kids look down on you. And no way did he want that for his daughter.

The town was in a position to take something precious from him again, just like they'd taken his freedom, and the thought had him scared shitless. And angry.

He looked up and realized Emily was waiting for an answer. "I hadn't planned to, but Reese had promised to bring Keira and he was delayed in Richmond. Again. Keira wanted to come, so here we are."

"Daddy's meeting us here," Keira put in.

And as soon as Reese was here, Tanner was out of there. He wasn't fit company tonight. And didn't trust his temper if anyone should come along and punch him. This time he wouldn't just lie down and take it. Not that he'd had much chance to do anything else last time.

He handed the tickets to Keira. "Here, pumpkin, look after these."

"Thanks, Uncle Tanner."

While she was studying them, her finger running along the writing as she read, he turned to Emily.

"You're not happy I'm here?" he asked quietly.

She blinked at him as though she hadn't expected the question and was searching for a suitable answer. She gave a little shrug. "I just don't want any…unpleasantness."

"And you can guarantee that where I go unpleasantness will surely follow?"

She opened her mouth to answer, but at that moment Reese appeared, and Keira squealed and ran to him.

Reese lifted her in the air and spun her around. He was great with her, considering he hadn't even known he had a daughter until a year ago. Reese had been in a meeting with the bankers that afternoon and looked almost as smart as Ryan. He strolled over with Keira in his arms. "Uncle Tanner is going to win me a pony," she said.

"Is he now? But can you eat a whole one?"

She pinched him in the shoulder. "I'm not going to eat it, I'm going to ride it."

"God forbid," he muttered. "Hey, Teach, my little brother giving you problems?"

"Not yet."

"Well, the night is still young. Give it time." He punched Tanner on the arm. "I'll leave you two to whatever it is you do. *We* have a date with the cotton candy man."

They watched as he walked away, tickling a giggling Keira.

"He's so good with her," Emily said.

"Maybe you should marry him," he snapped.

She widened her eyes. "I didn't know it was an option."

"He was going to ask you out before..." He nodded toward her stomach and his baby. Never going to happen.

"What you said before—about not wanting you here. It's not true. I do want you here. I just..." She shrugged. "I just wish you didn't have to go out of your way to antagonize people."

"Hey, I never start anything."

"No, but you finish it. They're not bad people. Most of them would back off if you just met them halfway."

"And what would that involve? You want me to wear a suit and tie. Turn myself into your ex. You think people would then forget I'm the son of the town drunk. That I'm an ex-con they think killed his best friend. If you think that, you're deluded and living in a dream world. Grow up, Emily. Not everyone is as nice as you are."

He needed to get out of there before they both said something they would regret. How had the high of that afternoon soured to this? Fear. He was scared shitless he was going to ruin her life, ruin his kid's life. He turned and strode away.

"Tanner."

She called to him, but he hunched his shoulders and pretended he hadn't heard. He was staring at the grass as he walked and almost bumped into the man blocking the way.

"You know the best thing you can do is just walk away from her. You're no good for her. You're no good for anyone."

He gritted his teeth. Fucking asshole. Well, Ryan might be smart and rich and from one of the best families in town. But in the end, Emily hadn't wanted him. She'd chosen Tanner. Though no doubt she was regretting it now. "You know she came straight from your proposal to me."

"What?"

"The night you asked her to marry you—the first time—she said no, then she came to see me. Threw herself at me. You think she'll marry you now because she has to. But you're wrong. She wouldn't marry you then, and she won't marry you now." He stepped up closer. "She fucking chose me."

Ryan stared at him for a moment, then swung around and hurried away. Asshole.

He hadn't noticed the woman at his side. Now he did, and he swore silently. *Fuck*.

"That was cruel. You didn't have to hurt him like that," Lanie said. "Haven't you cost our family enough?"

For a moment, he just stared at her. And wondered again how much she believed in her version of the past. In the beginning, it had probably never occurred to her that Sawyer was lying about his whereabouts that night.

But how long had it been before she started to question that?

Longer than Tanner would have believed possible, considering Sawyer's behavior—his ex–best friend reeked of guilt. But they did say love was blind, and there was no doubt Lanie loved Sawyer. Their families had lived next door to each other. Lanie had once told him she'd been in love with

Sawyer since she was seven years old. Sawyer had told him that Lanie had proposed when she was twelve and he was thirteen. Tanner had thought it a hoot. Sawyer had treated her like a kid sister until she had grown breasts. They'd been a couple since she was fourteen.

So she'd believed Sawyer's story. And Tanner hadn't denied it, expecting a slap on the wrist or community service for a DUI. Of course, that had been before Dwain had died. And then things got a whole lot worse. After Dwain was dead, his lawyer had warned him not to change his story. It didn't matter he hadn't been the one driving that night. No one would believe him over Sawyer—*and* his own confession. But that if he pleaded guilty, he'd get off with a suspended sentence. Look how well that had turned out. Two years of his life.

But now, according to Sawyer, she'd left him. Had she finally realized the truth? About fucking time. And yet she was still carping on about what he had cost their family.

And suddenly he was furiously angry. He hadn't felt that way since prison. He thought he'd put it behind him. But he was fed up with everyone looking at him like he was some sort of monster.

"You know what, Lanie. Get out of my fucking face. I'm sorry Dwain died. He was my friend. But if you give me that fucking—what I've cost your family crap, I swear I'll..." What? What would he do? Fuck all, that's what. He hadn't spoken up back then, and he wasn't going to now. What difference would it make? The whole lot of them would probably find a way to twist it around so it was all his fucking fault. He shrugged. "Just leave it." He made to turn away but, in that moment, she seemed to collapse in on herself. She blinked, and a tear ran down over her cheek.

Aw, shit.

She rubbed a hand over her face and then looked into

his eyes. "I'm sorry," she said. "So sorry. I just got so used to hating you. And now…" She took a deep breath. "You don't understand. Sawyer…" She pressed her fingers to her lips, closed her eyes for a second. When she opened them, all the coldness was gone, replaced by a look of…pleading. "You're so strong. You've never cared what anyone thought. Look at you." She waved a hand at him. "Everyone knows how successful you are. Yet you dress like a grease monkey. You never did care. You always stuck your finger up at the people who tried to look down on you. Laughed in their faces. Now you've got Ryan's girl."

"She's not Ryan's girl."

"She was. Until you took her away. Everything just works out for you."

How the hell did she figure that out? But before he could say anything, she continued. "Sawyer always looked up to you. You were his hero. Everything he wanted to be. That night changed him. He's never been the same."

"And what the hell do you think it did to me?"

"Nothing. Nothing touches you."

Was that how she really saw him? Was that how they all saw him?

"He was never the same after that night. It was like he was distancing himself from me, but all the same it never occurred to me… I never… For years. I can't believe how blind and stupid I was." She swiped her hand across her face. "Things got worse after you came back. Now he's drinking more than ever. He won't hardly talk to me or the children. I started thinking…why? And I didn't like the answers I came up with. But I couldn't make myself ask him outright. So I left."

Silent tears were streaming down her face now. "I'm sorry, so sorry for what happened to you. I know it's pathetic to say I didn't know, but it's true. Maybe I was hiding from the truth, but I'd just lost Dwain, and I couldn't lose Sawyer as well." She took a deep breath, straightened her shoulders, and looked him in the eyes. "Even now, whatever he's done, I still love him. And I want him back. I want the man he could have been if none of this had happened."

Tanner glanced away. Across the carnival grounds, he found Emily. She was smiling and talking, selling her tickets, but as she caught his gaze a worried frown crossed her face. She thought he was going to mess up again. Hell, she probably expected it. He turned his attention back to Lanie. She was wringing her hands in front of her. "And you think I can give him back to you?"

"You're the only one who can. But you won't, will you? And I can't blame you. What happened to you…what we've all done since—" And she whirled around and disappeared into the crowd. He gave one last look at Emily, but she was busy talking to a group of kids.

He ran a hand through his hair. It was weird that Lanie thought he didn't care. Or maybe not so weird. He'd perfected the blank look at an early age. He'd hated people looking down on him. The kid of the town drunk. Hated that they had no money and he wore hand-me-down clothes, and his shoes usually had holes, and his hair was never cut. And more often than not he'd sported bruises because he was always getting into fights. You had to stand up for yourself when no one else did. Lanie would never understand that. She'd always had everything she could ever want handed to her before she could even ask. Sawyer was the same. But still they'd been friends. Almost inseparable. He'd believed Sawyer would watch his back. Stand up for him whatever happened. Then he hadn't. He turned out to be no better than the rest of the goddamn town, and he'd looked after himself when it mattered.

And Tanner had done time.

But strangely, in prison, he'd finally managed to let go of

his anger. Or so he'd thought. He'd come back here because it was home, and in many ways, he loved the town. But he'd also returned because he wanted to say fuck you to the people of Saddler Cove. Yeah, he was successful, despite what they thought of him.

But he couldn't win. He'd never gotten drunk in his whole life, but if anyone even saw him with a beer in his hand, then it was clear proof that he was just like his good old daddy.

Okay, so maybe his anger hadn't *all* gone. Maybe there was a little bitterness and resentment still needling away inside him. So he couldn't get over it. Hell, he wasn't fucking perfect. And neither was Sawyer.

The situation had spiraled out of control. Lies were told and couldn't be taken back. But he'd agreed. He'd just never expected things to go so bad. He'd lost both of his best friends that night. And he realized that it wasn't the lies that pissed him off. It was the fact that Sawyer had turned his back on him. Sided with *them*.

He'd been scared. Tanner got that. Scared of losing Lanie. Scared of losing his whole charmed life. Hell, maybe he'd believed Tanner's life was so crap that it didn't matter if he lost it. And just maybe he was right.

He knew what Sawyer wanted. What he needed. He blew out his breath. And maybe, just maybe, Tanner was ready to give it to him. No one else would understand. They'd probably just see it as proof that he was as bad as they'd always said he was. Including Emily, and for a moment, he faltered. And he realized there was one person who he cared what they thought of him. He wanted her to see him as worthy.

But maybe he also needed her to see past the Tanner the rest of the world saw and know that he was better than that. He didn't want to change for her. So she could have a nice, glossy, smart version of a husband, who would go and suck up to the Jed Forresters of the world. *Never going to happen.*

He wanted her to love him as he was. And shit, had he just thought the *L* word? He was going crazy. She would never love him.

And there wasn't a goddamn thing he could do to change that.

So why worry?

He headed through the crowd, caught sight of Reese and Keira—she was sitting on his shoulders eating pink candy floss—and turned the other way. He didn't feel like talking anymore. He felt like fighting.

Everything was wound up tight inside him. Needing some sort of release. The kind you got with your fists. He searched the faces as he walked, finally caught sight of the man he wanted to see. He stared until Sawyer must have felt the weight of that stare and turned slowly. Their gazes caught, and something flashed in Sawyer's face.

At least he looked moderately sober. Tanner wanted a fight, not a fucking knock-down. He swung around and headed away, not looking back to see if Sawyer was following. He knew he was. He wound his way through the people until he reached the edge of the carnival grounds, where the crowd thinned out. Then he did glance back—he didn't want to lose Sawyer now. He headed around behind the back of the bumper cars, into the shadows, then he turned and waited, hands hanging loosely at his side. Anticipation churning in his stomach.

Sawyer came to a halt in front of him. "I saw you talking to Lanie."

"Yeah. We were reminiscing about old times."

"She looked upset."

"Talking to me seems to have that effect on a lot of people."

"What did she say?"

"Apparently, she's married to a drunken bum who's

setting himself up to take over my dad's old role." He needed to piss Sawyer off. "She's probably worried *her* dad will take away all his money if you don't shape up. Isn't that what you live on, Sawyer? Your wife's daddy's money? Because you're too fucking riddled with guilt to get on with your fucking life. What are you going to live on now she's left you?" He stepped up closer and prodded Sawyer in the chest. At the contact, something flashed in his ex-friend's eyes. Hope? "You know what, Sawyer?"

"What?"

"Maybe it's time to give you what you want. Maybe it's payback time."

Sawyer stood there. Hands hanging at his side. "It wasn't supposed to happen that way. Nothing was supposed to happen that way. Dwain wasn't supposed to die."

"But he did. He's fucking dead. And it's your fault."

Sawyer swung then, and Tanner held himself still as the punch landed on his cheek, and he swayed under the force of the blow. Then Sawyer launched himself at him, and they crashed to the grass with Sawyer on top, and they were grappling on the ground. Sawyer was hitting out wildly and furiously, and Tanner relaxed his control, let his anger grow, and he was fighting back. He got his boot between them, heaved Sawyer off, and then followed him down, on top now, and rained punches on the other man. A wild blow caught him on his nose, crunching the bone, and he felt the coolness of blood trickling down his face.

For a moment, they both went still. Then Tanner shook his head, spraying blood across Sawyer's white shirt, and they were at it again. He scrambled to his feet, kicked out, hitting Sawyer in the solar plexus so he folded over, and Tanner bashed him across the back of his neck, and he crumpled to his knees. He raised his head and looked into Tanner's face.

"You had enough?" Tanner growled.

"Fuck no." And he wrapped his arms around Tanner's legs and dragged him to the ground.

They fought until Tanner's muscles ached. He had to win this. He had to beat the shit out of Sawyer. For his sake as much as his own. And he gritted his teeth and slammed punches into the other man. Finally, Sawyer collapsed to the ground and didn't get up.

Tanner rolled off him and knelt, breathing heavily.

"I'm sorry," Sawyer said.

"Yeah. I know." He blew out his breath. "The thing is, I spent two years in hell so you could have your fucking perfect life. I didn't even get to go to my father's funeral. So don't piss it all way because you're too much of a fucking pussy to accept what you were given."

Sawyer looked at him for a long moment. "I won't."

"Well, halle-fucking-luiah." Mission accomplished. He pushed himself to his feet, just as a group of people appeared. Lanie in the lead, Ryan at her side, Emily close behind. Lanie looked at him, and then gave a small nod and sank down beside her husband.

Tanner sighed, wiped his hands down his jeans, and glanced down. His T-shirt was stained with mud and grass and blood. When he looked up, it was straight into Emily's eyes. And it wasn't hard to read her expression. Disappointment. Well, he'd always been good at disappointing people.

"Would it hurt you to just make a little bit of effort?" She shook her head.

"You have to accept me as I am," he said.

"Do I?"

And she walked away.

Chapter Twenty-Four

Emily took a bite of her sandwich—now that the sickness was gone, it seemed like she was hungry all of the time— and turned to study Josh, who sat in the truck bed beside her. They were parked across from the pony swim landing site on the east coast of Chincoteague Island. The place was packed—other trucks and a whole load of people on foot. It was just after dawn, but the sun was already warm.

She was trying not to think about Tanner, because that just made her so mad. She couldn't believe he'd gotten into a fight last night. And with Sawyer. Who just happened to be the head of the school board's son-in-law. Of course, he was also the father of the boy killed in the crash that had sent Tanner to prison. But best not to dwell on that.

Jed Forrester would always hate Tanner. All the more reason to try and be a little circumspect, not draw attention to himself around the man. But no, he had to go and get in a very public fight.

Why couldn't she have fixated on a nice man?

She shook her head and banished the thought. She wasn't

thinking about it right now. It was a beautiful morning. And she'd always loved the pony swim, from when she was a little girl and Mimi would bring her.

She'd met Josh a few times now but felt like she hardly knew him. He didn't give anything away. He was the most self-contained person she had ever come across. But presumably he must have let Mimi past his defenses. He'd been to the ranch a few times to ride and, according to Mimi, was now off the leading rein and in control.

Mimi had asked her to bring him along to the pony swim. She'd had to go earlier to setup. She'd said she wanted Josh to come, and he was likely to back out if he didn't have someone to keep him there. Apparently, he didn't like crowds. And there was a huge crowd here today. About ten thousand people usually came to Chincoteague to watch the swim. Locals as well as tourists.

She'd got some strange glances when people recognized her companion. She'd just smiled and introduced him to anyone who stopped by as a good friend of her fiancé's.

Maybe she should introduce him as Mimi's boyfriend. That would stir a few people up.

If she was honest with herself, she had to admit that he made her nervous. And it wasn't anything to do with the fact that he'd spent forty years in prison for murdering a man.

What would it be like to lose forty years of your life?

Tanner had told her that Josh had never denied the murder. So maybe he had deserved the sentence. Mimi said that Josh had been in a bad place after he came back from Vietnam. That today, likely someone would have recognized that he had a serious problem and gotten him some help. But back then PTSD wasn't really acknowledged. She said he was a good man, and he'd paid for whatever he had done. And more.

But he was just so self-possessed.

He was a handsome man, with a strong face and dark eyes. He seemed almost ageless, as though time hadn't touched him, though his black hair was flecked with white-like frosting. He had a long almost lanky frame and he moved easily. She could see what her grandmother saw in him—as old guys went he was pretty cool. But she didn't feel like she knew him at all.

And maybe that needed to change.

She didn't know if he was serious about Mimi, but she knew her grandmother liked him a lot. And that was something totally new.

"So, what are your intentions toward my grandmother, Josh?"

He'd been about to take a bite of his sandwich, and now he lowered it and cast a wary glance at her. "Intentions?"

"You've been seeing a lot of each other. I'm her only family. I just want to make sure you're not leading her on."

She was sure he almost smiled. "No, ma'am."

"Don't call me ma'am. I'm Emily. Are you serious about her?"

He put the sandwich down and returned her look, his expression hardening. "Serious? I'm a black ex-con with absolutely nothing to my name. She's a rich white woman. I doubt very much that it's serious."

She wrapped her arms around her knees. "My grandmother has been a widow for thirty years. In all that time, she's never invited a single man for Sunday lunch. She's pursuing you, Josh. You need to have an idea of whether or not you want to be caught."

"You approve of her and me?"

"I don't know yet. I don't know you—you're a hard man to get to know. And she's my only family. But I want her to be happy. And as far as I can tell, you make her happy. That's good enough for me right now."

She twisted the ring on her finger. She wasn't supposed to be thinking about Tanner, because that would ruin her mood, but she couldn't resist one quick question. "Did you see Tanner this morning?" He nodded. "How did he look?"

"Like shit."

She winced. "Oh."

"Broken nose, black eye, looked like moving hurt. What happened? Did you beat him up?"

"Why would I do that?"

"Probably because he deserved it."

She let out a short laugh at that. "You know him so well."

"I know him well enough."

She poured them both a coffee from the flask beside her and handed him one. "He told me you shared a cell."

He took a gulp, then nearly choked on the hot liquid. "Yeah."

"And that you probably saved his life."

"Maybe."

She studied him for a moment. "You don't give a lot away, do you?"

"No."

She smiled then. Maybe she did like him. "He got in a fight. With Sawyer Dean. He used to be a friend of Tanner's."

"I've seen him around."

"Does he do it on purpose? Just to annoy people. Does he want them to think bad of him? Or does he just not care?"

"He cares."

"So why…?" She heaved a sigh.

"Maybe you need to ask him why he was fighting with Sawyer." He glanced at her as though he wanted to say more, but in the end, he remained silent.

"Perhaps I'll do that."

"Tell me about this thing." He was clearly changing the subject, and she knew she wouldn't get anything else out of him. "What are we waiting for?"

"Slack tide," she said. "It's a period of about thirty minutes between the tides. When there's no current in the channel. It's easier for the horses to swim then."

"You don't think it's cruel? To round them up like this. Corral them."

"Maybe a little. But you'll see—they don't seem stressed. The older horses have done it before. They probably reassure the younger ones. And it enables the herd to survive. If they didn't reduce the numbers, they'd keep breeding until there were too many, and they'd starve to death. That's probably more stressful. This might not be perfect, but it's the better option. And it brings a lot of money into the town." A movement across the water caught her eye. "Look," she said. "They're coming."

Across the channel, she could see the first of the horses wading into the water, urged on by about twenty men and women on horseback. "There's Mimi," she said, waving a hand toward a rider on a colored pony on the far left of the herd.

"Hard to believe that woman is seventy."

"I know. She's amazing."

Mimi was riding her horse into the water now, and then she was swimming alongside the herd.

They watched in silence as the horses swam. She searched the leaders, saw a small palomino head in the water.

"See that little one, just off center," she said to Josh. "The first foal that comes onto land is named King or Queen Neptune and is given away in a raffle. I hope you've bought your ticket."

"Yeah, because I always wanted a pony."

The first horses were coming up onto the beach now, shaking and stamping. The little palomino was the first foal. She was a beauty, golden with a flaxen mane and tail. The cowboys kept them moving, herding them into a corral.

"They'll rest them now for forty-five minutes or so. Then they drive them to the carnival grounds for the auction on Friday."

Mimi rode up at that moment, and Emily uncurled her legs and jumped down from the bed of the truck. Josh climbed down beside her. Mimi halted the mare in front of them and dismounted. She was wet and smiling and looked happier than Emily could remember.

"Maybe next year you can ride as well," she said to Josh.

He looked vaguely alarmed at that, and she grinned. Emily turned and rummaged in her bag, pulled out a sandwich, and handed it to Mimi. "Here. Eat."

Mimi took it. "Have you two been getting to know each other?"

"We have. I've asked his intentions, and he's pretty much told me to mind my own business."

She grabbed an apple, took a bite, and then held out the rest to Mimi's horse. "You want me to walk her and you and Josh can…talk." Without waiting for an answer, she took the reins and led the horse away. When she glanced back over her shoulder, they were sitting on the truck, legs swinging like a couple of kids.

Her grandmother deserved to be happy. It was an unlikely relationship. But maybe no more unlikely than her and Tanner.

Was Josh right? Should she ask Tanner what the fight had been about? Maybe, but she would leave it a few days, because she was still mad at him, and underneath the mad she was upset. And scared. That she'd made a huge mistake. And he was going to break her heart and probably not even notice.

She knew he'd only agreed to the marriage because she was pregnant, and she'd asked, and it was supposed to help her keep her job.

But deep down, if she was honest, she wanted to marry Tanner. And she wanted him to want to marry her. For more than just the baby. She'd been living in a little fantasy land of her own devising, where Tanner realized he loved her and couldn't live without her and…

She was an idiot.

He'd never love her. Tanner O'Connor didn't do love.

And she was starting to realize that without love she couldn't survive a marriage to him. The pain of living with him and knowing he didn't love her would be unbearable.

And the way he was acting, it certainly wasn't going to help her keep her job.

For the sake of her child, she couldn't back out now. Her baby deserved a mom and dad, and she'd seen enough of Tanner with Keira to know that he would be a good father. With Keira, she was able to get a glimpse of the man he would have been without all the bad things in his life.

And she wished she could somehow magic those bad things away.

But she couldn't, so she just had to find a way to distance herself. Move their relationship onto a more impersonal footing. Well, as impersonal as you could be with the man you were going to marry.

Chapter Twenty-Five

"And the winner of Queen Neptune is…Tanner O'Connor."

The crowd greeted the announcement with a moment's silence and then a round of applause.

"I don't fucking believe it," he muttered.

Beside him, Keira was wide-eyed. "You won, Uncle Tanner. You won my pony."

She'd insisted he come today. Apparently, his name was on the tickets, and the rules said: if he wasn't there he couldn't win. He hadn't been able to say no. He never could to Keira. He was probably going to be a crap dad. One of those who spoiled their kid rotten because he couldn't say no. But he'd never for a moment thought he might win.

What the hell was he going to do with a fucking pony? He caught Reese's gaze over Keira's head. His brother wasn't saying anything out loud, but his eyes held a faintly panicked expression that said as clear as anything—this is your mess, clean it up.

He scrubbed a hand through his hair.

"Come up and claim your pony, Mr. O'Connor."

Keira was positively bouncing now, looking at him pleadingly. God, he knew exactly what it felt like to want something so much. With that thought, he searched the crowd around the auction ring and homed in on her immediately. Emily was standing beside her grandmother and Josh, and she was staring right back at him. Her expression was serious. She was avoiding him. She had been avoiding him since he'd fought Sawyer.

He held out his hand to Keira. "Come on, princess, let's go claim your pony."

A huge grin almost split her face. "Really?"

"Really."

She took his hand, and he weaved his way through the crowd to where the auctioneer stood on a podium.

Keira had the tickets clutched in her free hand, and she held them out to the man while her eyes never strayed from the pony who was being restrained by a couple of helpers and looked totally wild. One thing was for sure, he wasn't letting Keira anywhere near a wild pony until it had had some training. It was pretty, though, a sort of golden color with a silver mane and tail.

"You want to take your pony now, Mr. O'Connor?"

"Just give me a bit of time to sort something out," he said.

"We'll keep her in the pens for thirty-six hours."

Keira tugged on his hand. "Can we take her home with us, Uncle Tanner?"

He glanced down at her and rubbed her head. "You planning on keeping her in your bedroom?"

She giggled. "She couldn't climb the stairs." She thought for a moment, a little frown forming between her eyes. "Could she live in the yard?"

"It's not big enough, sweetheart."

"Then where is she going to live?" He could hear the panic in her voice.

"Let's go see if we can find somewhere." He picked her up and carried her through the crowd to where Emily and Mimi stood. Waiting for him. Emily's gaze lingered on his face. He had a great black eye, though it was turning yellow now.

Keira wriggled, and he put her down on the ground. "I've got a pony, Ms. Towson."

"I saw. She's a pretty one as well."

"She's the best pony in the whole world."

"She'll be a lot of work."

He cleared his throat. "I don't suppose... I know it's an imposition, but..." He tugged at his hair. He was crap at asking people for anything. Emily stared back at him, one eyebrow raised. He turned to Mimi. He could do this. "Can we take the pony to your place until we sort something out?"

She smiled, her eyes crinkling. "Of course you can, Tanner. We have the trailer with us. Why don't you and Emily take your new pony, and you can come back and collect my horses afterward."

Was she matchmaking? Again. It warmed something inside him, that Mimi was on his side.

He looked at Emily but couldn't read her expression. She was beautiful today, looking younger than usual in faded jeans and a pink T-shirt. He liked her casual. Hell, he liked her any way he could get her.

Finally, she nodded, and some of the tension left him. He'd been quite aware that she was pissed off at him. But how could he explain? However much he hated Sawyer— and strangely some of that hatred had dissipated since their fight—nothing could be gained from bringing the truth out now.

"Can I come?" Keira said.

He searched for a reason to leave her behind, because he craved some alone time with Emily. But he couldn't come up with a reason.

"Why don't you stay with me, and we'll watch the rest of the ponies?" Mimi said. And in that moment, he loved her. "You can go see your pony when she's settled in. She's going to be frightened for a while. You have to take things slowly, but I'll teach you if you want to learn."

"Really? How to ride?"

"Of course. Though your pony won't be ready to ride for a couple of years yet. She's just a baby. But we'll find something for you to learn on, so you'll be ready."

"Come on," Emily said. "Let's go get your pony." She sounded amused.

"This is all your fault, you know. You sold me those goddamn tickets. You said there was almost zero chance I would win."

"Keira's happy."

He sighed. "Yeah."

An hour later, he drove the truck through the gates of the ranch and pulled up outside the barn. They hadn't talked much on the drive. But it had been a comfortable silence. Maybe she hadn't wanted to break the fragile peace.

Emily jumped out and opened the double doors of the barn, and he drove the truck in. She waved her hand toward a stall, and he backed up so the ramp was directly in front of the stall door, then turned off the engine.

He climbed out and went around to the back, opened the ramp, and peered inside. The poor little thing was standing in the center of the trailer, trembling.

"Poor thing," he murmured. "She's lost everything she's ever known."

"They settle quickly," Emily said, coming up beside him. "And really they couldn't all stay on Assateague. The island couldn't support a bigger herd. She'll be fine. You want to get your pony out?"

Did he? She was small, only came up to his chest. He could do this. He strode up the ramp, and she backed away. Maybe he couldn't do it after all. He stood for a minute. And she stepped forward. And he stepped back, forgot the ramp was there, tripped over, and fell backward. The filly gave a huge leap over him. He stared up at the roof of the barn.

Emily giggled. "Well, it got the job done."

By the time he'd pushed himself up onto his elbows, his new pony was safe inside the stall with the door shut. He sat up, ran a hand through his hair, pulled out some straw.

"Come on, cowboy. On your feet." Emily held a hand out to him, and he slid his palm into hers and got to his feet. She tried to pull free, and he held on to her.

Reaching up with her free hand, she ran a finger over his face. "I'm still angry with you," she said.

"I know."

"I don't know why I expected anything different." She touched a fingertip to his nose. "You broke it."

Actually, Sawyer had broken it, but he thought it best not to bring that up.

"I'll make it up to you." Though he had no clue how. He couldn't be the man she needed him to be. That wasn't who he was. He could clean up as much as she liked, and it wouldn't stop people looking down on him. But he wished it was different. That he could be someone she could be proud of. That their baby would be proud of him and not ashamed, as he'd been of his own father, however much he denied it.

And the truth was, he'd been deeply ashamed. And more than that—he'd been ashamed that he was ashamed. He'd liked to pretend that he didn't give a shit what people thought. But it had been an act. An act that had become so ingrained that now he couldn't tell the act from reality.

"Will you play for me?" she asked.

"What?"

"Will you play the piano for me?"

She gave his hand a tug and led him out of the barn, down the drive, and to the house. She upended a plant pot on the porch and picked up a key. "Everyone is at the auction," she said as she let them into the house.

They had the place to themselves. There were a lot of things he would rather do than play the piano, but he followed her into the sitting room, with its grand piano in the corner.

He sat down on the stool and thought for a moment, chewed on his nails. "What would do you want me to play?"

She shrugged. "You choose."

Then he started playing. Schubert. The music was lilting and soothing, and he lost himself for a little while as he always did. He wasn't that good, he didn't practice enough, but for once the music came out flawlessly. As the last notes died away, he turned on the bench to face her.

She blinked away the tears in her eyes. Aw, he hadn't meant to make her cry.

She sniffed. "That was so beautiful." She waved a hand at the piano. "Why can't you let the rest of the world see this side of you?"

It was his turn to shrug. How could anyone from her background ever understand what it had been like for him and his brothers? What it had been like for him to come home from prison? To know they all looked at him and wished he'd died instead of Dwain. That he could never measure up. And that if he showed any sign of weakness, they would tear him apart.

If he even tried to show that he wasn't the piece of crap they all thought of him, he'd fail. And they'd see through him to the failure he was. To the scared little kid. To the shit-scared eighteen-year-old. One best friend dead. The other just gone.

He couldn't say all that to her.

He didn't want her thinking he was pathetic. Better she think him an asshole than he lower his guard and let her glimpse the real him. Because if he did that and she rejected him, then he knew he was finished.

So instead, he placed his hands on her hips and lowered his head so it rested on her stomach. They stayed like that for what seemed like an age. Finally, she lifted her hands and slid them into his hair, holding him tight against her.

She smelled of warm woman and a hint of flowers. He slid his hands under her T-shirt to touch her silky skin, then straightened and pulled the T-shirt over her head. Beneath it, she wore a pale pink lace bra. And he traced the edges, her skin so soft.

He was already hard—had been from the moment he touched her—and he wrapped his arms around her and picked her up, carried her the few steps to the big brocade sofa, and laid her gently down.

He knelt on the rug beside her and tugged off her boots, then her socks. His hand moved to her waist, and he flicked open the button on her jeans, slid down the zipper. She raised her hips so he could tug them down and off, tossing them on the floor behind him. Then he turned his attention back.

She was naked now except for her bra and panties, pink lace so he could see the soft blond curls beneath.

He traced a finger over her stomach, then rested his palm flat against the small bump—just starting to reveal that she carried his child—and a sense of tenderness filled him. He would try and show her with his touch everything that she meant to him. Even while part of him knew it could never be enough.

• • •

He was so beautiful, he made her heart ache. Maybe that

was shallow, but she couldn't help herself. The sight of him, kneeling beside her, nearly broke something inside her. She'd already been feeling moved from his music.

No one bad could ever produce something so wonderful.

Now his big hands, the nails ingrained with oil, lay flat against her stomach, as if he was feeling for the life inside. His skin was dark against her paleness. He made her feel fragile, breakable. And she had to be strong.

She'd told herself that she was going to distance herself, try to see their relationship objectively, somehow prevent the heartache she knew was heading her way, but surely she was allowed this. Her body ached for him, her breasts swelling, tender and needy.

He shifted his hand and lowered his head, pressing his lips to the spot where his palm had been. She was sure it wasn't a sexual gesture, but heat and need fused in her belly, between her thighs.

He must have seen something in her face, because his nostrils flared, and he rose to his feet. She didn't take her eyes from him as he tugged his T-shirt over his head and dropped it on the carpet behind him. He kicked off his boots, then unsnapped his jeans, lowered the zipper, pushed them down over his hips. He was already fully aroused, and her breath caught in her throat.

He was totally naked when he came down on her. She opened her arms to him, parted her thighs so he could lie between them, his weight held up on one elbow while he caressed her with the fingertips of his free hand. Trailing lightly over her cheeks, her throat, the upper swell of her breasts. He followed the touch with light butterfly kisses that made her skin tingle and her soul yearn for more.

She needed this.

One-handed, he somehow managed to unhook her bra—he might not have had a girlfriend for a while, but he'd had enough along the way to get very proficient—then she pushed such thoughts from her mind. This was just her and Tanner—no ghosts from the past. He peeled the straps from her shoulders and flung the garment away, then lowered his mouth to her breasts.

He kissed one nipple and then the next, sending heat shooting down through her belly to her sex. They were far more sensitive than they'd ever been before her pregnancy. He licked with his tongue, then drew one into his mouth and suckled gently. A pulse throbbed between her thighs, and she worried she might come just from his mouth on her breasts, and she wanted him deep inside her when she came. He'd been holding himself slightly above her, and she needed to feel him, had to know he needed her as much, though she could sense that in the intensity of his touch. She squirmed, and he raised his head and stared into her eyes.

"Please, Tanner."

"Since you ask so prettily..." He lowered his hips into the cradle of her thighs, so she could feel the scalding length of him pressed against her. He shifted his hand between their bodies, and for a moment he cupped her sex, his fingers pushing inside, sinking into the wetness. Then he was opening her, placing the tip of his erection at her core. He held her gaze as he filled her with one slow lunge of his hips, and she wrapped her legs around him as though she would never let him go.

He made love to her slowly. Before they might have had sex, but whatever his real feelings—or lack of them—for her, this was making love. The slow, intense glide and press of his body into hers. The excruciating drag of flesh against flesh as he pulled out, only to push back inside as far as he could go, rotating his hips against hers, massaging her sensitive clit with his pelvic bone, so the pleasure built inside her, spreading out from that spot until everything tingled and heat coalesced in her belly.

He wrapped his arms around her, burrowed his face against her neck as the first shudders trembled through her body. He kept moving, in and out, grinding his hips, and instead of dissipating the pleasure continued to grow, lifting her higher and higher, straining her tighter. When she thought she could take no more, he raised his head and kissed her mouth, his tongue pushing inside, and she finally shattered into a thousand pieces. For a long time, she lost herself as pleasure pulsed through her body. She'd think it was over, and he'd move, and she'd go off again and again. Finally, he went still. She opened her lashes to look straight into his silver eyes, his expression almost dazed as he stared down into her face. Holding her gaze, he pushed into her again, his back arched, and he came inside her, with a long shuddering moan.

He collapsed onto his side, still deep inside her, throwing his long leg over hers to hold her in place. Then his lips took hers in a slow, drugging kiss.

"That was the best," he murmured.

She would have agreed but wasn't sure she could still talk. So she closed her eyes and nestled herself against his sweat-slicked chest. She was sure she was equally sweaty, but she liked the idea. She'd think again in a minute, but it was hard to think with him still deep inside her.

They had to get back, pick up Mimi and her horses. But she didn't want to move. She thought Tanner was asleep, but when she shifted against him experimentally, his arm tightened around her.

Finally, and very unromantically, she had to pee. Blame his baby. She had no doubt he would understand, because he seemed to have read just about everything about pregnancy that was ever written. She couldn't fault him for not taking an interest.

When his arm tightened again, she admitted, "I need to

go to the bathroom."

"Oh." He let her go immediately.

She glanced around. Found her T-shirt on the floor and pulled it on. It covered her to the tops of her thighs. She crossed the room, then the hallway to the downstairs cloakroom, and had her pee, washed up, all the time managing to avoid looking at her reflection in the mirror, because she didn't want to know what she looked like right now.

She suspected she looked like a woman in love, and that wasn't acceptable. So she splashed cold water on her face and tried to scrub away any expression with the towel.

When she got back, Tanner was fully dressed and sitting on the sofa, arms resting on his outstretched thighs. He looked up as she approached, a wary expression in his eyes. What was he so afraid of? That she'd ask for more than he was willing to give? Probably. Because in her secret heart, she wanted all of him. Every last cell, every last thought.

She was an idiot.

She found her panties, pulled them on, then her jeans and boots, and came and sat down next to him.

"Thank you," she said.

That got his attention. He turned to face her. "For what?"

"For making love to me so beautifully and carefully and magnificently."

Maybe she'd gone too far; a faint flush colored his sharp cheekbones. She'd embarrassed him. But he was made of sterner stuff. "Thanks, babe. Best fuck ever."

She should have expected it. He was just staying in character. And she hadn't really expected anything different. And she supposed it was a compliment of sorts, but... No buts. She could do this. So she pasted what she hoped was a patently false smile on her face and patted his leg. "Well, I'd have been happy to be in the top ten."

He blew out his breath, and something flickered in his

eyes. "I'm sorry. That was a crass thing to say." He ran a hand through his hair, which was loose around his shoulders. "It's just you...scare me."

She frowned. That didn't seem likely. Though he had mentioned it before. "I do?"

"You want me to be something else, something I'm not. I know you like how I look, how I make you feel, but you hate who I really am. And I'm fucking up your life and..."

She studied him, then stroked her finger along his nose, the slight bump where it had just been broken, then along the yellowing bruising around his eye, while she thought about what to say, how to answer him. Because in some ways he was right. Just not totally right. But she had taken too long to answer, and he rose to his feet.

"I wish I could be the man you need me to be, but I can't, Emily. I can't turn myself into some sort of Ryan clone. No one would ever believe it anyway. You have to accept me as I am."

But the question was—who was he? The jean-clad, greasy, tattooed ex-con who stuck the proverbial finger up at just about everyone who he ever met? Or the piano-playing romantic, who could touch her so deeply and so sweetly he brought tears to her eyes?

If he would only try and meet her halfway. But what did that even mean? Cut his hair? Just the idea made her want to scream: no! She loved his hair. Shave? Again she couldn't imagine him without the facial hair—it tickled her when she kissed him. Cover up the tats? They were a part of him, and besides, covering up that killer body would be a crime. Stop purposefully annoying people? Yup, that would be a start.

But that couldn't come from her. He had to discover it for himself, and she suspected he was far too blind on this subject to ever see the light. She stood up and wiped her hands down her jeans. "Come on, we'd better go check on your pony and get back and pick up Mimi."

For a moment, she thought he was going to say something. Confusion flashed across his face, then he seemed to give himself a little shake and he held out his hand to her. "Definitely the best fuck ever," he said.

And that would have to do for now.

If they never had to interact with anyone else, she reckoned they could be happy. Unfortunately, that was never going to happen. They had to live in the world.

And soon she'd have to face the school board. And somehow, she'd have to convince them that, despite evidence to the contrary—her fiancé's very impressive black eye and broken nose—marrying Tanner did not make her immoral.

Chapter Twenty-Six

Five days later and he was still quite aware that he had fucked up majorly with how he'd ended that last conversation with Emily. But he couldn't think of a way to make things better.

When they'd parted on Friday night, she'd asked him to give her a little space. Not to come around and not to call. And he had fought every instinct that screamed at him to be with her, not let her out of his sight. He'd gotten used to speaking to her each day, and he missed the contact. He felt as though she was slipping away.

"Why don't you come with me tonight?" Josh said.

Josh had been spending most of his spare time at the ranch. For the first time since Tanner had met him eight years ago, he seemed...happy. Relaxed and at peace.

So at least things were going right for one person. Reese and Keira were also spending their evenings over there, learning how to look after Keira's new pony. It seemed like he was the only one who was persona non grata at the ranch.

"She doesn't want me there," he said. He sounded pathetic even to himself.

"Are things not working out between the two of you?"

He picked up a wrench from the bench, the bench where he'd…he cut off the thought and hung the wrench in its place on the wall. "You doing the counselor thing again?"

"No. I'm just a friend who's trying to stop you fucking up your life."

"She asked me to stay away."

"She probably doesn't mean it."

He shoved his hands in his pockets. "She did."

"She's just worried about her job, that's all."

And he could hardly help her there. Hinder, more like. "They can't fire her now. She might be pregnant, but she's getting married. If there's anything immoral about that, half the population of Saddler Creek will be going straight to hell. Fucking hypocrites."

"Let's hope you're right. Because Mimi will be going to war if Emily loses that job, and she doesn't need the stress."

"Is she all right?"

Josh shrugged. "She says she's fine. But she has MS, and stress is one of the things that can lead to a relapse."

"You been reading up on it?"

"Yeah. Just like you've been reading up on babies." Josh shrugged into his jacket. "Is it okay if I take the truck?"

"Of course."

"Sure you won't come?"

"I might call her after I close up, get a feel for what she's thinking. See if I've stayed away long enough."

After Josh left, he tried to lose himself in work. Everyone had finished for the day, and he had the place to himself. He couldn't concentrate, though, and after he squirted himself with oil from the engine of a bike he was working on, he decided to give up for the night. He wiped his hands and face on a piece of rag. There wasn't much he could do for his T-shirt—it was covered in oil.

He paced the floor a couple of times. Put away a few tools.

He was being a pussy. He should just call her and ask if he could come over. They still had to set a date for the wedding. That's if she still planned on going through with it. Before he could change his mind, he grabbed his phone off the table and pressed her number. It rang a couple of times, and his gut clenched. She wasn't even going to talk to him.

Finally, she answered. "Tanner?"

"Yeah. Look, I was wondering…" His stomach churned. He couldn't remember when he had wanted something so much.

"Tanner?"

"I thought I'd maybe come over tonight. We could talk."

She was silent for a moment, and his fingers tightened on the phone. *Come on, say yes.*

"I'm sorry, Tanner. Not tonight. I'm really tired, and I'm just going to have an early night and…"

"Please, I just want to talk." Christ, he was begging now.

"Not tonight. Maybe this weekend. Good night, Tanner."

And she ended the call. He stood staring at his phone for a minute and then threw it against the wall. "Fuck."

The bell on the door rang as someone entered the showroom. He combed his hands through his hair and pressed his fingers into his skull. She was driving him crazy. He'd said he was sorry about the fight. Though he wasn't. He'd done what needed to be done.

He took a deep breath and headed into the showroom, then stopped abruptly as he caught sight of the figure standing ramrod straight, staring straight ahead, at the counter.

What the hell was Jed Forrester doing here? In all the years since he'd been back, he had never known Forrester to voluntarily enter a room he was in. It was a small town, and occasionally their paths crossed. They usually pretended the other didn't exist.

Forrester was seventy, the same age as Mimi, though he'd aged much worse. He was too thin, though his figure was upright, his hair white, and as always, he was impeccably dressed. But Mimi radiated life, and this man never smiled.

He'd lost a son, but he still had a daughter. Mimi had lost her only child. But she still exuded a joy of life that kept her young at heart.

Tanner walked slowly over, came to a halt behind the counter directly across from the other man. Forrester glanced at him, then away, as if he couldn't bear to look at him. Tanner was used to it. But what the hell was the old guy doing here? It hardly seemed likely he was here to buy a Harley.

He cleared his throat. "Can I help you?"

"As a gesture of good faith, I want you to fire Joshua Simpson and ensure he leaves Saddler Cove and doesn't return."

For a moment, the words didn't make sense. He didn't know what he'd been expecting, something about Emily, maybe, but not this. "What?"

"He's a murderer and a danger to the town."

Tanner forced down the anger that was choking up in his throat. "Have there been any complaints I should know about?" He wouldn't believe that for a moment. But he needed to get to the bottom of this.

"The man has been spending time with Miriam Delaney. Taking advantage of a vulnerable widow."

For a second, Tanner had no clue who he was talking about. Then he realized he meant Mimi. A vulnerable widow? Was this some elaborate joke?

Hardly likely from Jed Forrester. He never joked, certainly not with Tanner. He was still thinking of how to answer when Forrester continued. "If you do that, then I'm sure I can ensure that the board will look more favorably on Ms. Towson's case."

Now that did get his attention, and not in a good way. He rested his hands on the counter and leaned forward. Forrester took a step back. Good. "Let me get this straight," he said quietly, because if he let his anger get away from him, he'd be roaring. How dare the fucker play with peoples' lives? "Are you saying that if I fire Josh, then Emily gets to keep her job?"

"It will prove that you have the good of the town at the forefront of your mind. I will put in a good word with the board regarding Ms. Towson."

"And why would she need a good word? She's getting married. She hasn't done anything wrong."

Forrester looked at him then, allowing his hatred to show, but still his words came out measured, emotionless. "Ms. Towson holds a position of trust. The young minds of Saddler Cove are in her hands. Many people believe that you are not a suitable husband for a woman in such a position."

He'd be calling Emily vulnerable next. "You think she's going to corrupt those kids just by being married to me?"

"You destroy everything you touch."

How could he argue with that statement? But for the first time since he'd returned to Saddler Cove, he wanted to. He wanted to scream that he was fucking innocent. That it wasn't his fault. That he hadn't been driving the car. That it wasn't fair.

Like a big fucking pathetic kid.

He turned away for a moment and stared at the wall. His hands were fisted at his side, and he forced his fingers to relax, one by one. He breathed deeply, and when he was sure he had his feelings in check, he turned around.

"I think you should leave now."

The man nodded. "I've said what I needed to say. Think about it."

"Never going to happen."

"Then Ms. Towson will pay the price. But isn't that your way, Mr. O'Connor? Someone else always pays for your mistakes." And he turned and walked away.

Tanner stared at the door for long minutes.

What a fucking mess.

But no way would he fire Josh. Never going to happen. And why did Forrester want Josh fired, anyway? Was it just another way to get at Tanner? Or was there something else behind it?

He needed to warn Emily. She was going to be devastated. But maybe she'd know how much power Forrester had. Whether he was bluffing.

At least this gave him an excuse to go see her. Talk to her. He locked the door to the showroom and went back to the workshop, grabbed his helmet. Two minutes later and he was revving down the road on the way to the ranch.

There was no answer at the door to the house, and he headed toward the barn where he could hear voices. They were all crowded around a stall. The one containing Keira's filly. Mimi, Josh, Reese, and Keira. But no Emily.

Mimi glanced up as he stood in the doorway, then came toward him. "Tanner, I thought I heard the bike. What is it?"

"I came to see Emily."

"She's not here."

"She's not? Is everything okay?"

"Fine. She just said she needed to get out. She headed into town, meeting with Susanne I think."

"What time?"

Mimi raised an eyebrow, probably at his brusque tone. "She left around seven."

Just after he'd called. So much for being tired. She must have known she was going out when she spoke to him, and she'd chosen to lie. Was she worried he might suggest he go along?

Hadn't he known it was all a fantasy? She was probably ashamed to be seen with him. Was regretting asking him to marry her. Was probably right now asking her girlfriend for advice on how to get out of it. He rubbed the back of his neck, trying to ease the tension.

"What did you want to talk to her about?" Mimi asked.

He shook his head, trying to clear it. Emily had lied to him. Told him she was too tired to see him and then she'd gone out.

Maybe she wasn't meeting Susanne at all. Maybe she was meeting Ryan. Had she decided he was a better choice after all? Tanner knew, even as the thought crossed his mind, that he was thinking bullshit. Emily wouldn't do that. But that didn't change the fact that she'd lied. And they'd agreed that if nothing else, at least they would always be truthful to one another.

Christ, he needed a drink.

"Tanner?" Mimi urged, and he realized she was waiting for an answer. There was no reason not to tell her. Josh had come up beside her, but maybe he needed to hear this as well.

"I just had a visit from Jed Forrester. He told me that if I fired Josh and ensured he left town, then he'd let Emily keep her job. If not, she'll lose it because marrying me makes her likely to corrupt the innocent minds of the children of Saddler Cove."

She stared at him for a moment, her eyes narrowed, nostrils flared. "Jed Forrester wants you to fire Josh? And did he say why?"

"You were mentioned. Forrester reckons Josh is taking advantage of a vulnerable widow. That's you."

"He actually called me a vulnerable widow?" Her voice was rising. Josh edged closer to her, put his hand on her arm in a calming gesture. It said a lot about their relationship.

"Yes, ma'am."

"Don't call me ma'am," she growled. "And what did you tell him?"

"Nothing. I asked him to leave."

"I'm going to kill the fucker."

Tanner raised an eyebrow. Obviously, he'd hit a nerve, and she was taking this personally. It made him wonder what history Mimi had with Forrester.

"Well, I'll not stand in your way. I'm heading back to town." He needed that drink. More than one, probably.

"I'll tell Emily you were here."

"Do that."

And she'd know that he'd caught her out in the lie. What would she do then?

. . .

Mimi watched him go. Things weren't going well for Emily and Tanner, but she couldn't think of that now because she was so furious her vision was tinged with crimson. Her jaw locked tight.

How dare he?

"I don't often hear you swear," Josh said. "I guess that means you're mad." His hand still rested on her arm. It was the first time he'd voluntarily touched her. She touched him often, at first under the pretext of a riding lesson, but now it just came naturally, the need to touch him, to feel connected. And he didn't jump quite so high these days. "I'm sorry," he continued. "I've caused trouble for you."

"What?" For a moment, his words didn't quite make sense. Then she realized he was blaming himself for this. She was going to eviscerate Jed. "Don't you dare think this is your fault. This isn't about you. It's about me." She glanced back over her shoulder. Reese and Keira were still by the stall—it was hard to drag Keira away—they were going to have to set some rules.

"Walk with me?" she asked Josh. Without waiting for him to answer, she took his arm and headed out the back of the barn and along the creek path. They were silent for a while, and she allowed her surroundings to sooth her.

"Maybe I should leave," Josh said, breaking the silence. "Help everybody out."

She halted, resting a hand on his arm to stop him, then turned, so she could stare into his face. "And maybe you should stay. You don't deserve this. Whatever you did, you've paid for. More than paid for."

He ran a hand around the back of his neck. "How can you know that?"

Reaching up, she touched his cheek. "Then tell me."

He looked away. For a moment, she thought he was going to clam up on her again. But he took a deep breath and started talking, fast, as though he wanted the words out. "When I got back from Nam I was a mess. Couldn't hold down a job. I was drinking…and other stuff. Hardly sleeping. If I did, I'd have nightmares…flashbacks to… It doesn't matter—you can probably guess. And I remember being angry all the time."

"Classic symptoms." It was what she'd expected, but all the same, her fury rose. "You should have had help."

He chuckled. "You sound so fierce. But there weren't a lot of folks around back then wanting to help a broken down ex-soldier with anger issues. Anyway, I lived in this shitty apartment block with an even shittier landlord. He was a white guy—thought that made him better than us. Some of the women, if they were late with the rent—he'd…you know. Probably thought he was doing them a favor."

He paused, and she silently urged him to go on. She guessed he'd never spoken about this.

"My next-door neighbor had a fourteen-year-old daughter. Nice kid. One day, I got home—I'd been at some bar or other, was drunk. I usually was. I heard a scream. I pushed open the door, and she was lying in a pool of blood. I thought she was dead—turned out she wasn't. Prosecution said I'd totally overreacted. Bastard had raped her, and *I'd* overreacted." He shook his head. "It was the smell that did it. The blood. Took me right back to Nam, and I lost it."

"You killed him?"

"Yeah, I killed him. Though I hardly remember doing it." He was silent for a moment, his gaze flickering over her face, searching for something. "So, that's it. You still want me to stick around?"

She stepped closer, wrapped her arms around him, and held him close, feeling the shudders running through him. Then she stepped back. "Yes, I want you to stick around. I was right—you've more than paid. It's time to let it go."

She hooked her hand in his arm and tugged him onward, walking slowly, giving him time to do just that. Let it go.

Josh leaving wasn't an option. Jed must be out of his mind to even suggest it.

She shouldn't be surprised by this. He was a man blinded by bitterness. A man who'd never gotten over the death of his son, and she could understand that. Losing a child was the hardest thing a person could suffer. She'd lost two. One she'd given away, and the other was taken from her. Both had brought her to her knees, but she'd struggled back up. Made an effort to go on for her family's sake. Gone through the motions of living until it had become natural, and she'd finally found joy in life again.

Jed had never made that effort. He'd wallowed in his bitterness. When he still had a daughter who needed him.

She'd turned Jed down numerous times over the last few years. She was aware that he saw her as some sort of way back to a better past. But that wouldn't work. Hell, it would never have worked back when they were sixteen. It certainly wouldn't work now. She didn't even like the man. But once she'd thought she loved him.

They reached an old wooden bench her husband had built for her because she loved this spot looking out over the creek to the mountains beyond. They sat, and she turned to face Josh, studied the strong lines of his face, his eyes that held so much pain and loss. But they also held peace now. She blew out her breath. He'd bared his soul to her. Now it was her turn.

"I went out with Jed back in high school," she said. "It's hard to believe it was over fifty years ago. We thought we were in love. Maybe we were in love."

"He was the father of your baby?"

"Yes."

Josh rubbed a hand over his chin as he thought it through. "You wanted to marry him? Keep the baby?"

"I begged him to, but we were only sixteen, and both our families were against it. We were banned from seeing each other, but I snuck out one night, went to see him. I told him we should run away together, have the baby. I was such a romantic."

"What did he say?"

"He said we were too young, that we'd lose everything—Jed always did like being someone in the town—he couldn't bear the idea of being a nobody. He told me that he loved me, that we could get married after college, have another baby." She could still remember the sensation of her teenage heart breaking.

Now she could only be thankful. She didn't think they would have suited in the long run. But it might have been worth it to keep her child. "The next day, I left Saddler Cove and didn't come back for five years. He tried to see me then, and I wouldn't. I told him I'd tell everyone what happened if he didn't leave me alone. I married Liam. I wanted a baby more than I wanted a man. I thought it would wipe out the memory of the loss. It never did. Jed married late, he was over forty. We went to the wedding. He cornered me and told me he'd always loved me, and he'd waited, but he couldn't wait any longer. A month later, Liam was killed in a car accident."

"I'm sorry."

"He was a good man. But I never loved him. I wouldn't let myself love him."

"So, this Jed wants you back. What happened to his wife?"

"Divorced. Still lives in town." She sighed. "Jed's a stupid old man. Who should open his eyes and see what he's already got instead of chasing after something he's never going to have."

Josh looked troubled, a frown between his eyes. "Can he do what he said? Have Emily fired if Tanner doesn't get rid of me?"

"He could. But he won't. Because I'll rip him limb from limb. Then I'll tell the town what happened all those years ago. He can shove his morality clause up his—" She broke off. "It just makes me so mad."

"I noticed."

"That he has the nerve to question my granddaughter's morals when he was in the same situation, and he refused to marry the girl he got pregnant."

"You don't mind people knowing?"

"I don't care who knows. In fact, I'm hoping..." She hadn't mentioned this to anyone, but then, apart from Jed, Josh was the only person who knew about that long-ago baby. She would sit down and tell Emily soon, but the poor girl had so much on her mind. "I contacted the agency that arranged the adoption. They couldn't give me details, but they said if I wrote, they would forward the letter to...my son. I sent it off a week ago. Maybe he won't want anything to do with me. But maybe he will."

He slipped his hand into hers, the gesture tentative. Likely it was a first, and the touch warmed her. "I hope so," he said. "You deserve it."

"Do I? I gave my child away." She toyed with his fingers, laying his palm in her lap. "I should have fought harder."

"You were a child yourself."

"Hmph. Anyway, in the meantime, don't worry about Jed Forrester. And tell Tanner not to worry. I will go pay him a visit tomorrow, and I promise you, he won't bother you again."

Chapter Twenty-Seven

Her head hurt, and she wanted nothing more than to crawl into bed, preferably with Tanner to hold her tight, and forget everything just for a little while.

But that wasn't going to happen any time soon.

She'd gotten the call that afternoon. There was a meeting of the school board that evening, and she was expected to show herself. She hadn't told Mimi—she would only get herself worked up. Time to get worked up if everything went wrong.

Were they going to fire her? They couldn't. Could they?

This time she didn't even think about asking Tanner. She still hadn't forgiven him for the fight with Sawyer. And he'd made it perfectly clear that he wasn't going to change his ways for her. She could take him as he was or not at all.

And she would.

Actually, she loved him as he was, every grease-stained, unshaven, long-haired, tattooed inch of him. But he would hardly be an asset at this meeting, and just the thought of losing the job she loved made her eyes prick and her hands shake. It was so unfair.

When he'd called earlier, she'd almost given in and asked him if they could meet up after the school board meeting. But she had a funny idea that she wouldn't be feeling particularly sociable if everything went bad. So she'd put him off. But tomorrow, she would go see him, see if they couldn't move forward.

Just get through tonight first.

Maybe it would be okay, and they'd give her a slap on the wrist and it would all be over.

She was getting married.

She wasn't going to be an unmarried mother.

She parked in the school parking lot and made her way through the empty building. The meeting was in the principal's office. Daniel Dawson, the school principal, was leaning against the wall outside the door. He straightened as he caught sight of her. A frown drew his brows together, and she had a feeling of foreboding.

"Look, Emily. I'm sorry about this, but for some reason the board is pushing to make an example of you. I'd like to help, but my hands are tied."

"How? How are they tied?"

She'd thought Daniel was her friend. Hell, his little boy had been in her class last year. He'd praised her for the good job she'd done. Told her how pleased the school board was with her work.

He gave an uncomfortable shrug. "You know Jed Forrester runs this board, along with the rest of the town. If he wants you out—you're out."

"It's unfair, Daniel."

He shook his head. "Why the hell did you have to go off the rails with Tanner O'Connor? You know him and Forrester's history. Anyone else…" He ran a hand through his hair. "Look, just don't antagonize him. Right now, nothing has been formally decided."

She wanted to scream that she hadn't gone off the rails. Then she had a sudden flashback to lying naked on the table in Tanner's workshop. Most people would consider that—if not completely off the rails, then sliding fast in that direction. It still wasn't fair, and the anger churned inside her.

Breathe deeply.

Both Mimi and Tanner had suggested they get a lawyer in to look at the case, but she didn't want to go that route. How tenable would her working life be if she took the school board to court?

She blew out her breath. "Okay, let's get it done."

He nodded, then pushed open the door and ushered her in. She came to a halt just inside the door. The room was big, but it seemed crowded with people. All nine members of the board were there, four men and five women. People she had known all her life, now looking at her as though she was some sort of creature of Satan. They had to be kidding. This didn't happen in this day and age. She was not immoral. She gritted her teeth and forced a smile. No one smiled back, and her stomach churned.

Not fair.

Is this how Tanner felt all the time? Facing the town's condemnation.

Jed Forrester sat in the center of the group. The superintendent, next to him. The rest fanning out on either side. All prominent members of the town. Daniel walked past her and stood behind the group, obviously making it clear whose side he was on. Could she blame him? If it came down to her job or his, of course he would let her go. He had a family to support. But so would she, soon.

"Please sit, Ms. Towson."

She took the solitary seat on her side of the table and put her trembling hands in her lap, holding her fingers tight.

"I think we all know why we are here," Mr. Dawson said. "To discuss whether Emily is in breach of the morality clause in her contract. Would you like to say anything first, Emily?"

She swallowed. "Just that I don't believe I am—in breach of the clause, I mean. I'm going to have a baby, but I'm also getting married. It won't affect my work."

"You're marrying the father of your child?"

"Yes."

"That would be Tanner O'Connor."

"Yes, sir."

They were all silent. Jed Forrester tapped his fingers on the table. Then cast a look at the woman on his left. She cleared her throat. "I'm afraid, Emily, that the board does not believe that Mr. O'Connor is a suitable person to be connected to a teacher in this school."

And there it was. She swallowed down the bitterness and the anger that was threatening to escape. She had to stay in control.

Jed Forrester spoke for the first time. "Tanner O'Connor is a violent ex-convict who only last week got into a fight in a public place. And he's brought other violent convicts to this town."

Did he mean Josh?

She wanted to say it wasn't Tanner's fault. And anyway, he wasn't going to teach the children. She was. What did they expect? That just spending time with Tanner would turn her into some violent sociopath? She had the urge to jab Jed in the eye with a sharp stick, but she supposed that would only prove their point. Tanner was wearing off on her. She was turning violent.

"Tanner has paid for his crimes. He' a good man, runs a successful business, he's—"

"His father had a drinking problem and was an embarrassment to this town, and it's a serious concern that

O'Connor will follow the same route."

That was so unfair. She'd never even seen Tanner slightly intoxicated. Probably because of his father. Unlike a lot of people in this town, including Jed's son-in-law, who was hardly ever seen sober. She gritted her teeth.

Stay calm.

"Tanner does not have a drinking problem. In fact, he hardly—"

At that moment, there was a loud bang as the door crashed open. All the eyes across from her shifted to stare at something behind her, eyes widening in unison. She had a premonition of disaster as she slowly turned in her chair. And there he stood. Her "good" man.

She closed her eyes for a moment. Maybe when she opened them he would vanish. But no, he was still there.

He was dressed in oil-spattered jeans, a once-white wifebeater, now liberally stained with oil and grease. His hair was loose around his shoulders, and if she wasn't mistaken— he was drunk.

How could he do this to her?

She'd never seen Tanner drunk before. He was usually quite abstemious. But he swayed slightly as he stood in the open doorway, his gaze slightly bloodshot as it fixed on her.

"Emily, baby." He walked toward her with careful steps. "Emily, having-my-baby. Hah, new name. Fancy seeing you here," he said. "I thought you were at home, too tired to see anyone."

"Tanner. Go away. I'll talk to you tomorrow."

He carried on as if he hadn't even heard her. "Then I spotted your car in the parking lot and I realized you must be here." He smiled, spread out his hands. "So here I am to offer my support." His gaze shifted from her to the board. "We're going to get married."

She pushed herself upright and turned to face him, trying

to tell him with her eyes that he was not helping her cause. She suspected he was beyond picking up anything as subtle as a facial expression. Probably nothing less than real daggers would have any effect. Pity she hadn't brought one. She could see her life as she knew it dissolving before her eyes. "Tanner, just shut up," she muttered. "You're not helping."

Right at that moment, she hated everyone. Why couldn't things go her way? Just for once. She jabbed him in the chest, but he was so hard and didn't even flinch.

"You know Jed here came to see me earlier."

She spun around and looked at Mr. Forrester. His eyes were narrowed on Tanner.

She swung back to face her fiancé. "I don't care, Tanner."

"Jed Forrester. Upstanding citizen of the town of Saddler Cove. I'm sorry Dwain's dead."

"Not here and not now, Tanner."

"All you other good people," he said as though he hadn't heard her, "we're going to have a baby. But Emily has agreed to be my wife. So fuck you all."

Oh crap.

Did he have to do this now? *Anytime* for that matter.

He smiled and looked dreamy for a moment. Then opened his mouth again and spoiled it all. "Sensible Emily Towson has agreed to become my wife. Except she's not actually that sensible."

At the word *sensible*, something snapped inside her. She'd had enough. She was fed up with all of them. She wanted to scream and shout and stamp her feet.

Instead, she tugged at her beautiful engagement ring. It stuck on her knuckle—probably her fingers were swelling. Just one more thing going wrong in her life. Finally, she got it off. "You know what, Tanner? I'm feeling a little sensible after all." She slammed the ring into his chest, and he fumbled for it. "Take your ring and go marry your goddamn hog."

He stared down at it where it lay glinting on his palm. Then up at her. "Aw, Em, you don't mean—"

"I do mean. I do. I've had enough. You can take your bad attitude and your ring and shove them—" She broke off. Probably just as well. She pushed him in the chest. "Just go. I can't take any more of this right now." She played her trump card. "It's not good for the baby."

Something flickered in his eyes. She'd gotten through to him at last. He glanced down at the ring. Back at her and then their surroundings. Then he gave a nod, whirled around, and strode out.

Her eyes pricked as the door closed behind her. And almost immediately she wanted to call him back.

Goddamn baby hormones.

She bit her lip, standing for a moment, then she turned and faced her accusers. They all appeared a little shell-shocked. She was guessing school board meetings didn't usually come with quite this much drama. She wanted to shout at them as well. But more than that, she wanted to go home, crawl into bed, but definitely not with Tanner to hold her tight, and hide her head under the pillow.

She straightened her shoulders. Stiffened her spine, stared Jed Forrester in the eyes. "I am not immoral," she said and followed Tanner out the door.

But when she got the parking lot, he was already gone. Ryan was leaning against her car. He straightened as she approached.

"I just want you to know: the offer is still—"

"Go away, Ryan," she snapped. "I won't ever marry you, so you might as well stop asking."

"Why?"

She blew out her breath. "Because I'm in love with Tanner O'Connor."

And what an absolutely appalling time to make that

realization.

She was in love with Tanner, and that was probably going to ruin her life forever. Because he didn't love her. He was too bitter and twisted to ever love anyone.

When she pulled up outside the house, Mimi was sitting on the swing on the front porch, swaying gently. Emily switched off the engine, got out, and slowly climbed the stairs. She felt pathetic, and tearful, and a failure, and probably sensible as well, which was the worst of all. She came to a halt in front of Mimi and sniffed.

"How did the meeting go?" Mimi asked.

"How did you know?"

"I phoned up Jed Forrester. His housekeeper told me that he was at a school board meeting. I guessed the rest." She patted the seat beside her. "Sit down. From your woebegone expression, I'm guessing it didn't go well."

She sank down onto the cushions and stared at the sky. "It went awful. They'd already decided. I'm immoral." She sniffed again, and a tear rolled over, and she wiped at it with her hand. "And they were horrible about Tanner, and I was defending him, and then he came in drunk and made an ass of himself."

Mimi pursed her lips.

"I threw his ring at him and told him to marry his Harley. Then Ryan asked me to marry *him*. Again. But the worst thing. The absolutely worst thing was—" She drew a deep breath. "I realized I'm in love with Tanner."

Mimi didn't appear shocked. "Are you sure it's love and not just infatuation?" she asked.

"No, it's love. I mean, I am infatuated as well, how can I not be, he's..." She gave a helpless shrug. "But I love him as well. I know people probably look at us and think we're totally mismatched, but if you think about it, we're opposite sides of the same puzzle. We've just learned to hide different pieces of ourselves." She'd tucked her wild side away when her parents died, determined to keep herself "safe." And Tanner had hidden his softer side behind a badass attitude because he'd been hurt so much in the past. "We fit."

"'*Whatever our souls are made of, his and mine are the same,*'" Mimi murmured.

Emily sniffed at the quote. It was so perfect. "*Wuthering Heights*," she said. "You've been playing the quote game with Josh."

"That man is well-read."

"So is Tanner. But it doesn't matter, none of it does, because Tanner doesn't love me. And he never will. Because I'm unlovable." And with that she let her control go and burst into tears. Her grandmother's arms wrapped around her and pulled Emily close, stroked her back as she cried. She smelled of horses and hay, and so familiar that Emily cried even harder, until her chest hurt and her eyes ached.

"I'm sorry," she mumbled. "I never cry."

"Well, it's about time, then."

Finally, the tears ran out and she pushed herself up. "It's the hormones, that's all. I'm a big, horrible, hormonal mess."

"Maybe a little. But maybe this has been a long time coming."

"Really?"

"You've bottled everything up for a long time. Since you parents died. Maybe even longer. Since they went away and left you behind."

"They had to go help people. They had a calling."

"Hah. Nonsense. They had to go and have fun, travel the world, have exciting adventures."

"I must have been an encumbrance."

"You were a child. They should have waited to have you. Got it out of their systems, but you were…unexpected."

So she'd been a mistake baby. That didn't surprise her. "Seems to be a habit," she said, patting her stomach.

"More than you know."

What did she mean by that? She pulled back a little so she could look Mimi in the face.

Mimi sat back, picked up her glass from the table, and took a sip, handed it to Emily. "It's only soda water."

Emily drank. "Come on, Mimi. You can't make statements like that and then leave me hanging."

"When I was a lot younger than you—"

"How young?"

"Sixteen. When I was sixteen, I fell in love, and I got pregnant. Our parents decided that it should be kept quiet. I was sent away. I had the baby and he was adopted. I came back."

There was a wealth of pain behind the simple words. "Oh, Mimi. I'm sorry. How sad. You must have been heartbroken." She put a protective hand instinctively over her stomach. She couldn't imagine giving her baby away. Never seeing her again. Couldn't begin to understand the pressure Mimi must have been under as a young girl back then.

Mimi shrugged. "I won't say I got over it. You don't get over something like that. It shapes your life."

"Couldn't you have gotten married? Kept the baby. You were young but, if you were in love…"

"I was in love. I would have run away, anything. He was the more sensible, and he was right in the end. It wouldn't have worked."

"You don't know that."

"Believe me, I do."

"The father? Is he still around?"

Mimi's face tightened. "Oh yes. He's still around."

When she didn't say anything further, Emily forced her brain to work. "Why did you phone Jed Forrester?" she asked.

Mimi's eyes narrowed, and her nostrils flared. "That asshole. You know he went to see Tanner tonight?"

"He mentioned it at the meeting."

"Tanner came here and told us afterward."

That must have been how he knew she was out. What had Jed come to see him for? As far as she was aware, the two never spoke. Ever. "Told you what?"

"That Jed had come to see him and told him if he got rid of Josh, then he would look more favorably on your case."

"What? Why?"

"Because Josh has been spending time with me. Jed called me a goddamned vulnerable widow. I want to rip his eyeballs out. How dare he abuse his power like that?"

It was slowly coming together in her head. "Okay, let me get this straight. Jed Forrester was the father of your baby?"

"Don't look at me like that, Emily Towson. It was fifty years ago, he wasn't the same back then, and he was such a handsome boy."

She couldn't get her head around it. "But Jed Forrester? He's just so…"

"Sensible? Stick in the mud? Hypocritical?"

"All those things." She pressed a finger to her forehead. Her headache had shifted, but her brain was sluggish. "So he wants rid of Josh because…"

"He wants me back, of course. He's been pestering me for years. I told him he'd had his chance, but he sees me as some sort of redemption. A way of getting back what he lost."

"Oh my God. You've got a more complicated love life than I do."

She couldn't get over it. Mimi had a baby. When she was sixteen. That would make him fifty-four now. Wow. "Do you know what happened to the baby?"

"No, but I'm hoping to find out. Which is something else I have to talk to Jed about. He needs to be prepared."

"He can't cause trouble for Josh, can he?"

"He'd better not try."

"You like Josh, don't you?"

"I do. But I doubt there's a future for us. Josh needs to figure out what he wants out of life, before he'll let anyone else close."

He wasn't the only one. She had a flashback to the hurt in Tanner's eyes when she'd handed back his ring, and she had a weird feeling that she had let him down. Everyone had always looked down on him. Expecting the worst, and he'd just given them what they expected.

She scrubbed a hand over her face. "I've messed everything up. This is all my fault."

"Actually," Mimi said. "I think you had a little help along the way."

"I wanted everything to be safe and nice. I was good. I did the right things. Everyone liked me. And now...I'm immoral."

Mimi's lips twitched. "Tell me something. If you're so keen on safe and nice, why did you want Tanner O'Connor? Who is about as far from safe and nice as you can get?"

"He was a secret. A fantasy. He was never supposed to be real. And that's your fault. You're a meddling old lady."

She smiled serenely. "I am."

"But what do I do now? It's a mess. How do I get Tanner to change? I know there's a good person in there."

"Perhaps before you start trying to change your fantasy man, you need to ask yourself a few questions. Do you think he needs to change? And do you actually want him to change? Into what? Ryan Forrester? Why would you ever want that?"

Why indeed?

She'd turned Ryan down because he'd said she was sensible. Which she was—or rather, she had been. But really, she'd been looking for an excuse, because she didn't love him, and somewhere deep inside she knew she could never love him.

"You could no more be happy with Ryan Forrester than I could with his uncle."

And Emily had a moment of blinding clarity. She loved Tanner. Not the man he could become, or the man he might have been had things been different. But the man he was now. She loved his edginess, his tattoos, his lovely long hair. His muscles and his bad boy attitude. She loved his music and even his Harley.

She loved how his eyes crinkled when he smiled. How he could play the piano with such emotion he made her heart ache. That he'd set up a scholarship so other children could get the chance to play. How he owned a pony because he couldn't say no to his niece. Everything he'd done for Josh. There was so much to love about him.

"You were never meant for safe and nice," Mimi said. "Perhaps it's time to get over your parents' deaths. You can't keep everyone safe, however hard you try. All you can do is enjoy the time you do have with them."

She was so right. "I love you," she said.

"I know. So, what will you do about Tanner?"

"I don't know. I'll go and see him. Ask him for my ring back—I love that ring, and I can always sell it if worst comes to worst and I'm out on the street without a job."

"I like your positive attitude."

"And I'll try and work out if there's a chance he can come to love me. Because if not, we can't get married. If I didn't love him, then maybe it could work, but if he can't love me back, it will be too painful. He can still be part of Sophie's life."

"Sophie?"

"It was Tanner's mother's name."

"It's pretty."

At least she could see a way forward now. She might still lose her job, but the sense of hopelessness had vanished. And inside, excitement bubbled through her veins. A tension she hadn't even known was her constant companion was easing its hold on her.

"You know what I'd like to do now?" she said.

"No. Should I be worried?"

"I want to go for a ride."

"What?"

"I want to ride Beauty."

"Now?"

"Right now."

Mimi glanced down at her black pantsuit. "Perhaps you should go and change."

"Nope." She grinned. "And you know why not? Because that would be the sensible thing to do."

And then she had to go see Tanner and fix this mess.

• • •

Tanner stood in the shadows and watched. He'd sobered up fast after she'd thrown him out of the meeting. Then he'd driven the bike cross-country to avoid the roads, but he'd had to see her. Had to apologize.

Christ, he'd messed up bad. He was a fucking idiot. The reason she hadn't told him about the meeting was because she didn't want him there. So, what had he done? Turned up drunk.

But she couldn't *not* marry him. They were going to be a family.

It was still early; the sun hadn't gone down yet as he pulled up at the gates. Leaving the bike there, he walked down the drive, needing to get his thoughts together. As he passed the barn, he heard voices out back. His stomach churned as he walked through, passing the horses in the stalls. He meant to make his presence known, but he stopped short at the sight of her. They were in the paddock out back, where Josh had had his first riding lesson. Emily was leading a horse with a glossy black coat and a star on her forehead. She stroked her and kissed her nose, and the horse nickered softly.

Mimi spoke, and Emily threw back her head and laughed. She looked happy. Earlier, in that horrible board room, in front of those judgmental people, none of whom were good enough to bow at her feet, she'd seemed so defeated. And he'd made things much, much worse for her. He hated himself for that. He knew he could never make her happy. But he had to try, because he couldn't face losing her.

She moved around to stand by the horse's side, and he realized what she meant to do.

He nearly stepped forward then. Should she be getting on a horse when she was pregnant? But he held himself still. Emily would never do anything to endanger her baby.

She swung easily into the saddle and leaned forward and patted the horse's neck. Then they were moving. Walking at first, then a slow lope, and finally she broke into a canter. And she threw back her head and laughed again.

He turned away then. Because it hurt too much. This was where she belonged. He would never be good enough for her.

He was no good for anyone.

Wasn't it about time he accepted that and let her move on with her life and find the happiness she deserved?

He'd write to her, tell her he was backing out of their agreement. Something cracked inside him at the thought. This was it. She'd been his one chance of doing something good, something worthwhile with his life, and he'd fucked it up.

Tomorrow, he'd talk to Reese about making a permanent move to Richmond. Maybe it was time to leave Saddler Cove behind him. Let his kid grow up without the stigma of a fuck-up for a father.

For the first time, he admitted to himself why he'd really come back. It had been for Emily. For a dream.

Time to wake up and smell the fucking roses.

Chapter Twenty-Eight

"You're a goddamn miserable bastard," Aiden said. "You know that, right?"

Tanner didn't even look up from the bike he was working on. "Fuck off."

Work was the only thing keeping him going at the moment. That and his bike. His first love. He spent the hours he wasn't working out on the open road, trying to forget.

"Yeah, very intelligent answer, bro. Show off your language skills, why don't you?"

Tanner straightened up from his crouch beside the bike and stared his brother in the face. "What is it you want, Aiden?"

"I want you to get your head out of your ass and cheer the fuck up."

"I am cheerful." And that was maybe the biggest lie in the history of some real whoppers.

"Six years. Six miserable years, we've let you get away with this."

"This?" Tanner asked softly.

"And don't think you're going to frighten me off with that mean-eyed stare. I'm not a kid anymore."

"No, you're not. And I don't have to listen to this crap." He grabbed a rag from the table, wiped his hands, and threw the rag on the ground.

"Oh no. You're not walking out on this conversation. You're going to stick around and listen for once. Reese!"

Crap. His brother was calling for reinforcements.

Their older brother appeared in the doorway. He was wearing a suit. He looked like a goddamn businessman. What was with that?

He strolled into the room, Josh behind him. Josh had informed Tanner that he should fire his ass and make sure Emily's job was safe. Tanner had told him to fuck off as well. Anyway, they wouldn't take Emily's job away. Not now that she wasn't marrying him. Being an unwed mother was way better than being married to him.

"Jesus, get that scowl off your face," Reese said.

They stood in a line in front of him, blocking his exit. He shoved his hands in his pockets and glared. Why were they making such a big deal out of this? Why couldn't they just leave him the fuck alone?

"Look at you," Reese snapped. "Have you even changed your clothes recently? You're a disgrace. And a bad example to Keira. You look more and more like Dad every day. He'd be so proud. A chip off the old block."

That was a low blow. Especially since he hadn't had a drink since the night he showed up pissed at Emily's meeting. He gritted his teeth and let them get on with it.

"We get it," Aiden said. "You had a shit deal. Your mom died, your dad was a drunk. So was ours, and we don't spend all day looking fucking miserable and making everyone else miserable as well."

He gave them his best are-you-shitting-me look.

"And we know you had a raw deal over the Dwain thing. We know it wasn't your fault."

How the hell did they know that? He'd certainly never told them what had happened that night.

"We know you," Reese said. "And the way you've been acting with Sawyer since you came back. It wasn't hard to piece together."

And he'd thought nobody knew. Who else had pieced stuff together? Lanie, without a doubt, though it had taken her long enough.

"And why won't you see Mimi?" Josh asked. "She's been trying to talk to you for a week. And you're ignoring her. It's not cool."

"What are you? My goddamn dad?"

They were all studying him with varying amounts of pity in their eyes. He didn't need their pity. Or want it. He turned away, paced the room a couple of times, but when he came back they were still standing there.

"What?" he growled.

"We get it. You're scared."

"No. I'm. Not." And he wasn't. Not anymore. Hadn't been since he'd made the decision to back away. Leave Emily alone. You couldn't be scared when you had fuck all to lose. He wasn't scared. He was...broken-hearted.

Shit. And there it was.

He was goddamned pathetic.

"You have to go and see her," Aiden said. "Beg her forgiveness. Whatever it takes."

"Try giving her the ring back," Josh suggested. "Mimi said she loves that ring."

"And maybe you could slip in the conversation how much it cost. That should impress her." Reese had come across the receipt from the jeweler's last week. He'd been shocked and horrified. Especially when he'd realized that the ring had been lying on Tanner's dressing table since Emily had returned it.

"Why?" he asked. "Why do you care? Why is this any of your business? Can't you just leave me the fuck alone?"

"To wallow in misery? I don't think so."

"I am not wallowing in misery." And yet another lie. He was sinking fast.

"Dude, for a little while there you were bordering on human. She made you a better person. We want that better person back. Just go grovel."

"He won't need to grovel. According to Mimi, Emily has been trying to see him for the last ten days. He's been skulking around. Running away."

She didn't really want to see him. Why would she? She was the one who had given him the ring back. "She's just feeling sorry for me."

"Well, why wouldn't she be? A fucking miserable bastard like you. She's probably praying right now that miserable-bastardness isn't hereditary."

"I'm doing the right thing. The people here will never let her forget who and what I am."

"And what are you?" Reese took a step closer, hands on his hips, a glare on his face. "Do you even know? You've been doing such a good job of convincing everyone what a badass you are that you probably have no clue who you really are under all that attitude."

What the hell did that mean? This was who he was. "It doesn't matter. This isn't about me. It's about Emily. I'm no good for her. She'll be fine once she has her job sorted out and once I've moved away. She can put all this behind her."

Aiden threw up his hands. "Ah, what's the point," he muttered. "Too goddamn stubborn to change." He got a sly look in his eyes. "Anyway. They're probably right about Emily. She's seriously lacking in morals. She deserves to lose her job." Tanner gritted his teeth. "Yeah, a woman like that shouldn't be around little kids."

Tanner leaped across the space between them. Aiden didn't budge, and he slammed into him, and the two of them crashed to the floor.

"Don't you say a goddamn bad word about her," Tanner snarled. "She's worth ten of every other person in this goddamn town, including you assholes."

Reese and Josh both grabbed an arm, dragging him away from Aiden, and Reese gave him a shake. "Behave." He turned to Aiden. "You, too. Stop winding him up."

"At least I got a reaction. Better than the Mr. Misery imitation he's been doing for the last two weeks."

Tanner forced himself to relax. He knew Aiden was only trying to get a rise out of him. He'd always been that way, even as a kid. Push, push, push. Until something gave way. And he'd always been able to push Tanner's buttons.

Aiden scrambled to his feet and brushed himself off, walked over, and came to a halt in front of Tanner. "You love her. Grow some fucking balls and go get her."

But he couldn't. What if he told her and she still walked away? What if he bared his soul and she didn't like what she saw there?

Was it so wrong to just want one person, just one, to see past the outward appearance, past the son of the town drunk, past the teenager everyone thought had stolen a car and killed his best friend? Past the ex-con who had supposedly paid for his crimes, but in the eyes of this town could never pay enough?

And there was the fear all over again.

He looked at his brothers and Josh. They were only trying to help. But how could they? How could he ever expect people to see him differently if he was too scared to let them see the real him? In case they still didn't like what they saw?

He forced a smile. It felt slightly unnatural. "I know you all want what's best for me, and I appreciate that. But I have to think about what's best for Emily and the baby. And it's not me."

He shoved his hands in his pockets and headed for the door. This time, they didn't try and stop him, though there were a few muttered words as he passed. He definitely heard asshole.

He let himself out onto the street and walked for a while, finally heading into his local bar on the corner of Main Street. The bartender glanced up. "Hi, Tanner. What will you have?" He thought about a bottle of scotch. That had been his dad's drink of choice whenever the old man could afford it.

He could drink himself to oblivion. Just like his dad. But he wasn't going to do that.

"A coffee."

The bartender nodded and turned away as someone came to a halt beside Tanner.

Hell. Could this fucking day get any worse?

He blew out his breath. "Hi, Sawyer."

• • •

He wouldn't see her. Emily had tried everything she could, but he always seemed to be one step ahead of her.

"He won't even talk to me," she said. "He hates me. I know he does."

Mimi rolled her eyes. "He doesn't hate you."

She could feel her lower lip wobble. "Then why won't he talk to me?" The words came out as a wail, and Mimi's eyes narrowed.

"For goodness sake, stop moaning," she snapped.

At the sharp words, Emily closed her mouth—which had been open to do a bit more moaning. She swallowed down the words. Then blinked a couple of times. "I have been, haven't I?"

"Yes. And it doesn't do a lick of good."

"But I don't know what else to do."

Mimi reached out and patted her leg. They were sitting on the swing on the front porch, drinking tea. "If it's any consolation, Josh says Tanner is even more miserable than you."

Was it a consolation? Maybe a little bit. Okay, more than a little bit. She'd probably be more than a tad upset if he was wandering around right now with a big grin on his face. But she didn't really want him to be miserable. She wanted him to be happy. But happy with her.

It had been two weeks since the night of the meeting. She'd called, she'd gone to the showroom and the workshop and his house. She'd even visited the new place in Richmond. But he was always conspicuous by his absence. He must have some sort of Emily radar that told him when she was close.

And tonight was the open meeting with the Board of Education. The whole town was likely to be there, and she felt sick just thinking about it.

And she missed Tanner. She hadn't even realized how much he'd grown to be a part of her life. Yesterday, she'd gone for the sixteen-week scan. Mimi had come along and held her hand, but she'd wanted Tanner there. And she'd cried when she saw the baby, because he wasn't there to see little Sophie as well. And he would have loved it, and it wasn't fair, and she was going to cry again. She clenched her jaw.

No more crying. Or moaning. She had to make a plan.

"Have you talked to Jed Forrester yet?"

"No. He's being even more evasive than your Tanner. But honestly, if he fires you tonight, I'll stand up in that room and yell out the truth about that hypocritical bastard."

This time Emily patted her grandmother's leg. "No, you

won't."

They'd already discussed it, and Mimi was not allowed to use her and Jed's lovechild as a means of blackmail. It just wasn't right. But Mimi did need to tell him that she had been in contact. If their son turned up on the doorstep, he was likely going to want to know who his father was. And she knew Mimi wanted to be able to be open with him.

The adoption agency had confirmed that they had passed on the letter, but Mimi still hadn't heard anything else. And Emily was aware it was driving her crazy. That she believed her son blamed her for giving him away, that she hadn't loved him, hadn't wanted him.

And Mimi didn't need the stress.

The sound of an engine approached, and for a second, her heart hitched. Maybe he'd come to hold her hand.

But it wasn't the throaty purr of Tanner's Harley. And her hope flagged.

Instead, a truck pulled up in front of the house. She stared inside the tinted windows but couldn't see who was in there. It wasn't Tanner's truck, but maybe…

Then the door opened, and a man climbed out, then another from the passenger side. Reese and Aiden. Mr. Tall, Dark, and Handsome and Mr. Lean, Mean, and Dangerous.

Beside her, Mimi gave a low whistle. "Makes me wish I was young again." Then the back door opened, and Josh jumped down. "Or maybe not."

. . .

"I saw you come in," Sawyer said, easing onto the barstool next to him.

"And thought you would join me. How fucking sweet. Maybe you thought we could get shitfaced together."

Truth was, he didn't know how he felt about Sawyer

anymore. Since the fight, the old bitterness seemed to have left him. He just didn't know whether there was anything left in its place.

"I haven't had a drink since we had that fight," Sawyer said. The barman put his coffee down in front of him and looked at Sawyer. "I'll have the same."

"How's Lanie?" Tanner asked.

"Sad. Relieved. Disappointed in me. But at least we're talking for once. It might take time, but I think we'll be okay."

"Good."

They drank in silence for a minute, but Tanner knew it wouldn't last. He wasn't ready for this. He had too many troubles of his own to try and deal with Sawyer's right now.

"I know the fight got you in trouble. I heard Lanie talking with her dad. He said it just proved you hadn't changed. That he was doing the right thing. That Emily Towson would see the truth of the matter and break off the engagement."

"Well, she did that."

"Only because you pushed her into it."

"What do you know?"

"I have sources. I heard you turned up at the hearing drunk and pissed her off."

"Yeah. She was pissed off. But better she knows who I am now, though, rather than later."

Sawyer snorted. "Yeah. That might be the case. Except it isn't who you are, is it?"

"What?"

"If it had been me turning up drunk, then that would have been typical Sawyer. But you? Tell me, how many times have you been drunk since you came back to Saddler Cove."

He didn't bother to answer, so Sawyer answered for him.

"Once, right? That night of the hearing. Once in six fucking years. Hell, even when we were kids, you wouldn't get drunk with the rest of us."

"Well, if you'd had my dad as a role model, you'd probably have been the same."

"Exactly. So you don't have a drinking problem. Hey, that doesn't mean you're *not* a bad guy. Let's look at your other claims to the title. Your father was the town drunk. Hardly your fault. And you kept your family together. Even after Reese left, you looked after Aiden."

"Sweet as this is, where are you going with this, Sawyer?" Except he suspected he knew, and he didn't want to go there. Not now. Not ever.

"Okay, we'll move on to the good stuff. You're a car thief and a killer."

Tanner's hand tightened on his mug, and he put it down slowly. "What do you want from me, Sawyer?"

"You mean other than two years of your life, your belief in human nature, and your reputation?"

He let out a laugh. "I hardly had one of those to start with."

"What's really gone wrong with you and Emily?"

The change in subject caught him out, and for a moment he floundered. "She deserves better."

"Better than a man who put his life on the line for his friend who didn't deserve it."

"You were drunk that night. It would have gone much worse for you."

"Yeah. I was drunk. Good old Sawyer, always ready to party. That's hardly an excuse. I was drunk, and I persuaded Dwain to take his daddy's car, then I drove it too fast, and we crashed. And Dwain died. But they weren't my worst crimes. Those came later."

Tanner held his silence, because he sensed Sawyer needed to get this out of his system. This is what he'd needed since Tanner came back. Confession and absolution. And Tanner was the only person he could get that from.

"I climbed out of that car and I ran. And you got the blame."

He remembered that night so well. It had replayed in his dreams. If he'd just done anything different.

"They can't find me here," Sawyer had said. "Another strike, and I'm in prison." Sawyer had already, at the age of eighteen, gotten two DUIs under his belt. "And Lanie will never forgive me."

"Go," Tanner had said.

Sawyer had hugged him in relief. "Look after Dwain." They hadn't known then that Dwain was fatally injured. That he would die two days later from those injuries. By then it was too late for Tanner to change his story. He'd considered it, talked to his crappy lawyer, who'd convinced him that changing his statement was a bad idea—he'd get no leniency for lying in a statement and likely get the max anyway. *Put your faith in the system*, the lawyer had said to Tanner. This was a first offense, most likely he wouldn't even do time. Hah!

Besides, who would have believed him? Sawyer certainly hadn't been talking.

That's what had hurt him the most. That Sawyer had just turned his back on him. They'd been friends almost all their lives. And then nothing.

"You never came to see me."

"I couldn't. My dad sent me out of town. He knew something was wrong." Sawyer shook his head. "Who am I kidding? I was ashamed. Ashamed of what I'd done and scared that if I came to see you, you would have asked me to tell the truth."

"Maybe."

He'd sometimes wondered: if he could do it all again, would he do it differently? Would he have protested his innocence? But the truth was—he didn't think so. It was more the fact that the choice was taken from him that pissed him off. But Sawyer had had far more to lose than Tanner. Sawyer had been in love with Lanie since they were kids. How would that love have survived Sawyer as good as killing her brother? How would her father have felt about his only remaining child marrying his son's killer?

"No, you wouldn't," Sawyer said. "Because you're a better person than me. But I want to make things right. I'm going to tell the truth."

Jesus. He'd suspected something like this. And it totally pissed him off. His fingers twitched with the need to punch Sawyer. Again. Punch some sense into his head. Did the man understand nothing? Maybe it needed to be spelled out in words of one syllable.

"I gave up two years of my life for you, and I can't get them back. Now you want to waste that. Just fuck it all away?"

"But—"

"No buts. None. It's done."

"Do you regret that night?" Sawyer asked.

"No, I don't regret what I did for you. But you know what really pissed me off when I came out of prison and back here?"

Sawyer shook his head.

"I gave up two years of my life for you, and you learned nothing. I come back and you're still drinking your fucking life away. Yeah, I thought I was all fucking noble—helping the path of true love. And are you making Lanie happy? Fuck no. You're making everyone fucking miserable. And that needs to change now, or you might as well have gone to prison instead of me. And let me tell you—you wouldn't have lasted one fucking day. So, go find Lanie, tell her you're sorry for being such a dick, and you'll do better from now on."

Sawyer nodded. And Tanner caught a glimpse of the boy he'd been. Christ, they'd had some good times together.

"Thank you." The soft voice came from beside him, and

he looked away from Sawyer and into Lanie's face. He nearly jumped. How the hell had she snuck up on them? She stared into his eyes, and he knew she was really seeing him for the first time.

"You have nothing to thank me for," he said.

"We both know that's a lie. Even if it did take me a long time to realize it. I'm sorry for what we put you through."

He shrugged. "It's the past. Leave it there."

She nodded and hooked her arm through Sawyer's, rested her head on his shoulder. It was the way they'd always stood.

"What are you going to do about Emily?" Sawyer asked.

He wanted to say none of your fucking business. "Nothing. I'm going to keep away, and maybe she can get her life back on track."

"Goddamn virtuous prick. You talk about not having regrets. I've seen the two of you together, and if you let this pass, you'll regret it for the rest of your life."

"It's too late. I'm leaving Saddler Cove."

"The fuck you are."

"And anyway, she doesn't want me."

"She must have wanted you at least one time."

"Ha-ha." He looked away. Acknowledging the hurt he still felt. "The last meeting. She didn't even tell me about it. She lied to me, told me she was tired. But really, she didn't want me along. I'm the last person she would want on her side."

"I see you now, Tanner," Lanie said softly. "You think that if you look like the bad guy, and act like the bad guy, there's no risk if everyone thinks the worst of you. But you're not giving anyone a chance. You're not giving Emily a chance."

Sawyer nodded. "You were my hero as a kid. You'd risk anything. You're still my hero."

Tanner swished the coffee around in his cup. He couldn't stand their penetrating stares. He took a deep breath. "This is too important."

"Well, maybe it's time to take a risk and let someone see what's behind the image. Hell, let everyone see. Go shock them. They'll all be there later tonight. No doubt badmouthing your girlfriend and definitely badmouthing you. Go prove them wrong." He wrapped his arm around Lanie's shoulder. "Come on, sweetheart, let's go cheer for Emily. Even if this loser isn't going to support her."

Tanner watched as they walked away. At the door, Sawyer hesitated and turned around. "I'd like to be friends again."

"Don't push your fucking luck."

But Sawyer was smiling as he left. At least one of them was. Tanner caught a glimpse of himself in the mirror behind the bar. There was a scowl on his face. His hair looked as though it hadn't seen a comb in weeks, his beard was scruffy, and a big black streak of grease bisected his cheek. He was a goddamned mess.

Yeah, he wasn't anything to boast about.

What did Emily see in him?

Could he be worthy of her? And if she still wouldn't take him back, then was he strong enough to go on? And it came to him then that he couldn't feel worse than he did right now. What did he have to lose?

Time to see if he could be the sort of man Emily could one day love. For now, he reckoned he had enough love for both of them. He'd better hurry if he wanted to get cleaned up before the meeting.

Somehow, he had to get Emily's job back.

Hell, he'd grovel to the whole of Saddler Cove if that's what it took.

• • •

Emily blew out her breath. "What do you think they want?"

she asked in a low voice. She wasn't above admitting that, with the exception of Tanner, the O'Connor brothers scared her to death. They were just so big and masculine and... intimidatingly gorgeous.

"I have no clue, but I'm sure we're about to find out."

They climbed up the steps side by side, came to a halt in front of the swing, and stood shuffling their feet. Emily had the impression they didn't really know what to say. That this was perhaps a spur-of-the-moment visit.

"Good afternoon, Josh, gentlemen," Mimi said. "Can we offer you a cold drink on this hot afternoon? A beer, perhaps." Without waiting for an answer, she turned to Emily. "Emily, would you?"

She didn't want to. She wanted to find out what they were doing here. Had Tanner sent them? And if so, why? But she hurried across the patio, through the open French doors, sprinted to the kitchen, grabbed three bottles of beer, uncapped them, and ran back.

"Here," she said, slightly out of breath as she handed them around.

She gave Mimi a look that said—have I missed anything?

"Not a thing."

Josh had taken her seat next to Mimi, so she took a chair across from them, resting her hands on her lap as the O'Connor men took seats on either side of her. They gripped their beers and looked uncomfortable. Finally she couldn't take the silence any longer. What were they doing there?

"Is Tanner okay?" she asked.

"It depends how you define *okay*," Reese replied.

Mimi gave a small smile. "How annoyingly cryptic, Mr. O'Connor."

"What Reese means is—Tanner is being a total asshole," Aiden said. "A miserable fucking—sorry about the language, ma'am—asshole."

"And is this not normal behavior for your brother?" Mimi asked.

"Well, a few months back, I might have said yes, ma'am. But not lately." Reese turned his attention to Emily. "For a while there, you made him happy, Teach." Reese was studying her, probably trying to work out what Tanner had seen in her. "It took us a while to recognize it—happiness is not an emotion we see from Tanner all that much. But he changed when he was with you."

"Started humming all that classical music shit around the place," Aiden added. "And quoting books and stuff. And we didn't even give him a hard time over it, because shit... Tanner, happy? It was like a miracle."

Her eyes pricked, and she gave a sniff. She so wanted Tanner to be happy, but happy with her. Reese's eyes widened in alarm. "Sorry, Teach, we didn't mean to upset you."

She sniffed, then waved a dismissive hand in the air. "Baby hormones. And I'm not upset. But I don't know what to do. He won't see me. Or talk to me. He can't hide forever, but—"

"Don't you believe it," Reese put in. "He's planning to move to Richmond. Take himself away from temptation. Ensure that you and your baby aren't contaminated by him."

He couldn't do that. No way.

"Is he crazy? He can't do that. He promised to be there for us." She took a few deep breaths. "I get it if he doesn't want to marry me. I can't force him, but my baby needs a father."

"Tanner reckons no father at all is better than him for a dad."

"Well, he's wrong. And an idiot. That man is just so... Grr. An asshole." She looked at his brothers, her eyes narrowing. "What are you doing here? Are you just here to let me know what a jerk the father of my baby is? Or do you have something constructive to say?"

Reese sat back. "Nothing *really* constructive."

"Actually," Aiden added, "nothing constructive at all."

"So why are you here?" Why were they torturing her like this? She needed solutions, not more problems. How dare Tanner even think about moving to Richmond. She was going to kill him. If she ever saw him again.

"I think they want to know your intentions toward their brother," Josh said.

"What?" She gritted her teeth. "I asked him to marry me, didn't I?

"But was that just because you needed a father for your baby?"

She thought for a moment, because it was an important question. But only a moment, because she already knew the answer. "No. Of course not. I love Tanner." There, she had said it out loud. Was there a collective sigh around the porch? "I think I've loved him for years, but I never thought we had a chance together because—"

"You think he's not good enough," Aiden interrupted.

"That's not what I—"

"Because if that's the case—"

She jumped up and stamped her foot. "Will you let me get a word in, please? I was going to say, because I'm not beautiful, and Tanner has hundreds of beautiful girls after him, and I'm not exciting, and he rides a Harley. What would he see in me?"

Aiden frowned. "You know, they just might be perfect for each other. They can sit around moaning and talking through their low self-esteem issues together."

Mimi sniggered, and Emily glared some more. "I do not have a low self-esteem, I'm just realistic. I'm ordinary, and Tanner is...special."

"You really think that?" Reese asked.

"Of course. But it doesn't matter, because your bonehead of a brother won't even talk to me."

"You're right. Tanner is special. Problem is—he doesn't see it. He's loyal to a fault, he'll put himself on the line for his friends. But he also learned to hide his feelings a long time ago. He thinks that if he presents an asshole attitude to the world, and they see him as an asshole, then that's okay, and they're too stupid to see anything else. But now he wants more, and he's scared. Because what if he lets them see the real Tanner—lets *you* see—and you all still think he's an asshole?"

She got to her feet and stood, hands on her hips, and glared. "Tanner is not an asshole...most of the time."

Reese shrugged. "That's all we needed to know." He grinned. "Emily Towson, we give you our blessing."

"Screw your blessing," she snapped. "Give me your brother. Because right now I don't have him."

Reese got to his feet. "I like you, Teach. You know, I should have moved a little faster and got in before Tanner."

She rolled her eyes. "Never would have happened."

He ignored the comment. "We'll get you a meeting with Tanner, if we have to drag him there tied and gagged. He will listen. But you have to convince him you love him just as he is."

"That won't be hard, I—" She broke off as a dark gray sedan came roaring down the drive, way too fast, and behind it a red open-topped Mercedes. The sedan skidded to a halt, and she looked at Mimi, one eyebrow raised. Mimi shrugged back.

The door was flung open, and a man climbed out just as the red sports car pulled up behind.

"Great," Emily murmured. Why didn't the whole town turn up? Perhaps they could hold the meeting here.

Sawyer Dean.

Just what she needed to get her in the right frame of mind for a town showdown. Except she really had no clue what Sawyer Dean and his wife were doing here, though she suspected it wasn't the same thing. In fact, from the way Lanie ran up to her husband and grabbed his arm, it looked like their goals were at definite odds.

"You can't do this, Sawyer," Lanie said. "You know what Tanner said. Leave it in the past."

"I have to. I owe him this much." He pulled himself free and headed up the stairs. Beside her, Mimi rose to her feet, sent Emily another glance and another shrug. Josh came to stand beside Mimi. Protecting her. It was sweet, really.

Aiden and Reese took a step closer.

Sawyer and Lanie seemed to suddenly realize how many people were present, and they hesitated.

It occurred to Emily that Mimi's lost son was in fact Lanie's half brother. Lanie was only a couple of years older than Emily, and her half brother would be fifty-four. How weird was that? Lanie had lost a brother. And now she was getting a new one. Maybe there was some balance in the world after all.

"Sawyer. Lanie," Mimi murmured. "How lovely to see you both. But we're about to leave for a meeting. So…"

"I need to talk to Emily," Sawyer said.

"No, you don't," Lanie snapped. She turned to look at Emily with pleading eyes. "Please. I'll talk to my father. I'll make sure he doesn't fire you over this. Just…" She ran a hand through her hair. "I love my father, and I love my husband, and this will take away everything."

"You don't need to talk to your father," Mimi said. "I plan on talking to him."

"All the same," Sawyer said, "there's something Emily needs to know. Something about the night Dwain died."

She got up and moved to his side. "It's okay. I can guess

what you're going to say, and you don't need to. Nothing good can come of it now." She'd guessed, almost from the start, that Sawyer was the one driving that night. And he'd let Tanner take the rap for it. But he'd clearly suffered because of that decision. Maybe everyone involved had paid enough. "Tanner was right. Leave it in the past."

He searched her face, then nodded. "You love him?"

"Yes."

He blew out his breath. "Tanner's a lucky man."

"We have to leave," Mimi said. "We're going to be late."

The porch cleared quickly. Emily climbed into the passenger seat of Mimi's truck and fastened her seat belt as they pulled out behind Lanie's red sports car.

"Mimi, I'm sorry if it will cause problems for us. And I know I'll likely lose my job, but I can't grovel to them. They're in the wrong, and I can't stand by and let them badmouth Tanner."

"I'd be annoyed if you did."

"I'm afraid it's not going to be the sensible option." In fact, she was going to give the Board of Education, and probably the whole population of Saddler Cove, a piece of her mind.

"All the better. Go do what you have to do, Emily Towson."

Chapter Twenty-Nine

He didn't even recognize himself.

He stared at the mirror.

Holy shit.

Is that really me?

Obviously, it wasn't the best haircut ever. He'd done it himself, just chopped it off and slicked it back with something he'd found in Reese's bathroom cabinet. He'd shaved—he couldn't remember when his face had seen the light of day—splashed himself liberally with something else from Reese's cabinet—that guy was turning into a pussy. He'd scrubbed his hands and nails until they were raw, but there wasn't a speck of grease left anywhere. And finally, he'd raided Reese's wardrobe. Luckily, they were the same size. The white shirt, dark red tie, and dark gray suit all fitted him as though they were made for him. With the tattoos covered, he reckoned he could pass for an okay guy. He tried a smile, but it came out as more of a grimace. Not a problem. He didn't think he'd be smiling that much anyway.

Only thing he hadn't been able to borrow from Reese

was shoes. Reese had fucking huge feet. Which meant he was wearing boots, but hopefully no one would be looking at his feet.

He grabbed the speech he'd written—all about how he was going to be a better person, and he wouldn't drink or fight or...hell, they just had to give him a list of things they didn't want him to do and he'd sign on the dotted line.

He ran a hand around the back of his neck. He was sweating.

Was it enough? But at least it showed he was willing.

Would anyone even try to meet him halfway? Would Emily?

Time to go. He could do this. He picked up his helmet on the way out, but as he opened the gate from the yard to the road, a truck pulled up beside him.

The passenger door opened, and Mimi shouted, "Get in."

For a moment, he hesitated. "What are you doing here?"

"Your brothers were going to come and get you. I said I'd come instead. I thought I might have more success if you were...reluctant. But we're running out of time."

As he climbed in beside her, she stared at him as though she couldn't believe what she was seeing. He narrowly resisted the urge to run his hands though his hair—that might mess it up.

"What?" he asked when she didn't move.

"Just—holy shit," she muttered. "What have you done to yourself?"

He swallowed. "Do I look like an idiot?"

"No. You just don't look like Tanner O'Connor."

"That was the point of the exercise," he said drily.

"Emily likes the way you looked."

Did she? Well, she had told him that she'd spent a lot of time fantasizing about him. But that was just fantasies and not real life. In real life, she no doubt found him an embarrassment. "Did Emily ask you to come get me?" Did he sound pathetically hopeful?

"No. But she wants you there."

"Then why didn't she ask me?"

"Duh? Because you've been refusing to talk to her."

Good point. She was still staring at him, a frown between her eyes. "So are we going?" he asked.

She seemed to give herself a little shake. "I suppose so. It's too late for you to go back and change now."

What did she mean by that? She wanted him to change back? After all that effort he'd put in.

She pulled out onto the road before he could ask. The streets were quiet, and she put her foot down on the accelerator, and they shot forward. "Hey, just don't crash or get caught speeding—they'd definitely blame me."

She didn't slow, but she flashed him a grin. "The police are all at the meeting. The whole town is at the meeting."

Shit. His stomach churned. He was going to have to stand up in front of them all and pretend to be something he wasn't. And they'd probably laugh at him, and Emily would lose her job anyway, and she'd hate him and...

"Stop chewing your nails," Mimi said.

He stopped. "So you don't like the way I look?"

She sniffed. "I just don't like you giving in to those sanctimonious do-gooders who think they're better than anyone else just because they go to church on Sunday."

"I didn't do it for them." He scowled. "I did it for Emily. So she can keep the job she loves."

Her hands tightened on the wheel. "She'll keep it."

"So why am I here?"

"Because you should be at that meeting. And Emily has been trying to talk to you for two weeks, and you've ignored her."

"I thought it was for the best."

She cast him a sideways glance. "Well, you were wrong."

"I know. I was on my way. I came to my senses and realized if I let Emily go without a fight, I'll regret it for the rest of my life. I love her. I know she doesn't feel the same, but maybe one day…"

"You'd be surprised what Emily feels."

A little twist of hope fluttered to life inside his chest. He shoved it down. He had to get through this meeting, then he could hope.

"Sawyer came to see us," Mimi said. "Tonight."

"Shit, what did he say? He didn't—"

"No. He didn't. Don't worry, your secret is safe. But everyone who matters knew anyway."

What did she mean by that?

"We've all seen the way Sawyer has behaved," she said, as though he'd asked the question out loud. "If that hasn't been a clear sign of a guilty conscience, I've never seen one. And the way he disappeared after the accident. It didn't take much to put it together." She pulled up with a squeal of brakes outside the school. "And Jed would have as well, if he hadn't been blinded by grief and anger." She switched off the engine. "Let's go."

He climbed out slowly and found she was already heading into the building and had to run to catch up. She opened the door to the auditorium, and they slipped inside. The place was packed, but Mimi elbowed her way through to the side, where they could see the podium clearly. The meeting was obviously already in progress. Jed Forrester was just sitting down, having no doubt said his piece. And there was Emily. She'd been facing the long table where the board members were seated, but now she turned to face the audience, looking so beautiful and perfect and good. Her lower lip was caught in her teeth, and she was shifting from foot to foot. It didn't appear like things had gone well for her. He willed her to look at him, but she was staring straight ahead. He made to move closer, but Mimi stopped him with a hand on his arm. "Let her speak."

She cleared her throat. "Good evening, everyone. I know it's not normal procedure for me to address you like this, but I'm sure the board have already made up their minds, so I'll talk to you instead, because there are some things I need to say."

The murmurings of the crowd ceased. She blinked a couple of times, then moved a little closer to the microphone. Christ, he hated the bastards for putting her through this.

"You've already heard what the Board of Education has to say. They want you to believe that I am in breach of the morality clause in my contract. That I am an unfit person to teach your children. Most of you have known me all my life, and I truly hope that you don't see me that way."

The crowd had gone quiet.

"Go Emily!" Someone shouted from the back. So she had some supporters. They hadn't all been turned against her.

"It's true, I am pregnant. And I am unwed. But I hope to change that in the very near future. I wouldn't have chosen to bring a child into the world this way, but now it's happened, I'm happy and will do the best for my baby. Including marrying her father."

He was breaking up inside. She still wanted to marry him—after all his fuck-ups, she was still willing to give them a chance.

"And there we have the crux of the matter," Emily continued. "Certain people in this town do not want to see me married to my baby's father. They tell me he isn't a suitable husband for a teacher. That I'll be morally corrupted just by spending time with him."

Pausing, she glared over her shoulder at the board. What was coming next? He held his breath.

She turned back. "Well, you know what I say to that? I say bullshit."

Shocked laughter ran through the crowd.

Behind her, Jed Forrester rose to his feet, but the woman beside him tugged him back down and spoke to him. Tanner couldn't hear the words, but he sat, albeit with a scowl on his face.

Tanner couldn't move. What was she doing? She was supposed to be getting her job back. He'd come here ready to grovel, and she was going to mess everything up before he even had a chance. He tried to tug free of Mimi's grip, but she held him tight, and he really didn't want to get into a fight—he was supposed to be proving he was a changed man—and certainly not with Emily's grandmother, who'd probably beat the crap out of him.

"She's doing a great job," Mimi whispered. "Let her finish."

"I'm going to marry Tanner O'Connor. And if you had a brain cell between you, then you'd realize what sort of man he is. He's a good man. A man who didn't have the advantages of some of us, a man who's suffered tragedy, a man who despite all that has made a success of his life. He works hard, runs a thriving business, brings money into this town."

Christ, she was going to break him. He felt like his insides were all knotted up and his heart ached and—

"You," she said, pointing at a man in the front row. "Mr. McBride. Do you know who pays for your daughter Lucy's piano lessons? And you, Mrs. Daily. Are you aware of who keeps the bus going that takes your grandmother out on her weekly trips? Martin Lopez—who fixed your grandma's boiler while you and your family were on holiday in Orlando, and then visited every day to make sure she was okay? Tanner O'Connor. That's who. And much more. You'd all know that, except, unlike most of the do-gooders in this town, Tanner doesn't go shouting about the things he does. He doesn't need your thanks, or your pats on the backs, or a mention in church every Sunday."

How the hell did she know this stuff? He was sure he'd covered his tracks.

"Yes, he's made mistakes—who hasn't—but he's also paid for them. What happened eight years ago was a tragic accident. It could have happened to anyone, no matter who was driving." She took a deep breath, and he worried she'd say more. But all she did was turn briefly to look at Jed Forrester, and the man's shoulders suddenly slumped, as though facing a weight he was tired of carrying. "But that's *all* it was," she said, turning back. "And it's time for us all to move on."

"Yay!" That was Sawyer. He should keep his mouth shut.

"Maybe Tanner doesn't look all smart and nice and tidy. And he has tattoos. And maybe he could smile more. So what? It doesn't make him bad. Just take a look behind all that and see what I see."

She licked her lips. "The truth is, I'm not marrying Tanner O'Connor because I'm going to have his baby, I'm marrying him because he's the best man I know, and I love him."

Holy hell.

She loved him? She really loved him? She wouldn't say it in front of the whole town if she didn't mean it. He blew out his breath. His legs were weak.

"And that's all I have to say on the matter," Emily said. "If you're expecting me to beg for my job, then you're all going to be disappointed. And if that means I lose my job, then so be it, you'd not be the sort of people I want to work for anyway. And I feel sorry for your children, growing up within such a narrow-minded, mean-spirited attitude." She looked around the room. "But one last thing. If I do keep my job, no more morality clause. Because if what I've been doing with Tanner is immoral, then I'll be in breach of that clause every single day. Hopefully more than once. And I don't want to take up all of your time with more of these meetings. Tanner and I will have better things to do."

She fell silent, no doubt worried as she waited for some sort of reaction. But the crowd seemed numbed. Mimi whispered to him. "You can move now." She sort of pushed him forward, and he took a step toward the podium. Emily must have sensed him, because she turned slightly. She blinked a couple of times, as though she didn't recognize him. Then her eyes widened, and she burst into tears. Mimi patted his arm. "Don't worry. It's the hormones."

He didn't care. She loved him. And she couldn't take it back because he had hundreds of witnesses. She could cry as much as she liked. He'd be there to hug her better. But one thing was for sure. She wasn't losing her goddamn job.

He walked to the podium and came to a halt in front of her. He ignored everyone else, though he could almost sense Jed Forrester's glare.

"You've cut your hair," Emily said softly.

He smiled. "For you. I'll do anything for you, don't you know that yet?"

She sniffed, then reached up, rubbed his clean jaw. "And your beard. I liked your beard."

She seemed really upset. Shit. She was starting to cry harder, and he just wanted to calm her down. He wiped the tears from her soft cheek. "It'll grow back, baby."

He stared into her warm eyes until the tears stopped falling, and then he cleared his throat, pulled the piece of paper out of his pocket. He stared at it but couldn't make the words make sense. They'd sounded okay in his head earlier. Now after Emily's heartfelt speech, the words seemed stilted and lifeless. He crumpled the paper and dropped it on the floor, then realized that he should have put it back in his pocket—they'd probably arrest him for littering. Too late now.

God, she did this much better than him.

He ran a hand through his hair, then realized he'd messed up his "style" too late. The goddamn tie was strangling him. He pulled it off and shoved it in his pocket. Someone in the crowd wolf-whistled.

He looked across the faces all staring up at him. He recognized all of them. Had known them all his life. Reese was there, and Aiden. Sawyer and his wife. Ryan Forrester. The woman who ran the café across the street from the garage. She smiled at him.

"I grew up in this town," he said. "I've known most of you all my life. And to be honest, most of you I've always considered complete assholes."

"Way to go, bro," Aiden shouted. "Tell it like it is."

"I always believed you all looked down on me. And all this time, I've blamed you for that, when I should have blamed myself. So this is a one-time thing, and it will likely never happen again." He took a deep breath. "I'm sorry. I've been an asshole as well." A ripple of laughter ran through the crowd. Maybe he could do this. "But this is about Emily. And I don't think anyone would disagree that Emily is one of the best people in Saddler Cove. Actually, not one of…she *is* the best."

A few people cheered at that.

"She's a truly good person, the best teacher ever—or so my niece tells me—she's sweet and kind and would never hurt anyone. And yet there are people here who would call her immoral." He took a step closer to the microphone. "Anyone want to come up here and say that to my face?" He waited for a minute, scanning the audience. Nobody moved. "Good. Because I don't want to mess up my brother's best suit showing you to the door."

Another ripple of laughter ran through the crowd.

"Anyway, what I wanted to say was Emily shouldn't be

punished because I'm an asshole who can't keep his hands in his pockets and apparently carries a three-year-old condom in his wallet."

Another ripple of laughter.

"My speech"—he waved a hand at the crumpled paper on the floor—"gave a list of things I planned to do better. It went into a whole load of detail about how I was gonna try and be less of an asshole. I'm not going to go into that now. Instead, I'll just say that if Emily takes me on, then I'll do my goddamn best to be worthy of her." He looked down at her, a smile splitting her face open wide, and his heart cracked open wider.

Get a grip and finish this.

"I'm sure I'll fail sometimes, because as my brothers will tell you, I can be a cantankerous bastard and hell to live with."

"Too right, bro."

He ignored the interruption. "I just hope my best will be good enough." He turned so he faced Emily, then pulled the ring out of his pocket and held it out to her. "Please take it back. Say you'll marry me."

She reached up and touched his hair, hooked it back behind his ears. "Do you promise to grow your hair?"

"If that's what you want."

"Lose the suit?"

"Anything for you, baby."

Her eyes narrowed on him. "Get a tattoo with my name on it?"

"Consider it done."

She swallowed, and he could see the nervous flutter of her lashes. "Do you love me, Tanner?"

He thought for a second. "'*Do I love you? My God, if your love were a grain of sand, mine would be a universe of beaches.*'"

Her lips curved into a slow smile. "*The Princess Bride.*"

She sniffed. "I love that book."

"I love you."

"Then yes, Tanner O'Connor, I would be proud to marry you."

He slipped the ring on her finger as the crowd cheered. He didn't know whether Emily would keep her job, but even if she didn't, they would find a way through. She loved him, and that was all he'd ever wanted or needed. "I love you so much," he murmured and lowered his head and kissed her.

"Let's get out of here," she whispered.

"Don't you want to wait and hear what they decide?"

"Hell no. We're going to go somewhere and get a little grease beneath your nails. I don't recognize you like this." She backed away a little and spoke into the microphone. "We're off now, to celebrate our engagement. But if anyone wants me, I'll be getting down and dirty with the town saint. So I suggest you leave it until tomorrow."

She tugged his hand, and together they walked down the steps. The crowd parted, and they headed for the door. As they reached it, they turned and looked back.

Jed was on his feet. He stared at Tanner for long moments, then gave a small nod. "The Board of Education finds that Emily Towson is not in breach of the terms of her contract, and she will be reinstated as first-grade teacher in the coming school year."

They could still hear the cheers as they walked out of the school building.

Chapter Thirty

Mimi sat on the porch. She was tired but happy. Josh was beside her, and the lawn was scattered with friends.

Emily and Tanner came toward them, hand in hand. The happy couple. And they did look happy. She'd never regret that trip into the O'Connor's showroom, even if it had been a somewhat bumpy road.

They came to a halt in front of her. Emily sniffed and wiped her eyes with a napkin snatched from one of the tables. "Sorry. Baby hormones. But I'm just so happy." She sniffed again.

"Maybe you'd better stop crying, or they're all going to think you didn't want to marry me," Tanner said. "And it's only been an hour."

"I know, but it was so beautiful."

Mimi had been in charge of organizing the ceremony. It was supposed to have been small, but somehow at least half the town had gotten in on the act. Josh had given Emily away. And Sawyer had been Tanner's best man. He'd said it was because if he chose one of his brothers, then he'd never hear the end of it from the other. Sawyer was the logical choice.

Mimi wasn't sure she would have been so forgiving. But she was glad Tanner was finally putting the past behind him.

The service had been beautiful. They'd been married under a canopy on the lawn in front of the ranch house.

Tanner was wearing dark gray pants and a white shirt loose over the top, sleeves rolled up to show the tattoos on his forearms. If Mimi wasn't mistaken, he hadn't shaved since that night of the meeting, and he already had a half inch of golden beard on his face. Emily didn't seem to mind. She couldn't keep her hands off her bad boy husband.

"I'm going to show Emily her wedding present," Tanner said. "And then we'll be off."

Tanner was taking her away for a week before school started.

Mimi rose to her feet and kissed Emily on the cheek. And then Tanner. She sighed. He really was the most gorgeous bad boy she had ever seen. A sense of melancholy filled her. Lost opportunities. They shook hands with Josh, and then disappeared into the house.

She stepped up to the railings and looked out over the lawns. She'd made this happen. One good thing to set against the bad. She still hadn't heard from her son. And she was starting to believe she never would. She wouldn't pursue it any more. He had a right to ignore her, and she deserved nothing better.

Josh came up beside her, and she turned to him. "If I ever get the urge to meddle in anyone's love life again—you tell me to go right ahead."

He grinned. "I will."

She searched his face. He looked at peace with himself. "So now my granddaughter is settled. What about us?"

A wary expression entered his eyes, and he looked at all the people on the lawns as though they might overhear. She didn't care if they did. "Us?"

"You and me, Josh." When he didn't say anything, she heaved a sigh. "Come on. It can't have escaped your notice that I'm in love with you."

He almost choked.

"Tell me I'm just a stupid old lady and people our age don't fall in love."

"And then you'll...?"

"Persuade you otherwise, of course. We're never too old for love."

"I'm not good enough." But his words lacked conviction.

"You're more than good enough. I don't care where you came from, or where you've been, or the color of your skin. You've made me remember what love felt like. You've given me hope for the future. And I'm hardly a good bet. I'm seventy years old and I have MS and—"

"And you're the most beautiful woman in the world. Inside and out."

"So you *do* care. I wasn't sure."

He took a deep breath. "I care."

She reached up and cupped his face and, in front of at least half of the population of Saddler Cove, she kissed him. It was a tentative kiss and ended way too soon. But it was a start.

She raised her head to find everyone watching them, including a woman—or rather a girl—she looked early twenties at the most. She was a stranger, and Mimi had never seen her before. In faded jeans and a black T-shirt with some sort of logo on the front, she certainly wasn't dressed for a wedding. But there was something familiar about her. She was tall and slender, with long black hair and pale skin.

She was watching them with narrowed eyes. Green eyes.

Mimi swallowed. "Can I help you?"

"I'm looking for Mrs. Miriam Delaney," she said. Her

accent was not local. English, Mimi guessed.

"That's me."

The girl shrugged. "I think you might be my grandmother."

• • •

"You've already given me a wedding present," Emily said. "Is this another one? What did you get me? Where are we going?"

He grinned. "Stop nagging, wife."

He pulled her close and wrapped an arm around her as they walked beside the creek, heading away from the ranch house. He was glad that was over. Weddings really weren't his thing. Even his own—but he'd wanted to give Emily a wonderful day. She deserved it. Even if it was a shotgun wedding.

She snuggled close to him, and he said, "Do you remember this place?"

"It's where I used to come swimming as a child."

"Yeah." He gave a leer. "It was where I saw you skinny-dipping."

"I was so not skinny-dipping."

"Christ, you were hot."

"I was plump."

"You were thinner than you are now." He patted her belly. "Stop interrupting me. Believe me, you were the hottest thing I'd ever seen, and from that moment on, you were mine, even if neither of us knew it."

She heaved a huge sigh. "Destiny."

"Yeah. You can't get away from your destiny, and you can't get away from me."

"I don't want to."

"Good. Because you and I are forever. I know now that you were the reason I came back to Saddler Cove. You were my home."

"Would you ever have done something about it if I hadn't come to you that night?"

"Probably not. Just gazed at you from afar. You were way too good for me."

"And I thought you would never look at someone like me. It's scary, isn't it?" She looked around. "So, where's my present?"

He waved a hand around him. "This is your present. I bought the land from your grandmother. I've been looking for a house but couldn't find anything that was just right. And while I love your grandmother, I don't want to live with her forever. And I certainly don't want to live with your grandmother and Josh."

Her eyes widened. "You think…?"

"No doubt. The women in your family are tenacious once they get their hooks into a man."

"You're going to build me a house?"

"A perfect house for you and me and little Sophie and anyone else who comes along."

Her eyes filled with tears. "It sounds wonderful."

"It will be. You want me to show you where the bedroom is going to be?"

She nodded, and he held out his hand. Emily slipped her palm into his. He stepped back and tugged her into the shade of a magnolia tree, lowered his head, and kissed her. His hands moved to the curve of her spine and the zipper that ran down the back of the dress. He kissed her again and slipped it open. By the time he raised his head, the dress was gaping open, and she held it to her breasts with one hand. He still found it hard to believe she was his.

"What if someone comes?" she asked.

"No one would dare," he said, slipping the dress from her shoulders so it pooled around her feet. "It's private property. Your private property." She was in a white lace bra and panties, and his breath caught in his throat—she was so perfect, her stomach softly rounded with his baby.

"Show me your tattoo," she said.

"You just want to get me naked." He opened the buttons down the front of his shirt and parted the material. She trailed her finger over the heart directly over *his* heart. *Emily forever.* He'd gotten it the day after the meeting. As promised.

He shrugged out of the shirt, then kicked off his boots and was out of his pants before she could blink.

"Oh my," she murmured. "Very impressive." Her hand moved to the front of her bra. She flicked the hook and peeled the material from her breasts. They were bigger, the nipples prominent, and they took his breath away. She slipped her hands under the lace at her hips and wriggled out of her panties, and she was as naked as he was.

He closed the space between them, scooped her up, and lowered her to the grass. Came down over her. "With my body, I thee worship," he murmured and took her lips in a long kiss and filled her with one sure flex off his hips.

And now he really was home.

Epilogue

She was so not having this baby until Tanner was here. He'd promised to be with her at the birth, and she was not going to let their daughter make a liar out of her daddy.

Another pain, and she threw back her head and screamed. Where was he?

"Push, Emily," the midwife urged.

She didn't want to push. She wanted Tanner.

She'd only been in labor for an hour. Little Sophie couldn't be coming yet. Another contraction, and she lost herself in a world of pain. She was splitting in half. This could not be normal. She was going to die, and Tanner would be sorry because she'd be dead, and he'd never get to say goodbye and...

Then he was there. A hand slid into hers, and she opened her eyes and stared straight into his stormy gray ones.

"Push," he encouraged.

And she pushed. It felt like something popped, and she had a moment of blissful release.

"Oh my God. She's coming. She's actually coming. It's a

baby, Emily."

"Really," she growled. "Not a Harley?" Then another pain, and then the pressure was suddenly gone, as if a switch had been turned off. What was happening? Tanner was staring between her legs. Ugh. That couldn't be pretty, and she almost giggled at the thought. She'd heard of men who had been put off sex for life by being present at a birth.

But Tanner was made of sterner stuff.

"Is she okay?"

"She's beautiful. She's the most beautiful—second most beautiful," he amended quickly, "thing in the whole world."

Emily closed her eyes for a moment as relief flooded her. When she opened them, Tanner stood at her shoulder. He had a streak of grease across his cheek, his hair was halfway to his shoulders, and he wore dirty jeans and an oil-stained wifebeater. He was perfect.

The midwife handed him a bundle, and he took it almost reverently.

The baby snuggled against his broad chest. She was like her mom and clearly loved the smell of oil. The man and the baby. Her man, her baby. Together they were the most beautiful thing Emily had ever seen.

How easy would it have been for them to never have come to this point. One turn in the wrong direction. It frightened her for a moment. Then Tanner caught her gaze, and a slow smile curved his mouth. And the fear vanished.

You didn't know what life was going to throw at you. But you couldn't live in fear, or you missed out on the very things you feared losing. She held out her arms, and Tanner lowered their baby to her, laid her gently on her chest, and Emily felt the warmth seep into her skin.

"I think we should get her a pony," she said. "At next year's pony swim. You can't start riding too young."

"And maybe a hog," Tanner said. "A little tiny baby hog.

And a little baby leather jacket to wear when she rides it."

She bit back a smile. "Are we going to be sensible about this?"

He grinned. "Hell no, baby. I never married me a sensible woman."

"Thank goodness."

Acknowledgments

Thank you to the usual suspects: the fabulous ladies at Passionate Critters, who take the time to read my work and offer their wonderful insights and advice. And to my husband, Rob, without whom none of this would be possible.

And thank you to everyone at Entangled Publishing, especially my fabulous editor, Liz Pelletier. Liz has been an amazing support, teacher, and inspiration, since I sent my first book to Entangled many years ago.

And I've even more reason to thank Liz this time around as she actually came up with the original idea and plot for *Handle with Care*. It came about during a plotting workshop, hosted by Liz, so an additional thank you must go to all the wonderful authors who participated.

When Liz sent me the plot and asked if I was interested in writing the book, it was love at first sight. The story grew a little from the original outline—as a whole bunch of secondary characters appeared demanding to be included—but the essential romance is still the same. So thank you Liz!

About the Author

Growing up, Nina Croft spent her time dreaming of faraway sunnier places and ponies. When she discovered both, and much more, could be found between the covers of a book, her life changed forever.

Later, she headed south, picked up a husband on the way, and together they discovered a love of travel and a dislike of 9 to 5 work. Eventually they stumbled upon the small almond farm in Spain they now call home.

Nina spends her days reading, writing, and riding under the blue Spanish skies—sunshine and ponies. Proof that dreams can come true if you want them enough.

If you'd like to learn about new releases, sign up for Nina's newsletter here.

www.ninacroft.com

UNSPEAKABLE

THE THINGS TO DO BEFORE YOU DIE SERIES

HIS FANTASY GIRL

HER FANTASY HUSBAND

HIS FANTASY BRIDE

THE BABYSITTING A BILLIONAIRE SERIES

LOSING CONTROL

OUT OF CONTROL

TAKING CONTROL

THE MELVILLE SISTERS SERIES

OPERATION SAVING DANIEL

BETTING ON JULIA

BLACKMAILED BY THE ITALIAN BILLIONAIRE

THE DESCARTES LEGACY

THE SPANIARD'S KISS

What Happens in Vegas
a *Girls Weekend Away* novel by Shana Gray

Tough-as-nails detective Bonni Connolly is on a girls' getaway in Vegas with her friends and she splurges on a little luxury, including a VIP booth in an exclusive club. That's when she sees *him*. Professional poker player Quinn Bryant is in town for one of the largest tournaments of the year. What starts as a holiday fling soon turns into something more, as Bonni learns to see the man behind the poker face. Even though Bonni's trip has an end date and there is another tournament calling Quinn's name, their strong connection surprises them both. And by the end of the weekend they start to wonder if what happens in Vegas doesn't have to stay there…

One Night Wife
a *Confidence Game* novel by Ainslie Paton

Finley Cartwright is the queen of lost causes. That's why she's standing on a barstool trying to convince Friday night drinkers to donate money to a failing charity. And hot venture capitalist Cal might just be her ticket to success. Professional grifter and modern-day Robin Hood, Cal Sherwood is looking for a partner, and if sexy Fin sticks with him, her charity will thrive, and she'll help him score billions to fund his social justice causes.